Bad Blood

A Long Island Mystery

David E. Feldman

This book is a work of fiction. Places, events, and situations in this story are purely fictional. Any resemblance to actual persons, living or dead, is coincidental.

ISBN: 1-4033-0291-X (Ebook)
ISBN: 1-4033-0292-8 (Softcover)

This book is printed on acid free paper.

Printed in the United States of America

1stBooks - rev. 4/29/02

Dedication

To my parents.

For all Bill's friends.

Acknowledgements

I would like to thank the following people for their invaluable medical, law enforcement and editorial expertise: Carole Butler, Maria Heinz, Joseph Villari, Michael Jamison, Gary Onks, Debbie Leonard, Ellen Feldman.

Bad Blood

A Long Island Mystery

Also by David E. Feldman:
Born Of War: Based On A True Story of American-Chinese Friendship

1

1995.

RAGE

The roller coaster ride evened out; uncontrollable shaking calmed to a continuous minor tremor. Mountains and valleys became more manageable hills and dips, and monstrous rage chilled enough to allow the evening's plan to unfold.

The materials, leather and glass and steel, were spread out neatly on the red and blue plaid cotton blanket. Swollen fingers put them in their places, vials of blood ready to visit so many potential helpers. So many beds, all filled, all ready to help. So much potential revenge. The irony drew a coughing laugh which twisted the stomach into sudden nausea and ended with a quick rush to the toilet. Dry heaves.

Time to go to the healing place. Healing? HEALING! What sick hypocrisy! Healing. They knew nothing about healing there! Hilarious! Healing! But don't laugh; don't even think of laughing. This was not the time for irony nor even the time to let the animal out from behind its steel bars. Tonight was business. Just business. And a good business plan must be executed. Now was the time for execution.

* * *

BEN

Two walls of the huge, sunlit "creative" room were painted in massive brown and beige geometrics and covered with framed prints from successful ad campaigns. The other two were of glass that faced other departments of the small ad agency located at the northern end of the Meadowbrook Parkway, just a honk of an SUV from the Garden City Mall. Bookshelves lined the short ends of the room and two gold statuettes—"Addie's"—served as bookends on the shelves one saw first upon entering the room.

"Every hospital is suffering budget cuts. We're all in the same swiss cheese boat," said Lou, looking up from his easel. "If you have a crisis in health care you don't solve it by taking money away from the hospitals and expecting businesses to take over." He adjusted his glasses, their thick black rims standing out against his prematurely white hair. He turned back to the comp he was sketching, occasionally frowning and looking at the point of his pencil as though it were responsible for an error that had appeared on the page.

Lydia shifted her ample behind in her chair and blinked at her computer screen. Finally, she looked at Lou. "How was your weekend?"

"Great," said Lou.

"Fair," said Art, at exactly the same time. From his perch at the front of the room, he craned his neck and looked over the desks before him, like a mother goose over its brood.

"What Wide World of Sport over there means, is: he had a great weekend of fishing, whilst I actually went backwards with my script."

Lou lifted his glasses up above his eyebrows. "Now, Arthur. We had a wonderful dinner. Your tofu marsala was magnificent, and we found another new antique store I can vouch to Lydia you enjoyed. So while your sitcom may not have had the perfect weekend, we had a lovely time, I'm sure."

Art sighed, set his square jaw and flipped a brown bang out of his eyes. "I suppose you're right. Yes, Louis is correct, Lydia, we had a lovely weekend thank you. How's the hospital's copy coming?"

"I've been researching to get a feel, you know?" said Lydia. "And what I've found is that we have some particularly talented Senators running the health care system, and they need to look good to the folks who voted for them." Lydia worked her jaw in an exaggerated chew and pretended to spit. "Y'all just let us businessmen handle it. You womenfolk gather behind that thar desk and jes' watch. We'll rassle this healthcare varmint to the ground." The glow of her computer screen was reflected in her black eyes. Her expression turned sour. "Gimmee a break!"

Lou looked up. "The truth is, if we expect anyone else to take care of us, we're in for a let down."

"A letdown," said Lydia, "would be a Christmas present in this world. I'll bet that if we all did mind our business there's all sorts of great stuff just waiting to brighten up our day. Why look at the Oklahoma bombing, or that Senator who so wonderfully represented his constituents by equally and fairly molesting every one of them, male and female, he could get his hands on." She held up a piece of paper. "Okay, how does this sound?" Her voice softened and sweetened. "The New York Metropolitan Medical Center—Making the World A Better Place." She looked to her left at Art, the head writer, "dot, dot dot, 'for you.'"

"It might work, Lyd. Put it in with the others." Art's fortyish features betrayed no emotion. "Just try not to let yourself be overcome with optimism." His phone chirped and as he turned to pick it up, Lydia stuck her tongue out in his direction and looked swiftly back to her computer screen, her dark hair whirling.

"Selling Sight and Sound. This is Art. Uh, no, you want the art department. Well, yes, I did say this is Art but that's because it's my name, short for Arthur, you see. The people who would tell you when the comps will be ready would be in the—" he smiled, "certainly, I'll transfer you." He exhaled noisily and pushed the "hold" button. "Bennett, for you!" he cupped the receiver with one hand. "Lydia," he said softly, "you're fired."

"Yeah, right," Lydia muttered. "You'd all sink like stones." Her mouth clenched in an amused pout and the rest of her features lined up in support—nostrils flared, eyebrows bulged around darkened eyes, olive skin tightened and lay flat over prominent cheekbones.

Seeing she was happy, Art smiled to himself.

"I've got it. Thanks, Arthur." Bennett James, the newly anointed Three S Art Director, swiveled in his chair and waved through the glass. He had been daydreaming about camping with Beth, their sleeping bags zipped together under a moonless sky alight with stars, the fire warming them until they began to warm each other. He smelled pine needles and the dizzying fragrance of Beth and her famous coconut lotion, as a lifetime of cynicism melted away—until a blinking red light blotted out the stars.

The hold button continued to flash. "Hello, Bennett James," he said, feeling the sad weight deep in his throat and behind his eyes. He swallowed, forcing the weight away. "I sure did, Vince. Right after you called. Would I forget your comps? Yes, I know we got the...Sure, they're a big...Vince, this year's medium sized account is next year's big grosser." He sat up and made a motion as if to slick back his hair which was already in place, parted and solid with gel.

Ned Doyle, the agency's president and majority partner, peered into the office. Bennett laughed. "No, that's Ned's line." He winked at Doyle's questioning nod. "No, Vince they won't be on time. They'll be early. Yeah, I love you, too, Vince. *Ciao.*"

He followed Ned onto the main floor, looking down at the back of the smaller man's steel gray head of hair. When he got to the center of the room Ned clapped his hands together twice, hard. Like gunshots.

"Okay, everybody, listen up. Annie—!"

A mop of red hair in the back of the huge room popped up from behind a computer screen. "Okay, Mr. Doyle, I'll get the phones."

"...get the phones while we're talking." His bony features relaxed fondly as he interrupted himself. "I knew you would, Annie." He surveyed the room, his expression granite-like.

"How much do you people know about the outbreaks of AIDS at the NYMMC?"

Lydia shrugged. "Any urban hospital must get its share."

Art held up a finger. "I know two guys in their ICU." He paused. "Both have been HIV positive for eight years—well, one's more like nine. Neither was in a high risk category, but I thought it was just one of those bizarre things..."

Ned hopped up and sat on the long cherry wood table that ran down the center of the room. He tilted his head back and gave a slow, exaggerated nod. "Well, there've been a lot of those bizarre things going on for quite a few years over there." He gave another slow nod as everyone began to understand. "Umhm. And we're being brought in to stop the bleeding, so to speak."

Lydia crossed her arms. "To cover their asses, you mean."

Lou shrugged. "Business must go on, I guess. And the truth is, a hospital is a business..."

"Listen to you," said Arthur, his arms folded. "The surgeon general. And look at those pants. My goodness, more wrinkles than creation! You know, I ironed your gray pleats. You didn't see them on the—"

Lou held up a hand and mouthed "I'm sorry."

"Excuse me," Ned interrupted. "If Tracy and Hepburn are through?"

"More like Myrna Loy and…" Art began.

"Oh, I'll be William Powell!" Lou straightened an imaginary tie.

Lydia sounded annoyed. "Aren't we participating in a coverup? If the hospital's incompetent or negligent, why should we cover for them? Oh, I know, because they're paying us…"

Ned pointed to her. "The hospital's not doing anything wrong. They're complying with every agency that's checking them out. This is about public perception."

Lydia sulked. "Isn't everything?"

"So let's get back to what our role is," Art suggested.

Bennett was thinking about what sort of campaign they might create for his first major project. Would there be a photo shoot at the hospital? Would they hire models to simulate scenes with patients? Would he and Lou sketch scenes including doctors and patients, or perhaps the building itself? New campaigns thrilled him in much the same way new girlfriends once had. He looked forward to having a few drinks and planning the campaign—his ritual.

"Before I go on," Ned was saying, "I want to make clear that this meeting is confidential. The extent of what has appeared in the papers—some of you may have seen it and some of you may not have—is that a few people seem to have contracted HIV over the last eight or nine years at the New York Metropolitan Medical Center through, who knows—the incompetence of a particular worker or a series of unfortunate coincidental circumstances." He gave a helpless shrug. "Anyway, that's the official version."

"I'm sure those folks' moms're thrilled by that version," said Lydia.

"Easy, girl," Art chided.

"I am not an easy girl."

"Really?" Lou grinned. "Ralph Marx? Jason Weiss? Malcolm—did Malcolm have a last name, or just a big old—?"

"That's enough, Louis."

Ned glanced at the door. "In truth, seventy four people have contracted AIDS at that facility over this period. Fifty one of those have died and none, not one, had the virus upon entering the facility. How did they contract the virus? Is the blood supply safe? Mr. Franklin, the CEO of the facility, has personally taken me on a tour of the blood taking, testing and storage procedures, much of which aren't even at the hospital. These are state-of-the-art procedures and they do appear secure."

"Another comforting…"

"Lydia!" His voice whipped through the room and even street tough Lydia jumped in her chair. "This is a client. If you don't trust their integrity, you're saying you don't trust my integrity. You do seem to trust my signature on your check each week…" He waited and when Lydia didn't answer, continued.

"There are a series of computerized and human monitored checks on the system. All appear to be working correctly and, as I said, the blood supply does appear to be safe. It has appeared safe throughout this period. No one has had any reasonable explanation for these deaths. The facility does not link them, officially. Now, that being said, word has been spreading about this situation, slowly at first, and lately more rapidly." He looked in Lydia's direction. "I'm not comfortable with it either. People on staff at the NYMMC have learned about what's been going on and have begun to talk. Seemingly unrelated deaths have begun to be connected. A panic could develop, and that's not good for anyone."

Art interrupted. "But shouldn't people *be* informed? Isn't it natural that word get out about a dangerous situation? I wouldn't want my loved ones staying at that hospital..."

Lou turned slowly. "*You* have loved ones?"

"A cocker spaniel, two gold fish...and you."

Lou looked at Lydia and Ned and pretended to swoon. "That's the closest he's ever come to telling me he loves me."

Art sighed and rolled his eyes.

"Now, here's where it stands now." Ned hopped down from the table. "The blood supply does not originate at NYMMC. It comes from independent blood banks that supply other facilities, none of which are having this problem. In addition patients are being encouraged to give autologous transfusions..."

"Do you mind telling me what that is," said Lydia. "What do I look like—Marcus Welby?"

"Dating yourself!" Lou called, in the opposite direction.

Art nodded. "And you know I think you *do* look like him, a little, around the eyes. And if your nose were a little more—"

"Arthur, please." Ned looked at Lydia. "An autologous transfusion is when a patient gives his or her own blood in anticipation of needing a transfusion." He took a deep breath. "Now, the other aspects of the hospital are fully functioning. Police and medical experts are looking into finding out what's been going on and fixing it."

"Police?" Bennett asked. He had been daydreaming about Beth, but the threat to a new account brought him back to the moment.

"Well, they may not be necessary, but there's always a possibility that some nut or group of nuts is responsible for all this."

Art sat back, a hand over his heart. "Someone giving people HIV on purpose?"

"I'm sure that isn't it. Look, for us, for Ben particularly, this can be a triumph or a tragedy. It's certainly a challenge, and for you, Lydia, just being comfortable with it might be the challenge."

Her eyes narrowed. "Just what I need, a challenge."

"Now, we don't have the account yet. I'm meeting with the hospital's CEO this afternoon and I'm going to pitch our ideas to him."

Bennett perked up. "Ideas? What ideas?"

"The three terrific options you'll have on my desk by two o'clock."

"Ah," said Bennett. "Those ideas."

* * *

David E. Feldman

FEAR

The airplane roar silence was impossible to control. Blood through veins behind the ears. If you sat quietly you could tolerate it for a moment, build a wall of willpower and experience a moment without thoughts or feelings—no anticipation, intent or fear. The wall held for a moment and then gave.

Once the car made the turn from Ocean Avenue onto Sunrise Highway and pulled into the parking lot, the fear returned, but it was barely a resonant ghost of its former self. The leather packet of full syringes and spare vials dug into the waist from its hiding place under the long, leather coat, a reminder of tonight's purpose.

The two RNs on overnight waved and called friendly "hellos" from the nurses' station and went back to their monitors and paperwork.

The corridor turned just past their station, and the hall at this point became a maze of IV stands and beds. The ward was so full that patients had been situated temporarily in the hallway. Disgusting.

Coughing and labored breathing echoed through the ward; heart monitors beeped and hummed. Someone cried out. Pain shrieked through tired lips. Shuffling steps, vomiting, more shuffling. Uncontrollable giggling. An old woman groaned.

The gloves were too tight; they pinched the base of each finger, cutting off blood and causing a vague pulsing that was an echo of a heartbeat. The tip of each finger was numb but there was no loss of dexterity. Turning the belt and removing the vials and syringes from the dual chambered carrying case was easy. The dull pain in each finger had been adjusted to long ago.

The first patient was propped up on three pillows. Her hair was dyed black and fell about her shoulders; her prominent cheekbones, large eyes and thick lashes suggested that as regally beautiful as she was today, she had once been more so. Her tanned, lined face suggested that she was well to do and had, perhaps, retired to Florida or some similar climate. An endotracheal tube was connected from the base of her throat to a respirator. A sphygmomanometer checked her blood pressure at regular intervals. The ICD-9 number on her chart was meaningless without appropriate decoding paperwork; the same could be said for the CPT Code. Her chart indicated lung cancer. Thoracentesis, the removal of fluid from around her lungs, had been performed, and tumor cells detected. The high level of CEA in her blood confirmed the diagnosis, as did the prescriptions: an antiemetic for nausea, and Cytoxan, the prescribed chemotherapy. Keeping CPT and ICD-9 paperwork with the syringes might be a good idea, to keep track of the patient. Anyone who would die before the virus blossomed into full blown AIDS would serve no purpose.

But the woman's prognosis appeared good, and there was no time to consider the heavy, sore fingers or vague nausea. A moment bent over her, and the syringe came quickly out of its holster. The sight of the dark liquid easing into the needle was pleasantly relaxing and brought the nausea down. The woman sighed in her drugged sleep. The syringe was returned to the far chamber of the carrying case.

On to patient number two.

* * *

BEN

The long conference table was set neatly with white coffee cups and saucers, each bordered with red striped trim. Each empty. Ned had been too preoccupied to remember to make coffee or to ask Annie, the designated coffee person, to make a pot. Annie knew he had forgotten, but saw his intense preoccupation and wisely left him alone.

Ned Doyle moved some notebooks aside and sat down on the table, clapping his hands for attention. "I know you've all been working hard, the ideas and comps have been great, but if we don't close the deal, none of that means a thing." He paused long enough to look each of his creative staff in the eyes. "I want to know that I've got your support, that you're behind me on this." He waved a hand and raised an eyebrow, his eyes focusing, narrowing, gaining intensity. The 3S staff shifted in their seats.

Ned's hard baritone echoed through the cavernous room, bouncing off the drawn green blinds which seemed to ripple from the sound. "I don't want you to think this is trivial public relations. I'm not bullshitting here. I need to know, I need to feel you guys're behind me when I go in there with Mr. Franklin. We're a team, whether we're physically together or not. There's strength in numbers, whether we're together or not. When you have a closely knit family, it makes you stronger—think of that. I know my wife and kids love me, so I carry that with me." He touched his heart and closed his eyes. "And I'm more effective for it." He waited, his eyes shut, then smiled. "See, it's coming. I can feel it." He opened his eyes. "You guys're coming on board. I know you're with me now." He lowered his voice and bowed his head. "Thank you." He walked from the room, which remained quiet for a full minute.

"Yeah, we're on board," said Lydia, rapping her knuckles on her desk. "The good ship cuckoo! Good thing the client is a hospital. Maybe they'll give Ned a freebee."

Art was examining several catchphrases on his computer screen. "I don't know about a cuckoo, but he is a strange bird, isn't he? You know, tough as he is, he needs us the way he needs his family."

Bennett was thinking of his own family. His father's face appeared on the other side of a chessboard, expressionless, looking at him as though he were a minor piece—a rook or, more likely, a pawn. His mother sang nursery rhymes to him when he was a child. That must have been nice.

He went to the row of beige Macintosh computers lined up against the brick wall at the back of the creative room and called up the hospital's files. He began scanning through the "for position only" photographs Lydia had found to see which would convey the friendliest, most familial image under a headline in an ad or on the front cover of a brochure. He was so intent on the computer files that he did not notice Annie watching him from her desk, a sad smile on her lips.

* * *

NED DOYLE

"I have no control over any of them. I can only do my best." Ned was staring at himself in the mirror of the mens' room, talking in a low, even tone. His voice bounced off the green tiles and came back to him, reminding him of what he so easily forgot. "I can think straight, I have a great job, a beautiful wife, two wonderful kids." He closed his eyes and rocked back on his heels, took a deep breath and looked in the mirror. "Thank you."

He walked slowly from the room, smiling to himself, and stopped at the pay phone in the rest room foyer. He dialed and waited. "Hey, Sam. Just wanted you to know I'm going to meet with that CEO now. Yeah, I'm fine. I'll be there tonight. Sure, I'll be at the church or outside a half hour early and...Yes, Sam, I'll make sure to have good coffee tonight." He laughed. "Hey, give me a break, it's not that bad—though since I don't drink coffee...You're right. Why should you give me a break? I appreciate it, Sam. Thanks."

* * *

George S. Franklin was in his mid 50s, a shade over six feet tall and perhaps thirty five pounds overweight. The grayish cast of his face and his brown rimmed glasses were frequently obscured by a cloud of smoke that curled upward from the cigarette adored by his fingers. His thinning hair was dyed a deep brown and punctuated by red highlights. When he spoke, his deep, radio-announcer's voice deepened further at the end of each sentence with the "mwah" of a drag on his cigarette. He listened carefully and politely. His affability had taken him far in business, and now, the pleasure of his cigarette intertwined with that of the conversation, and when it was time to respond, his words were preceded by a whoosh of air and smoke that gave a finality and resonance to his answer.

George Franklin radiated the kind of power that allowed the CEO of a major metropolitan hospital to rise above many of that institution's most fundamental rules. No other employees or board members dared smoke anywhere on the premises.

"Have a seat, Mr. Doyle." George Franklin guided Ned lightly by the elbow to a chair on the side of the board room's table, pushed aside a telephone and smiled down at the diminutive ad man. He sat at the table's head, before a small notebook and a heavy glass ashtray which appeared not to have been emptied in a long time.

"Take all the room you want, Mr. Doyle. I know you folks like to spread out." His voice dropped from its low baritone to a barely audible bass. "By all means. Make yourself comfortable. Coffee?"

"No, thank you. I don't drink coffee."

"Tea, then?"

"Thanks anyway."

"You don't mind if I smoke?" Without waiting for an answer, he drew the small blue cigarette pack from inside his suit pocket, shook one out and lit it from the end of his current cigarette.

Ned thought to say "You're already smoking," but remained silent.

Newly alert and fortified, George Franklin lay his palms flat on the table. "What have you got for me?"

Breathing deeply from a point several inches below his navel, Ned Doyle reminded himself to relax. In his mind's eye he saw the concepts and layouts he would present and how they related to the hospital's dilemma and its potential future. Calmly and carefully, ignoring the ever present fear of failure, looking the man opposite him directly in the eye, he began to speak.

His opponent came into the tiny ring, his coarse ghi or dobuk as it was called in Korean, riding high on his wrists and calves. He was tall for Ned's weight class, something Ned had not expected, which forced him to consider an entirely new set of attacks and counters. He remembered them well. Taller opponents were difficult. They often could kick you before you could kick them by virtue of their longer legs. Lateral motion was vital as was the need to block effectively.

"Say jok!" *cried the ref, and the tall opponent moved slightly from side to side, his black belt with its two white stripes twirling after him. He stayed in an upright fighting stance, sixty percent of his weight on his rear leg. His arms swung in counter motion to his body and suddenly he leaped and Ned bounded to one side. It had been a fake. He had only switched to opposite stance to see what Ned's response might be.*

"The illustration's interesting, Mr. Doyle," said Mr. Franklin. "*Mwahh.* I'm not sure I like the slogan, though. An accessible family atmosphere is crucial to us. The older generation, who find themselves in hospitals more, as well as their children, who might be here having babies of their own—all must be included and it must seem effortless." He smiled at Ned but the smile had no emotion behind it. "*Whoof.* What else've you got?"

Ned circled and shuffled-stepped, a footwork distraction. The tall man threw a front snap kick as a defense against Ned's attack.

But Ned was not attacking. He was spinning on his front foot, pivoting until he faced away from his opponent and for an instant could see the row of spectators and judges behind him. His other foot came up high at the knee and powered straight back. A spinning back kick toward the tall man's chest.

But the man was fast, he had slid back. So Ned came forward with the kick's momentum and punched twice, more for distraction than for impact. The kick behind the punches had his full momentum behind it, yet there was still control enough to stop and turn, should the tall man block or evade or have his own counter ready. The roundhouse knocked the tall man's blocking hand out of the way and was followed by a jumping spinning kick, which slammed into the tall man's ribs.

There was a cracking sound and the air rushed from his lips and his eyes opened wide.

"*Whooo.*" George Franklin reeled at the sight of the mockup ad. "Now you've got me. The illustration of the building is nice and I like the way you've incorporated it with the type and placed it at the bottom, near the 800 number. Mmm. *Mwah.* And the copy is good. Could use a little work, perhaps, but not bad."

Ned smiled slightly and looked down at his fingers. "Of course, your expertise is, I'm sure, exactly what we need to round out the details. We may be a little off here and there." He looked as respectful as he could.

"A good thought, Ned, but I'm rather busy. Perhaps someone on my staff..."

"Exactly what we had in mind. Now if you look at these comps, you'll see that we've incorporated that same concept of caring for generations by showing pictures of residents, interns, nurses, technical staff, all happily helping and interacting with happy patients."

"I like it, Ned. You folks do nice work." George Franklin jabbed his cigarette at Ned, forming tiny o's in the air. "I want you to be sure and compliment your staff for me. Too often the people who do the most real work get the least credit."

"I promise you I will do that, Mr. Franklin."

"Call me George. Now tell me, Ned. Exactly how many ads and brochures were we talking about, and if we include the radio and television spots and web pages, what would you say we were talking about for the year, moneywise? Ballpark." He shook his head. "I won't hold you to it, of course, until it's in writing and we've gone over the details and the lawyers've seen it. But a big part of the decisions around here are made and broken at the numbers stage."

Ned's eyes went hard on the inside. He focused on what was before him. He carefully measured his position until he knew he was at exactly the right distance—as far as his long side kick would extend, minus about three inches. He concentrated and breathed. His lower stomach area tightened with each breath. He felt that knot, the tonghun, where the power lived.

The two men were braced on either side of the boards, arms locked into position, faces showing their concentration. He had taught them well, knew they would not flinch.

With a screaming kiaiii he slid forward, his knee high, the side kick smashing toward the boards.

He ignored the failure image, the old tape in his head that said that he could not possibly accomplish this thing, that his foot would slam into the unyielding wood and bounce off.

His foot approached the wood, pointed at the heel, and passed lightly through. There was no impact, only four small splintered boards where there had been two large ones.

George was nodding. "That sounds fair." He lowered his cigarette voice. "I'll tell you, it's a whole lot less than those boys on Madison Avenue wanted us to pay.

I know it's unprofessional to tell you that, but I'm sure it's something you know already."

Ned smiled. "No comment, sir. Can I buy you lunch?"

"That new place over in Merrick okay? And it's George, Ned. By the way, what do you drink?"

"Mineral water."

Mr. Franklin, who had stood up and was in the act of lighting another cigarette, stepped back and appraised the smaller man for a moment. "You don't have to hold back on my account, Ned. I enjoy a couple of good 'meeting enders.'"

Ned shrugged, still smiling. "Haven't had a drink in years, George. But you go right ahead."

George Franklin looked surprised. "Well, I appreciate a man who looks after his health. Me, I could use a drink."

* * *

BEN

Bennett yawned, closing his eyes, and when he opened them, Beth was standing by the side of the bed, her nightgown rippling. He inhaled a breath of coconut hair as she sat down on the bed beside him, cupping his face in her coffee-warm hand. She leaned forward, kissing him on the forehead and then on the lips.

Ned hurtled into the office, slamming his black leather briefcase onto Bennett's desk, shattering the daydream. "I don't know about these ideas of yours!"

Once again, Beth was gone. He looked at the blinking green words on his computer screen. "A Friendly Place to Make You Well," the words said, topping the illustration he and Lou had been working on, a collage of hospital personnel and patients.

Ned smelled of alcohol, but Bennett knew better than to wonder about it. Ned had never made a secret of his alcoholism; he had, in fact, made sure everyone in the office knew about it so he would never be able to hide a slip. Every employee of Selling Sight and Sound had Sam's telephone number and was instructed to call that number if they thought Ned might have had a drink.

It had never been necessary in the three years Ben had been with the company. Ned took all the clients to lunch, particularly new ones, and more than half of them drank. That was business, Ned explained. Besides, even when he had been drinking, he had never had cocktails at lunch. He had whole bottles of whiskey for days at a time in his basement, but never, ever cocktails at lunch.

Why play around?

Ned slapped the stack of notes from the business meeting down in front of Bennett. He pointed to the red scribblings on top of one of his comps.

"This illustration is too realistic. I wanted you to suggest these peoples' faces and what they're doing, not show every detail. And look here," he flipped to another page. "What they're doing is physically impossible. This guy's arm couldn't possibly be here. It wouldn't fit around the tray and look, no hospital bed sits this way. And what's this piece of machinery supposed to be? Did you get it from a science fiction magazine? And look at this," Ned shook his head, his eyes rolling back and looking at the ceiling. "Is this a nurse or a hooker? Come on, these are supposed to be family ads!"

Bennett remembered that there were two other agencies in this part of the county. He knew the art director at one and might be able to get a job as an assistant there. The other he knew only too well. They had accused him of stealing a visual concept for a series of shoe store ads. The way the man was holding the shoe, the fact that he looked like a particular movie star...both had been reminiscent of their ads. But similar ads are not necessarily stolen ads. They are complimentary. Anyway, they would never hire him. He wondered if Ned would give him severance pay.

"Look, Ned, why don't you just get it over with, and instead of tearing down my work, tell me how much notice you're giving me."

Ned had been leaning over the desk, pointing at details of the illustrations, his jacket scraping the desktop, but now he stood up and became quiet, looking at Bennett. "Why would I give you notice?"

"Exactly! Just throw me out in the street then, without even the courtesy of a few measly day's notice!" Ben shook his head, the annoyance plain in his voice. "But please don't rip my work. This isn't stuff I just churn out; this isn't clip art."

Ned spoke slowly, staring at Ben with granite eyes. "Don't be so sensitive, Mr. James. I'm not being any tougher on you than that hospital board's going to be."

Bennett didn't say anything for a moment. "This is how you tell me I've got a new client?"

A smile tugged at the edges of Ned's mouth. "*We've* got a new client." A hint of satisfaction glinted from his eyes.

Bennett sat back, crossing his arms. "Some day you might consider getting into therapy."

"Just what I need, a dysfunctional relationship I have to pay for."

* * *

Bennett started the white Cougar and threw it into first gear, still revved up by the thought of handling the biggest account of his life. A hospital with an AIDS epidemic within its walls would be a public relations nightmare. The problem had to be identified, isolated and contained for any public relations repair work to be truly effective.

He pulled out of the parking lot and onto Sunrise Highway, heading west, toward Valley Stream. The Cougar sputtered slightly and lurched into third and then fourth gear. He had to remind himself that the disease was not something he could do anything about. His concern was the perception of the disease, though he could not help wondering what the powers that be were doing to learn the cause of the epidemic and stop it. He breathed deeply, put on a meditation tape and relaxed to the woman's soothing, hypnotic voice and the soft bells and tones that carried her words to him. He drove easily, weaving in and out of traffic, letting the Cougar do the work.

At Horton Avenue, a dirty white van with a logo made of multicolored squares reading "Today's Tiles" was moving too slowly in this, the fast lane. Bennett flashed his brights and waited, still relaxed and at one with the road.

The van slowed down. Bennett swung out to the right, but the van swerved just in front of him and Bennett had to slam on the brakes to avoid crashing into its bumper.

He rolled down the window. "What the hell's the matter with you!"

The van's driver gave him the finger and, furious, Bennett inched the Cougar up until the grill of his car was nearly touching the van's rear bumper. After a moment, he changed his mind. What was he doing? What if this guy had a gun? He popped out the meditation tape and replaced it with some head banging rock 'n roll.

He decided to go to the gym, but first he had a stop to make.

* * *

In a tiny cul de sac off Cochran Place in the Gibson section of Valley Stream was an enormous, desolate gray house amidst an unmowed tangle of weeds and vines. A drainpipe along one side of its front had come loose at the top and was tilted crazily to one side. Long gray tongues of paint peeled down from old shingles.

Bennett rang the bell and waited. He looked up. One small window near the roof appeared to glow faintly blue.

He rang the bell again, heard nothing, not even the bell itself, and decided to go inside. The floor and walls of the foyer were made of dusty wood. Wires hung from a lone empty fixture in the ceiling. The door banged shut behind him and Bennett found himself in near darkness. To the right of the winding stairway was the kitchen and he could just make out the countertop and a few used dishes and cups and what might have been bits of food strewn about. He went up the stairs, which bent and strained under his weight, until he reached the top and listened. He heard a series of faint clicks, followed by a loud screeching and he hesitated before moving toward the noises. A blue-green light shone through the doorway at the end of the hall.

Bennett went toward the glow and, when he reached the doorway, he peered inside. The room was bare except for a plate of food here or a piece of clothing there. A light was shining from on top of an old roll top desk on the far side of the room and, in the middle of the light, a profile was illuminated.

The eyes were those of an old man but the rest of the face was that of a man in his late twenties. The hair was brown, but in the glow it appeared gray or even silver, and it sprang out, Medusa-like, in all directions. The eyes were small and dark and the rest of the face was long and sagging as though held up by pins attached just below the eyes. The mouth seemed to be saying the letter "o."

It glared out from the glow.

"What the hell do you want? Well, are you going to come in and talk to me or are you going to WAIT until I DIE of the suspense?"

Bennett stepped into the room. "What're you doing?"

"I'm having SEX! What does it look like I'm doing?" The apparition turned back to the glow and the clicking resumed; the back of the apparition's head shook every few moments and Bennett saw that the shaking and the clicking were the result of feverish typing. Every now and then the room would fall silent, the head would stop moving and remain still for a long pause, and then the typing would resume again, with more intensity than before until finally, the head and its tiny body, which was clad all in black, sat back, exhausted.

"Goodbye," said a voice out of the glow.

"Okay, I've hung up." The apparition relaxed and swung around in its chair. "What's it about?"

"What's that about, Mattis?" Ben pointed to the screen.

"I told you. I was having sex. Over the Internet. Nothing better, dude. I can be who I want and she can be who I want. It's perfect. No games."

Bennett sat down in a faded red loveseat. "No games? Looks to me like it's nothing *but* games."

Mattis scowled. "Well, then the games don't have to end, if you want to look at it that way." He glared at Ben for an extra few seconds. "If we stay in the game, then it stops being a game, doesn't it?" He stood up. "And I'll tell you something else. Some people ought to learn to take their lives as seriously as I take these games, as you call them." He pointed a thin finger and shook his head, the computer's glow reflected in his eyes. Every few words rose to a near scream. "I might not be too sociable, but maybe it's because I KNOW I don't fit in and I KNOW what MY shortcomings are so I'm courteous enough to keep the hell AWAY from people." Without warning, he sat down on the floor, never putting a hand down to steady himself. His legs simply folded beneath him. "And I'll tell you something. Some people, hell MOST people don't even think of others THAT much. They just go around doing whatever they want, in anyone's face, no matter who they hurt or how in-fucking-appropriate their actions might be." As quickly as he sat down, he jumped back up. "The world is full of bastards, Ben-ster. Gigabytes of 'em. They're everywhere! EVERYWHERE!"

Bennett calmly looked at his watch. "All right Mattis, what happened?"

"It was that car! That station wagon. It just pulled up in front of the house across the street." Mattis ran to the window and leaned out and Bennett instinctively lurched out of the loveseat to catch him before he jumped. But Mattis turned slowly, the breeze fluttering the wire strands of his hair. "And they sat there, eating. Three of 'em. EATING."

"Three people? Three men? When?"

"Around noon."

"They were probably eating lunch."

"Oh, they were eating lunch, all right. And when they were done—that's when it happened." Mattis was breathing quickly, his adam's apple jumped and fell. His old man eyes squinted.

"What happened? What did they do?"

"They threw the wrappers out the car window."

"They, they littered?"

Mattis nodded, waiting for the impact of his words to sink in. "And the government just stands by." He nodded, lips clenched. "They don't care, Benevolent. No one does."

Bennett took a deep breath. "C'mon, let's go work out."

"Work out?" Mattis looked at him, not visibly reacting.

"Yeah, let's go to the gym."

"I gave up my gym membership."

"Whaddya mean? You love working out."

"And I'm going to keep working out, but I'm doing it online."

"Online? You're going to work out on a computer screen? Isn't that a little like having sex…excuse me, isn't it like, I don't know—say, eating, online? I mean, aren't there some things that you have to do in a three dimensional world?"

Mattis nodded towards the door. "It's getting dangerous out there." He pointed a thin finger toward the window. "People l-l-littering and d-double parking…inconsiderate, unfriendly…!" His finger shook. "Double PPARKING!"

Bennett didn't answer. He had noticed recently that his friend was shying away from venturing out of the house, preferring the dark room and his computer screen to the outside world. He tried to think of a way to get Mattis to relax.

"Well, forget the gym, then. If you change your mind, you can come in as my guest for five bucks. How 'bout we have a few beers here and go out somewhere?"

Mattis brightened. "The beers sound great, but don't think I'm going anywhere."

Four beers apiece later, they were at a club where the music was so loud they had to play "Charades" to understand one another. Mattis met several people he knew in the bathroom, where the unisex elite drug party-within-the-party was taking place. He stayed there for over an hour while Ben let the crowd carry him along with the crashing drums and thumping bass. He made eye contact with a few women, dancing a bit as they eddied past, swaying his body since there was no room to move his feet outside his immediate space.

By 1:30, Mattis had come out of the bathroom, high on a variety of pills and powders in addition to his beer, and insisting on seeing his "Cyberbabe," so Bennett brought him home, then went back out to find a dance club where he might have a few drinks, resigned to having no sleep before work tomorrow.

2

BEN

The antiseptic smell of the hospital frightened Bennett and inhibited his concentration. He had mentioned the problem to Ned with an eye toward trying to move the meeting to the agency's office, but Ned had said to "use" that fear to become more aware of the hospital environment. Better understanding of what it was like to be in the hospital from the patient's point of view would help bring about a better ad campaign. So, he had thought, what would alleviate this fear? He looked at Art, who, as the senior copy writer, had come along to contribute ideas, but as usual, Art was content to watch quietly, his eyes sharp, noting everything.

Bennett took a sip of coffee from the styrofoam cup, then held up the first illustration. "First we personalize the staff; show why a stay at the Center is a friendly, warm experience. Give the potential patient and his or her family confidence in the caregivers."

George Franklin was concentrating. He took the comp from Bennett and examined it.

"We would use photographs?"

"Oh, of course. These are just to give you an idea." He laughed. "We don't want to waste your money on models until we know exactly which scenarios we'll portray."

Mr. Franklin sat back, still holding the comp, and took a pack of cigarettes from inside his suit pocket. He made a little motion and a single cigarette slid up from the pack. He lit it and exhaled with a whoosh. He nodded as he spoke. "It's good, Ben—I can call you Ben, can't I?" He leaned over and touched Ben's arm. "I'm sure you'll be here a lot over the next few months, so we'll get to know one another pretty well, right?"

Ben smiled. "I hope so."

"Mmm. It's good, but too sterile."

The room grew cold. Bennett tried to breath evenly. "How so?"

George frowned and folded his arms across his chest. "I'm not sure." He shook the comp in front of him. "This is friendly, all right, and we do want friendly." He dropped the paper on the table, shaking his head. "It's just...missing something. I can't put my finger on what."

Ben's mind raced in circles. He wanted to yell: "Am I supposed to read your goddamn mind? If you don't like it, fine, but tell me what you want, you hypocritical, nicotine-addicted old bastard!"

"Missing something," was what Bennett said, tapping his lips with a pointed finger. "Missing something."

"Why not address the problem head on?" Art said. He looked thoughtful, one thin eyebrow down, the other raised. His perfectly groomed rugged good looks gave him a James Bond appearance.

"What do you mean?" asked George.

"Well, we want to convince folks not to be afraid to stay here, that there's no problem with the competency of the staff or the integrity of the blood system and so on..."

Ben was cringing inside. He had pointedly avoided mentioning the hospital's AIDS crisis so as not to offend the senior administrator.

"...so why not meet people's fears head on?"

A river of wrinkles ran across Mr. Franklin's forehead. He leaned closer to Art, his eyes narrowing. "And how might we do that?"

"We say the unsayable. Show the hospital's state-of-the-art procedures with an accent on the blood screening process, show AIDS patients being cared for, show the newest treatments being administered." Art looked up at the ceiling, thinking. "Show the bond that develops between the caregivers and those being cared for. Show the awards given to the Center for its quality of care and its, I don't know, its attention to the patients' needs above and beyond the usual requirements." He waved one hand and took a sip of decaf. "Something like that."

Mr. Franklin was appraising the clean cut copy writer. He waited a long moment before answering, shaking his head as he spoke. "Son, to be honest, we've never received an award like that."

Art giggled. "So we'll make one up, and we'll find someone to give it to you."

Bennett was aghast. He wondered for an instant where Art might find another job in Nassau County. As a newspaper editor, perhaps.

Mr. Franklin slammed one of his heavy hands on the tabletop. He threw back his head and laughed, a deep, wheezing laugh that reminded Ben of a Chevy Impala he had owned fifteen years earlier. It had been his first car and he and Beth had lost their respective virginities in its back seat. He allowed himself a sad inner smile, remembering the frosted windshield and the bite of the cold air on the backs of his thighs and the red marks the plastic upholstery made on her hips while the look on her face told him she didn't mind.

"I like it," Franklin roared, unable to catch his breath and starting to cough. He alternated between laughing and coughing and finally calmed down enough to look at Art with red rimmed eyes. "Oh, you've got balls, buddy. Like goddamn cantaloupes. An award! Yes!" He began to laugh again, gasping and snorting.

* * *

DESPERATION

The Man with the Hat was late! Maybe he wouldn't come at all! No, no no! What, how? Help! Where, where, where was he! That son of a bitch! That whore!

Down the street was a jewelry store and the thought of robbing it came and went—without a weapon, that might not work. A stick could pose as a weapon if you held it right, but maybe not. Maybe run up to a cop and steal his gun and run back to the jewelry store and—

There it was! The Hat! A black speck in the distance! He was coming! Help was on-the-goddamn way! Ha! The cavalry! The trumpets!

Standing still while shaking was a helluva job but when trying to keep an eye on the Man with the Hat, miracles were possible. Stand on tiptoes and concentrate. Don't blink. He's coming isn't he? Isn't he?

Noooooooooo!!!!! The hat had been a picture on the side of a bus! That irresponsible...!

A wailing scream pushed up from deep inside. Startled shoppers backed away. A man lurched into the street, ignoring the oncoming traffic; a woman clutched her purse. They think you're crazy, the voice said.

Maybe they were right.

The Man with the Hat, the Man with the Hat! Where the hell was the Man with the Hat! Help came from that, the Man with the Hat.

"Yo, my friend, howya been?"

And there he was. He had come from the other direction. What a new, different, wonderful idea. What a fabulous thought. What a delightful man! He could appear from anywhere, hat and all!

Thank God!

The exchange was made. Now, be very, very careful. Don't let anyone guess. Run to the house without running; get there, don't drop any, have everything you need, get it ready, don't break anything, be careful, don't let anyone steal it. And remember, they're watching. They're always always watching.

Boot Buddy would be there; he'd be waiting. He'd been given half the money and would have half a bundle waiting. Walk, don't run. Be a part of the pre-Christmas crowd. You've got your present, so smile and keep walkin' in the winter wonderland. In a few minutes we'll be deckin' some halls.

The house seemed pitch black inside after the white snow and early afternoon sun. The windows were boarded and there was a combination of smells: old overcoats, urine and butane. Half closed eyes watched from corners, disinterested, nodding. Hungry, wary eyes, having used up theirs, waited for an opportunity to steal.

Boot Buddy was on the floor, in the corner, his once handsome features carved into a whacked half smile.

His top pocket was empty.

"You piece of garbage. You couldn't wait for me, could you?"

While his ears had heard, the comment had not yet registered. "Whoa, all right." He grinned, eyes rolling back into his head.

"I paid for half of what you did, you shit. Well, know what? I knew you'd do this and copped my own. And I'm sharing with the Teacher." The faint hope that Boot Buddy might feel some remorse or apologize vanished. He had nodded and was already snoring, his chin bouncing on the snot coated corduroy shoulder of his dusty overcoat.

The Teacher, a math teacher at the local high school, was one of the hungry pairs of eyes. He had shared his yesterday so he would be today's lucky winner. A deal was a deal and, unlike Boot Buddy, here was a man with integrity!

A faint discomfort called out from somewhere low in the chest. What was that sensation? Familiar, but not too important...Hunger. The ten dollars given to the

Man with the Hat had been the only money that could be expected for several days. With a shrug, works were laid out on the floor and the wonderful process begun.

Science. Better living through chemistry. Experts at work. Mad scientists.

Once the mixture of heroin and water was cooked and the syringe filled, it was handed to the Teacher, who knew exactly what and how much to do. His leg was drawn up close to his body, his sockless ankle exposed. With practiced precision, he identified a vein and pushed the needle in and held it steady, slowly drawing back on the plunger. Blood mixed with heroin—a vein had been hit. The Teacher took a deep breath, blinked and pushed slowly on the plunger, and the mixture of blood, water and street heroin eased into his body. When it was half gone he responded to the tap on his arm by pulling the needle out and handing it back.

For a while no one moved. The Teacher waited and his partner and benefactor watched carefully, looking for signs of strychnine seizure or overdose.

The Teacher leaned back suddenly, his neck muscles gave way and his head banged back against a board. Something wet puddled on the floor near his hands. Blood. His head had struck a nail; no one noticed.

"Ohhhh," said the Teacher, as a smile tried and failed to appear on his face. "Ohhh."

He fell back on an elbow, his eyes all but shut. His steamy breath came in bursts from his open mouth. "Ehhh," his shoulders moved in tiny circles of ecstasy and his hand moved ever so slightly and squeezed the friend who had brought this light into existence. His lips smacked together, tasting. Then his body went limp. This was where you had to watch. Was he breathing? Was the batch too good?

The batch...was fine.

"How's it taste?" The question was redundant, and soon to be answered anyway. The half filled needle pushed easily into a new, barely used spot behind the knee. Once the syringe was empty and in the moment before the fix hit, the plunger was drawn back and new blood drawn in and emptied into a vial which was shut and stored in the leather waist pouch. This was the Game. The Race. Beat the Fix! Hey! Can this week's contestant get the blood back into the syringe, pull the needle out, insert it into the cork and push the blood into the vial...all before the fix hits your system?

You get the prize either way.

The process was repeated just as the heroin kicked in and that warm, loving glow began to spread. And in the dark, lonely basement, flowers began to bloom.

Time for business. Off to the hospital. To find IV lines, Broviac catheters, Foley catheters—doorways to the body! That irresistible smiling hunger was back and we all knew what that meant! The nurses and cleaning people in the quiet, pre-dawn halls minded their own business, never suspecting. All part of the game! The only sounds were of medical machines and quiet voices. The roar that had grown like a migraine before the arrival of the Man with the Hat had crawled off into its hiding place for now. The Fear was gone from the stomach and bowels and that warm campfire glow, that singalong of friendship, fellowship and illusion was growing, cradling, like a hot blanket on a winter night.

* * *

BEN

The temperature in the main room at Selling Sight and Sound was nearly ninety degrees, despite the crisp late Fall weather and the open window. Towards the front of the room three models in green hospital gowns were seated on a bed, around which stood a variety of hospital equipment. Twin light banks shone on this scene, around which a small dark-haired photographer darted, clicking a hand held light meter.

Bennett James and George S. Franklin sat in two oval backed white wicker chairs behind the light banks. The rest of the 3S staff stood, fidgeting, along the back wall.

"Now, this ad," said Bennett, stepping back from the hospital room set, "will show the patients at the Hospital—"

"No names, now," George Franklin interrupted, pointing a warning finger as Bennett sat down next to him, several feet from the makeshift stage. "Not even fictitious ones."

"No, the reader won't know who they're supposed to be, but we will."

"What difference does that make?" Mr. Franklin wanted to know.

Ben paused a moment longer than necessary, the way he'd seen Ned pause to show impatience. "We've found that we can achieve the best sense of realism if the ad is based on a real situation. This also helps the Art Director—"

"That's you?"

"—get to know the people in the ad, how they interact, and better understand the ad's composition and feel."

"Feel?"

The actors were shifting and sweating in the hot lights.

"If you want to discuss it further, Mr. Franklin, perhaps we ought to shut down the light banks and give Charlie a break."

George Franklin sipped his coffee. "No. No discussion necessary. Go right ahead." He turned towards the door and cleared his throat. "Who are they?"

"You remember Art and that's Lou, head writer and artist." He beckoned them over. "Guys, this is Mr. Franklin, he's the—"

"Of course, Mr. Franklin, a pleasure." Art stepped toward them and put out a hand.

Lou smiled and followed suit.

Art turned the bulky administrator towards him. "Have you ever had any construction on your home?" He looked at the ceiling. "Well, if you haven't, don't. And if you have, well, I'm sorry for you."

Mr. Franklin nodded. "Actually, I—"

Art interrupted. "They start late, order the wrong materials, don't do what they say they're going to do, show up if and when they feel like it—"

"Arthur," Louis chided, "Mr. Franklin doesn't need to hear about our dirty laundry." He smiled at Mr. Franklin. "Actually the wear and tear on Art has been much worse than on the house, and he's come up with a brilliant idea for a sitcom as a result of all the *tsouris*."

"Tsouris?" said Mr. Franklin.

"Louis!" Arthur was aghast. "You promised!"

"Oh that's all right," said Mr. Franklin. "I have aspirations in many areas, but television is not one of them. Tell me about your idea."

Art sat down, crossed his legs and leaned back. "Well, it's called *The Addition* because it's an addition to both this family's home and their household."

Bennett, who had been listening patiently, leaned over the back of Art's chair. "Tell him why."

"Well, because the family in the program hires a construction company to build them a second floor and they procrastinate so much and there are so many obstacles to their getting the job done, that they never leave. The construction company is permanently part of the show. Each episode starts with a glimmer of hope that they'll get the job finished, but it always falls through and they become an addition to the family. Maybe they pull the family's kid or dog out of a well, date the daughter, give the mom inadvertent cooking advice."

"I see," said Mr. Franklin, looking a little alarmed.

Louis nodded proudly. "It happens to be a very good idea and eventually, I believe Arthur will be able to sell it. He's very good at what he does." He gave Art's shoulder a squeeze. "He just lets it affect him a little too much."

Art nodded. "Anyway, it's based on our own little construction project in the Hamptons, which seems like it'll never end. Writing it was a way of making lemonade."

Mr. Franklin looked confused. "Your project?"

"Mine and Lou's."

"Yours and..."

Bennett was watching Mr. Franklin's face. "Places everyone!" he said suddenly. "The actors are overheating in the lights. Everyone ready! Let's try to get it right in one take."

Arthur sighed. "Listen to Louis B. Mayer."

Mr. Franklin rubbed his palms together, looking around. "You fellas are welcome to stay but keep it down."

Lydia snickered behind her notepad. "No comment."

Bennett felt a fleeting helplessness, as though his ship were about to sink and he could do nothing to stop it.

He went to the stage and moved the IV stands closer to the actors, who had begun looking toward the camera with frozen expressions of yearning and pain.

"Okay, Charlie. Whenever you're ready." He motioned to the photographer to begin shooting his Polaroids. He turned to George. "Now the headline, which will be in bold but not too bold type, will be above the photo. It will say 'Where There's Hope' dot dot dot. And below the photo we'll have two short columns of text running around the facility's logo, which will be centered at bottom...What?" The CEO was shaking his head.

"It's not right."

"But we discussed—"

George S. Franklin stared hard at Ben. "I know what we discussed, young man, but it just isn't right. Don't take it personally. This is business." He eyed Ben. "If you don't like it, bill me. Now, I don't mean the text or the headline, that's all fine, but the image, the people, the layout. It's all wrong." He lit a cigarette and puffed noisily, his wing tipped shoes tapping the polished wood floor.

Ben nodded to Charlie to take a break. The light banks were shut off and the actors were shuttled off to one side and given coffee. Lou and Art edged closer, so they were within earshot and available for help without seeming intrusive. Lydia grinned into her notebook, loving every minute of any confrontation or controversy.

Ben took a deep breath. "If it isn't right, Mr. Franklin, we'll fix it. Now what aspect…?"

His mouth and the active part of his brain safely on "autoplacate," Ben was in London with Beth, riding a bright red double-decker bus around Oxford Circus. The streets were crowded with shoppers, and they held hands and necked until they arrived at their stop, where they got off and, arms around one another's waists, and spent an hour window shopping.

Afterwards, they went to a pub reputed to be several hundred years old, and received a new perspective on Colonial American history from the bartender while drinking pints of the house brew. They shared a shepherd's pie and took the bus back to the bed and breakfast, where they dropped a few coins into the room heater and snuggled close under red wool blankets. Chilly England was warmed and colonized by Bethness.

Lydia was crossing her eyes, Lou was taking notes, while Art was shooting him warning looks. Bennett could hear his own voice rising and overriding Mr. Franklin's.

"The composition won't work that way. If you're going to use a graphic like that—"

"Excuse me?" George Franklin barked, standing up. "I told you, this isn't right." He jabbed a nicotine-stained finger and, without another word, turned and walked off the set.

Ben chewed the inside of his cheek and looked at the scene they had set up. The models were playing cards at his desk. Lou, Art and Lydia were coming toward him. He looked at the open window and thought briefly of doing an end run around them and launching himself through it.

Lydia slapped him on the arm. "You can see how a guy like that made a career out of healing, can't you?"

Lou shrugged, his eyes understanding. "Clients. Can't live with 'em, can't live without 'em." He patted Ben's shoulder and went over to the table with the food. "I'll take cold cuts any day," he called over his shoulder.

Lou sat down where Mr. Franklin had been. "Why don't we brainstorm for a while? We'll let the models go for the day, send Charlie home and figure out another angle. I'll think of something to tell Ned."

Arthur clapped a hand on the back of Bennett's neck. "You've got to get your mind off that pretty young thing and back on your work full time."

Bennett frowned, annoyed. “I wasn’t thinking about Beth!”

“I see…”

Louis, who had begun to sketch, looked up from his pad. “Why don’t we have him out to Tara for the weekend? The ladies at The Mill will never let him leave the Hamptons.”

Arthur’s eyes twinkled. “Lou’s right, you know. You can check out the lake—it’s a pond, really, but we call it a lake—you can fish with Louis, shop with me, maybe find a little companionship…”

“Jeez,” called Lydia. “You never invite me to the Hamptons for the weekend.”

Arthur let go of Ben’s neck and stood straight up. “That’s because to find you companionship we’d have to rent a day boat and go shark fishing. They’d have to strap you in one of those chairs.”

“Hey,” she called back. “At least that’s the only time I’d be strapped into something, you cross-dressing…!”

Arthur waved her away. “Keep your alternative lifestyles straight, so to speak, white trash.” He smiled at Ben. “Ignore her. You just let Aunt Arthur and Uncle Lou take you in for the weekend and everything will be fine.”

Bennett smiled, feeling better. “Thanks, Art, but I need to do something creative.”

“What’s more creative than coming with me to the Arts Center?”

“Or, the Art’s Center,” Lou laughed, “with an apostrophe. Arthur practically lives there.”

“Thanks, guys. I’ll think about it.”

* * *

Within an hour the set was dismantled, the camera equipment and lights gone, and the floor covered with crumpled yellow pieces of paper. Bennett, Art, Lou and Lydia sat around the conference table surrounded by pads, pens and white styrofoam cups of coffee.

The phone rang. Lou picked it up and Ben glanced in his direction. The look on his face kept him from looking away.

“It’s Franklin,” said Lou, as he hung up. “We’ve got to get the photographer back. He’ll be here in an hour with his own models.” He looked around, hands on chubby hips. “Are there any more jelly donuts? You know, I think we need more food.” He took a small but thick notebook from his left pants pocket and began leafing through it. “Chinese, no. Greek, no. Deli, no. Ah, Tex-Mex…”

Bennett’s back broke out in a sweat.

“I’ll page Charlie,” said Art, remaining calm. “See, Ben? Franklin’s coming back. We didn’t lose the account. He probably just had to bring in some people he thought looked more realistic. Some clients have to feel like they’re in control.”

Lydia sipped her coffee. “Or maybe he went home for his gun.”

“He’s bringing models, dear,” said Lou, nodding subtly towards Bennett.

“Oh, don’t worry about hurting my feelings,” said Ben. “After dealing with Franklin, you’re a walk in the park.”

"Maybe these models're his gang, coming to see to it that we do right by the Medical Center." Lydia smirked. "Maybe he just says they're models."

Lou smiled. "Your cup is so half empty, isn't it?"

Lydia perked up. "I know, maybe Franklin's responsible for the outbreaks of HIV. Like it's some kind of insurance scam or something."

No one answered.

Art was organizing the pages of copy he had written over the last hour. "If you'll climb down from your broomstick, dear, we've got to have this in some kind of order by the time Franklin gets back."

Despite Lydia's comments, Bennett relaxed. Franklin hadn't canceled! He was coming back!

* * *

George S. Franklin returned full of energy. He had left his jacket and tie behind and rolled his sleeves up. He began issuing orders, lighting cigarettes, jotting notes. The three models he had brought certainly looked their part, Bennett thought. Two of them did, anyway. They were a tall, bony man with very short gray hair who appeared to be in his early fifties and a short, fair skinned woman with a page boy haircut and bright blue eyes. Both were emaciated, gaunt, although they were smiling and chatty at the moment. Their expressions would change, Ben assumed, once the shooting began.

The other man was different, and Ben thought that perhaps George had decided to go with two models rather than three, and had brought along an assistant of some sort. This man was rugged and athletic, with a freckled, sun-weathered Major League Baseball complexion and a bright smile to match.

"Ralph, Carolyn, Tim. Meet Bennett. He's the art director at Selling, Sight and Sound, better known as 3S. Ben," George put a hand on his shoulder. "These folks are patients at the Center." He turned to the patients. "Can I get you guys some coffee?"

Ralph and Carolyn shook their heads. Tim, the athletic-looking one, nodded. "Dark, no sugar."

George nodded and smiled and looked inquiringly at Ben. "You?"

Ben shook his head. Art, Lou and Lydia had come over and stood, waiting to be introduced and Ben slowly turned. "Yeah, Art, Lou, Lydia, these are…"

"Ralph," the tall man stepped forward and offered his hand, which was shaken all around. Carolyn and Tim introduced themselves and did the same.

"We're outpatients at the AIDS clinic at the Medical Center. George asked us to stop by and help you guys out with your ad campaign."

"You're…patients?" Lydia asked.

Ben inadvertently stepped back, and looked down at his hand. Art stepped forward, slapping Ben lightly on the back of the head. He leaned toward Ralph, and said something into his ear, after which the two men embraced and spoke softly for a moment.

George Franklin brought in the 2 coffees. With him was the photographer and his assistant.

"Okay, let's get started," said George. He took Carolyn by the hand and led her to the set. "Okay, dear. Where would you like to sit?"

Everyone else moved to the set area. The patients were given scripts.

"Tim, aren't you cold?" George asked, taking off his own coat. "Here, why don't you wear this? You sure? It's a big studio and kind of drafty. Okay. How 'bout you, Ralphy?" He leaned over to Bennett. "Can you make this room 5 or 6 degrees warmer, Ben?"

Ben nodded. "Sure, though the lights'll warm it up pretty quickly anyway."

"Charlie!" George called to the photographer. "Let's do this in one take, okay?"

"That's up to you and to them."

"They'll get it right," said George.

And they did. The ad was shot in a half hour and within an hour, Charlie and his assistant were packed and gone, the film promised for the following day.

As soon as the shoot was done, George huddled with his patients. "I'm proud of you guys," he said, his arms around their necks. "Thanks so much for helping me out today."

"Anytime, Georgie," said Ralph.

"Let's go into the city," said Carolyn.

"You did say you'd buy us dinner," Tim said, shooting George a look.

"Ah, I never said that," George said, turning quickly and mouthing "watch this" to the Selling Sight and Sound staff.

Ralph stood up, staring at George. "You bastard," he said.

Carolyn nodded, hiding a smile. "Doesn't surprise me," she said. "Typical of the medical community, nowadays. HMOs don't pay the caregivers, the caregivers lie to the public..."

George looked at Ben, his eyebrows dancing, eyes alight.

Tim stood up, squared his shoulders and began walking toward George, wagging a finger. "Georgie. Now you promised, right in front of all of us..."

"Okay, okay!" George got up and began backing away, lighting a cigarette and puffing frantically. "All right, all right! Where to you want to go? A show? Italian food? No, no, not French!" He stepped forward and hugged the patients to him.

Ben watched, fascinated.

* * *

STRUNG OUT

The nod was long gone. The alertness was deteriorating slowly into that uncomfortable, skin crawling restlessness. Ants, normally admired, now turned against you, transforming your skin into the irritant. Take a deep breath. It would get worse, and soon. Only one way of stopping it.

The discomfort was becoming an irresistible itchiness. The sweats would start soon, and you might sit for hours in the dark, sweating and scratching, knowing it would get worse. Then the pain, retching, convulsions. No money, so what could you steal or pawn to get more? Who could you rob, what could you do to stop these damn ants? Look around. Do something. Right now! NOW! What would he want? What did any man want? What kind of deal could you make with the Man with the Hat?

* * *

BEN

"Shut the goddamn window!" Mattis cupped his hands over the green tray in his lap. Marijuana was spread across the tray's bottom. He had begun rolling joints and, after a few minutes, felt the need for cocaine.

Ben took a deep breath and closed his eyes for a moment. "Do you have to do that here?"

Mattis looked at him as he unfolded a square of white paper. "We can pull over if you whoa—now look what you made me do!" A gust of wind had blown the white powder out of the packet.

Ben looked hard at the road, his attitude that of the protective older brother or parent of a misbehaving child. Better to keep him within sight and earshot even given his bad behavior, than sending him off where he might find some more dangerous mischief.

Ben shook his head. "Mattis, it's bad enough that you smoke that stuff in the car. Can you keep the blow in your wallet until you get someplace private? I really don't want anything to do with any of it."

"What you want is your problem," Mattis muttered.

Ben drove from Mattis's house, east on Sunrise Highway, through Lynbrook, Rockville Centre, Baldwin and Freeport, to the Meadowbrook Parkway, which he took north to the Northern State East. "Who does this Franklin he think he is? I had the situation under control, but apparently he knows everything, not only about hospitals and administration, but about advertising! I mean, why doesn't he work nights at the hospital and do my job during the daytime!"

"He's a goddamn Renaissance man!" crowed Mattis, who, despite his dismissal of Ben's request, had put away his drugs and was now popping open a beer, his fifth. The first four had been necessary to give him the courage to leave his house.

"Whoa!" Ben slammed on the brakes. "You believe that guy swerved into the lane right in front of us?"

"I'll hang out the window and flip him the bird." Mattis rolled down his window, leaned out, then rolled it quickly up again and crouched in the back seat. "I know that guy! He's a friend of my old man's! He's, he's...hey, he's after us, man!"

Ben gave his friend a casual glance; none of this was new to him. "Mattis, he's just a guy who cut us off. He wasn't sent by anyone."

"He was, I tell you! He swerved from right over—" He pointed to the next lane. "Oh my God! That guy was looking at us, and he said something. I'll bet they're together. I'll bet—holy jeez, I know! FBI."

"Uh, huh. Just what you need. Feed your paranoia with a little blow." Hoping to distract him, Ben put on a tape and turned the volume up. The inside of the car vibrated from the bass as Ben gunned the engine and the car hesitated, and then jumped forward.

"We're doing a photo shoot for the Metropolitan Medical Center over on Sunrise Highway near Ocean Avenue," Ben yelled over the music. "It's kind of a public service announcement with 3 real AIDS patients."

Mattis nodded, sniffling. He was examining the label on the front of his beer bottle. "Did you ever hear that there's a coded message somewhere on here that only men between the ages of 18 and 30 can see?" he asked.

"It's a pretty screwed up situation," Ben continued.

"Sure," said Mattis, "if you're under 18 or over 30 and spending your money on beer just to see a message you'll never—"

"No," said Ben, "I mean, patients at the hospital seem to be getting AIDS out of the blue. They just go into the hospital for whatever reason and all of a sudden they're HIV positive. That's what this ad campaign's supposed to contradict."

That got Mattis's attention. "Really? Aren't you supposed to keep that a secret?"

Ben nodded, then shrugged. "I trust you, man."

"So you guys're supposed to," he waved the beer bottle, searching for the right phrase, "make the Medical Center look good."

Ben nodded.

"I say that place gets what it deserves."

Ben looked at his friend, whose eyes had a distant, intense, calm-before-the-storm look. "Yeah, well that's my job."

"You know I was in that place eleven years ago," Mattis said. "My parents had me locked up on the fifth floor—the detox unit. Said I had a drug problem. I say I had a parents problem."

"Your parents put you in a detox?"

"Oh sure. I had to go to therapy, twelve step meetings, the whole bit. What a load! Those people tried to get me into religion." He took a small glass vial with a black screw on its top from his pocket and held it up so Ben could see. "Here's all the religion I need."

Ben slapped his hand downward. "You have more of that? Get it away from me! You want someone to see it?"

Mattis shook his head. "And I was just going to turn you on, too. Whadda shame!"

"No thanks. I'll wait and have a beer at the bar."

Mattis slipped the vial back into his pocket. "God, I hated that place. They made me scrub toilets, which might not have been so bad if I could've dropped a few tabs of blotter first, but I had to do it straight! I tell ya, I hate everyone there. They should all drop dead!"

They had left the parkway and were at a stop light; a faint tone could be heard over the music. The car next to them was honking its horn and its driver, a man in a business suit, was pushing a palm downward; he put a finger to his lips.

"He wants us to turn it down?" Mattis said. "Oh, really?" He gave the radio knob a vicious clockwise twist as the light changed and the Cougar shook with the roar of overloaded speakers. From the back seat came two deafening bursts of static.

Ben turned the radio off. "Dude." He paused, and let the ringing fade from his ears. "You blew my speakers."

"Oh," Mattis said. "Sorry, dude."

They pulled into the bar's unpaved parking lot, which was packed with cars, found a spot in the back and got out of the car.

"Funny," Ben began.

"No, not funny at all," said Mattis, closing the passenger side door. "Those're expensive speakers. I'm sorry, Ben-factor."

"No, I mean about this thing at the hospital. We started the shoot for their ad, and the head of the hospital, this guy George Franklin, who's turning out to be one real bastard, blows us off, then comes back with these AIDS patients, and it's like he turned into a saint or something."

"Probably guilt," said Mattis, getting his wallet out and checking to see how much money he had. He glanced around before handing Ben three hundred dollar bills. "Here, for the speakers."

Ben took the money without comment.

"You can't go around harboring guilt," said Mattis. "Just figure out what the right thing is, and do it." He returned his wallet to his pocket. "I feel bad for any patient at that hospital who winds up with the virus, but the staff, the doctors—screw 'em. It's probably just the hospital staff screwing up that's getting all of them sick, anyway."

Ben thought about this. "Could be. Could be." They approached two burly bouncers who stood at either side of the entrance, allowed themselves to be patted down for weapons, loose bottles or cans and entered the bar.

* * *

The nature of time and space seemed to change in the bar. The red lit air moved more slowly than the blue air outside and air particles, the molecules themselves, seemed to gyrate against one another, creating warmth and dispelling loneliness. To Ben, it was a comfortable oasis of sound and atmosphere.

To Mattis, it was more. He appeared to Ben to have grown several inches taller the instant he entered the bar. His eyes looked outward rather than toward the cuffs on his pants. His voice deepened and strengthened. He smiled and nodded to the regulars with the comfortable ease of a fish returned to water.

The patrons were divided into two groups. There were the regular customers, who came to drink and dance and mingle. They stood on line outside, paid their admission, and remained until last call, dancing, watching and occasionally meeting others of their kind. The second group was the one to which Mattis and Bennett belonged: the specials. None of the specials paid monetary admission. Many of them did not have homes in the usual sense of the word. Few had health insurance, most were jobless. A collection, called "the door pot" was taken up during the early part of the evening and, once collected, was split in half. The first half went to the two owners, who were twin brothers who had come over from the other side: Bay Ridge, Brooklyn. The second half went to the four bouncers, two of whom worked the door while the other two worked inside the bar.

This collection consisted, not of money, but entirely of every kind and classification of drug. There were pot and pills, a wide variety of speed and tranquilizers, and cocaine in its snortable, smokable and shootable states. There were a variety of opiates and pills, like Dilaudid, that mimicked them. There were even the newest drugs, like Ecstasy and OxyContin, and these the two owners, Tony and Frank, took for their girlfriends.

"Nothing doin' out here," said Mattis, heading for the mens' room. "I'm going in." The mens' and womens' rooms were where the heavy drug use was centered. They were divided into the public sector along the sinks and counters where cocaine and pills were openly used, and the private stalls where needle use and crack smoking dominated. Mattis was a mainstay in the public sector.

Bennett, who stayed away from drugs in favor of beer, was thinking about how he might meet one of the women who was coming out of the ladies' room. He stood at the wood paneled strip of wall between the bathrooms, telling himself that he just didn't have the guts to say hello to a strange woman. But just then some kind of "what-the-hell" motivation took a hold of him. Perhaps he was tired of daydreaming about Beth and living in sensations that were years old. He decided to strike up a conversation with the next woman who came out of the ladies' room.

The ladies' room door swung open and a woman in blue leggings, a green blouse and very big gold hair walked out.

Well then, the next woman.

A short, African American woman came out wearing red lipstick, braided hair and an orange dress so tight that it forced her to take very small steps.

He didn't say a word.

He took a step towards the door, which opened, nearly hitting him in the face. A pale young woman with reddish hair and very blue eyes came out and looked at him, surprise on her face. She was wearing a black button-down tank top with white lace trim, tight, low-cut jeans and black satin gloves which extended to several inches above her elbows.

"Why are you looking at me like that?" She smiled when she spoke. Her voice was low, creamy.

"Like what?"

"Like you've really gotta go and I took your place on line. There's no line, you know. You can just go right in. The mens' room is over there." She indicated the appropriate door. "This is the ladies' room."

Well now she's here, so talk. And try not to sound stupid.

"That's an interesting pendant you're wearing."

She touched the gold ornament, rubbing it lightly between her thumb and forefinger. "I got it from my grandmother."

He tried to look interested. "I never knew either of my grandmothers. Were you close to yours?"

The young woman nodded. “From when I was a little girl until she died, when I was a teenager, she was the only person I trusted, except for—”

“Except…?”

“Never mind. He’s dead, too.”

“Oh.” He tried to think of a way to steer the conversation in a more positive direction. “So, who’d you trust after she died?”

“No one…yet.”

He nodded, understanding.

“Excuse me.” Some women had come out of the ladies’ room and had to step around Ben. He touched the woman’s upper arm with the tips of his fingers, guiding her out of the flow of traffic. Her arm jerked away and his ego began the downward spiral that began so easily when women did not react the way he had hoped.

But she followed him to the side of the room and leaned against the wall facing him, the lacy trim on her black tank top bunched together as she clasped her hands in front of her.

“I’m Ben.” He put out his hand. She looked in its direction without seeing it. Instantly, he was ashamed; who, in this day and age, shook hands?

But she extended her hand, her fingers undulating, then drew it away with an amused giggle. “Eleanor.”

* * *

NED DOYLE

Ned Doyle was giddy with exhaustion. After meeting with Ben and going over what had occurred at the photo shoot for the first Medical Center ads, he had spent an hour and a half bent over the green blotter on his desk, writing longhand notes to himself outlining the next series of moves he or Ben would propose to George Franklin. He was elated that Franklin had thought enough of 3S to bring his own patients, whom he obviously loved, to the shoot. He had joined the process. He had signed on and was now officially a client. Time to make him happy. Franklin ought to see the ads using different shots, different headlines, typestyles, and layouts. And he had to see them fast. The comp ads could be created in a day or a day and a half and proofs made overnight.

This thrill of anticipation was exactly the same as the one he received from sparring or a tournament after dancing around his opponent, sizing him up and knowing which techniques would work and what the response would be.

It was time to dazzle Franklin with speed, accuracy, footwork!

But that would be tomorrow. Now, it was time for what made it all worthwhile. Little Ned loved to be read to. The book was unimportant. He could be listening to the dictionary; as long as he could lean his little head on daddy’s leg and breathe softly while daddy’s soothing voice washed over him, all would be well in his world. And in daddy’s world as well.

Ned smiled to himself. That was certainly a two way street. Seeing that little chest rise and fall and seeing his boy’s loving attention to his own voice and knowing that he filled this beautiful child's world—he told Sam again and again, that's what it's all about. Any hot night his mind and taste buds started to stray to a cold beer, he could remember nearly losing those moments forever and he was right back on course. That was how it worked. And if he forgot, he called Sam. The only thing better than reading to little Ned was reading to both boys. If little Ned liked it, then it was good enough for little Frankie.

He had to strain to focus his eyes on the road, leaning over the wheel of his family car, a red Voyager, as he drove the 15 miles to his split level ranch. He made a mental note to have his eyes checked.

When he arrived home, he was surprised to see that the light in the den was on. He would have thought Maureen and the kids would be asleep.

He tiptoed into the kids' room. He'd been right; they were sleeping. He stood quietly for several minutes, watching their tiny chests expand and contract.

What have I possibly done to deserve these beautiful little faces in my life?

Then he remembered and he swallowed and went into the den, hanging his coat on the rack where the lower tier of the split level began.

Someone on the television was saying something about love meaning never having to apologize.

And then he heard Maureen's sobs.

* * *

BEN

"So, you come here a lot?"

Eleanor nodded. "Yeah, most nights."

Ben looked surprised. "Really? I don't remember seeing you."

She shrugged, looking around. "Well, I've been here."

She was getting bored; he had to think of something. "Want to go out for a bite to eat?"

She shook her head, looking pained. "No. I don't eat much. But I would like to dance."

Grateful to be able to stop trying to think of things to say, he took the hand she had floated behind her and followed her to a spot on the crowded dance floor, where they moved in place, looking everywhere but at one another. After a while, he saw she was smiling at him in a way that said they shared something, a way that told other men to leave them alone. Was that strictly for the benefit of those other men? Was she just using him as a "Do Not Disturb" sign?

She was pretty; she was interesting. And something about her reached out to him and drew him in. It was as though she had a sweeping emotional cape that billowed out, catching and enfolding him until he was part of her world.

As they danced, he casually put a hand on her hip. She continued dancing, looking away, but her hips seemed to respond, like a cat stretching under a petting hand.

"You live around here?" he asked, during a break in the music.

She ignored the question, nodding toward the dance floor. "Flaco's my favorite band."

"Does your family—"

"Know what I've wanted to do for a long time? Get a tattoo!" She grabbed his hand. "Come on. Let's get tattooed."

He stared at her, thinking she was joking. Then he heard himself say, "Yeah, why not?" in the most casual of tones.

* * *

NED DOYLE

Ned stood at the kitchen counter, slicing a tomato for his sandwich and remembering the argument he and Maureen had earlier. He had asked her to rearrange the toys and clothes little Ned had outgrown. Had he asked nicely enough? Had there been some inappropriate inflection in his voice?

The tomato was becoming puree, as the slices became chops, the knife echoing against the white formica counter top. Couldn't she be less sensitive? Couldn't she see how busy he was...? His mood shifted to one of readiness. He was filled with edgy energy, his muscles poised for flight or fight, his air conserved for a sudden yell or *kyai.*

And then he remembered who he used to be and he smiled to himself. He remembered the old fury and felt the impulsive, irresistible rage that used to take hold of him, and which he was powerless to control. He remembered the shame of knowing he had hurt people and he remembered how utterly unable to admit how wrong he had been. He remembered all he had gone through to change.

Slowly, his muscles relaxed. He exhaled, visualizing a calming blue light. Gratitude replaced the fury. The movie had been wrong. Love was *being able to* apologize.

Carefully wrapping the tomato in cellophane and putting it in the appropriate drawer in the refrigerator, Ned went into the living room, put his arms around his wife, and told her he was sorry.

* * *

BEN

Charlie's was in East Rockaway, near the train station. He must have driven past it countless times. How odd that he had never noticed the tiny storefront with its red and black sign before.

Bennett's mind was racing far ahead of the white Cougar. While he had left Mattis at the club, a forty minute drive, he wasn't worried about his friend. Mattis knew everyone. He'd either get a ride or would pass out on someone's floor. His mind searched for a face-saving way out of getting the tattoo. Beside him, Eleanor was calmly directing.

"All the way down Ocean Avenue, then right, just over the tracks."

He hadn't believed her when she told him where Charlie's was. She lived five minutes from there, she said, in Oceanside, in an apartment around the block from Jimmy's, the huge hotdog and cheesesteak emporium that dominated the supermarket shopping center in the middle of town. Friends had brought her to the club, she explained, so she wouldn't need to go back for her car.

"Used to be only certain sorts of people got tattoos," she explained. "Pull in here. Now, the kid sitting across from you in science class might be getting one. Hell, his science teacher might show up with one. You can just park right there. Good. Well, this is it! You ready?"

He didn't answer for fear of throwing up.

They walked to the back of the building, which was overgrown with grass still shining beneath the thin layer of sleet that had come down that morning.

"Charlie's open late for anyone who knows the code." She pushed the bell three short times and one long.

A corpulent man with very short, orange hair and bright eyes opened the door and allowed them to pass down a musty hallway that must have once been painted white, and was now streaked with dirt. The carpet was of some indeterminate color. A few old chairs lined one wall. At the end of the hallway was a medium sized room whose walls were entirely covered with pictures of tattoos. Each wall contained a different illustrative style. One was the old fashioned patriotic eagle and snake or heart variety, many of which contained banners for names of wives, girlfriends or mothers. Another wall contained skulls, roses and motorcycles, many in flames. Yet another wall was adorned with cartoons: devils, small birds, butterflies, while the fourth wall contained abstract designs and old Indian motifs.

"I'm Charlie Spoon," the man said, not offering his hand. "Have a look around. Take your time." He wore a perpetual smile that somehow wasn't a smile since only his mouth was smiling; the rest of his face did not move. His bright eyes along with the grin gave him the exaggerated malicious look of a villain in a B horror movie.

"Don't mind him," said Eleanor. "He's got Graves' Disease. Makes his eyes bug out."

Ben looked at her. "You sure you want to do this?"

She held his gaze for a long time; then walked over to him, their eyes met and he could feel some part of her reach out to him. She wanted him, needed him. The feeling was strong, yet delicate. She grasped his arm at the elbow and squeezed. "I do if you do."

At that moment, he would have done anything for Eleanor, a fact he realized was absurd since he had only known her an hour and a half. He wasn't particularly drunk, yet he hadn't been so excited by a woman since Beth. Eleanor made him feel as though nothing in the world mattered but the two of them.

"I like birds," he said, indicating an eagle. "And that dragon's cool."

"What about her? You like her?" Eleanor pointed to a realistic illustration of a woman, her breasts exposed, a coquettish expression on her face.

"Um, not on my arm." He turned to her. "What'll you get?"

"I was thinking of a ghost—something to do with death."

"What about a skull?"

"Too common. I want something more…ethereal." She took her hand away from his arm and let it fall to her side, where it brushed lightly against his leg. Ben felt an odd sensation on the back of his neck, turned and saw Charlie Spoon watching them from the doorway.

"Settled on anything?"

"I was thinking about that Charlie Chaplin guy over there, for the back of my calf."

"If you're sure, we can get started. That one's ninety dollars." He peered at Ben. "You're not drunk, are you?" His eyes thought the idea amusing.

"No, sir."

Charlie Spoon gave a giggle. "And I know *you're* not drunk."

Eleanor looked annoyed. "Just take care of my friend, okay?"

"So, you're getting a ghost?" Ben asked, trying to keep his voice from shaking.

"I was thinking of a spider and a web."

"Very appropriate," said Charlie, giggling again.

Eleanor shot him a look. "I'm going to use your ladies' room, okay?"

Charlie Spoon nodded. He took a long, sealed package from a drawer and tore it open.

"What're those?" Ben asked.

"Needles. I have to use new ones every time. AIDS, you know? Damn disease changed the whole tattooing industry. We have autoclaves now, and sealed, disposable needles, all sorts of protective gear." He shrugged. "I guess it's a good thing for you. Pain in the ass for me, though. Expensive. Have a seat." He began to fiddle with a machine that looked to Ben rather like a dentist's drill. "So, what do you do for a living?"

"I'm an art director at an ad agency."

"Selling Sight and Sound?"

Ben nodded. "How did you know?"

"Only one around here. What're you working on?"

"Well, right now, the Medical Center is the big one."

Charlie gave him a funny look. "Oh," he said, and went back to fiddling with the needle, the drill and some packets of ink. He took the Charlie Chaplin stencil from the wall, positioned it on the back of Ben's leg as Ben lay down on the table in the center of the room. He held a small mirror up for Ben to see. "That ok?"

Ben nodded.

Charlie Spoon rubbed the back of Ben's leg with something cold.

"Alcohol," Charlie explained. "I have to swab it every few minutes to get rid of the blood."

"Oh," said Ben.

Eleanor came back into the room and sat down on the floor in a corner, humming to herself. She appeared to be falling asleep.

"So, what do you think of that place?" Charlie asked.

"What place?" Ben had begun to feel faint. He took a deep breath.

"The Medical Center. What do you think of the way they treat patients? The staff? The nurses?" He was holding the tattoo machine now, poised, over the back of Ben's leg.

Ben fumbled for an answer. "Ah, ah, it's okay, I guess. I don't really know. I've never been connected with them that way—only professionally, as an artist."

"Think they…know what they're doing over there?" Charlie switched on the machine, which buzzed and hummed. Ben's answer was lost in the noise.

The needle burned and Ben squirmed, trying not to move his leg. After a few minutes, Charlie shut the machine off.

"The outline's done," he said. "Gotta change needles. Anyone who uses a needle is at risk now. And it's all thanks to those people."

"What people," Ben asked, trying to be polite.

"Those men who couldn't keep it in their pants with other men. They could at least use protection or be a little selective. But no! They've got to ruin it for the rest of us!"

"Eleanor!" Ben called. "C'mere. How's it look?"

But Eleanor's head was angled forward; her eyes were closed.

"Taking a little nap, she is." Charlie pushed the back of Ben's head down. "Sons of bitches ruined it for the rest of us."

"Um, how did you get into tattooing, Mr. Spoon?"

Charlie laughed and looked at Ben. "Really want to know? I wanted to be an artist. My father was an art critic, classically trained with high standards. He wanted all his life to be a painter but never encouraged me. He wasn't even against it; that would have been better. At least he'd've cared." He turned on the tattoo machine again; the coloring apparatus must be different, Ben thought. It made less noise and didn't hurt as much.

"My friend, Marcy," Charlie continued, "she's a painter. And the day she sold her first painting her mother said: 'I always knew you could do it. I'm so proud of you.' Man, I wanted that. I wanted to hear it from him. But I drew and sketched anyway, despite the fact that my dad the damn art critic didn't notice. Some of my best work is as strong as it is because I'm disgusted by his disinterest in what I love most. He never gave me the money for art school so," he shrugged, "here I am."

Charlie colored in silence for some minutes.

"Well, this is art," said Ben.

"Don't get me started on that," Charlie said. "Okay, you're done. I've got to put some ointment on that and tape it over with gauze. Make sure you keep it clean, so it can breathe. By tomorrow it'll scab over and within a week the scab'll come off and you'll be all set." Charlie shook a finger at him. "Don't pick at it or the color might come out."

"Okay," said Ben, craning his head to see. "Cool," he said, catching a glimpse.

Charlie went over to Eleanor. "Wake up, Sweetie."

"Mmm," said Eleanor. "Ready to go?"

"Your turn," said Ben. "Still going to get the ghost?"

"I don't think so. I changed my mind." She smiled at Charlie Spoon. "Nothing for me today, thanks."

Ben paid Charlie Spoon and walked out, shaking Eleanor's hand away from his elbow and walking quickly in front of her. She had tricked him! And he had been so attracted so her! He'd leave her behind. He'd walk home!

"Ben, come on. Get in the car. Give me a chance to explain." Her voice had softened, becoming apologetic. She held the door open.

He got in, thinking "you bitch." He would take her home, then never see her again and never go to that club again. This was all Mattis's fault!

He started the car and drove out onto the road. She pointed off to the left. "That way."

"That's not the way back," Ben said.

"I know," said Eleanor. "I wanted to show you something." She turned and looked at him, her clear eyes unblinking. Deliberately, she unbuttoned her blouse.

A strip mall was under construction on the side of the road. Tall piles of lumber stood alongside dump trucks and bulldozers. Behind them rose mountains of dirt, blocking one's view of the rest of the area. Eleanor looked in the rear view mirror.

"We're hooome," she sang, with a sleepy smile. Ben pulled the car around behind the machinery. Eleanor breathed deeply, sighing as she exhaled. Her right hand rested just above Ben's knee.

She directed him to stop the car and instantly was straddling him, kissing him hard and sensually, first on the mouth and then on the neck and chest. One hand unbuttoned his shirt while the other unzipped his fly.

He was not quite so angry anymore.

The cool clean night sweetened by Eleanor's sweating urgency erased his painful memories, exorcising the sad place he had reserved in his heart for Beth.

Later, he sat back and looked with wide eyes at the starry night as she put her shirt on and pulled up her pants. She combed her hair in the mirror, and turned on the radio while chain smoking two cigarettes.

"I can't believe I met you three hours ago," Ben said.

"Four hours," said Eleanor.

"Charlie Spoon's a funny guy," Ben said.

"Hilarious," she said, turning to him and licking his neck with the tip of her tongue.

He held her close. Her body had a delicate smell—sweet, vulnerable. "He asked me what I do for a living and I mentioned that I work at Selling Sight and Sound and that the Medical Center's one of our accounts and he had this weird reaction."

She lifted her head from his shoulder, blinking. "The Medical Center's one of your accounts?"

"Yeah. He was very homophobic. All this stuff about gay men ruining it for the rest of us. And then he asked me what I thought about the hospital—if they knew what they were doing. Why would he ask something like that?"

She kissed him softly on the mouth, stroking the side of his face. "I don't know, I think something happened to his daughter there."

"Oh," said Ben, and for an instant he pictured the angry look in Charlie Spoon's wide eyes when he spoke about the hospital. Then Eleanor was kissing him again, a soft, wet trail down the side of his face, onto his neck and chest, evaporating in the cool night.

* * *

DOPESICK

Lying on the bathroom floor, the sky of pink and black squares was cool against the side of your face. Stomach cramps stopped for a moment. But it was a trick. They were recouping their strength for another round. Your stomach was taking a beating. Aches traveled deep into your bones, up and down your skeleton. Everything shook.

The second phase had set in and the only thing keeping this from degenerating into the deepest hell imaginable was knowing that the body crunching third phase was coming, with its paralysis and shaking. These stomachaches would have nothing on those gut wrenching cramps. And like a freight train whose light had just become visible from far off in the night, they were coming.

3

BEN

Friday morning was so cold that smoke from the industrial buildings in Oceanside and the Rockaways stood out against the clear sky, the billows frozen and clearly defined. The white Cougar was sluggish in the cold, jumping and shifting as it idled.

Ben tried to remember why he was so hung over. The tight ache on the back of his calf reminded him about the tattoo. He remembered having sex with Eleanor in the car—twice. They had gone back to an after-hours club she knew about someplace on the North Shore, and he had waited at the bar while she had gone to the ladies' room. That was it! She had been gone awhile, so he had ordered himself a shot of tequila. And then another. She had been gone long enough that by the time she came back he was too drunk to ask what the problem had been.

The biting cold pierced his hangover but not without a fight. For a moment, he thought he was going to throw up, and when the feeling passed, he put the Cougar in reverse and started off to work. Twice he pulled onto the road's shoulder, nauseous again, swallowing hard against the burn in his throat, but he opened the door and gulped cold air each time and felt better.

"Helluva morning, isn't it?" Ned grinned and slapped him on the back.

"Uh, yeah," Ben said. *Did Ned mean that sarcastically?*

"Howya feeling?" said Lydia, glancing up from her computer terminal.

"Why, do I look sick or something?"

Lydia looked up. "No, why? Are you sick?"

He squatted down next to her desk. "I got a tattoo last night."

A grin spread across her face. "You got a—?" She stood up, cupping her hands to the sides of her mouth. "Hey everybody! Bennett got himself a tattoo!"

Ben put his hands over his ears, moaning.

"Oh, you're hung over. I'm sowwy baby, sweethawwt." Lydia patted him on the head. A crowd had already gathered around them.

"So, let's see it," said Art.

"What'd you get?" Lou asked.

"I know," Annie said. "Your mom's name in a heart."

Ben looked daggers at her. "Not funny, Annie." He pulled up his pants leg, showing them. "It's already scabbed over."

"Charlie Chaplin!"

"What'd you get that for?" said Lou, walking away.

"Classy," said Art.

Ben started walking towards his office. Annie followed him, her green eyes searching. "Bennett," she said.

He stopped.

"Did you uh...you know, last night?"

"Sometimes, Annie, it might be better if you kept your insights to yourself." He turned and walked towards his office.

"That's a yes, isn't it?" She sounded disappointed. He could feel her eyes on him.

He turned. "Just don't make like the town crier over there and start shouting for the world to hear." As he went into his office he heard Art's voice call after him.

"Don't forget this weekend, Bennett. We'll pick you up at six."

As the memory of his agreement with Arthur and Lou came back to him, Ned peeked in. "Better get over to the hospital shoot. The photographer called. He's all set up and waiting for your instructions."

Instantly he was up and moving, trying to do four things at once. "Oh, my God. I forgot. Ned, I'm sorry. I'll get right over there."

Ned looked at him for a moment, his blue eyes opening a doorway into a larger room of concern. "Little hangover today, Ben?"

"Yeah, a little." He couldn't keep the annoyance out of his voice.

"That's how many this month?"

"I don't know. What're you, the hangover police?"

"You don't have to live like that if you don't want to, Ben."

He looked hard at his boss. "I know I don't have to do anything."

Ned shrugged and smiled easily. "Sunny out there, today, isn't it?"

All the way to his car, Ben wondered exactly what Ned had meant by that.

Does he mean I ought to get out more? Was that a non sequitor meant to change the subject away from an uncomfortable one? Could he have meant that I'm somehow not capable of noticing something so subtle as the weather and he's got to point it out to me...?

The photographer, his assistants and the patients taking part in the shoot were standing around having coffee and reading newspapers when Ben arrived. No one commented on the time or his condition. With minimal fuss, everyone took their places. The lights were switched on and the photographer began clicking his hand-held light meter around the set.

A nebbish in a rumpled olive suit and yellow tie appeared at the door alongside a thin, blonde woman in a lab coat.

The nebbish cleared his throat. "I'm looking for Mr. Franklin."

George Franklin came up behind the two. "What can I do for you, Mr. Archer?" He shook both their hands and ushered them into the room. "Excuse me, people. We can take five. You can turn the lights off, Charlie."

The photographer rolled his eyes. "We've been taking goddam five all morning."

"Well then, we'll take ten." He snapped the fingers of one hand in the air. "Folks. This is Mr. Stephen Archer and Doctor Adrian Lord. Dr. Lord is assisting us in keeping tabs on the incidence of the HIV virus here at the Center, in addition to her regular duties as Chair of Internal Medicine. Mr. Archer is from the Board of Health."

The photographer had sat down on the floor and crossed his legs. "...most expensive damn coffee break you'll ever see."

"Excuse me, Charlie. Was there a problem?"

The photographer's eyes widened. "Yeah, there's a problem. I'd like to get to work here, that's the problem."

George spoke with patronizing patience, as though to a child. "We've got a bigger problem here, Charlie. A life threatening problem, for hundreds, perhaps thousands of people. You don't mind if we deal with that, do you?"

"Oh, don't stop on my account. Go right ahead." The photographer waved and George waited a few moments to make sure he was finished, then turned back to the officer and the doctor. "Mr. Archer?"

"Mr. Franklin. Our information is that the incidence of infection is up again. Way up. It appears to be on the order of six to ten new cases per month."

"Jesus Christ. Wait a minute. What do you mean by 'appears'?"

Dr. Lord interrupted. "Because the virus may take up to six months to present in tests, counting actual cases at this time is difficult."

"Mmm." George Franklin appeared deep in thought. "Excuse me." He glanced across the room, his head tilted back, lifted his glasses and looked under them. "Ben?" He waiting until Bennett walked over. "Ben, I'd like you to meet Dr. Lord and Mr. Archer. In light of the focus of our ad campaign, it's important that you hear this."

Bennett shook both their hands.

"Since this increased incidence of HIV infection at The Center became evident, nearly ten years ago," Mr. Archer began, "ever stricter controls have been instituted on the blood supply. Doctor?"

"Let's move over here." George Franklin guided them to an isolated corner of the room.

Doctor Lord nodded. "All donated blood is tagged by computer, bar coded and rigorously tested."

"Bar coded?" said Bennett, thinking of the many food packaging designs he had worked on and the UPC codes he had placed on them to be scanned on supermarket checkout lines.

"We can track every donated pint of blood to every donor," said Doctor Lord.

"And each donor is given a checkup before being allowed to donate blood," said Mr. Archer. "So the upshot is, it's virtually impossible to transmit diseases such as hepatitis B and C or the HIV virus via donated or stored blood."

George Franklin pointed a finger. "What about someone newly infected?"

"That's right," said Ben.

"If the virus takes six months to show up, you wouldn't know—"

"No blood is used until after the incubation period and thorough testing and retesting," Dr. Lord explained. "And we've been tracking donors throughout the ten year period. No, that isn't it."

"I don't understand," George said, scratching his chin. "So, if we don't have a contaminated blood storage system, what do we have?"

"Exactly the question we've been working on all week," said Lord, folding her arms. "I've narrowed it down to several possibilities and bear with me because some of them are a little far fetched."

"Oh, God," said George Franklin. "I know what you're going to say. It's already occurred to me." He began patting his chest. "Where're my cigarettes?"

"You understand," Archer said, looking at George Franklin, "that we've got to look at every possibility."

George nodded. "I wouldn't have it any other way."

"Doc," Bennett began, "if we know these cases are originating here, why is the hospital still open?"

"Young man," George Franklin pointed a finger at Bennett. "It's exactly that sort of irresponsible—"

Dr. Lord interrupted; her tolerant smile showed that she was accustomed to answering difficult public relations questions. "We don't want to cause a panic. That would also be irresponsible. So far, all we have is a statistical anomaly. We don't know anything until it is proven and nothing's been proven. The public's health interests are not so easily determined. If we closed the hospital, hundreds, possibly thousands of people would lose their care. Is it so easy to say that's the right thing? Meanwhile, determining where an infection occurred, in this case, how and where individuals contracted the virus, might be extremely difficult."

"Exactly," George Franklin glared.

"The first possibility," Doctor Lord continued, "is an outbreak of some new strain of AIDS. It is possible. This is a virus that mutates. That's how it stays ahead of our efforts to defeat it. It changes, so the various agents we send after it cease to recognize it. Could the HIV virus for instance, become airborne?" She shook her head. "We think not. It is a fragile virus that only lives for minutes at a time outside the body. We've examined and tested the patients who've begun testing positive. The virus or viruses in their bodies are not substantively different from those we've found previously."

Bennett was trying to clear his mind. The headlines from this current series of ads—promises, guarantees of safety—were appearing in huge, bold letters in his mind's eye.

Dr. Lord shifted her weight and continued. "The second possibility is that there is a major flaw or series of flaws in the hospital's screening procedures: We've examined this from the human error standpoint and there's just no way to explain the infection of so many people who seem not to have been previously infected in one year. Our procedures are sound. The accidental infection of dozens of people is just not possible."

George Franklin had been looking at his shoes, now his head jerked upright. "You're saying this was intentional?"

Archer shrugged. "We're eliminating possibilities."

Franklin shook his head, moaning. "Oh, I was afraid of this. The insurance people alone will—"

Doctor Lord folded her arms. "It is beginning to look like someone, or some group of people…"

George Franklin threw his arms in the air. "But who would do something so insane? A doctor? I can't believe it!" He drew a pack of Marlboros from his inside jacket pocket and flicked a cigarette from it. "One of the staff? Never! And no one else could get past my nurses. They'd be seen! Someone would know!"

The man from the health department spoke gently. "I know it seems far fetched and your question is certainly appropriate. Who would do such a thing? Why? How could they get away with it in a tightly controlled, efficient environment like this?"

"These are our questions as well," Dr. Lord agreed, smoothing the front of her lab coat. "I'm afraid it's the only possibility left."

Bennett spoke suddenly, and the other three people looked at him as though he had not been there. "Are you telling us this because you know who…?"

"Not at all." Archer shook his head and folded his arms across his chest, causing his tie to bunch up. "We're here to tell you our conclusions and also to discuss…"

George Franklin interrupted. "This meeting's over." He was in charge again, an air of authority in his voice. "Ben, we'll pick up on this tomorrow." He lit his cigarette. "Mwah. Archer, Doc. *Mwah.* Stick around. *Mwah.* We've got to talk."

* * *

Autumn's cold snap disappeared as suddenly as it had come; Ben saw it as a good omen for his weekend away. Where the air had been cold and clean, it was warm enough now to carry the odor of raked leaves. Ben had long associated late autumn with danger, its smells were of fear and the unknown. Perhaps this was a vestige of years of midterms, perhaps it was older, from a time when Halloween goblins and ghouls preyed on the nighttime consciousness of a little boy.

This autumn was no different, but a ride east with Art and Lou, cheerful enough for their own cable show, was enough to send any goblin scrambling for a different time of year.

The happy couple chatted in the front seat and listened to Oscar Peterson's cascading piano riffs. Now and then they asked Ben an isolated question about his affinity for a particular musician or food, but for the most part Ben was left with his thoughts, which were a jumble of fear and confusion. The strange and exciting night with Eleanor had been blunted by the possibility that the Medical Center's crisis involved criminal intent, an idea which made Ben's head spin; what was left of his hangover didn't help.

He had a nagging feeling that he ought to withdraw from the account.

He watched the thin gray clouds disappear into the dark orange of the day's last light. And then there was that hungry hole in his heart. Would he see Eleanor again? Should he?

They followed the Long Island Expressway to its eastern end, then headed south on Route 111 and then east again on Sunrise Highway, which was Route 27, until the road narrowed.

"You're awfully quiet back there," Art said over his shoulder.

"Listen deary," said Lou. "Once we get settled in, Arthur will cook us up a bite. You froze some of that delicious sauce from our dinner with Jonathan's crowd, didn't you?"

"What a great idea." Arthur turned around and shook his head. "It was a marvelous sauce, I must say. And afterwards, homemade cannolis and espresso. Ooh, la la."

Lou crowed, "This isn't Long Island, it's heaven!"

The road weaved through the Hamptons, past farms and wineries winding down from last year's season, and boutiques that boasted trendy fashions and antiques along the roadside. Finally, they arrived at the little house on the western shore of Fort Pond, in the town of Montauk.

Within minutes of opening his suitcase on the guest bed and brushing his teeth, Bennett's face was buried in a fat pillow and he was fast asleep.

* * *

When he woke up Saturday morning, Bennett felt more rested than he had in quite some time. And when he ventured into the kitchen, Arthur and Lou were sitting at the breakfast table, each reading a section of newspaper. Four different cereal boxes were lined up in the center of the table, next to which was a multi-sectioned serving dish sporting various fruits, raisins and toppings.

"How'd you sleep, deary?" Lou asked.

"Coffee?" asked Art, getting up.

"Thanks," Ben nodded, and sat back in the chair. "You know, there's something strange about this," he swept his hand over the table.

"We don't eat bacon, eggs or any of that," Art said.

"No, it isn't that."

"Oh," said Lou. "Well, perhaps you've been conditioned by society to only accept a conventional…"

"No, no." Ben shook his head. "This is a good thing. This all strikes me as so, so—"

Arthur grinned as he poured the coffee. "So nice?"

* * *

Lou sat in the center of the row boat, the tackle box and both fishing rods next to him. He did the rowing. Ben sat up front and watched the surface of the lake. Each time the surface rippled he imagined that a fish was swimming just below and pointed it out to Lou, but Lou said to wait. They were going to one of several premier spots on the lake.

He looked back and was able to see just how unfinished the construction on Art and Lou's summer home was. The framing of the second floor was complete and the windows were installed, but the wood was bare and Ben remembered Lou explaining that if it were left this way much longer, the rain and moisture from the particularly wet autumn would have so affected the materials that it would all have to be redone.

Arthur had stayed behind to work on his manuscript. Afterwards he would need to shop for supper.

"This is it." Lou removed the oars and oarlocks and placed them towards the side of the boat. He took up one of the fishing rods and quickly attached a swivel, hook and purple rubber worm, then handed it to Ben. "Fished before?"

Ben nodded. "A little. In grade school."

"Good. Just drop your line down, oh, about over there." He indicated a shady area beneath a weeping willow. "The big bass wait in a hole under there for bugs to fall off that tree. Wait a while after you cast to let the worm settle and attract a little attention, then draw it back a little at a time. Try to imagine it undulating, wormlike, looking mighty tasty to some hungry fish."

As Ben tried to follow Lou's instructions, Lou rigged and baited the second rod and cast it in. Within seconds he had caught a splashing, jumping bass. The silver morning light shone off its scales as it twisted in the air. Lou held it with one hand by its bottom jaw as he quickly, easily removed the hook with the other. "Whatdya think? Two, maybe three pounds?"

A rush of adrenaline focused Ben on his own fishing.

Lou caught two more.

"I don't know about this," Ben began.

"I want you to relax," said Lou. "Somehow when I'm calmer, I catch more. And try to be more patient. Let the worm sit a while, attract a little attention."

Ben nodded and recast, then sat back and tried to relax.

Lou watched him. "Lot of pressure having your first account."

Ben didn't answer.

"And it's not some little account. It's one of our biggest. Ned trusts you. He doesn't trust many people."

"Like you said, big responsibility."

"You're up to it."

Ben looked at Lou to see if he was kidding. He wasn't. He was smiling, nodding, as though stating the obvious.

"And the fact that there's this crazy situation with the account kind of ratchets up the pressure, doesn't it?"

Ben hesitated. "You're trying to help me relax?"

"I'm pointing out that you didn't cause that situation and you're not going to make it go away. There isn't anything you can do."

Ben shrugged. "Actually, I had thought to look into it on my own."

"What're you, Barnaby Jones?"

"I'm involved, in a way. I just wanted to see what I could see."

Lou had hooked another fish, this one was long and thin and looked dangerous. "Pickerel, hand me the pliers. I'm not putting my fingers in this guy's mouth."

Ben leaned towards the tackle box but was startled by a tug on his fishing pole. Followed by another, harder.

"Set the hook!" Lou ordered. "Set the hook. Pull back on it!"

Ben pulled and reeled in the bass, held it up for Lou to see. "At least two and a half," Lou admired. "Nice job." He threw back the pickerel and Ben did the same with the bass.

"I'm not going to tell you what to do." Lou kept his eyes on the spot where his line went into the water. "Just remember that you're not responsible for the situation. And if you do get into a jam, you can always count on me or Art. Run it by one of us."

Ben looked at him and was surprised at the emotion gathering at the back of his throat. "Thanks."

* * *

He stayed in his room for a while in the late afternoon, reading a mystery, and neither Art nor Lou disturbed him. The mystery made him think about the hospital and what sort of person would purposely spread the HIV virus. The only answer he could come up with was a villain in a book.

He heard Arthur come in and begin to unpack paper bags from his trip to the store, and Ben resisted an impulse to poke his head into the kitchen and ask what was for dinner. Instead he went outside and walked down to the lake, enjoying the way the grass tickled the spaces between his toes. From the woods around the lake came a symphony of chirps, twitters, and animal chatter. The lake lapped at the reeds at the water's edge and Ben closed his eyes and breathed in the scent of the countryside.

He felt a warmth, a connection, as though he were part of something much bigger than himself. He thought of his camping weekends with Beth, and knew that this feeling was more than an appreciation of animals and foliage, though it was that, too.

He felt more a part of a family when he was with Art and Lou. Their kindness toward him, which asked nothing in return, was unfamiliar but welcome. It fit, somehow with the natural beauty around him.

He knew he had no real, long-term place with them, but sensed that maybe, if he remembered this feeling, he might someday recognize it when he encountered it with someone else.

Taking a last breath, he showered and climbed back up the hill into the house, and went into the kitchen, where he found Arthur cutting vegetables.

"You wiped your feet?"

Ben laughed.

Lou was asleep and snoring on the couch, his feet up on its arm, blending somewhat with the pinkish brick surrounding the fireplace on the far wall.

"Want to help? Grab a knife." Arthur pointed with his knife to a rack on the wall, then to three green peppers next to the cutting board on the countertop.

Ben did as Art suggested.

"How's the tattoo healing?"

Ben shrugged. "Haven't thought much about it, so I guess it's not too bad. It feels a little tight. That's all."

"Ah," said Art, then after a moment, "You had that done…of your own accord?"

Ben laughed. "You know me, don't you? No, I met a girl."

"A fine influence, I see."

"It's just a tattoo."

"Which came with a horrendous hangover on the biggest morning of your professional life."

"Well, there's that. But as Lou says, I have to place accountability where accountability lies."

"Lou's an artist."

Ben went on cutting. "I know."

"Miss Beth much?"

Ben waiting a long time before answering. "I think of her now and then."

"Is this woman like her?"

Ben shook his head. "Other than the obvious…"

"Yes, Bennett, we know she's a woman."

Ben put down the knife. "Arthur, I appreciate your concern, but it's been a while, you know? I'm not rushing out to replace her. I got laid, that's all."

"Strike up the band."

"I don't mean it that way. I mean I'm not trying to replace Beth with, with—"

"Yes, I forgot to ask her name."

"Eleanor. At least I think it's Eleanor."

Art was looking at him with paternal concern. "I'm not suggesting you're trying to replace Beth with anyone or, if you are, that you shouldn't be doing it. Look, I can only speak for myself. You know I lost someone? About five years ago. The whole thing was pretty horrible and the emotional loss was the worst." He paused, but Ben didn't respond, didn't move. "What I learned was that I had to find a way to be with myself, to be alone first, before I was ready to be with anyone else. That way, when I found a real relationship, it was for the right reasons."

"I see," said Ben.

"But that's just me."

"Yes, it is," said Ben, pushing the diced peppers to the side of the cutting board with the broad blade of the knife. "I'm done." He put the knife down, went to the far end of the living room and started building a fire.

* * *

"This shish kabob's amazing!" Ben shook his head. "You hardly have to chew at all."

"It's the marinade," said Lou.

"Thank you," said Arthur. "A little wine, soy sauce, honey, mustard—and a dash of this and that."

"Excellent," Lou agreed. "Pass the rice."

"Tell me, Lou. Art and I were talking before and I want your opinion. What makes a successful relationship?" Ben waited, his fork in midair.

Lou answered without hesitating. "Comfort. Feeling safe. I have to feel relaxed with a person, like I can enjoy myself, be myself, have fun." He broke off a hunk of bread and dipped it into a bowl of dark marinade. "And trust, of course. I have to believe you're not going to leave if we argue. And that I won't be hurt. I guess we've got to have things in common." He chewed the bread thoughtfully. "But first comes being comfortable, having common interests."

"Or contrasting interests," said Arthur, with a private smile.

"Complimentary interests, Mr. Writer," Lou laughed.

"What about," Ben hesitated, "fireworks?"

"Oh, that'll come later," Lou waved him off.

"Maybe much later," said Arthur, and looked quickly at Lou. "Kidding, kiiidding," he sang, then looked more seriously back at Ben. "Truthfully, a person has to decide for him or herself what's important. I need to feel comfortable and safe and loved. Passion can flow naturally from there."

"Amen," said Lou, holding up his wine glass. Arthur held up his glass and they touched, giving off two complimentary tones.

* * *

RESIGNATION

Coughing blood into a handful of tissues, then stuffing them into your pocket on the way to the hospital. There had been few symptoms until a year and a half ago. Now the symptoms were intermittent. But so what? Copping, getting off, paying back the old debt—those were the priorities. Those were owed. The rest of life followed: eating a little, getting laid, talking a little, maybe catching a movie. Nodding. But the virus? Old news.

Get to the hospital, park the car and head up to the hospital floor, check the time. Ten years ago, things had been different. Lots of people didn't know what they had. Being around doctors and nurses had its advantages. And there had been a terrifying period right after the diagnosis, but life had been full of terrors back then.

We're all going to die.

In a closet you play and win the game: how fast can you get the blood into the syringe and squirt it into the vial? Can you do it before the dope hits, before that dope taste hits your mouth? Can you do it even after the dope hits you? Life had boiled down to little games, and waiting for symptoms was also a game. Were the dizziness, the exhaustion, the little spot on the side of your neck symptoms of the virus? Stay in the game and you'll find out.

You wait at the elevator until you know the change-of-shift signout meeting has started and the floor would be staffed with only a skeleton crew of doctors and nurses. You likely won't be noticed even during a full shift, but the precaution makes sense. Once the time is right, you tap the supplies strapped to your belly, relieved to feel that everything's in place, and buzz for the elevator.

* * *

NURSE SARAH

Sarah stepped onto the elevator; she had been on duty in Med. Surg. 2 for fourteen hours. The person getting on with her looked as tired as she was. "Long day, huh?"

No response. She knew that feeling; too tired even to talk. She headed back to the nurses' station and sat down heavily behind the counter, glancing over the charts, paperwork and rows of room monitors before her. Chilly sweat stuck her uniform to the small of her back. The floor was crowded, as always, and there had been more to do on her shift than there were hours to do it in.

She had been starting IVs, inserting urinary catheters, emptying urine bags, checking inputs and outputs, turning and positioning patients, checking for bed sores and generally prepping patients for those operations not prepped in the OR. For a Med. Surg. nurse this primarily meant bowel preps—administering laxatives and enemas preceding intestinal surgery—as opposed to skin preps, the shaving and washing, which would be done by the OR nurse.

She blinked, trying to stay awake, and looked up every few minutes to see that the nurse or doctor going by was someone who belonged.

She glanced again at each of the room monitors. Admitting physicians made their rounds, barely nodding to her as they hurried past. More friendly were the RNs or LPNs—Licensed Practicals—who, in addition to the physical care, looked after patients' states of mind, held hands, assuaged fears.

* * *

NUMB

You unbutton the coat's top two buttons upon entering the room, exposing the leather case. The patient, a young woman with short, dirty blonde hair and tiny freckles on her nose, is sleeping, one hand under the green blanket and oversheet, the other, the one connected to the IV, laying over the edge of the bed. She has a child's fingers, half curled, the skin fresh and clean and uncalloused.

You bend over her, reaching into the front of the belt for the syringe, ever cognizant of the camera behind and above you. Authoritative footsteps approach and there's a faint twinge, a distant hello, but your best friend keeps it away, and you take hold of the line, turn the port toward you…

"Ah, excuse me."

A distant siren screams and you slowly respond, letting the syringe drop back into the pouch with one hand while you maintain a grip on the IV line with the other. You turn your head but not your body.

"Where would I find 207? This is 206, isn't it? I would have thought 207 would be right next door."

"Oh, the hallway makes a U shape," your voice says. "You've got to go to the end, make a left past the nurses' station, then another left, and you'll see it on your right. The odd numbers are all over that way."

"Thank you."

Your mouth remembers to smile. "It can be a little confusing."

Back to business.

* * *

NURSE SARAH

Sarah glanced at the monitor for 206. What was going on there? She frowned and studied what she saw, watching the figure hunched over the patient.

"Hey, Sarah, how's your mom feeling?"

She looked up. "Much better, thanks for asking, Kim. Her hip's sore, but it'll be okay." She watched the elderly LPN walk away and pictured her mother, struggling to walk with her new hip. She looked back at the monitors, then at her watch, the shift was nearly over.

* * *

BEN

It was eleven o'clock Monday morning and Ben's next meeting was with Ned, at noon, to review the photo shoot. He went to his car in a daze, not feeling the chilly air on his cheeks. Before driving through Lido Beach to the Meadowbrook Parkway, he drove the few blocks to the boardwalk, parked on West Broadway, and walked slowly up one of the ramps to the boardwalk, and leaned against the metal railing. He stared out at the ocean; the horizon was empty save for a low, gray barge several miles out to sea. A trio of gulls flew low over the water, then rose, laughing, and floated overhead.

The Medical Center campaign was to have been his coup, his grand entrance into the world of Corporate Accounts. He was in charge of making the world, or at least Nassau County, aware of the Medical Center's safety.

He went back to the car, dialed the office on his cell phone, and left a message for Ned that he would have to postpone.

He got in the car, but instead of heading to work, he drove in the other direction, towards Long Beach Road and the bridge into Island Park. The Cougar took him over the bridge, through Oceanside and East Rockaway, over Peninsula Boulevard and into Valley Stream.

He wound up at Mattis's house. The hazy blue/green light was shining faintly from the top floor window and Ben was careful to knock when he got to the bedroom door.

"C'mon in," Mattis called from the computer. "Just selling some cyber real estate. What're you doing here at this time of the morning?"

"I could use a little hair of the dog. Let's go to the Ten Spot. It'll open soon and I'm buying."

Mattis shook his head. "You know I can't just go out there." He nodded towards the small window at the back of the room. "It's so light and there are so many people…"

Ben waited while Mattis drank three beers to keep his agoraphobia at bay. "Did I mention that I've gotten into therapy?" Mattis said, once they were in the car and heading towards the bar, which would be open by noon, in fifteen minutes.

Ben tried to sound natural. "Oh?"

"You might have noticed that it's hard for me to leave the house."

"Really?"

"I've already had one session. Beth says I've had some sort of trauma and they've got to find out what it is. I don't necessarily agree."

Ben blinked. "Beth? Your therapist's name is Beth? What does she look like?" His hands gripped the wheel, his foot involuntarily pressed the accelerator.

"Whew, this car can move! Lookit that! Woh, cop at two o'clock. Slow down. I said slow down. She's about forty five, I guess. My therapist, not the cop. Hair in a bun, collar up to here." He tapped his chin with the back of his hand. "You know the type. Living somewhere in the middle ages. Anyway, I did learn something. It's really parks and open spaces I'm avoiding. I don't know why, yet. Weird, huh?"

Ben shrugged. "Cool, if she's helping you…" He let the rest of the sentence hang in the air.

* * *

"Hey Rick. C'mon over." The man at the bar was talking to Mattis.

"Hey Jess, Eddie."

Bennett looked at Mattis, then across the bar at the man who had called out when they walked into the bar. Rick? The man was tall, in his early twenties, and wearing a green and black checkered flannel shirt. His skin was dark, even for an African American. His recently shaved head showed perhaps two days of stubble. He looked back at Mattis. "He calls you Rick?"

"It's my name, man. Mattis is just a college name. You knew that, didn't you? I'm Ricky Hatters to these guys. And they don't think I'm 'mad as' a Hatters, you know? I feel almost normal around these guys. It's kind of nice."

Stung by the inference that Mattis did not feel "normal" around him, Bennett followed his friend to the far end of the bar, where the three men were standing.

The tall man in the flannel shirt put out a hand; Mattis shook it. "Rick, how are you? Been a while."

"What's up, Jess?"

"Guess you heard about my dad."

"Josh? No. I knew, I mean, I was aware that he's positive, but—oh, by the way, this is my friend, Ben."

Jess put out a hand. "How are you, Ben? Jesse Abraham. And this is Eddie," he pointed to a tall, graying man in an old corduroy coat, "and Bud."

Bennett shook Eddie's hand. Bud, who was on the bar stool on the other side of Eddie, and was nearly as wide as he was tall, smiled and waved a finger.

"Yeah, well, he's full blown now. T-cells dropping like rocks off a cliff."

Mattis shook his head and clucked his tongue.

"I'll tell you, he's dealing with it," Jesse said, shaking his head. "I'm learning how to be a man just watching him." Jesse smiled sadly. "This is the best we've gotten along since I was a little boy."

The bartender was looking at them, waiting.

"Beer and two shots of Jack," said Mattis.

"Um, I'll have a burger and a soda," said Ben. "I've got to go back to work after this and I don't want to smell like alcohol."

Mattis pointed to Ed's glass. "That's not alcohol. That's beer. Besides, wasn't it you who wanted that hair of the dog?"

"Yeah, I guess you're right," Ben agreed. "Bartender, better make that a beer. No, two beers." He smiled uneasily. "Save you the trouble of coming back."

"So," Mattis was saying to Ed, "did you ever get back to work?"

"No, and two of my kids're sick at home with bronchitis. My wife's staying home today to take care of them. You know how it is. Finally got health insurance and the HMOs don't pay for a damn thing."

Mattis shook his head. "HMOs, man."

Bud said, "Um, hmm!"

The television above the bar was showing the afternoon news. A tidal wave in Japan had killed twenty seven people, including a family of four.

"So, what're you doing?" Mattis asked.

"I'm going to have two more beers, hang out a half hour, then me and Bud're going to work out at a gym he goes to."

"No, I mean about your job, and your kids'n all."

"What do you suggest?"

"I don't know."

Ed shrugged. "Tell you the truth. I just try to stay out of the way. We end up fighting, otherwise. See, lookit that."

On the news was a story of a famous actor who had been accused of spousal abuse.

"Me and my old lady fight like that all the time." Ed laughed, waving his fists. "We been beatin' each other with pans. She hits me hard as I hit her! That ain't abuse, that's marriage!" Jess smiled and Bennett noticed that Bud laughed a little too hard.

He had been wondering why he had allowed himself to be persuaded to have two beers when he had already made the decision to have a burger and a soda. Sometimes he wished he didn't drink quite so much.

"So when're you going to see Beth again?" he asked Mattis.

"You don't have to say her name. You can just say 'your therapist.' Next Monday. I'm going to talk to her about this remembering my birth thing." He saw the men looking at him. "I'm going to a therapist—trying to get it together, you know?"

"Oh," said Jess.

"Right," Ed agreed.

The beers and drinks arrived and Ben quickly reached for his, ready to drown his discomfort. "I don't think you really remember your birth. You just think you do."

"I guess I'll find out."

Bud raised an eyebrow. "My old lady says she remembers things that happened in her previous life."

"Um, hmm," said Ben. The newscaster was a red headed woman. Though she looked nothing like Eleanor, she somehow reminded him of her. He was beginning to regret having slept with her. Had he used a condom? He tried to remember. Yes, he had. He sighed, relieved. She was not the most virginal-looking of women, and, you never knew. This was not the sort of thing he often did and after thinking about it for a few days, he had come to the conclusion that he had done it to exorcise Beth from his consciousness. He had found himself doing all sorts of uncharacteristic things lately. Why was that? He looked around the bar, trying to clear his mind and allow the depression he knew was there to well up from his belly so he might find comfort in feeling sorry for himself. It didn't come.

Mattis was pointing, his voice rising. "I'm telling you, man. I remember my birth. It was a traumatic event. It affected every aspect of my life."

Jesse laughed and slapped Mattis on the back. "All right, all right. So you remember your birth." Ben's head was beginning to hurt. Must be from last night, he thought, a little annoyed that he wasn't getting depressed. He felt as though he were waiting for a bus that had never been late before. Where was that depression? It ought to have been here by now! He tried to think about the hospital, and realized that until now, he had been avoiding that subject, too. Fortified with beer, his mind opened. He would, of course, have to inform Ned that the AIDS cases in the hospital may be intentionally transmitted, the thing he had been avoiding.

Whether the campaign would continue would be up to Ned. An idea had been brewing in the back of his mind since the meeting, and it moved forward now, to the spot, perhaps, once occupied by his Beth depression. It grew into a plan. Why not look into this himself? Ask a few questions, get to know some of the hospital staff. That might be considered part of his job, given the nature of this ad campaign.

"I hate that bastard," Mattis was saying, and the words reminded Ben of something else he remembered hearing his friend say. He could be wrong, but Ben was ninety nine percent sure he had heard Mattis say that he hated the Medical Center and wished everyone in it were dead.

* * *

JANICE

"The snow'll kill you, if you don't watch out." Janice ran the scanner over the bar code on the first plastic packet of blood, pressed a button on the computer and handed the packet to Marilyn, who put it on the top shelf of the refrigerator. Janice had been scanning and storing blood in the Clinical Pathology Lab for hours, and she welcomed the company. Janice Rosen generally worked alone and she liked it that way. Marilyn was one of the few nurses she would tolerate in her lab for an extended period of time. That was how she thought of Clinical Pathology—Janice's Lab.

Janice's eyes were smaller than they appeared through her thick glasses; her eyelashes were long and thin. Her fear of even the smallest exposure to the sun had left her skin powder white, and her perception of exercise as dangerous had left her body thick, her shoulders stooped. "If you don't slip and break your back, the weight of the snow'll cave your roof in." That it would snow so early in the season was a personal affront. She swivelled her neckless body to look at Marilyn.

"I suppose," said Marilyn, her thoughts elsewhere.

Frowning, Janice scanned another packet of blood. "Eleanor and I are going out for coffee after work—I'll have tea of course. Do you want to join us?" Her eyes went over Marilyn's features, examining every freckle, impatient for an answer and ready to extrapolate further conclusions from the way the answer was delivered.

"Thanks, I don't think so."

Janice paused. "I don't blame you," she weighed her words. "You've got to be careful about what you eat at those diners. We could go to Karp's Fish Emporium in Merrick…"

Marilyn was reading the label on a packet of blood, lost in thought. She blinked and looked at Janice. "Actually, I'm going to therapy this afternoon."

"I didn't know you went to therapy," Janice said, eager to press this tack, but trying to keep the eagerness out of her voice. People's vulnerabilities were weapons to Janice, to be locked away and brought out when she needed them. Though Marilyn was her friend, the fact that she was attractive—tall, with blue eyes and striking red hair—created a need for a weapon.

"Mmhmm. Dr. Dale says I have a lot of anger." She put the packet of blood in the refrigerator.

Janice nodded, as though she understood. She was hungry for more details and knew from experience that sympathy would bring them out. "I know how that can be."

Marilyn looked at her, eyebrows raised. "You do?"

"Well, maybe not exactly, but I know the feeling you mean. I've been angry at my family for years. Haven't spoken with any of them since the sixties. You wouldn't believe the way they treated me!"

Marilyn took the last packet from the gurney. She looked up. "Who said anything about my family?"

"I'm sorry."

Marilyn continued to work. Janice touched her shoulder. "You're welcome to have a piece of pie with Eleanor and me after therapy. We'll wait for you. Of course, I won't be having pie, I'll have a bowl of fresh fruit. You don't need to watch your weight."

Marilyn jumped at Janice's touch. She had never liked to be touched unexpectedly. She managed a smile. "Thanks, Janice."

Janice pointed a chubby finger. "If you come, be careful of the intersection on Merrick Road just before the Meadowbrook. It's dangerous."

"Thanks. But I don't think I'll be able to make it. I have some things to do after therapy."

Janice didn't answer right away. "I understand your sister has a new boyfriend."

"Um, yeah. I guess. I don't keep up with El's boyfriends." She laughed. "That would be a full time job and this one keeps me pretty busy, what with all the overtime."

Janice winked and flicked the side of her nose with her forefinger, the way she had seen Robert Redford do in "The Sting." Now, she and Marilyn were partners in gossip, and she had a powerful new weapon against Marilyn—not that she'd ever need it. But, you never knew. All in all, a very successful day.

"Oh, shit, look what I did!" Marilyn held the packet of blood up to the light. "I made a little hole with my nail." As Janice watched, Marilyn sat down and examined the hole in the packet, glancing once at Janice and then back at the packet of blood.

* * *

As she signed out and fetched her coat from the closet, Janice's mind was racing. She had a wealth of new information to process, categorize and evaluate. Everyone had been under so much pressure since the rumors had spread about the HIV being intentionally administered. Everyone looked funny at everyone else. And why not? Hadn't she been right to be so suspicious?

Something about Marilyn's therapy was not quite right. Janice weighed her view of Marilyn against what she imagined a murderer would be like and concluded that more information was required.

She put her coat on, trying to decide whether to put her gloves on now or when she got in the car. She opted for the car and began buttoning her coat. As she passed a supply closet, she heard a sound that made her stop and listen. It sounded like a moan.

Instantly, she was terrified, her brain in overdrive. Should she run for the police? What if someone were hurt and died while she were gone? It would be her fault and she might lose her job. She had to open the door! But what if the person in the closet were the killer and he was only wounded. He might lunge from the closet and kill her!

Leaning forward with all her weight on her feet, so that she might spring backward or to the side in an instant, the way she had seen numerous detectives do on television, she turned the knob on the supply closet door and inched it open.

On the closet floor, under the sink was a pile of white clothes and it was only after her eyes adjusted to the dark that she saw the man amidst the clothes.

"Dr. Sticker! What have they done to you!"

Dr. Sticker smiled up at her, calmly rolling down his sleeves. His carefully combed brown hair was neat as ever. The only difference in his appearance was a slight redness to his face, which might have been due to the circumstances. "Hellooo, Janice."

It did not occur to her to ask what the Chairman of Hematology was doing in a supply closet holding a needle and tourniquet.

"Janice, I'm going to confide in you, so you've got to promise to keep this information quiet." He cleared his throat, standing up and putting an arm around her shoulder. He put the syringe and tourniquet into a small, leather bag that was strapped to his waist. "Until the proper time, of course." He did not wait for a response. "I've found a clue to the spread of the virus, Janice. These items," he pointed to the bag around his waist, "were down the hall in one of the rooms where two newly infected patients were staying. I hustled them in here to get them out of sight."

"So, you're saying…"

Doctor Sticker smiled faintly. "You know that the AIDS virus can take quite some time to appear in an individual?"

Janice nodded. Her mind had become the Indianapolis Speedway.

"Well, these items were hidden in the room of a woman who stayed here six months ago and who now, inexplicably, has the virus. What I need you to do, if you don't mind, is to check up on all the people who've been in that room since then. Can you do that for me?"

Janice nodded. "Of course, doctor."

He grasped her shoulder, sending a tingle down her leg. *Was it sciatica?* She made a mental note to have it checked.

"I knew I could count on you." Doctor Sticker gave her shoulder a squeeze, pushed past her and walked purposefully down the hall, his rubber soles squeaking.

As she finished buttoning her coat she realized that Dr. Sticker had forgotten to give her the room number. She had to talk to Eleanor. She was the most level headed person Janice knew—the more sensible of the Franklin sisters. Eleanor was sure to be able to make some sense of it all.

* * *

DETACHMENT

Sometimes, occasionally, the original fire was there. Like a charcoal, it had to be lit from another source, some anger from the day that could recall the old, real fire. When it was there, it was glorious. An aurora borealis of the soul, a crusade of armor and lances and the sharpest, glinting swords and all for the greatest glory. The righteous glory. And occasionally, the fire was pierced with an icicle of revenge and then the fire was so strong it was sexual. Occasionally the excursions through the Medical Center were like mythical tasks that had to be performed, steps to be climbed despite distractions and obstacles. Did Jason focus on anything but the Fleece? Did Ulysses heed the sound of the sirens? Or did he plug his ears and sail on?

Most often, though, there was no quest, no Fleece, no fire. Not even revenge. A round robin of visits to the Man with the Hat—all on his terms, waiting on street corners until he showed or didn't show—followed by hours on the floors of dirty basements of abandoned buildings with spoons and cigarette lighters and small bore needles trying to find a vein that would hold up. Then the Game: get the blood back into the needle and the tiny vial before the dope hit or, if the dope won the race, try to do it high. Then it was a field trip to some ward of the hospital and a new game. This one Deception. Fool the nurses. You're part of their ordinary evening. Blend in. Be a chameleon. That was easy. And then, easy gratification: administering a dose of revenge, of survival. The only hard part was starting it all over again the next day. And the next.

* * *

NED DOYLE

Ned gripped the steering wheel and breathed deeply to that point low in his diaphragm that the Japanese call the *Chi* and the Koreans refer to as *tonghun*. The meeting with the hospital CFO had gone well, better than expected. The photos and preliminary layouts for the public relations and advertising campaigns had been well received and the project was more or less on budget.

Sweat broke on out Ned's forehead as he concentrated; his breathing deepened.

During the meeting, he had mentioned what a shame it was that funds had to be appropriated for such worthy causes as treating the sick and elderly. Barbara, the CFO of the Medical Center and an attractive woman with curly brown hair who was secure enough to allow some gray to show, had confided that she had always wanted to be a playwright and had, in fact, written four plays. When he asked about them and saw the light in her eyes, he had known that the meeting would run longer than its scheduled two hours.

They stayed late and talked. He had been mesmerized by her exuberance for her art. Creating from one's heart was a feeling he understood viscerally but had given up on years ago to support a family. Barbara awakened that old joy...and more. And now, he was frightened by his feelings.

He had watched her eyes as she described each of the plays. The genesis of the characters, the structure of the plot, the setting, the ebb and flow of dialog. She listened carefully on the street and wherever she was, furtively jotting down phrases and thoughts and saving the slips of paper for early Saturday mornings when, over a cup of coffee, she could fit them coherently into her creative process—God's creative process, she called it. Her eyes were eager, shining and consumed with the love of creation.

And that old buried longing began to stir and pull at his consciousness, that involvement and personal tie that came with drawing portraits and scenes, using his heart as a brush and his memory as a model. Barbara understood this private feeling as Maureen never had and sitting opposite her and seeing the animated love on her face, he told her of his own creative past and how he missed it. And he felt himself edging toward a cliff and toppling over its edge. He had met Barbara before, yet somehow never noticed how beautiful she was. He had an overpowering feeling of falling in love, not of sex and lust because this wasn't that; this was a teenage, breathless love where your heart swells and shares and squeezes the air from your lungs and tears of gratitude and fear fill your eyes and concentration on anything but the moment is impossible.

How could he be falling in love? He had been married for fifteen years and was deeply in love with Maureen. He was the father of two boys whom he cherished with all his heart.

He stopped his breathing and meditation and checked his feelings and found that he did love his wife and his boys as much as ever. This new love was separate. Distinct.

He thought of Aldo, the CEO of Barrutti's, with whom he had traveled to Italy to see the manufacture and packaging of product. Aldo had a wife and five daughters whom he claimed to love, as well as a mistress on the side. And Aldo swore that one had nothing to do with the other. He had laughed and felt morally superior to Aldo, clutching his fidelity around himself the way a politician clutches the Constitution. But now he thought of Aldo and wondered.

These new feelings were so powerful that he knew that to nurture them would be an infidelity. But how could he not?

He needed to talk to Sam. He needed to get this out in the open. His sobriety, his survival depended on it.

Little Ned was at school but Frankie was in the den, lining up his toys in neat rows.

"Daa!" Frankie ran to him and clutched his knee, rubbing the snot that filled the space between his nose and the top of his lip onto Ned's pants leg. Ned bent down and hugged his son to his shoulder, and Frankie lay his head down and sighed. Tears of love and guilt came into Ned's eyes. This was gold to him; he would never give up his boys, his home, his wife. Even if he had to be emotionally dishonest. He had hurt so many people in his earlier life. He would never, ever do that again. He owed it to them, to himself.

"Hi." Maureen was smiling in the doorway. He kissed and hugged her, trying to remember whether Barbara had been wearing perfume and wondering if he smelled of it. It didn't matter; Maureen trusted him.

"I've gotta give Sam a call."

"Okay. Come on Frankieboo. Daddy has to make a call. Let's go watch a tape in the bedroom."

"Baa!" Frankie exclaimed, waving and blowing kisses.

Ned smiled and returned the kisses. "Bye, bye, Frankieboo."

Sam was at work but, as always, took a moment to listen. He was quiet for a few moments, then said, "Umhmm."

"Is that a good 'Umhmm' or a bad 'Umhmm'?" Ned asked.

"There are no good or bad 'Umhmms'," said Sam. "Not everything is so black and white. You're entitled to your feelings, you know. You don't have to feel ashamed for feeling attracted to this woman and what she represents. I'm glad you're talking about it."

The air burst from Ned's *tonghun* as though he had broken three blocks of concrete.

"What the hell was that? A water main?"

"No, nothing."

"I have a suggestion."

"Uh, oh. I mean, what is it?"

"Reach out. Find someone who needs help and help them. Make yourself available."

"How the hell am I going to do that?"

"Wait and see."

"Umhmm." Ned tapped his foot. Sometimes listening to Sam was like reading a mystery novel.

"What kind of answer is that?"

"Sam, there are no good or bad 'Umhmm's. I have that on good authority."

"That's the first time I've ever heard you call me 'good authority.'"

"It was a slip. It'll never happen again."

"Thanks for calling, Neddy. Have a good day."

The pain in his heart had faded to a dull ache and, after a short prayer for guidance, he kissed Maureen and Frankie and drove back to work.

* * *

Blankets of heavy clouds were rolling in from the northwest. The car shifted sideways, buffeted by a sudden wind surge and when the rain came, it was torrential—huge splattering drops. Streetlights had come on as had the headlights of oncoming cars. As he drove around the curve of the off-ramp, the streetlight at the apex of the curve went out. Ned looked up but the sky was, if anything, darker than before. Ribbons of black laced the gray billows and all rushed toward the southeast. As he drove into the parking lot, another car, one he had never seen before, was exiting. Its headlights were on, but just before it went by, its left headlight went out.

Ned slowed his car as he approached his assigned spot. He glanced skyward, scanning the clouds. He whispered, "What're you trying to tell me?" A car had taken his personal parking space and he stopped his car, feeling the adrenaline anger surge within him. Just as quickly he let it go. He pulled into a guest spot, got out of the car and winked up at the sky before going inside.

* * *

Ned had called to reschedule and, feeling guilty over cancelling, Bennett made sure to be leaning back in one of the rolling gray chairs, watching his boss approach through the glass partitions at the appointed time. Crumbled note paper was cluttered on his normally organized desk. His green suit jacket lay across another chair.

Ned processed these details without comment. "Let me get settled, make a few calls and I'll be right with you."

"No. You wanted to reschedule and, as it turns out, I need to see you. Now."

Ned thought he smelled alcohol, so he sat down at his desk, arranged the pictures of Maureen and the kids while he composed himself, breathing from down low. He gave Ben his full attention.

"The Board of Health came to the shoot. They have an explanation—at least part of one—for the AIDS cases."

"Well?"

Ben's face was flushed and sweating. He rubbed his mouth with the insides of his fingers, then kneaded the sides of his face and his chin. "They were transmitted intentionally."

Ned did not react.

Ben looked at the floor. "Look, I know what this does to the whole ad campaign and since you've trusted me with this, I feel like I've let down the whole—"

"How do they know?"

"More by process of elimination than by anything else. So many cases of HIV could not have occurred any other way, given their analysis of the procedures."

Ned was shaking his head. "Meaning there's a murderer out there? Hard to believe. Who would do such a thing? What would be the motive? Hard for me to believe."

Ben nodded. "I know. The Board of Health guy, Archer, and Dr. Lord went over the procedures, the bar coding and tracking of blood, and showed how that and the lack of a pattern in the infection, left no other possibility. The patients have different doctors; not all received blood transfusions. It doesn't make sense."

Ned stared at Bennett, running his hands through his hair. "Jesus. I'll have to think about this and talk to Mr. Franklin."

"It was Franklin who cut the meeting short when the subject came up." Bennett tapped his foot. One two, one. Syncopation.

Ned looked up sharply. "What do you mean?"

"As soon as Archer explained his conclusions and Dr. Lord told us the whys and wherefores, he cut in and said the meeting was over." Ben was breathing heavily; his eyes were red.

Ned smiled and the smile startled Ben. "I'm sure you feel you've let us down, Ben. Well you haven't. In fact, I want you to know that you're doing a helluva job. I don't know whether to believe all this or not. But it certainly isn't your fault. Maybe instead of cancelling our appointment you might have called me and apprised me of the circumstances sooner but, okay. It is what it is. We've been hired to do a job and we'll do it to the best of our ability—and you've been doing that. Now if it stands in the way of the truth, we'll have to step aside. Wouldn't that be the right thing to do?"

Ben tried to smile but only succeeded in looking more miserable. "But how can we know?"

"Right now, we don't. But we'll find out. We'll ask questions. Now, how about you? You look like you're taking this pretty hard. I know it's your first real chance to direct a big account. There'll be others."

Ben shrugged, looking down. He sat down heavily in one of the brown leather chairs opposite Ned's desk. "It isn't just that."

"Oh? What else is on your mind?"

Bennett took a deep breath. "I met this girl the other night and I can't get her out of my head."

Ned brought his palms together in front of his face. "Sounds nice. You met her casually? You went out with her?"

"I sort of slept with her."

"Oh."

"In my car."

Ned smiled. "That brings back some pretty fond memories. Not real comfortable, though. Back seats were vinyl back then."

"Well, I don't know what to think. I've really missed my old girlfriend."

"Beth. I know."

Bennett looked at his boss, amazed. "How did you—"

"Oh, I'm no mind reader. You've managed to work her into twenty or thirty conversations, that's all." A tiny smile played at the corner of his mouth. He managed to suppress it.

"Oh." Ben rubbed his eyes with the fingertips and thumb of his left hand. "And, and, and I've sort of been thinking about all this over drinks." He shrugged, looking a little sheepish. "More...drinks than usual, I guess."

"I see." Ned quieted his insides, listening carefully. "Let me ask you, have you ever, say, been somewhere and not quite known how you've gotten there?"

"Well, maybe...once or twice."

"Do you keep a little something, one of those little bottles of whatever you like, maybe, around your apartment? Maybe," he waved a hand casually, "to help you wake up, or for a few swigs to help get you ready to go out..."

"Yeah," Ben brightened, "you do understand."

"Oh, I understand, all right." Ned leaned forward, looking Ben in the eyes. Suddenly, he changed the subject. He had made his decision. Ben remained in the office for fifteen minutes and the supervisor and employee chatted as friends. And, as the door closed behind Ben, a gratified smile appeared on Ned's face and he glanced up at the ceiling. "Thanks for the help," he said.

4

DR. EPSTEIN

Dr. Richard Epstein ordered another scotch. If you asked him, the stuff wasn't strong enough. He wished he had something stronger, but there was no time for that right now. He had to get to sleep so he could get to the damn staff meeting. Department heads and specialists and subspecialists—it made his head spin. Finding the right specialist and the right surgeon, dealing with these HMOs, and trying to get paid was as complex as the surgery itself. It *was* surgery in fact: extracting money from these bastards!

The scotch arrived and Kenny, the bartender, served it with a smile and a raised eyebrow. He looked concerned, but that was his job, wasn't it? Looking concerned. It got him a goddam bigger tip! It probably got him laid! The look reminded him of the goddam patronizing look on George Franklin's face. He hated that. If things had been different, he rather than Franklin might have been the hospital's CEO. But goddam times changed exactly at the wrong moment. No more General Practitioners performing surgery. Now you had to have three extra years of school to be an internist, then three for Cardiology, then a few more for Cardiothoracic Surgery. By the time you could perform so-called specialized surgery, you were eighty seven goddam years old!

And then this HMO mess. *Bureaucrats making medical decisions!*

The whole thing made him sick, disgusted and wanting to rip someone's throat out—the very thing he had never been qualified to do! So what happened? He switched his focus and ended up with the losers in Pathology. He was a goddamn medical detective! In this hospital Pathology was a dead end!

He had once had such plans, such dreams and they had been attainable, if the whole damn focus of medicine had not changed at exactly the wrong time!

He swallowed the scotch, exhaled noisily and looked around the high class wood paneled bar. He had done the right things, made the right choices, and the goddamn rug had been pulled out from under him. Someone had to pay!

* * *

SARAH

Sarah glanced at the people walking by the desk. The couples hand in hand made her think of Henry Roy. She wished she were home, snuggled next to him under the covers. A wide eyed man hurried past, glancing at her, then up at the numbers on the doors.

"Can I help you, sir? Who are you looking for?" But the man hurried on without stopping to answer. He was followed by a more familiar figure in a white coat.

"Good evening, Dr. Sticker," Sarah said, but as usual, he didn't answer. He didn't even wave. So she went back to her paper work, glancing occasionally at the video screens and listening to the beeps of the heart monitors. From her desk, she could hear any serious fluctuations on the heart monitors in the unit and she had learned to keep her ears tuned to that frequency. Any major change tripped an alarm in her mind, as well as the more mechanical alarms in the unit. She glanced at the screens every few minutes. She was exhausted, but alert and able to function.

A red-headed nurse went by. She nodded, and the nurse nodded back and smiled distractedly. She's probably as exhausted as I am, Sarah thought, nodding to Dr. Epstein and then Dr. Ryan, who barely acknowledged her as they hurried by.

She was startled when George Franklin strode past, carrying a black leather case. She was not used to seeing him in this part of the hospital so late at night. The sight of him woke her up, and she straightened in her chair, her back protesting. Sweat broke out on her forehead. "Hello, sir!" she called. He didn't respond.

* * *

BEN

Music screamed at Bennett from all sides—instruments he couldn't identify blended, rising and falling, pulsing. He sat where Eleanor had put him, in the middle of the room in its only chair.

"Sit right there," she had said, her upper lip curling with amusement at whatever she had planned. She had pulled his shirt off, then stepped back, looking at him, her fingers running up and down his bare arms. "I know what we need," she said, and she went into the kitchen and came back with the newspaper. She pulled it apart and placed sheets around him on the floor. "We don't want to make too much of a mess."

She grabbed him by the hair on the back of his head and pulled him close, kissing him hard. Then she left the room.

He sat in the near dark, half naked, surrounded by old news and minimalist furniture. Music washed over him and he closed his eyes and tried to trust, to relax for a few minutes. Her apartment was not as warm as he would have liked. Goosebumps rose on his upper arms and he felt rather than heard her come back. He opened his eyes and tried to turn his head but she was directly behind him. He heard two sounds, one a light slapping and the other a distinct buzz of machinery. He spun in his chair.

Eleanor was wearing a white terrycloth robe, tied at the waist. On a table immediately behind his chair sat a bowl of water. The buzzing noise came from a long, narrow piece of black machinery she held in her hand.

"I've been waiting to do this to you," she said, her face turned downward towards the floor but her eyes remained on him. A sly smile played at the corners of her lips. She waved the vibrating machine, flicking it off and placing it on the table. "But first, out with the old."

She lay a towel over the back of his chair and forced his head back so that he was staring at the ceiling. She straddled him, holding his face in her hands and kissing him passionately and pressing herself against him. He could feel her heart, delicate but strong, through the robe.

"Keep your eyes shut," she said. "This won't take long."

And then she was off him; he tried to see where she had gone but his head was suddenly doused with water. The music dulled as his ears were drowned and warm. He tried to sit up, sputtering.

"Whoa, whoa, don't do that!" She tried to pull his head back but he coughed and spun sideways.

"What is this, some kind of weird baptism?" he said, looking at her.

The animation drained from Eleanor's face; her robe had been pulled half open at the top by the struggle; a creeping resentment crept into her slack features.

"The only way to get that gel out of your hair," she explained, "is to wash it out."

He looked at the bowl and then at the metallic implement. "That's for…cutting hair."

"Well to make you look right I can't just use a scissor."

"I…see."

She looked impatient. "With the right look you could look hot—not that you don't already, but that shirt with those stripes. I mean, you're not at the office! And the gel in your hair makes you look like the Fonz, you know? A little pomade and the right jeans and the right hair and I'll probably have to fight for you when we go out." She wrapped her arms around his neck, "if I ever *let* you out."

He pulled her around so she stood in front of him. "You think I could look, you know, like one of the guys you'd want to meet when you're out for the night?"

"That *is* how we met." A sly smile teased her mouth.

"I know, but you didn't, like, just want someone for one night or feel sorry for me…?"

"Don't fish for complements and don't insult me. Yeah, I think you could look hot. I know it. You have great cheekbones and killer eyes. It shows on your face that you're a great kisser." She sat on his lap and kissed him. "So I'm gonna make you over: clothes, hair—everything."

"Maybe so," he pulled her to him, "but first let me leave you with a good impression."

Afterwards, they sat, naked, on the couch, and she talked about her disappointments—how she had wanted to be a nurse and then a social worker, but how neither had worked out for her. Financial reasons had been partly to blame, she said. But she had also felt alone, unsupported. Though her father and sister were in the medical field, they were busy with their lives; her mother lived for her garden. And until now, there had been no lovers beyond one night stands.

"So you cut hair for a living?"

She smiled. "I did a nice job, didn't I? No, I don't do this for a living."

"So what *do* you do? You do have some kind of job, don't you?"

She turned to him and stroked the side of his face. "I haven't really talked to anyone like this in, I don't know, ten years."

"Well, it hasn't been quite that long for me, but this really is nice. There hasn't been anyone for me to trust in a long time." He pulled her to him and kissed sweat from the base of her neck. "I've missed this."

* * *

HOPE

The sun peeked out from below the horizon, casting pink rays upon low clouds, warming their bottoms a pastel shade of purple. Were all Christmas eve mornings so beautiful? Had the last noticed sunrise been so long ago?

Normally an exhausting chore, climbing out of bed had been a pleasure, throwing on clothes fun—there had even been a lucid moment of color coordination!

But how to enjoy the moment. How to draw this out and make it last. With what friend could this appreciation of beauty be shared, however fleeting it might be?

Pop was the original never failing friend who never abused, never talked back, and brought that loving, warm sunrise from out there into the heart. Pop was only an arm's length away. Pop, the original love, the first among firsts, would gladly enhance any moment, enrich any feeling. Poppy heard, poppy saw. Pop understood and never left.

But The One was sweet and soft and caring and so easily embarrassed. The One would understand the sunrise even if called later in the morning, even if hearing of it second hand. The One gave love tenderly with an oh-so-warm body. And afterwards, The One cried! The One was unpredictable, a risk that rewarded. The One brought new possibilities, like a visitor from another planet.

A new and daring idea trapezed into your consciousness. The daring idea could be felt around the eyes and cheeks where it broke into a smile like white waves on a shoreline that had only known parched rage. Its possibility had always existed, yet where had this daring notion been before?

The blue plastic syringes were in the leather case and, once they were on the counter it was a moment before either black boot could be located.

Like dirt covering a grave, an old green bath towel was perfect for wrapping them, so they would not shoot shards onto the floor or damage the countertop.

The rage had disappeared. That had never happened. The retribution that had started it all and the satisfaction that once came with it were gone, leaving no aftertaste of victory nor remorse for the dead. Someone else had done it all.

I was not responsible. See that green towel?

The heel of the heavy boot smashed down on the towel, crunching the thin glass within. There was a moment of clarity, air gone from lungs. There was still work to be done! Three bags left! A mad dash across empty space, as though someone else might get them first—and someone might. The daring idea might jump back on the first trapeze out of town, or fall, no net below.

Flinging open the window and pausing only a moment to look down on the empty street, that was barely lit by the pink dawn sun, the bags fluttered in the light breeze and skipped and twirled along the concrete.

Why not go out for breakfast and then call The One to share these new perceptions! Why not have a normal morning, a human morning? The first breakfast of the first morning. Life's possibilities were endless! The adventure, the love! And after breakfast, Christmas shopping with money that might have gone to the Man with the Hat! And then a call to The One to share the experience! Now that's freedom. Like that other man said: "Free at last!"

For the first time in fourteen years!

* * *

BEN

At Selling Sight and Sound colorful holiday cards were folded over a string that ran the length of the creative room. Candy boxes and fruit baskets had been wrapped and sent to clients who were called each Christmas eve and wished well. The extra boxes and baskets had been opened and, as they did each Christmas eve, the staff shared their contents as an appetizer while work went on casually. A lazy day. At noon, work was put aside and a catered hot meal brought in, after which Ned handed out bonuses.

Lou hurried by carrying a manila envelope stuffed with papers. He nodded through the glass at Ben, stopped, turned and came into Bennett's office. "Isn't that something?" he said, arms folded, looking at Ben.

"What? Is there some egg salad on my face?"

Lou shook his head, speechless. Arms still folded over his chest, his hands made evocative little circles in the air. "Your hair. It's shorter and it's—you washed out the greasy kid stuff. It, it glows, like, like hand-rolled pasta or some exotic dessert—no, really! I mean it as a compliment!"

Annie came into the office as though she had heard, though of course she couldn't have. She shrugged. "I liked you before."

From over the glass and across the creative room came Lydia's playground catcall: "Hey, custard head!"

Ben looked at Annie, and when he met her eyes, her expression wilted and she looked at the floor. "Of course, I still like you. I didn't mean that, I—"

"Annie." Bennett stood up and reached with an index finger toward the side of her face. She shrank back. "You don't usually wear blush. Did you hurt yourself?"

"No, I mean it's nothing. I'm retaining water, I—"

"Come here." He touched her and a faint spot of purple appeared where the makeup rubbed off. "Annie!"

"Oww! What're you doing? Leave me alone!"

Ben brought his face close to hers and touched her elbow. "It's Kenneth, isn't it?"

Her eyes filled with tears; her lips bunched together, quivering. She nodded. "Please don't tell Ned," she managed to say. "He'll go after him and Ken'll, Ken'll—"

"He *belongs* in a kennel," Lou said.

Annie turned around. "I didn't know you were still here."

Lou put a palm to the base of his neck. "I thought you knew everything."

Ben didn't know what to say. He slowly shook his head. "Oh, Annie," was all he could manage.

"Get the phone," she said, pointing. Ben took a tissue from a box on his desk and handed it to her.

They heard Art, through the glass. "Selling Sight and Sound. This is Art. No, I *am* Art. I *don't* mean to be grandiose, ma'am, it's just that Art's my name. You must want the art *department.* Well, tell that to my mother! Bennett!"

Lou guided Annie out of Ben's office. Ben picked up line one.

The client was thrilled with the concept, the illustration, the fonts—it was all exactly the way she had pictured it! Unfortunately, her boss had a different idea in mind. Her boss? Where had her boss been while they were in the planning stages? "Of course, we'll work on another concept," Ben said cheerfully. He held the receiver away from his face and looked into it as though the client were captive in the piece of plastic. Another concept...and another invoice.

Ben hung up the phone and looked over the typed list of the hospital department heads. A knock on his doorjamb made him look up.

"Hey, stranger. I brought you some coffee." Arthur set one of the two mugs he was carrying in front of Ben. "So when're you coming to visit us again?"

Ben shrugged. "I don't know. Spring, maybe?"

"Sooner, I hope. How's your lady friend?"

Ben nodded. "We've been having a lot of fun. She's different. Maybe not the sort of girl you settle down with, but maybe that's what I need."

"Louis and I were talking about you last night at dinner...we know you're still unhappy about the account, even though you've been able to keep the campaign going. You're doing a great job, by the way."

Ben sipped his coffee. "I just wonder if I'm doing the right thing."

"You're an art director and you're art directing. Your job, right?"

"I can't get away from feeling like I'm covering something up. So I've been..." He nodded towards the list of hospital department heads.

"Working as a cop in your spare time? Maybe you and your lady friend could do the Thin Man routine. You said she's sarcastic, and you both drink. Does she look like Myrna Loy?"

Ben made a face. "Who?"

Art waved him away. "Uck, you're *so* young."

"How's the construction going?"

Art shrugged. "It's going. So I'm going. Meaning when they're working I can't get a thing done on my manuscript. I run off to Amagansett or Bridgehampton. The good news is they finally got the bathroom in. The bad news is they burst the sewage pipe in doing it, so now when Louis tells me I'm full of shit, well, anyway…" His eyes sparkled. "We're thinking of adopting the foreman. I think we can do it legally, he's been there so long."

"But overall the script is coming along. I know it's your baby."

Art nodded. "It? You mean she! And I may just send her to college, she's getting so old! Oh," he touched Ben's arm, "did Louis mention he met an agent who supposedly knows someone at a network? One of Louis's bowling buddies, of all people. Who'd've thought an agent bowled!"

Ben shook his head. "Imagine if you got the show produced!"

"Produced? It's in syndication, in here." He tapped the side of his head. "In fact I'm already over the cancellation." He walked to the door. "I just wanted you to know that Louis and I are there for you and we're rooting for your campaign to—" he laughed. "I was going to say knock 'em dead, but you know what I mean. We're also rooting for you, relationship-wise. Say, you know who'd love to go out with you?"

"Annie, right?"

"I thought she was the extra sensory person around here!"

"I'm not blind. Annie's cute and sweet." Ben shrugged. "I don't know."

Art winked. "Be a shame to let all that go to waste. But I know, you're spoken for."

"Time for you to get back to work," Ben deadpanned, but as Art left he was gratified to know that he was in someone's thoughts, and that moment of spiritual clarity he'd had at their lake rushed back to him.

And then he looked down at the list of names on his desk and it was gone, replaced by a vague dread.

The two departments that jumped out at him were headed by Doctors Sticker and Esptein. He dialed the numbers next to each. Epstein answered his own phone and issued Ben a warm invitation. Sticker's number was answered by a machine with a short, curt message. Ben announced that he would be there before noon and hung up the phone. He went quickly to the coat closet, folded the list of department heads and slid it into his shirt pocket. He patted his back pants pocket, feeling for his private note pad. As he put on his coat, he felt something pressing against his chest and he reached into the left inside pocket and pulled out a pamphlet. It was folded in half so that the back, which was gray and nondescript, faced outwards. He took it out and unfolded it.

Large, plain yellow and red letters: "Are You An Alcoholic? A Simple Test."

When he got back from the hospital, he'd have to have a word with Ned.

From behind a computer in the back of the room, Annie called out: "Ben, that's for you." But Ben was already gone.

The phone rang three times before Annie picked it up and explained to the woman on the other end that Ben had gone out. Before she could ask if the woman wanted to leave a message, the line had gone dead.

* * *

Blood was everywhere. On ivory colored trays, on the countertop, on two gurneys that sat near the doorway. The blood was stored in packets, which was apparently the way it arrived from the blood bank. Outgoing blood, to be processed or analyzed, was in vials which were labeled and bar coded.

But it wasn't the blood that startled Ben; it was one of the two technicians in the room. The tall one with the freckles and red hair. She looked at once familiar, yet unfamiliar.

He stood in the doorway, looking at the woman, forgetting entirely why he had come. She looked at him and then at the technician who was with her, a shorter, heavyset woman who wore red framed glasses. The shorter woman, whose skin was pale, nearly white, spoke first.

"Was there something we can help you with?"

It was a moment before he could bring himself to speak. "I, I'm Bennett James, the Art Director for the ad agency who's representing the Medical Center."

"Well, then, you'd want to see Mr. Franklin," said the woman-who-looked-like-Eleanor. "His office is down the hall," she leaned toward the door and pointed to the left, "and directly downstairs."

"Uh, no. I know where Mr. Franklin's office is. I'm here researching our campaign. Would you ladies mind answering a few questions."

They looked at one another, shrugging. Bennett took out a pad. "What are your names?"

"Janice Rosen."

"Marilyn Franklin."

He pretended to look surprised. "Marilyn, do you have a sister?"

Marilyn nodded. "But she's not connected with the hospital."

"Eleanor?"

Marilyn looked surprised. Delicate eyebrows arched and pretty blue eyes altered slightly from oval to round. He'd seen the same look on Eleanor's face. He stopped himself from sinking further into the daydream. "I, I ran into her downtown. Anyway, can you tell me who might have access to the hospital's blood supply?"

"Depends what you mean by access," said Janice. "Around here, pretty much anyone can go pretty much anywhere, except specialized wards like the OR. But if you mean who could tamper with the blood system. No one. This stuff's all tagged, bagged and computerized. It's checked and rechecked. No one's messing around with this. We've already had the cops and the FBI in here, so believe me, you're not going to find anything they missed."

"I see," said Ben. "Well, what other ways can people get the HIV virus?"

"All the ways you know about," said Marilyn. "Unprotected sex, sharing needles, bad transfusion."

"What about being injected with it directly?"

Marilyn nodded. "It's possible, I guess. But if it's in blood, that blood ought to be the same as the person's it's going into. There might be a reaction otherwise, though compared to the HIV, it might not be much."

"Can't it be taken out of the blood?"

Janice leaned back against a metal sink, folding her arms. "You mean isolate the virus in saline? Not easy. You'd have to have one extensive lab to pull that off."

Marilyn looked doubtful. "I really don't think anyone's injecting the virus into patients here."

He nodded. "Okay, but if someone were, who might stand to gain?"

"No one," said Janice. "Maybe the families, if they had insurance policies."

"Or someone who wanted to ruin the hospital," said Marilyn. "Or maybe a maniac."

Ben jotted some notes in his pad and slipped it back into his pocket. "Thank you very much, ladies." His eyes lingered on Marilyn's for a moment; then he turned to leave.

"Say hello to my sister," she said.

* * *

Dr. Sticker, Chair of Hematology/Oncology, was tall, perhaps six foot three, and wore his delicate brown hair parted and combed neatly to one side. His hair, however, was his only neat attribute. The bare once-white walls of his office were gray streaked. A gilded picture frame on the desk contained a photo of an achingly beautiful young woman wearing too much makeup and too little clothing. "Love ya, doc - Tammy" was scrawled across the bottom in felt tip marker. He'd met her two weeks earlier during a bout of insomnia that even his pills couldn't cure and she'd followed him around since, like an eager puppy.

Papers littered the floor and desk; what books lined his shelves were in disarray and, most startling to Bennett, the room smelled of cigarettes.

"Yes, yes, what can I do for you?" Doctor Sticker asked. "Excuse me," he picked up his phone, dialed, leaned back in his chair, chewing on a pencil. He said a few inaudible phrases into the phone and hung up. He frowned up at Bennett, scratching at the base of his neck. "And you are…?"

"Bennett James, sir."

"Never heard of you. Now I'm busy." He shifted in his chair, looked hard at a spot on Ben's arm and scratched himself under his right eye.

"I'm the art director for the Medical Center's upcoming ad campaign."

Dr. Sticker began rooting around the papers on his desk, pushing one pile into the next and back again. He scratched his forearm through the sleeve of his shirt. "Where was that chart? I can't believe—art director?" He looked up, then pointed to the door. "Then direct yourself out of here. You're in the wrong wing of the hospital. Franklin's office is…"

"Why do people keep trying to send me to…I know where Mr. Franklin's office is."

"Give yourself an award." His face was flushed; sweat stood out on the Doctor's forehead. "Just make sure he pays you." Dr. Sticker stopped what he was doing and sat back again in his chair. He threw the pencil he had been chewing into a garbage pail next to his desk. Ben watched it fall and saw that half a dozen chewed pencils lay amidst the garbage and some clear liquid. "My department hasn't received its assigned budget correctly or on time in sixteen years and it's entirely his fault—excuse me—his responsibility. He has it in for me and there's nothing I can do about it."

"Ahm, I see."

"Do you, really, Mr. James? Do you know that the prestige and effectiveness of this institution have been irreparably harmed over the last decade and a half because that selfish son of a bitch has been running the show? Hmm? Did you know that, Mr. James?"

Ben took a step back. "Well, no, actually."

Sticker leaned forward. "Well, I guess you don't see, then, do you?"

Ben took his notepad out and wrote down Dr. Sticker's name and put two stars next to it. "So, I guess you'd rather see someone else in charge of the hospital."

Dr. Sticker's response was drawn out with sarcasm. "You could say that, yes."

"So, if Mr. Franklin were somehow discredited, that might serve your purposes…?"

A trickle of sweat ran down Dr. Sticker's neck and onto his shirt collar, just above his dark blue tie. "I have no purposes, other than healing the sick." He scratched his chest in quick, jerky motions. "And any disagreements Mr. Franklin and I may have are of a business nature. They are not personal. Now, if you'll excuse me…"

"Just one more question, Doctor. Who might have access to the various wards around the hospital?"

The doctor laughed—a single sharp bark. "This isn't an Army base. Just about anyone can bullshit their way into any part of any hospital, Mr. James."

"I'd have thought that wards like the OR might be specialized—"

"Sure, but if you're clever and think up a good lie, prepare yourself—" He gestured with both palms up. "Just look at your own presence in my office." He laughed again, and by the time he stopped, Ben was down the hall and in the elevator.

* * *

The simulated wood sign on the door was embossed with white script that read "Dr. Richard J. Epstein, Chair of Pathology." Ben knocked, and after a moment, a deep voice said, "Aahem, come," and he pushed open the door.

Flashes of gold foil reflected florescent light from black, brown and red texts lining the wall behind the doctor's desk. Above the neat rows of books, black framed medical degrees spoke arcs of Latin. On the green file cabinets along the right wall sat colorful three dimensional models of the pulmonary, digestive, and skeletal systems. Dr. Epstein, who was in his early sixties, balding, with a clear complexion and equally clear blue eyes, shook Ben's hand and motioned him to one of the two chairs along the left wall. Folded neatly on the other chair was a herringbone coat on top of which sat a pair of fancy red leather driving gloves.

"What can I do for you, young man?"

"Well, I'm working on the hospital's ad campaign to restore confidence following this recent and I guess not so recent spate of AIDS cases." He shifted in his seat. "The explanation for these cases is...disturbing."

"Yes, I've heard." The doctor nodded. "The virus is said to have been transmitted intentionally. In an isolated case, I might believe that. The result of a grudge, perhaps, but dozens of unrelated people over a period of a decade? A bit far-fetched, don't you think?"

Ben agreed. "But there doesn't seem to be any other..."

"Diagnosing a disease, like Alzheimer's for instance, via the process of elimination, may be acceptable. Solving a crime, if that's what it is, through that process—well, I'm not so sure."

Ben shrugged. "I'm not a doctor and you're not a cop."

Dr. Epstein smiled. "Forgive me. You're...an advertising executive?"

Ben nodded. "Art director. And you certainly don't have to answer any of my questions. They are totally unofficial. Background for the campaign, actually."

The doctor held up a hand. "No, no. I'm happy to help in any way I can. This whole thing is so awful, on a personal, professional level—in every way. And I do try to work with the Department of Community Relations. They run the campaign, correct?"

"Actually, Mr. Franklin has been hands on, and thank you. I do appreciate your help. Now, who might have access to patients and areas where blood is handled?"

Doctor Epstein paused, looking down at the stack of papers on his desk. "Hospital staff assigned to that area: doctors, nurses, custodial staff, technicians. Quite a variety of people, I'm afraid."

"And who might stand to gain from giving people the virus?"

"Another hospital perhaps." He sighed. "I don't really know." He set his lips tightly together. "I must tell you, as difficult as it is for me to believe that someone might be giving people AIDS intentionally, it's more difficult to believe that our precautionary systems are that faulty. What's the answer?" He shrugged. "I'm a doctor, a scientist. I deal with facts, and any conjecture or hypothesis must be carefully analyzed before it is assumed to be true. One avenue I would certainly explore is the possibility that these are people who have the virus to begin with."

Ben nodded. "Well, thank you for seeing me, doctor. You've been most helpful."

* * *

INSANITY

"Buffalo gals won't ya come out tonight..."

"Turn that damn thing down!" It came out as a croaked whisper. Yelling loud enough for the people in the next apartment to hear was impossible with this headache. Besides, getting out of bed was physically impossible. The floor was too cold, and there was no leaving this blanket. What kind of stupid, ridiculous idea was this?

"Won't ya come out tonight..."

Freedom was horrible—terrifying! What did it matter if, underneath it all, you were crazy? That was it, that was the feeling. Out of control...crazy.

"Won't ya come out tonight."

Fingers of fear reached up from the stomach. Someone was watching. Someone was outside with a camera. The FBI. In a tree. In the apartment next door. In a car downstairs. Their knowing eyes crawled over your skin like bugs and the only time you forgot was when the nausea was stronger than the fear.

"Buffalo gals won't ya come out tonight."

Christmas Day and not a friend in the world. Lonely and terrified. Again. How had it happened? Was this blanket wool? It itched! Lonely, terrified...and itchy! Rub your legs together, kick the blanket off, but oh, there goes the stomach again! Gotta throw up but nothing left to puke so you sit there and make noises like a small van backing up without a muffler. You really are crazy.

"And...dance by the light of the moon."

This is not going to work. It was a good idea, yes, give yourself credit for the thought, but you can't make a race horse out of a pig. Once an addict always an addict. Who was out there? Who was watching? What are they going to do? Was it only Jimmy Stewart and Donna Reed in the next apartment? And The One. Ha! The One was like all the rest.

Fear was an iron hand in a leather glove, squeezing your chest, making you say "oh" softly, and ripping tears from your eyes. Can't go out for food, can't get out from under the blanket. Have to close your eyes to roll off the couch and shuffle to the window and crouch off to one side so the FBI won't see you. Peek through a lifted corner of the old yellow curtain and try, try to remember why you did this ridiculous thing. It had only been yesterday but that seemed like years. You were a different, foolish person then. Close your eyes and picture yourself standing here, somehow deluded into feeling good and thinking it was the right thing to do. You opened the window and took out the bundles and you threw them out. Now think, and remember. Which way had the wind been blowing? What was the weather report? Wind out of the east? Which way was east? Now look hard down and to the right. Could those white spots next to the curb across the street be two of them?

Hope appeared suddenly, like a red ribboned Christmas gift. There was a way out of this madness. A temporary reprieve, yes, but it was there and it was familiar and understood. The Man with the Hat! He had the answer. Only he could battle the FBI!

Fear was forgotten in a mad, barefoot dash for the elevator.

* * *

CHARLIE SPOON

"I'm sorry," Charlie said, covering the phone with his free hand. He held the tattoo needle away from his body with the other. "This is sort of an emergency." His eyes shifted away from the client. The person on the other end of the line had come back on. He listened, then exploded. "What do you mean they've cut her program!" he bellowed, and the client sat up straight in the chair. "You've screwed around with my little girl since day one. Your 'best damn medical staff on the east coast' as your ads say, caused her 'problem' in the first place and now her therapy's not covered? Screw the HMO! I don't buy it. And let's quit calling it a problem, okay? She's retarded. My little girl's retarded and it's because of your damn staff at your damn hospital. If they had gotten that cord from around her neck a fucking decade ago, if they'd been paying attention..." He covered the receiver with his hand, taking two deep breaths. "And now I have to pay for a program that I can't afford?" He slammed the phone down, raised it and slammed it again, harder. A piece of black plastic broke off and shot across the room. The client followed it with her eyes.

"Excuse me." She got up and ran to the bathroom.

"Eleanor, I'm sorry. I got a little out of control." Charlie's eyes filled with tears, increasing their Graves Disease prominence. He put down the tattoo needle and dialed another number.

"Veronica? Charlie. I just got off the phone with Adriane Curley. They're not covering Robin's therapy anymore." He shook his head and looked up at the ceiling. "No, that's not why I'm calling. I'll pay for it. I'll pay for it. Veronica, you know that where Robin's concerned I'd do whatever's...well I'll find a way." He listened for another moment, then slammed the phone down again. He leaned down, his mouth close to the phone. "Don't believe me, then, you bitch, you bitch!"

The bathroom door opened and Eleanor came back. "Ready." She smiled. Charlie Spoon looked hard at her.

"Maybe I ought to finish some other time."

"No!" Eleanor said. "I've got to show my boyfriend tonight. I need to see him tonight and I can't show up without this tattoo—finished. I'm going to surprise him. Come on, Charlie. Talk to me while you finish. What's all this about Robin? I heard you."

Charlie picked up the needle, hit the footpedal and the dentist-drill whine filled the room. He sat in front of Eleanor, placing her arm on his leg, and leaned his bulk downward, pinning her arm. "Now don't move, or you'll have a permanent line across your arm."

Eleanor giggled.

Charlie began coloring in the outline he had begun earlier. "Watching Robin come into this world was the most beautiful event I've ever witnessed," he said. "But they screwed up. Didn't we pay them enough? Should I have slipped the doctor a few bucks so he'd have paid attention to what the cord was doing? I mean, I'm here, doing your tattoo, paying attention to what I'm doing. I'd better, right? You're paying me. And you know what? Even if you weren't, I'd still do right by you. I'd never screw up. But doctors? They don't give a shit. As long as the Mercedes is paid for." He paused, sat up and examined his work, spraying her arm with alcohol and wiping away the blood. "So now I have a 10 year old retarded daughter and you know what? There's not a thing I can do about it except drink myself into a stupor every night."

"Mmm," Eleanor said. "Doesn't sound so bad."

"I tell you. I love that sweet little girl more than anything. She's not angry about her condition. She loves everything and everyone. She'd love those doctors or technicians who did that to her if she saw them today. I hate the whole goddamn system." He took a deep breath. "So, what's that boyfriend of yours like?"

Eleanor laughed, then leaned forward, not moving her arm. "Charlie. If I give him what he wants, he's there for me, you know?"

"Yeah, Eleanor. I know."

* * *

BEN

Ben sat back, watching the trees and fields through the dirty glass. Eleanor bumped and jostled against him. The train lurched out of the Long Beach station, over the tiny steel bridge spanning Reynolds Channel, and into Island Park. A blue uniformed conductor called out the stops, drawing out the names on the vowels with old fashioned cadences.

"Iislaaand Paaark. Oooceansiiide next! Tiiickets pleeease! All aboooard!" The Long Island Railroad cars creaked into motion, groaning as though waking from a long sleep. Sunlight shone through the ice coating the tree branches and what was left of last week's snowfall turned to white flashing light as the train gathered speed.

"You'll love the Matisse. The colors, the lines. They're the most beautiful paintings in the world." Eleanor looked at him, her eyes searching his face. At times she seemed like two, even three different people. This was the Eleanor he understood and cared for—he was not yet sure he loved her. The curious, innocent Eleanor who gazed at him with eyes that asked for him by name. Her expression became playful. "Oh, I didn't show you what I did!" She wriggled out of her jacket and, rather than roll her sleeve up she stretched the v-neck of her gray polo shirt down over her shoulder to reveal the still healing red and blue bird.

"I'm really glad you did it," Bennett said, leaning close and kissing her. She clutched his arm through his coat with her fingernails and pulled him close, kissing him hard, open mouthed. This was what he loved about her, her daring, to-hell-with-everyone attitude.

The sidewalk outside the museum was a sea of fur-lined green hoods, wool mittens and steamy breath. Bennett and Eleanor pressed against one another, kissing and playing the idle physical games of comfortable lovers.

The Matisse were as beautiful as she had promised. She described the flow of color and shimmer of line so that he saw and understood for the first time, and he stepped back and saw a continuity of image, color and motion he had never noticed or understood. Today, she was the art director, she teased, laughing.

She suggested he squint and look around the big display room and when he did he saw the subtle play of luminosity and hue that was lost in the detail of the finished image and he had a childhood memory of pure color and feeling, older than thought or consciousness. And for some reason he thought of Art and Lou. His epiphany at the lake had touched something equally old. He took her hand to steady himself.

Here he was an art director with years of study and she was...what was she, anyway?

"What exactly is it that you do for a living?"

She didn't answer right away.

"I said, what—?"

"I heard what you said."

And there she was. That other Eleanor. The one who avoided his eyes, who wanted someone there, but whether the someone was Bennett James or not seemed unimportant. They walked toward the exit. He let go of her hand.

"Excuse me. I have to use the ladies room."

While he waited, he watched people in the lobby. Parents with children, elderly couples, lovers like himself and Eleanor though perhaps not like them at all. Did these couples know and understand one another better than he and Eleanor did?

He looked at his watch. She had been gone ten minutes. The sky between the buildings outside had gone as gray as old snow plowed to curbside. Lines of dirty yellow cabs waited in front of the museum. He could tell by the way people clutched their coats, bodies angled forward, that the wind had picked up.

"Excuse me, Miss?" Bennett stood up and asked a middle aged woman wearing a long scarlet coat and a blue scarf, "could you see if my friend is okay? She's thin, has red hair and is wearing jeans and a gray v-necked shirt. Thanks so much. She's been in there a long time."

A moment later the woman came out, a confused expression on her face.

"There's no one like that in there. I even knocked on the stalls."

A hot sweat broke out on Ben's forehead. "Thank you, ma'am." He looked around the lobby, spotting a security guard.

"Is there something I can—?" The woman looked concerned.

"Oh, that's okay. Maybe she came out when I wasn't watching or—it's okay, I'll figure it out."

With a sympathetic look, the woman disappeared into the outgoing crowd.

Ben approached the elderly security guard and started to explain what happened. The guard, a coffee-skinned man with a wrinkled face and tired eyes, frowned, raising an eyebrow and rubbing his chin between thumb and forefinger. A fat gold wedding band gleamed from his hand.

"Ben, where'd you go to?" Eleanor was tugging at his sleeve.

"Is that her?" The security guard smiled.

"I, I sent a woman in after you. She said you weren't in there."

"You'd better screen your detectives better." She was in a much better mood and he was glad to see it.

"I'm hungry," he said. "How 'bout you?"

"Not really," she said. "I'm more tired."

"Well, maybe you'll get an appetite on the way to the restaurant."

"What restaurant?"

"I know a great Chinese place downtown."

The little restaurant was a storefront down a half flight of stairs. Thin strips of red pork, their edges charred, hung in the steamed window. The single room was nearly empty and Bennett and Eleanor sat next to one another, his right leg entwined with her left at the tiny table in the corner, with its red table cloth and bright white napkins. They sipped tea from small ivory cups until the spicy bean curd and purple eggplant arrived. Ben unwrapped a packet of chopsticks. "You use these?"

She shook her head.

"Why not try?"

She made a face. "I'm not so good with my hands."

He looked at once surprised and amused. "Could've fooled me."

She giggled and tried her chopsticks, fumbling until Ben showed her how. He was surprised by the thickness of her fingers. He had never noticed that. One of her sticks clattered onto the plate.

"Never mind. I'll use a fork."

"No, it's okay. It just takes a little—"

She picked up a fork and began eating.

"So, tell me about your job…"

"Well, you know I work at the 3S Ad agency and I'm the new art director."

"What kinds of projects are you working on?"

"All kinds. Most are just production jobs, though, since I wasn't the art director when they started. This Medical Center job is the first big one for me." He shrugged. "I'm kind of nervous about it."

"Why?"

"Because it's such a big job and because of this problem they're having at the hospital."

"What problem is that?"

"People're getting HIV who aren't supposed to be getting it."

"No one's supposed to get AIDS, Ben."

He looked at her. "But you know all this, don't you?"

She looked at him, putting her fork down on the plate deliberately. "Why do you say that?"

"You know about what goes on at that hospital."

Eleanor glanced around the room and began to cough. Ben patted her back, softly at first, then, when she didn't stop coughing, harder.

She caught her breath. He gave her some tea.

"Thank you," she said.

"The other day, while I was looking into this AIDS thing, I met your sister."

Eleanor had been looking into her food. Now she picked up the fork and began turning over bits of eggplant. "Oh, you met Marilyn."

"She looks like you."

"I look like her."

"So you must know what goes on there."

She lifted her eyes and looked at him. "We don't talk much."

"What about your father? George Franklin's your father, isn't he?"

She nodded, still without expression. "I haven't talked to my father since 1984. Neither of us has. He's got his own problems."

"And you?"

She put the fork down and turned to him, sliding her hand up his leg. "I've got you. Is that a problem?"

He took her hand away. "I thought knowing a little about your sister and maybe your dad might help with the investigation."

She turned back to her food. Her shoulders seemed to close around her chest; her head drooped just enough for her red bangs to hide her features. "What're you now, a cop?"

He looked up at the ceiling, took a deep breath. "No, Eleanor, I'm not a cop." He stroked her hair.

She pulled away from him. "What? You think my sister or my father are involved with people getting the virus?"

He spoke softly. "Apparently it's being given to people purposely and I don't have any idea who's involved. But I have to find a way to get information. You—your family may be able to help. No one over there will talk to me." He pressed his lips together, waiting. "And now you won't talk to me."

She didn't answer.

He liked that she seemed easily hurt. She was so tough sometimes. He decided that she must have been hurt in some past relationship and he made a mental note to be more tender and gentle. He smiled to himself and lightly touched the tip of her elbow with his finger. Her body jumped.

"El. It's okay. We'll talk about it some other time."

Later, as they sipped second cups of tea, the waiter brought fortune cookies.

"Read yours," Bennett said.

"I don't believe in that stuff." She ate the cookie, dipping it into her tea.

Bennett unwrapped his, and read the fortune. He smiled. "You will find love in an unlikely place'." He took out his wallet and slid the fortune in with his driver's license.

When they were back in Long Beach, and approaching his car, Eleanor took him suddenly by the hand and pulled him into the the back seat.

"Would you call this an unlikely place?" she giggled, pressing against him.

* * *

After driving to Oceanside and dropping her off at her apartment, he drove home slowly, his mind still filled with the exciting sweetness of the moment. A car flashed past, cut in front of him and slowed so suddenly that he had to slam on the brakes. The birds-egg blue Mercedes sped up again and turned off to the left. Ben caught his breath and sat back, the easy memory of Eleanor gone in a rush of adrenaline.

A half mile further along Long Beach Road something blue streaked across his peripheral vision. The Mercedes had run a light and was cutting in from a side road, barreling right at him. He cut the wheel to the left, and barely managed to avoid the back end of the car, which continued to the other side of the cross street.

A half mile further along the road, something smashed into the back of his car and his body slammed backwards, his head slapping the headrest. He looked at the rear view mirror but all he saw were lights. He gunned the accelerator, pushing the terror away. Okay, you crazy bastard. Let's see you catch the White Cat. The Cougar jumped to respond, accelerating down the straightaway, and up the hill towards Oil City. The Mercedes, if that's what it was, was either no match or hadn't the stomach for a chase, so he circled around, taking the fork through Island Park and came back north along Long Beach Road, glancing to either side for any sign of the blue Mercedes. He turned left onto Atlantic Avenue in Oceanside, drove over the train tracks, through East Rockaway and turned right onto Broadway in Hewlett, then left onto Rockaway Avenue, into Valley Stream.

* * *

He sat in the car for a long moment in front of Mattis's house, breathing while his body slowly unclenched. Upstairs, the blue light was on, so he tried to make as much noise as he could upon letting himself in and crashing up the stairs. Halfway up he stopped, remembering something Mattis had said a few weeks ago. He hated that hospital as much as anyone he had yet spoken to. Why? Ben couldn't remember. A spider crawled up the wall and stopped not far from Ben's hand. He considered his best friend and the crimes that had been committed. Mattis certainly could not have been in that car. He almost never left his house, for one thing. And he didn't drive. And of course, he didn't own a car.

The spider hesitated, extending a leg tentatively toward Ben's hand. Ben coughed several times and continued up the steps. He had to trust someone. When he arrived at the attic apartment, he banged his fist hard on the doorjamb.

No answer.

He knocked on the closed door. Faint blue shone through the crack below the door. He pounded on the door with his fist.

"Well, come in already! What do I have to do, print up invitations!"

Ben exhaled, his cheeks puffing with relief. He pushed open the door. Mattis was seated at the computer, typing, then staring at the screen. He didn't look up.

"Mattis, I just got..."

"Shh! Don't interrupt. I'm making a big sale."

"But some guy just—"

"I said shut up! What're you, deaf?"

"What?" He folded his arms and considered leaving. His leg was still trembling and some kind of pressure was invading his sinuses. He realized that it was an urge to cry. He reminded himself that he was safe.

He listened to the clatter of computer keys and Mattis's occasional grunt and "ahaa" until, finally, Mattis said, "Done," and turned to face him. "A seven thousand dollar system. And I get twelve percent. Not bad for working out of this hole, is it, Benito? No, it isn't. And it's my hole, that's the difference. No commuting, no dealing with idiots, except you, of course. Just kidding. Hey, know what I found out today? I learned why I'm agoraphobic. I was buried alive in a construction site by a neighbor's kid after witnessing him and other kids doing things to Lynn Palmer who lived two doors down." He looked delighted. "Merry Christmas, huh!"

Ben's eyes opened wide. "Really? When was this?"

"Twenty years ago. Well, more like twenty two years ago. I was four or so, I guess. That's part of why I'm so angry, but the bigger reason is that my uncle sexually abused me. Isn't that great?"

"Wonderful."

"No, I mean it. What a breakthrough! What a therapist! I'm learning new things. We're moving, finally. At least that was my first reaction." His expression darkened and his mood abruptly changed. "But I realized, what good is all that?" He got up and went to the tiny box refrigerator that sat on the floor next to the couch. He took out a 16-ounce beer. "Want one? Come on, take one. You look like you saw a ghost. I know, hearing this stuff can shake anyone up. It shook me up. But, I thought, what good is therapy? What good is finding out what happened to me in the past? Just how does it relate to today? And why are folks so fixated on this sort of thing anyway? It's all in the past. The real trick would be finding out what's going to happen to me now, or later on. Don't you think?"

"I—"

"Sure." He popped open the beer and took a series of long gulps. "That's the important stuff."

Ben opened his beer and took a sip. Immediately, the trembling in his leg relaxed to an occasional twitch. "Well everyone wants to know…"

"Of course. Exactly! So, I did something about it. I went to a fortune teller with next week's therapy money. Do you know how hard that was? To get out of the house and get to therapy I have to spend fifteen minutes on the phone with my counselor, a pretherapy session! That fortune teller wouldn't go for that. Believe me, I tried. And when I got there she scared the crapola out of me! She found this big line that cut across my lifeline like a freakin' machete. Right across, snuffing the life out of me like some big truck or something was going to come barrelling right through my life—and soon, too! It was right there in the middle of my lifeline. Jesus." He took two swallows of beer and tossed the empty can across the room in the general direction of a metal, outdoor garbage can which sat in the middle of the hallway, outside the bathroom.

"So, what are you going to do about it?"

"Well, first I'm having another beer. Didn't finish that one yet? Here, take another for when you're ready." He threw Ben another beer and opened one for himself. "Well, I realized what the deal was when I got home. See the way I work?" He sat down in front of his keyboard, staring at the screen. "This is the way I sit when I'm reading email, price info, and so on." He sat straight up, his hands pushing against the edge of the table, his head thrust forward. "Notice my hands, my palms. See how they're pushing against the edge of the table? Well, that makes a line across them. Get it?"

Ben started to laugh. "You mean that's what was cutting off your lifeline? They do say working too long at computers can—"

Mattis was staring right through him. "Hey, I just had a horrible thought. What if my pushing against the table created this truck coming into my life? Like, what if it's really going to happen because of the way I treat my hands? Oh, my God!"

"Oh, please. If you follow that logic, well, then people who use their hands a lot for manual labor would have crappier lives than say concert pianists and surgeons."

"And they do! Exactly! See?"

"Mattis!" Ben barked. "Stop it! You can't think like that. You're driving yourself crazy."

"What a lovely thing to say, Benwah!"

"Mattis, just go back to your therapist, okay? I'm here for a reason. I need your help. Snap out of it for a minute."

Mattis was subdued. "Yeah, what?"

Ben explained about the attack by the Mercedes.

"Hey, what if this line on my hand affected your—?"

"Would you forget about that! Let's consider the possibilities!"

Mattis sat back at the desk. He motioned for Ben to sit on the couch. "Oh, let me put on a CD. I can think much better with the Pumpkins in the background." He cranked the stereo to top volume.

"You call that the background?"

"What? I can't hear you! The music's too loud!" He turned it down.

"I said—never mind. So, what do you think?"

"Well, who would have access to the various wards, Benola?"

"A lot of people. Technical people, janitors."

"And the obvious. Doctors, nurses. Even visitors. But who would have the expertise to commit this crime, if that's what it is?"

"It is what it is. I've talked to the cops and one of the doctors who's assisting them. Every other possibility's been eliminated. They even looked into whether these people had the virus in some latent form before they came into the hospital. So if it's being administered by syringe, you could eliminate the janitors, visitors and at least some of the technical people."

"Unless they were drug addicts or had medical experience," Mattis said.

"Maybe one's a diabetic. But for now, let's go with the likeliest scenario. Now, I'd've thought that the most likely person, motivewise, would be the family of an earlier patient. Maybe someone who got poor treatment."

Mattis shook his head. "We don't know that. Besides, let's stick with our approach from the other end. Who could have done it? We've eliminated the janitors, visitors and most of the technicians. How was this done? Injection? Transfusion?"

"One of those." Ben sipped his beer. His leg was calm now.

"It's in blood?"

Ben nodded. "Yeah. Isolating it out of blood to put in water or saline solution is pretty tough, I'm told."

"Then why wouldn't that blood be rejected by some people? Different blood types, you know?"

"I don't know. It's a good question. But let's go on with our thinking. We're left with doctors and nurses. Maybe a doctor who's been accused of malpractice?"

"I just don't see doctors doing it. They're too visible. Not anonymous. And wouldn't a doctor be noticed around a patient who wasn't his? Maybe we should look into whether or not all the people who died had the same doctor?"

"Good thought. But we did. It's a wrong tree."

"You mean a dead end."

"No, a wrong tree. Barking up the wrong tree."

Mattis snapped his fingers. "Let me ask Dr. Botts."

"Dr. Botts?"

"Sure. I sold him a computer system two weeks ago over the Internet. He's in Minnesota. He ought to be willing to help. He'd better be, after the price I gave him." He starting typing. "And look at that. He's online now! This is our lucky day."

"Maybe yours," Ben said.

"Who - would - have - access - to - wards - to - be - able - to - give - injections - unnoticed? There." Mattis stopped typing. "Let's see what comes back. Oh, jeez. Look at this. Come here."

Ben got up and looked into the screen. "Everyone."

"Well," Mattis threw the second beer can in the direction of the first, "who have you questioned that might have gotten a little antsy? Obviously you got too close somewhere along the line. You got warm, pal, too warm."

5

OBSESSED

It was like living in a bubble. No matter where you were, no matter who you were with, you were alone. Even when you were doing your duty, your job, there was no one to say "hey what a great job" or even "yeah, that's right." You were alone. Even ants, as methodical and efficient and unfeeling as those unstoppable little automatons were, even ants had each other, even if they didn't know it.

The gaps were getting bigger. All of a sudden you were here or you were there and how the hell did you get there? What were you doing and how did you come to be doing it? The last thing you remembered was the Man with the Hat and the cold dirty tiles of the basement floor. And here you were at the hospital again, sticking needles into old ladies and little kids. Making things right again.

And not because you wanted to. Because you had to. The chain had become unstoppable, its links unbreakable. You'd become an ant. There was no feeling anything. Except rage, which was not like hot anger. Rage was cold, calm. A prickling of the skin. That was allowable but nothing else. *Hello. Nothing personal but you have to die. It's part of the big picture. The greater good. Just doing my job.*

The symptoms are mild now. No Kaposi's sarcoma; those purple splotches will probably never occur. Well that's a relief. You can at least die looking reasonable. But these colds don't go away. Some breathing difficulty but nothing major yet. A pain in the lower left side. Swollen fingers slipping on the syringe, falling off the plunger.

No one at that hospital is going to get any credit for healing anything; if they do, then someone's not doing their job. Not even the virus can stop the process. We're the lonely, the damaged, the proud. Killing is what we do. Feeling isn't.

Like ants.

* * *

ANNIE FLOWERS

"Should Auld acquaintance be forgot…"

The creative room at 3S was filled with staff and clients. Along the glass wall ran a long row of portable metal tables covered with white tablecloths and tins of catered Chinese food. On the far wall, under the window facing the street, sat a small help-yourself open bar and a CD stereo system.

"Ned, you know my husband, Kenneth?" Annie patted her red curls and opened her eyes wide in what had come to be known as her Orphan Annie look.

"We met at the awards show." Ned smiled and put out his hand. "Nice to see you. You folks know Barbara, from the Medical Center?"

She had been sitting behind Ned on the long cherry wood table, sleek and shiny in a too-tight black gown. She peeked out, mock shy. "Nice to see you, Annie, Kenneth."

Annie didn't return her smile. "Likewise." She adjusted the front of her cocktail dress, which was a turquoise and yellow floral print. Her eyes flickered back to Ned and held his gaze a moment too long.

Kenneth twitched his thick moustache and stared into his drink. He was a short man, perhaps five foot five, and his red rimmed eyes were devoid of emotion. His brown hair was thick, matted and falling over his ears and into his eyes.

Annie looked around, hoping to see Bennett, but he had not arrived.

"What're you looking for?" Kenneth mumbled.

"Just, just looking around."

"Oh, hello, Annabel!" Lou waved a fistful of M&Ms and wandered over. "This must be your husband. I'd shake your hand but mine're occupied at the moment. Kenneth, isn't it?"

Kenneth nodded, biting his upper lip. He looked at Lou out of the corners of his eyes.

"Nice party," said Annie. "Where's Arthur?"

"Around." Lou looked into his fist. "Red, yellow, brown. No blue?" He pretended to glare at Kenneth. "What kind of party is this—no blue M&Ms! Pisses me off. Know what these need?" He shook his fist. "Scotch!" He glanced in the direction of his other hand, in which he held a glass, and did a mock double-take. "Well, will you look at that! Ask and ye shall receive!" He took a swallow and followed it with the remaining M&Ms. "Do you guys want a drink or something?"

"I could use one," Annie said, looking at her husband.

Kenneth looked Lou up and down and then nodded slowly. "I'll be right back." He ambled to the bar.

"Why is he looking at me like I'm a fly in his soup?" Lou asked.

"He thinks you're coming on to me."

"Me? To you?" Lou laughed easily, looking in Kenneth's direction. "That would be incest!" He lowered his voice. "You've never told him about...your co-workers?"

"Oh, I have. He's so self-centered, he forgets. So zoned in on me and his own insecurities, he can't see anything else."

"He still hits you, doesn't he?"

Annie looked up at Lou, his face all kindness and concern. Her eyes welled; she swallowed.

"Last year," Lou said, looking away, "they had a combination dim sum platter that was out of this world but turned your stomach into the Space Shuttle. This year, we went healthy, or as healthy as Chinese can get—you know, tofu, wheat gluten, veggies—steamed, not fried..."

"He thinks everyone's in love with me or looking for some kind of confrontation." She started to reach for Lou's arm, saw her husband arriving with two drinks and forced her arm back to her side.

"Here." Kenneth handed a drink to Annie. "Vodka tonic." He held his beer up and nodded to Lou, as though making a little toast. "I had one while they were pouring hers." He gulped and half the beer was gone. White foam adhered to the bottom of his moustache.

"I'll be right back." He strode back to the bar.

"Of course," said Lou, and he looked at Annie.

"Where's Bennett?" she asked.

"Not here yet. I understand he's bringing a date."

"Oh," she looked at the floor.

"Annie do you really…?"

"Think he's right for me, even with Kenneth…?"

Lou nodded, smiling. "That's what I was going to ask *you*."

"I know he is, just like I knew what you were going to say."

"Would that put Ben in any danger?"

The animation drained from her face. "You said the Chinese food was healthy this year?"

"No matter what state your marriage is in, dear," Lou took her elbow, "remember, you are married."

She saw Kenneth returning and shook her elbow free.

* * *

BEN

Bennett's finger hurt but he continued to press the button and the channels changed yet remained the same. News, talk shows, infomercials, cartoons, sitcoms, sports, news, talk shows, infomercials, cartoons, sitcoms, sports…

He heard a noise from the bedroom, hit the mute button and listened. Perhaps it had been a car. When would she wake up? He wanted to go to the office party as much to show Eleanor off as for any other reason. He switched off the TV and went to the bedroom, opened the door and stood in the doorway. She was curled up in the far corner of the bed, covers up around her neck, one freckled shoulder peeking out. Her clothes were on the floor beside the bed.

"Hellooo…"

"Mmmmahh—"

"Ahem." He waited, but she did not add to the initial groan, so he sat next to her on the bed and touched her hair. She started and was suddenly sitting up. "Whaa—?" She grabbed both his shoulders, her nails biting into his skin.

"Hey, relax!"

She blinked and her eyes cleared, dimmed and nearly closed again. "Ooh." She fell against his chest and he cradled her head. "Let me go back to sleep."

"No, get up. We've got to go to my office party. Hey, who sleeps through New Year's Eve?"

She made a sleepy chewing sound. "I'm not going."

"El, come on!" He stood up, panicked. "My boss is there, clients're there. I'm the one with the big new account. How would it look—"

"And I'm the one with the hangover." She looked at him out of one eye, blankets protectively to her chest. "How would it look if I puked on your boss or…cut me some slack, okay?" She sat up, crossed her legs and looked down into her lap, the covers around her like a shawl. "If you loved me so damn much, you'd show a little compassion instead of thinking of yourself every—"

"Hey, this is important. And it's something you knew about!"

"When I'm fast asleep, I don't know about anything!" Her voice hardened. "You want to be like that?" She jerked her thumb toward the door, "you can get the hell out!"

Stunned by her tone, he stood up, and for a moment no one said anything.

"What?"

"You heard me."

He sat down again next to her, lightly touching her shoulder. "I'm sorry. I should have been more gentle."

She turned away.

He kissed the back of her shoulder, running his fingertip along the curve of her neck. She turned to him and pulled him on top of her, kissing him with sudden passion. "So, we'll be late," she gasped. "We'll make an entrance."

Sometimes, he thought, preserving harmony in a relationship required compromise.

She lay on top of him, sweat dripping from her neck onto his face. They both breathed heavily as hot muscles relaxed. Her fingers brushed his thigh.

He started, his body cringing away. "Oh…sensitive."

"Since when are you ticklish?"

He kissed her neck.

"Ha! Stop!"

"Oh, so you're ticklish, too! The woman has a sensitive side!" He could see she was trying not to laugh. She sneezed. Once, and then again.

"Bless you. Ooh, that didn't sound good. Bless you! You okay?"

"Just a cold." She took the tissue he offered. "Well, what're you waiting for? Let's get dressed. The party's waiting!"

* * *

THE PARTY

Lydia was laughing so hard that bits of food were shooting out of her mouth. "Oh, my Gawwd," she muffled, still chewing, when she saw the mess she was making. She put a hand to her mouth and turned her back on Arthur, Big Bob and Stein, a client who manufactured artificial flowers.

"I gotta wash this down!" She took a big swallow of white wine. "Mm, better. So, what were we saying?"

Arthur raised an eyebrow. "You were explaining to Mr. Stein how he might increase his company's productivity."

Lydia's eyelids drooped. "Well, I didn't mean anything by it, Mr. Stein. I was just talking, you know?"

Stein, who was dressed in a rainbow madras shirt that hung loosely outside his jeans, scratched his head, which was entirely bald except for a strip of curly gray hair above each ear. "Oh, not at all. I welcome any suggestions."

"Well, in that case—"

Arthur rolled his eyes. "Oh, boy, *carte blanche.*"

Bob took his elbow and tried to steer him away. "Let's get some dip."

Lydia cackled. "You've got a dip! On your arm! Haaah!!" She held her glass up to the light.

Bob, who was in his mid fifties and wearing a huge pompadour-toupé, chuckled politely. "Well, at least I've got someone."

Lydia glared at him. "Y'know, this is New Years not Halloween, Elvis."

"Don't antagonize her," said Art. "Remember what happened when you threw peanuts at the gorilla?"

"Excuse me?" said Lydia. "Exactly where do you see the comparison?"

"Well, I would never compare this place to a zoo, for one thing. The excrement's not on the floor; it's in the air." Art wrinkled his nose. "And possibly mixed in with that eggplant."

Stein was smiling and pulling a vial out of his coat pocket. "Valium?" He offered it around. Everyone stared at him; no one responded.

Against the wall next to the bar, Annie and Kenneth stood shoulder to shoulder, not looking at one another. He held a beer, she a Diet Coke. "This is some party," he said.

"I would have been happy to come alone."

"Oh, I'll bet. You'd've had a great time."

"So you came along to make sure I didn't."

"I came along because I'm your husband." He took her elbow between his thumb and forefinger and squeezed. "In case you've forgotten, you promised the priest you'd love and cherish me forever."

"Well, could you cherish my arm a little softer?" She caught Ned's eye from across the room. He was talking with the Medical Center's Chief Financial Officer. Annie watched as he excused himself and walked over.

"Annie, Kenneth. How're you enjoying yourselves?"

Kenneth forced a grin. "I'm amazed by how many male friends my wife seems to have."

"Well, we love our Annie."

"Oh, I'm sure."

Ned's expression didn't change. He just looked Kenneth in the eye. Kenneth looked away. "Quite an interesting group of people you've got here."

"Thank you. Our employees, our clients. They're all—"

"Have you seen Bennett?" Annie asked.

Kenneth turned slowly to look at her. "Bennett?"

Ned shook his head. “As a matter of fact, I haven’t. He should be here, though. I spoke with him yesterday and he said he and his new girlfriend would be here.”

“What’s it to you?” Kenneth looked at his wife.

“I, I’d just like you to meet him, that’s all.”

Ned looked from Kenneth to Annie, his eyes lingering on her face, taking in her expression. His hand gripped Kenneth’s bicep; there had been no noticeable motion. Ned’s fingers seemed to simply appear around Kenneth’s upper arm. They squeezed as Ned smiled, his deepset eyes locked on Kenneth’s.

“You be sure and enjoy yourself, Ken. And see to it our Annabel does, too.” He let go of Ken’s arm and walked back to the Medical Center’s C.F.O.

Kenneth rubbed his arm, then looked in the direction Ned had gone. “He’s crazy.”

Marvin Pflug, of Pfug ‘N Spence Beverage of Manhattan, was standing with Jeremy, the tall, redheaded 3S salesman who handled his account, trying to figure out how to leave gracefully, though it was not yet midnight. On the wood floor next to him lay Mrs. Pflug’s shiny black pumps. Mrs. Pflug was in the center of the room dancing by herself, her emerald gown and its lace slip flying up on either side of her; she was having a far better evening than her husband.

“Aannnywayy,” Lydia said. “You ought to give women more responsibility. Actually,” she giggled to herself, “we ought to take it for ourselves. But annywaaay, studies have shown that women really do handle, you know, interpersonal relationships better. Everything’d run smoother aannywaaay.”

Stein laughed. “Well, I can see you have the diplomatic touch. Women, huh? It’d work—except for one week out of the month!” He guffawed, looking to Lou, Arthur and Big Bob for support. Lou shook his head, looking at the floor. Arthur looked amused. Big Bob took a pack of cigarettes from his shirt pocket.

“I see your point,” he said.

“You see his point?” Lydia cried.

“Have some more wine, dear,” said Big Bob, slapping the top of the cigarette pack against his palm. “If, if women were running things, don’t you think mandatory coffee klatches would be a problem?”

Lydia’s eyes closed just a fraction, rather like a batter cocking a bat before a big swing, or a boxer setting himself before the knockout blow.

Stein agreed. “And making deals over sewing instead of golf—think of all the caddies that’d never make their college tuition. Hoohah. But I guess they could all get jobs as chauffeurs since bad driving would also be mandatory.”

“Really?” Lydia tapped her foot and looked thoughtfully into her glass. “Well, I guess you’re right. Some things would have to change and, I don’t know, it might not be so bad. Like, I guess, let’s see.” She looked hard at Big Bob. “Child care at work. Guess we’d have to make a little nursery out of a storeroom, so the boss’s kids would be taken care of. Hmm, don’t know if that’d be such a good thing, do you? And, what else? Hmm? Oh, I know. The pay. Women would have to be paid according to how much they work rather than according to how much some rughead decides to let them have! Ooh, equal pay. Yeah, guys, guess it’d be a nightmare. Oh, and maternity leave…”

Stein was edging towards the dance floor. Big Bob looked confused. Arthur was looking coyly at Lou.

"Dance?" he said.

* * *

NED DOYLE

Ned Doyle was half sitting on one edge of a conference table along the side of the room. He'd pushed the Chinese food to one side and had one foot on the floor, the other black loafer tapped to the Motown beat. "Oh, they did a helluva job. In the first place, the photos were terrific, and the way the ads were built up around them and brought together with the different headlines, well," he shook his head and held out a hand, "it all came together as a campaign. There was this look that inspired confidence and gave off a feeling of professionalism."

Barbara's eyes opened wide for an instant in appreciation, a little flash that said "how wonderful, not only the ads, but you." Her lips parted as if to say "Ahh" but she said nothing, only stared at him, her eyes on his. "I'd like to see," she said in a low voice, barely above a whisper. For an instant he forgot what it was she was referring to.

Then he nodded slowly. "I don't think showing them to you would do any harm. They're in the file cabinet in Ben's office. Come on." He took her lightly by the fingertips and led her out of the conference room.

Out on the dance floor, Mrs. Pflug hopped and twirled.

* * *

THE PARTY

Arthur had gotten up on a chair. "Hey, thirty seconds 'till 1996, folks! Grab your partners if you've got 'em! Ow, Louis, that's not what I meant. I meant dance partners." He held up his arm, looking at his watch, nodding with the seconds. "Okay, now. Ten, nine, eight, seven, six, five, four, three, two, one—Happy New Year!" A cheer went up around the room, and a sweet saxophone coaxed everyone to the middle of the floor.

Next to the bar, Annie took Kenneth by the tips of his fingers. "Come on, Ken. You haven't danced with me all year."

He shook his head, not meeting her eyes. "Nah."

"Aw, just this once." She danced provocatively at the end of his hand. "Well, I'll just dance with your arm, then. You won't get jealous of your arm, will you?"

He looked sleepily at her, his blue eyes faded to dull gray. Continuing to look at her, he pushed himself away from the wall and onto the dance floor, entwining his fingers with his wife's. When they got to the center of the floor, Annie stopped, waiting for him to set himself, but Kenneth continued to walk, tightening his grip on her hand and, as he passed her and their arms extended he gave a yank that dragged his wife after him, nearly pulling her off her feet.

"Hey, what're you doing? Ken! I just wanted to dance for a second. We're not leaving are we? Well, let me say goodbye to Ned and some of the—Ken, no!"

Her voice was cut short by two quick slaps which were barely audible over the saxophone. Lydia turned toward the door, frowning and unsure, shrugged and went back to dancing.

* * *

NED DOYLE

Inside Bennett's office, Ned's usually sure hand fumbled in his pocket for keys, coming up with coins, old tissues and a Captain Zap charm belonging to Little Ned. Finally he found the keys and opened the cabinet. He took out the manilla folder and turned around, opening it and bumping into Barbara, who had stepped closer to him. Her face was inches from his, her eyes upturned, her expression expectant.

"Yeah, they're right here, somewhere. Oh, here." He took the stack of proofs from the folder and stepped to Ben's desk. "See the way these work together? Here're pictures. This batch is duotones, the others full color, but all have that finished, very professional yet personal look."

Barbara took the folder from him, brushed her hair out of her eyes and looked through the ads. "Ooh, this one's terrific." She touched Ned's forearm and pointed to one of the ads. "I love the way this typeface sets the tone and the way you did the shadow and what's this called? The way the edges just fade off?" She looked up at him.

"Feathering. Aren't they great? Bennett and Lou do a helluva job." He took the folder from her and put it back in the file cabinet, closing and locking the drawer. "I think we might have to suspend the campaign, though." He looked at her but she didn't react. He walked back to Bennett's desk; she followed, standing a few inches from his arm.

"Ben was attacked, you know. Someone tried to run his car off the road."

Her mouth opened; her lips moved like some underwater living thing. It was a wide, dynamic mouth with lips that appeared to have extra muscles, enabling them to move independently. "I had no idea! Is he okay? I noticed he wasn't here tonight."

Ned nodded. "He's okay. I can't blame him for wanting to protect his first big account, but it would be nice if he were a little less inquisitive. Someone apparently doesn't like the way the investigation's going or who's talking to whom about what. And there's the original problem, the one this campaign was designed to deal with, in part, anyway. It has us under the gun with the health department."

She bit her lip. "The public's perception of the HIV situation."

"And the situation itself. New cases are still turning up. The police and the doctor assigned to the case say it's no accident."

She stepped closer to him. Her hand went to his shoulder. "I've heard that too, of course, but, don't you think it's a little far fetched?"

"I'm only telling you what I've heard." He shook his head, reluctant to continue. From the conference room, all that could be heard of the music was the vibrating bass. "It's gotten past the point where it's appropriate to try to restore the public's confidence via an ad campaign, as much as it hurts to say it."

She drew back, her hand dropping to her side. "That's not really my decision."

"I know. Franklin's—"

Her arm returned to his shoulder. "You really ought to talk to George about it. Now, what were we talking about before?" Her mouth did some kind of gymnastic he had never seen before; his eyes followed, unable to look away.

"Before?"

And then she was kissing him.

* * *

Ned got out of his car trying to figure out some way to change his clothes before stepping into the bedroom. If Maureen could smell alcohol from across a room, would she be able to smell another woman? The love of artistic creativity that had overwhelmed him and drawn him to Barbara had drowned in a sea of guilt. Overcome by fear, his mind reverted to its old, hide 'n seek way. How could he hide this, what could he say, what cologne could he wear, what would he tell Maureen, how could he cover up at the office? He had forgotten how much work coverups entailed.

He took a deep breath and sat down on the couch in the den, digging his nails into the navy blue velour. He closed his eyes and saw Barbara's face up close to his, her eyes impassioned and her mouth slightly open. He felt her breath on the side of his face. Nothing in the last ten years of his life had been so real, so perfect. How could he regret that? That she had wanted him, that she had to have him and shared the same passion—one that had been absent from both their lives—had been irresistible. And afterwards, it was plain from the way she clung to him, her head on his chest as they lay on the white shag rug of her living room floor, that she had not been disappointed.

A noise in the doorway startled him.

Little Ned was rubbing his eyes. "Hawy, Daddy."

Heartburn lapped at the back of his throat.

"Mommy says we can all make pizza tomorrow but Frankie can't have any because he's not supposed to have cheese the doctor said. I watched Planet Zoom tonight and Doctor Zark had a gun that shot colored rays and they have one just like it at the Toy Store. Can I have it tomorrow Daddy?"

Ned got up and went over to his son, kneeling beside him. He pulled him to his chest.

"Aww, Daddy. Not so tight! Can I have it, Daddy?"

"We'll see. It's late now. Come on, I'll put you to bed and I want to kiss Frankie, too." He lifted little Ned up so that the 5-year-old was sitting on the inside of his forearm, his legs around his Daddy's chest.

"You're gonna kiss me too, right Daddy?"

"That's right, Neddy."

"What time does the tooth fairy come, daddy?"

"What?"

"I put my tooth under my pillow and it's still there. Maybe the tooth fairy's too busy for me tonight. Can the tooth fairy come in the day?"

"Don't worry. The tooth fairy's never too busy for anyone. She'll be here." He kissed Little Ned on the nose and placed him gently on his bed, went over and looked at Frankie, who was curled up with his blanket bunched against his cheek. Then he went back to the den and switched on the television, taking two dollars from his pocket to leave under Little Ned's pillow once he fell asleep. After changing the channels a few times, Ned sat back and stared at the test pattern.

* * *

OFF

It was time to write, but the writing had become exhausting. The water lillies on the wall were shimmering, inviting you in to swim amid their oranges and yellows. The pink sky invited you up for a fly. And so you went.

The music was taking you, too. After you cook yourself a spoon, you join the music for an indeterminate time, swirling high and red and over and curling back down, racing blue through your own loop. You spread out, a string quartet, in perfect concert with yourself. You've become symmetrical, all mathematics and wood grain, no longer a frail, finite human being but a texture with new and different properties. Then you flare with the horns and shine and glow gold and proud and shout your sound and fill the void with yourself. And suddenly you go quiet and purple and roll up into a ball of subtle whispering, murmuring. Your folds, which are no longer arms, wrap close and shadowy, holding the light at bay but then open slightly, trying to trust the light, but unwilling. And finally you let a single ray of sunlight creep inside, and it spreads, leaping here and there with lilting trills, and your own murmuring becomes a steady voice, gaining strength and confidence as you raise up and come out of yourself. The folds open and stretch into wings, shining in the new sun, raised to the light as the brass shouts proud gold once again, soaring skyward.

Sometime later, you awaken. Something is wet on your face. Vomit. You're face down on the beige rug in your bedroom. The mahogany table, that beautiful gift shaped like Mexico, towers over you. How did you get here? Where's the music? What are all these bugs doing in your skin? You need to write a log in your journal. Suddenly that's the priority. But first, you need a boost.

A little pill. You have access to thousands, of course. Nothing big or important. A little morning boost to jump start your coffee before you really get off. Just something to enhance your journal entry. You wait twenty minutes for the Benzedrine to work. Then you write.

When I learned I had the virus, I wasn't really scared; I was thrilled. I had this, what's it called, the Japanese word for a tidal wave? Tsunami—tsunami of anger. It had never been there before. Waves of violent anger. And I enjoyed them. I was screwed again. I've been getting screwed all my life and here it was, the ultimate fuck! And I started all of a sudden to look back at who'd really screwed me. I'd never done that before. I was always afraid. But now, I didn't care. I was going to die. But not right away, you know? So I looked back and this one name kept popping up. That's who was really responsible. I'd never looked at it that way before, but it was true. It was like a religious experience. The truth was suddenly right in my face! And I decided I'm going to get that bastard like no one ever got anyone. And it must have been God talking to me or at least the very best dope I'd ever had because I had this great idea. The final solution. That's my little joke because the answer was in liquid form—solution, get it? I saw how I could take this bastard with me, and lots of other folks, too. And it would all be laid on him. I laid down all my life for people, let them walk all over me and now that was going to end. With a bang. A repeated, never-ending bang.

* * *

BEN

Bennett leaned over and shut off the alarm, resigned to go through the morning pre-work ritual. Shower, shave, coffee, newspaper, dress, brush teeth, white Cougar, work. More coffee. More work.

Then he realized it was Saturday and he remembered the night before, Eleanor kissing him all over. She had been so eager, so emotionally needful. Or maybe it was physical need. He rolled over and reached for her, but he touched empty cold sheets. He rolled to the edge of the bed, but her jeans were gone, and her shoes. Probably out on another of her meditation walks. She says it's where she gets her ideas. As an artist, he can appreciate the way she has to replenish her well of ideas for painting and writing. She wasn't a professional painter or writer, but she loved both and spoke often in visual terms. He had never been able to talk about art with Beth. She had a mathematical mind, she had said. Very linear.

He remembered dreaming about what happened the other day. That blue Mercedes was chasing him again. Only this time he was on foot. He'd dreamed about it twice this week and each time the car bore down on him, he had been about to see the driver's face and then it had gotten too close and he'd had to jump out of the way.

He went into the kitchen and dialed the phone on the phone/fax machine under the window, shooing a bug off one of the long light-green leaves of the spider plant hanging over the microwave.

"Mattis, I'm surprised you're not working. You are? But how could you be if you're on the phone with me. No, what I mean is how can you be on the internet and talking to me on the phone at the same—you did? Well, I know you can afford another phone line. I'm just surprised you let the phone guy in the house."

Cradling the beige receiver between his ear and his white Islanders shirt, he took a fork from the drawer and used it to split open an English muffin, which he slipped into the toaster. While he waited, he poured a cup of yesterday's coffee from the coffee pot and put it in the microwave.

"Hey Mattis, who're you talking to? Sure I heard that. You got a girl there? No, I'm not kidding. Your what hurts? Well, when I have something like that, I figure I slept on it funny. Sure, I get cricks now and then."

The bell on the microwave sounded and he took the coffee out. The mug warmed his palm. He took a sip, made a face at the day-old bitterness, then took another sip. "Well, I don't know if it's a crick, but I seriously doubt it's a tumor. No, I'm not a doctor. Listen, I'm calling about that guy who attacked me with the car. Yeah, the Mercedes. I agree with what you said yesterday. Somewhere, when I talked to someone, I hit a nerve, so doesn't it make sense that I go back and question the people I've already talked to? It's got to be one of them." He pulled a paper towel from the roll that hung over the sink, pulled too hard and unraveled a dozen towels into yesterday's cereal.

"Well, I wouldn't antagonize them," he said as he bunched up the paper towels and attempted to stuff them into the overflowing garbage. "I guess I'd just ask subtle questions to get an idea of who attacked me. Why don't I what? *You,* telling *me*, to go to the *police?* What's today's date? I'm writing that down. Get back to work!"

He hung up, then took the top off the garbage, and lifted the heavy inner bag out. But just as it cleared the lip of the beige plastic bin, the sharp lid of an empty tuna fish can burst through the side near the bottom and out spilled half of last Wednesday's garbage. He fought off a sudden wave of nausea, rebagged the garbage, left Eleanor a note, left the key under the Islanders doormat outside his apartment and went down to the parking lot.

He stopped on the outside stairway, smiling at the cement flower pots, empty now, except for a residual dirty ribbon of snow. He'd really forgotten Beth! An easy, no strings attached romance was the perfect cure for lovesickness! He had a sudden impulse to call a radio talk show and share this discovery with the world—or at least with the greater metropolitan area. He got to the white Cougar, its rear end still dented, and saw that she was sitting low. He looked down and his shoulders sagged. Well, at least he had an excuse to get the dent fixed. Someone had slashed his driver side rear tire.

He went back up the stairs, into the apartment and took a blue down vest from the hall closet and slipped it on under his jacket, then took the mountain bike from the back of the closet where it stood on its front wheel, removing shoe boxes in order to clear a path to the hallway. Leaving the hall strewn with boxes, he carefully navigated the stone stairway to the street, his body bent forward, his head tucked against the biting wind.

A short time later he banged on the door of the Chair of Hematology/Oncology. No one answered. He heard a voice; someone coughed.

"Hello? Someone in there?"

A long pause, then the door opened a crack. "Well? What do you want? Oh, it's you, young man. Didn't I answer enough of your questions last time?" Dr. Sticker's eyes were blood red and teary, as though he had been crying. He noticed Bennett staring. "Well, haven't you ever seen an overworked doctor before? What do you do for a living? Oh, I remember!" His black eyes bore into Ben's; brown freckles stood out against the pale skin of his face. "You're an art director. Oh, you must work very hard."

"I'm sorry to bother you again, doctor." The office was hot and Ben was about to take off the heavy winter coat and his down vest, but he had no desire to stay around this difficult man any longer than he had to. "Just a few things about procedures." He asked a few innocuous questions, thinking furiously about how he might ask about the Doctor's car. "...and, you commute to work?"

Doctor Sticker looked startled, then laughed. "Brahh! No, I live here. I sleep on my desk. Of course I commute."

"And you drive your, your, whatever..." It was a horribly transparent effort, he knew. Why hadn't he thought this out better. Mattis would have known some way to—

"My 1995 BMW? Yes. Is that what you want to know? You want to taunt me about my car? Think I make too much money, do you? Well you don't know very much about HMOs!" Doctor Sticker scratched his cheek; a bead of sweat formed on his eyebrow and ran down along the edge of an eyelid.

"You're not really here about those deaths, are you? You're not really connected with the ad campaign. You're here from Franklin. To taunt me into resigning." He stood up to his full height and leaned forward on his palms, looking down at Ben, who was a head shorter than he was. "I have every right to my salary and to my position here, young man. And you can go back to Franklin and tell him that. What I drive, the way I live, is none of his business, as long as the job here gets done." He pointed a shaking finger. "You tell him that!"

* * *

"Well, come on in, son." Dr. Epstein smiled, looked Ben in the eye and shook his hand. "How's your investigation going? Are you and the police getting any closer to an arrest?"

"Well, I'm not exactly working with the police, so I wouldn't know..."

"Umhm, umhmm." The doctor folded his arms across his chest. He seemed genuinely interested.

"It's really warm in here," Ben said. "Do you mind if I take off my coat?"

"Not at all. Be my guest. You can just put it on that chair."

He wriggled out of his coat and laid it over the empty chair next to him, then took off the vest and, since the coat was damp from melting snow that had dripped down from the roof as he entered the building, he draped the vest over the bookcase on the other side of the chair.

"I really wanted to get a handle on who has access to the various areas, as well as who in your department might have access to AIDS contaminated blood."

The doctor looked down at the green blotter on his desk, and smiled to himself. "In truth, young man, procedures and rules are regularly bent around here. Now, I wouldn't say that too loudly because we have rules for a very good reason, but on a day-to-day basis, they're broken all the time in the interest of getting things done, which translates into taking care of our patients. So, I'm afraid..."

"Wouldn't a person have to have access to different batches of blood? Forgive me, doctor, I have so little medical knowledge that it's embarrassing—"

The Chair of Pathology gave a bland smile.

"But wouldn't this killer have to have access to lots of different batches of AIDS-tainted blood?"

"How so?"

"Because the victims have different blood types." Ben sat back "I don't know this for a fact, but someone surely would've noticed if they were all the same blood type."

"I'd think so," Dr. Epstein agreed.

"So, to give them transfusions of AIDS-related blood, their blood type would have to be matched or they'd develop symptoms not of AIDS or not only of AIDS but of incompatible blood."

The doctor nodded. "Good point. But these secondary symptoms would vary and may well be minor, particularly when compared with their ICD-9—their Chief Complaint."

"So, who would have repeated access? Who could just come in, anytime, take various samples of tainted blood and leave?"

"A good question. Now, we don't store AIDS-tainted blood, except for testing." He rubbed his chin. "We don't need large amounts of it to store, the way we do the various components of healthy blood. We draw blood, and it's sent off to a lab."

"So, maybe a lab technician, or maybe the nurse or doctor who does the testing." He leaned forward. "Maybe the nurses who work in the lab here?"

"I suppose it's possible."

"Thank you, you've been very helpful. Oh, by the way, doctor. What kind of car do you drive?"

Dr. Epstein looked surprised. "Why would you want to know that?"

"As I came in, I noticed that someone's lights were on in the lot."

"A green Olds. What kind of car was this?"

"A, ah, red Pontiac." I guess I can tell them at the front desk." He grabbed his coat and went quickly to the door. "Thanks, doc, you've been a big help."

* * *

He headed toward the hospital's laboratory wondering exactly who was in on a Saturday. A nurse would be the perfect killer, he realized. She, or he, would have complete access to much of the hospital, yet might retain a level of anonymity a doctor might not. A doctor might be noticed as an individual; a nurse would be just another nurse. He passed through a waiting room; on a stained wood shelf along one beige wall a row of green planters sprouted red begonias. They reminded him of something Dr. Epstein had said and he tried to picture a nurse keeping different blood types of AIDS-contaminated blood. Something about that bothered him and he could not figure out what it was.

Only one of the two women he had met earlier was at the lab—the shorter, heavyset one with the red-rimmed glasses.

"Oh sure, I remember you," she said, smiling. "Mr. James. The ad man." She snapped off one of her white rubber gloves and shook his hand, then put the glove back on.

He smiled back. "And you're Janice Rosen. I remember you, too. Where's your friend?"

"Which friend was that? You don't mind if I work while we talk, do you?" She was sorting packets of blood from a gurney into rows on the countertop.

"Not at all. By all means. That red-headed nurse who was with you when I was here last time."

"Ah, Marilyn Franklin. She's a Well Baby nurse."

"Hmm. I guess I can catch up with her later. You ladies are friends?" He took out a pad and pen, leaning back against a metal sink.

"Marilyn and I have known each other for years."

"And you've worked your way up the hospital ladder together?"

Janice laughed, and there was a bitterness to her laugh that showed through the smile on her face. "Oh, no. I was here for a year and a half, working my way up through the dishwashing circuit."

"The dishwashing circuit?"

"Sure, I was an assistant, like just about everyone else around here. And I did all the scrubbing and washing, and day sweeping, and tidying up and prep work, long before they let me handle anything sterile, much less blood." She looked very serious. "Most people have to work their way up, no matter what their department or specialty."

"And Marilyn?"

Janice looked amused. Her white complexion reddened and again there was a hint of bitterness to her voice. "You mean you don't know about Marilyn?"

"Know what?"

"She's the boss's kid."

"Oh, that. You mean George Franklin. Well, sure. I knew that."

"Well then, you know she never had to work for anything."

"I thought you said you were friends."

He thought he glimpsed an instant of pain on the technician's face.

"Oh, we're friends. As much as you can be friends with anyone around here." She looked at him in a softer way; her eyes moved lightly over his face.

"I don't know what it's like at an ad agency, but a hospital's such a serious place, there's so much at stake, it's hard to get close to anyone."

Ben cleared his throat.

"How hard would it be for someone to get a hold of, say, various blood types of AIDS-tainted blood?"

Janice raised an eyebrow. "I wouldn't really know how to go about it. I'm stuck in the lab all day and I have access to only what happens to pass through this room." She paused. "Now, a nurse—"

"A nurse could do it?"

"I would think so. She would have access to infected patients, would have the knowledge to read their charts and know who was who, would have the know-how to draw and store blood." She stopped talking and put a packet of blood down on the countertop and turned to him. She spoke directly to him, her eyes holding his, an intimacy in her tone that had not been there before. "And you know, a nurse is often nearly invisible—as a person, I mean."

He stopped writing and lowered his pad. "That's exactly what I was thinking. A nurse is relatively anonymous."

She smiled. "See? We think alike."

He smiled back. "Thank you, Janice, you've been a big help."

"Oh, before you go. Two other things."

"What's that?"

"I wouldn't be surprised if Marilyn wrote down whatever she's involved in—not that she's involved in anything. I just mean that whatever she does she writes down. She keeps a journal, you know?" Janice slipped off the white rubber gloves that stretched up over her wrists. He saw that her hands were red from the gloves' pressure and, as the pressure was relieved, they returned to their natural white. "As long as I've known her she's written everything down."

"Really? Interesting. Oh, you said there was something else?"

She came slowly toward him, her eyes wide and hopeful. "I know a lot more about Marilyn. Listen, I'm off in fifteen minutes. Would you like to go to the diner and talk about it over coffee?"

He'd seen that look before. The mystery and all its details disappeared from his mind as an ancient fight or flight instinct took over. "Thanks anyway," he said, as he hurried from the lab. "But there's something I have to take care of."

6

BEN

The parking lot had been nearly full when Ben arrived, so he had parked the Cougar, its tire newly fixed, in the back row, against the stone wall. Now, the Cougar was alone and the lot was dark, except for a single street light that cast a yellow oval on the dark asphalt. He looked down, at a colony of ants swirling over a half eaten candy bar in a torn red wrapper. When he looked up, he saw a half dozen teenage boys congregated in the corner of the lot nearest the Cougar. They wore jeans and denim jackets. Probably drinking and listening to radios, Bennett thought, remembering when he had hung around "looking for trouble" as his mother had called it. "Boredom" was what he had called it.

As he approached the car, a bottle skidded across the pavement towards him. He looked in the direction from which it had come. A short, stocky boy with deep set eyes and curly brown hair had broken away from the group and was walking towards him, one fist jammed into a pants pocket, his head cocked to one side.

"I think you lost something," Ben said, indicating the bottle.

The boy's head thrust suddenly forward, his eyes wide, expression incredulous. "What did you say?" His voice was high, and it occurred to Ben that it had not yet completely changed.

A strip of hair fell across the boy's eyes and he jerked his head to one side, flipping it back. He turned to his friends. "Hey, this guy's startin' wid me!" The group stood as one and walked over.

"What is he, nuts?" someone said.

"Who's he think he is?" said someone else.

"What's he got against us?" wondered a third.

The boy opened his hand in front of him, gesturing as though pleading. "Why would you want to start with me? I was minding my own business."

Ben tightened his lips. "Hey, I wasn't starting with anyone. I'm just getting in my car, and going home."

"Aw, jeez," the boy said wearily. "Now, you did it. You called me a liar. Hey guys, he's saying I'm lying. And I don't even know this guy. Who's he think he is?"

"I don't know. Who is he?"

Ben took a deep breath. He rolled his eyes. "I don't think you're lying. I just want—"

"Don't make no face at me. And why is what *you* want so important? A little selfish, don't you think?"

"Listen. I'm sorry. This is a mistake. I'm on my way home. I don't want to bother you guys. I just want to get in my car and—"

The boy pushed Ben's chest. "I don't care what you want. You're definitely a selfish guy. Bad upbringing, prob'ly." He waggled a finger. "Very, very rude. You interrupted us, you started wid me. And it's too freakin' late to apologize."

Without thinking, Ben caught the arm of the boy's jacket, stopping him. The boy stepped back, his expression shocked. "Whaddya grabbin' me for? You're a little touched in the head, doncha think?" The boy tapped a forefinger to the side of his head, then pointed at Bennett, who was waving a hand in a windshield wiper motion.

"I grabbed you because you pushed me. Now I'm getting in the car."

"No, I don't think so." The boy swung his fist at Ben's face but, because he was so much shorter than Ben, the punch caught him on the shoulder. Ben pressed forward, grabbing the boy's shirt and shoving him backwards. Instantly, bodies converged on him, punching and pummelling his head, face and stomach until he fell to the ground. The punches did not hurt terribly, but once he hit the ground, the kicking started; heavy construction boots slammed into the side of his head and ribs. Within seconds, the blows ran together and faded away.

* * *

He woke up in a cloud of white. And when it came into focus he saw it was the curtain around his hospital bed. The bed was also white, as were his sheets and the gown he was wearing. His head and side throbbed. Something moved to his left but he could not turn that way. He heard a familiar voice.

"Nothing's broken. Just real bad contusions. I'm glad you're awake." A hand touched his thigh. "This doesn't hurt does it?"

"Eleanor, ohh, what happened? I remember these guys…"

"The hospital janitor came out with a broom and chased them away. There was an ambulance already around the side, at the emergency entrance. They came around to the parking lot and brought you in."

"Guess if you're going to get the crap beat out of you, a hospital's the place to do it. Ooh, laughing hurts. My ribs!"

"Then don't." Her voice held a softness he had never heard. "I'm glad you're okay, Ben."

He tried to turn his head, but the pain was too much and he was dizzy for a moment and thought he might vomit. The feeling faded and his equilibrium returned. "El, your sister…I was talking to her co-worker, a technician, heavyset girl, red glasses, and it really sounds like a nurse had something to do with this, and…"

"You think Marilyn's a killer?" There was laughter in her tone.

"I didn't know your father was the CEO of this hospital."

She paused. "And that makes Marilyn a murderer? My father's the psycho."

"I'm told he's not very nice. In fact, I've seen it for myself around the shoots."

"The only people he has any real compassion for," Eleanor said, "are patients. Particularly the AIDS patients. That part's true. Treats them better than his own kids. But that doesn't make Marilyn a murderer."

"Her co-worker says she's an angry lady."

"Yeah, she's angry. If you grew up in my house you'd be angry, too."

"But you aren't angry."

Her hand went to his shoulder, her thumb gently stroking. "Marilyn's got her problems, I've got mine."

They sat for a while, the silence broken only by the occasional echoing voice from the hallway, or by a car horn or siren from the emergency entrance below the window. Ben tried to imagine what having a sister or brother would be like. If he had a brother and he murdered someone, would he protect that brother?

"I just thought of something," Eleanor said. "The guy we went to for our tattoos hates this place. I remember hearing him talking about it. What was he saying? He was on the phone with someone. His ex-wife. I don't remember very much of it, but they were talking about this hospital and how much he hates it."

"Why would he…? El, did they give me anything for pain?"

"They're giving you shots every few hours and I think when you leave they'll probably prescribe something. It had to do with his daughter. That's right! Something happened to his daughter in this hospital and now something's wrong with her."

"Really?" He tried to sit up and was overwhelmed by a dull red tidal wave that formed at the base of his spine and rolled upward, cresting just above the bridge of his nose. He lay back, trembling; Eleanor's warm palm massaged his forehead. The last thing he heard was her voice calling, "Nurse, can we get something for the pain here?"

* * *

When he woke up, Eleanor was gone and the pain a fraction less. Seated in a chair at the foot of the bed was a blur that looked a lot like Lou. Ben blinked and saw Arthur standing over him.

Ben smiled. "This is like the last scene in *The Wizard of Oz*."

Art threw a hand in the air. "There you go. Everyone just assumes we like Judy Garland."

"That's not what I mean—"

"Easy with the kidding, Arthur. The boy's weak."

"How're things at work?"

Art shrugged. "The place collapsed without you. Okay, Louis, I get the message. Status quo, actually."

Louis held up a white bag. "We got you a little gift package at your favorite deli. I'll just leave it on the night table."

"Thanks, guys. What about my account?"

"It'll be waiting when you get back," Lou reassured.

"But the HIV cases are increasing. I heard…"

"Never mind what you heard," Lou chided. "Your account is doing fine. No matter what happens, Ned knows you're doing a great job."

Ben smiled. "He said that?"

"Several times. And Annie's been asking about you."

"She shouldn't have to. She should know how I am."

"Well, she is."

"I saw your lady-friend leaving as we were coming in," Art said.

"Yeah, she's been great. Taking good care of me."

"I think that's why Annie hasn't come."

"Arthur," Lou frowned. "He doesn't need to hear..."

"We've been having a lot of fun," Ben said. "I mean a lot of fun." He widened his eyes.

Art looked around. "What, here?"

"Well, no. But she's exciting. Unpredictable. I feel so, I don't know, alive. I don't know what she'll do next."

"I know the feeling," Lou said, and Art shot him a look, then sat down on the side of the bed. "Sometimes we need an edge."

Ben nodded. "Though stability's good too. Um, about my account. I've been looking into who might be behind these infections..."

"Bennett, why don't you leave that to the police," Art said.

"He's right," Lou agreed. "The Mercedes was strike one. This was strike two. We like having you around. Been getting kind of used to you."

"How's the construction?"

"Oh, don't ask," Lou said. "They were about to start the spackle and tape—"

"Sounds like a vaudeville act," Art said, "And here, for you comedy devotees, Spackle and—"

"—and they heard noises in the wall and it turns out we've got squirrels."

Ben laughed, then winced. "Don't make me laugh, guys. Hurts. Guess that means your script's going well."

"It is," said Art. "The writing, anyway. The selling, I'm not so sure." He stood up, stroking his chin. "I'll say this. You look good in white. When you get out, I'm taking you to Roosevelt Field and buying you some stonewashed cotton chinos and one of those hats, you know, the old fishing sort with the brim—what're they called, Louis?"

"Crushers."

"Exactly, a crusher. And all white, with white pants and a white polo. And we'll have lunch at Sofi's."

Lou smiled. "Maybe not. The waiters'll be all over him."

* * *

By the time he was allowed to go home, two days later, the pain had receded to a steady drumbeat on his left side and a dull pressure behind his forehead—as though someone's hand were trying to push him to one side. He had been given a prescription, including one refill, for some kind of pain narcotic, to be taken three times daily for a week and a half.

Eleanor had moved in. The attack had changed her, brought her out of herself. It was as if she were a different person when she was caring for him. Her voice softened and took on a sweet, caressing tone. Her warm, dry fingers stroked his forehead and held his hands. She sat by his bedside, spoon-feeding him soup she made herself from vegetables and boiled meat. When he tried to wash and was overcome by pain, she drew a warm bath and made him sit while she gently scrubbed him with a washcloth. She cooled his forehead with soft, wet kisses.

Four days later, he was well enough to go out, and, after twenty minutes of arguing, he managed to convince Eleanor that he would be fine if he went over to Mattis's house as long as he promised not to drink.

* * *

"Hear that?" Mattis's head twitched. His eyes rolled to one side, then the other.

"What?"

"Hear what he said?" Mattis barked.

A rolling, frantic harmonica twittered from the computer as a mouse and a duck danced on the screen.

"Never mind," said Mattis, turning back to the screen.

"What're you doing there?" Bennett asked.

"Music clips. I'm downloading and cataloging music websites for a client. Don't ask. That bandage looks very chic, by the way. Gives you that 'Bridge Over the River Kwai' look." He started to whistle the familiar theme.

Ben started to laugh, then remembered not to. "Yeah, all I need's a fife and drum."

Mattis frowned and turned from the screen. "I thought a fife was a piece of land in old England."

"No, a fife's a flute."

"No, I don't think so. Didn't you ever hear of a fiefdom? How 'bout we plug it into a search engine and see what the web comes up with?"

"No thanks."

"Hear it?" Mattis pointed a finger straight up. "There it is again. That same voice." A look of intense concentration had come over Mattis's face. He turned his head this way and that, trying to pinpoint whatever it was he was hearing. His long, curly hair twirled wildly. After a few seconds he pushed a key and Beethoven's Fifth bam-bam-bam-boomed from the computer.

Ben tried to look sympathetic. He thought of saying, "Guess we're both a little damaged."

"Damn, there it is again. Voices. And I've heard them before." He paused, listening. "They're whispering and I can't quite hear what they're—but it's about me. They're talking about me, the mothers. Oh, my God. They're driving me crazy!"

"Mattis." Ben rolled his eyes, thinking "They don't have far to drive."

"Shh! They're saying something." Mattis frowned. He shut off the computer and cocked his ear. "Wait, wait. Shit, they're gone. I wonder if they were coming from that website we had up. I wonder if that site had a background sound track. Insidious, but interesting."

Ben decided not to point out that Mattis had been hearing the voices while visiting the previous site as well. "I don't know."

"Hmm, Ben-coni? You have an opinion on everything. Whatdya think?"

"I said, I don't know. What I do know is my girlfriend says that the guy we got our tattoos from has some kind of vendetta against the hospital. That means he has a motive."

Mattis looked at him, then shook his head. "Why didn't you tell me?"

"I've been trying to—"

"Wait! There they are again! The voices are back and I didn't even turn on the—wait!" He leaped up and ran to the window, resting his arms on the sill and pressing his face against the glass. "Ah, false alarm! It's the pizza boy." He sighed and went back to his desk, switching on the computer. "So, Ben Casey, what about the hospital and this tattoo guy?"

"Well..."

"Want a beer? I always think better with a beer. Something about hops or barley or something that stimulates the brain."

"You sure it's not the alcohol that stimulates the bullshit?"

"Ben-factor! Why would you say something like that?"

Ben sat down on the couch. "No thanks. I'm not supposed to drink while I'm taking my medication. That reminds me," he looked at his watch. "Time to take my pill. Got any water?"

"What does this look like, a reservoir?" He pointed to the sink.

Ben took out his pills, squeezing the child-proof cap. "Damn, I can never get this—there. I thought there were more left than that. Guess I'm more fried than I thought." He put one of the white pills on the back of his tongue and jerked his head up and back.

"So he has a vendetta against the hospital?"

"Uh, huh. He's hated them for years. Something about his daughter."

"How many years?" Mattis popped open a beer, dropping the pop top on the floor. "And how old's his daughter?"

"Good question. I don't know."

"Want to bet a tattoo artist would probably be acquainted with a crowd of tough kids who'd have no problem pounding some guy for a few bucks, or whatever?"

"Another good point. Hey, you're on a roll."

Mattis stood up. "And while I'm on a roll, what do you think are the odds a tattooist is competent with needles?"

"Well, I'd think they're a different kind of..."

"Leave the thinking to me. Hey, you know what I've always wanted. I mean, it's been like...my dream?"

"What's that?"

"To get a tattoo." Mattis grinned wildly. "Let's check this guy out!"

After drinking four beers to garner the strength to leave the house, Mattis decided he desperately needed a cigarette. "I can taste it," he said. "Besides, I can think better with a cigarette in my mouth, like Sherlock Holmes." He rolled down the Cougar's passenger window. Two middle aged women wearing long wool coats and carrying heavy leather handbags were window shopping along Rockaway Avenue. "Hey, old bags!" he shouted, then ducked down low in his seat, giggling.

The ladies frowned up at Ben, who shook his head and made an 'I don't know where that came from' gesture.

He slowed the Cougar and pulled over next to a deli. "From what I know, it wasn't that pipe that helped Sherlock Holmes think. I've got no change for the meter, so I'll wait in the car, okay?"

"Uh uh. Come in with me. You know I can't go into a store alone."

"Oh, right."

They waited at the end of a short line. "Oh, man, I can't wait to have a cigarette," Mattis was saying, as he rocked forward onto his toes and back again onto the heels of his boots. "Ohh, yeah, I can just taste it. Hey, there they are again. You hear them?"

"What's that?"

"The voices. The same—never mind. Hey, I'm next. Ooh, la la."

The customer at the counter took her sandwich and Coke, put a straw and a napkin into the bag, paid and left. The counterman, who was bald and wearing black rimmed bifocals on the end of his nose, beckoned to Mattis, who hesitated and stepped aside. "Go ahead," he said to the man behind him.

"But it's your turn, sir," said the man.

"Well, I'm not sure what I want."

Ben looked at his friend for a moment, trying to figure out what he was doing. There was a fine line, Ben knew, between genius and madness.

The man at the counter finished and left. The counterman waited.

"Go ahead," Mattis said to the couple behind him. They didn't ask; they went right up to the counter.

"What's going on?" Ben finally asked. "We're in a hurry to get to East Rockaway and you know exactly what you want. A pack of cigarettes. Or, did you change your mind?"

"Oh, no," Mattis said. "I want a cigarette. I want one so badly I can taste it. But that's just it. I'm next. I'm about to taste it. This is better than actually having the cigarette. That...anticipation—it's like when the girl opens your zipper—"

"Yeah, like when have you experienced that?"

"Hey! I have. Just...not with a real girl."

"Oh, my God!"

"Don't look at me like that. I just like being next! I want to savor that feeling. Okay, okay, we'll go! Sheesh!"

* * *

Driving home along Lawson Boulevard, Mattis peeled the bandage off the Indian pattern Charlie Spoon had tattooed on his upper arm. "I like it. What do you think?"

"It's fine. So what'd you think of Charlie Spoon?"

"Well, he sure had no problem talking about his daughter. See over there? That's the place I got my boots. Remember I was telling you about—"

"Yeah, I remember." Ben sighed and looked out the window at the shoe store Mattis was talking about.

"And he sure is angry at that hospital. We had no trouble getting that out of him."

"He was forthcoming with the whole story," Ben agreed. "You wouldn't think that of a murderer."

"No, and besides, it isn't him."

"Why's that?"

"Because he's dealing with it appropriately."

"What do you mean?"

"Well, he's angry as hell, but didn't you hear what he said? He goes to Neal's every night." Mattis lit a cigarette.

Ben rolled down his window as he slowed down for a light. "Yeah, I heard him say that. Who's Neal?"

"Neal's not a who. Neal's is a corner-type bar. You know, pool table, crowd of regulars. He gets drunk there every night to forget about it. That's the appropriate way to deal with that kind of grief."

"That's appropriate?"

"As opposed to murder?"

"I don't know." Ben wasn't convinced. "Couldn't HIV be transmitted via tattoo needles?"

"And where would he get the blood—the virus? How would he get access to those areas of the hospital? Aren't they restricted?"

The light turned green and the Cougar shot forward. "I've heard it's easy to get anything more or less anywhere in that hospital if you're a little creative about it," Ben said. "Like, you're not supposed to have access, but no one ever actually stops anyone or asks for credentials or anything. Pretty much everyone takes the path of least resistance. He could pose as a technician, a delivery person. Maybe he has a girlfriend who—"

Mattis waved the cigarette in a gesture of dismissal. "What I'm saying is, Charlie Spoon didn't do it."

* * *

Lydia looked up from her computer as Ben came through the door. "We knew you wanted a longer vacation, but that was a long way to go to get one," she said.

"Yeah, Lyd, I missed you too." He grinned.

"You all healed?"

"Yup, and now I'm ready for you to beat up on me."

Art got up, came over and hugged him. "Welcome back. We're all glad you're okay."

Ben went into his office and sat down. The Medical Center folder was exactly as he had left it a week earlier. He sat back in his chair and started to close his eyes, thinking how much he had missed this job and these people, when something yellow and red caught his eye and he sat forward. A rectangular pamphlet lay, face down on his desk. It had not been there before. He turned it over.

"Are You An Alcoholic?" asked the letters on the front. "A Simple Test," read the subhead.

He heard footsteps and a door close; he folded the brochure in his pocket and walked out of his office and into Ned's.

Ned was dialing the phone, looked up, and immediately hung up, a huge grin on his face. "Benjamin!" He stood up and came out from behind his desk. "Wonderful to have you back! How are you feeling? Did you change your mind about telling the police about this thing?" He squeezed Ben's shoulders.

Ben took the brochure out from his pocket. "Did you leave this on my desk?"

Ned looked steadily at Ben. He nodded, waiting.

"Let's talk about it."

"I was hoping you'd want to."

Ben pointed to the cover. "I think the blue is all wrong."

"The…what?"

"Yeah. I wouldn't use a solid color with these geometric backgrounds. I'd use something a little more modern. Maybe photos of all the different sorts of folks who might be alcoholics—sort of dispelling the unshaven bum in a trenchcoat myth, right?"

"Ben," Ned looked at the floor, "I was hoping you'd want to talk seriously about your—"

"May I speak frankly, sir, without fear of losing my job?"

"Of course. You can always speak frankly. I would never—"

"Great. Then get off your high horse! Leave me alone." He took a step toward Ned, pointing his finger. Ned did not move back. "I won't be late anymore, okay? So it won't affect my job. When it does, you can take me to task. Fire me. Whatever. But what I do when I'm not here is none of your business. So stay the hell out of it, okay?"

Ned put up a hand, looking him in the eye. He nodded.

Ben started to walk out. He turned at the door. "Oh, there was something else I thought you could help me with. Give me a few minutes and I'll talk to you about it."

* * *

The storefront karate studio—the *dojang*, Ned called it—filled up with students, perhaps twenty or twenty five, of all ages. Bennett stayed close to Ned. "That's Master Elliot," Ned explained, pointing to a slight, middle aged man wearing thick glasses and a gray-blond ponytail. "We bow when he comes in the room. The senior member will say *"Chiriat!"* which means come to attention, then you've got to bow. Here, let me help you with your *do-buk*."

Everyone bowed. Master Elliot said, *"Goman,"* and everyone went back to what they were doing.

Ned helped Bennett tie the long white belt around the heavy cotton uniform. "*Do-buk?* I thought this was called a *ghi.*"

"*Ghi* is Japanese, *do-buk* is Korean. We use Korean terms here. *Taekwondo* is a Korean martial art."

"So this is the young man I've been hearing so much about?" Bennett and Ned turned; Ned bowed and Bennett imitated him as best he could. The master's voice was gentle, placid. His black belt with its five white stripes swung as he moved and all his movements were easy and fluid. Even his walk was graceful, his weight perfectly distributed, each motion exactly as necessary for its purpose.

"I understand you are an artist."

"Yes, sir," Ben said, unsure of how to address the instructor.

"I'm sure you will find this art to be like your own in many ways—graceful and beautiful, sometimes hard, sometimes yielding. You may call me Master Elliott or *sabumnim*, which means teacher. We'll be doing exercises first, warmups, then some motions—blocks, strikes and kicks that the rest of the class has learned. Just follow as best you can, all right? If you cannot do, don't. Ned explained you have injuries. Whatever hurts, don't do. The rest, try. Try is most important." He tousled Ben's hair and inclined his head to Ned, who bowed. Bennett tried to bow again as the instructor went back to the front of the room.

* * *

The exercises and stretching were not too hard, though he had never realized how tight his legs and back were. Students were pressing their faces to their knees, doing splits. His new, white uniform was quickly sweat-stained. Now and then he saw Master Elliot smiling at him, holding up a hand as if to say "easy does it." The stances, blocks and punches were difficult. Several times, the instructor froze the class in position to come over and correct Ben's stance, squaring his shoulders, pushing his knee forward, straightening his back leg. Ben was embarrassed by the attention but Master Elliot reassured him several times, commenting that he was doing very well for the first time. The kicks were harder and required a turning at the hip that his body did not yet understand. The instructor's strong fingers showed him how, but his body resisted. This was normal, he was told. Next time, perhaps, it would be easier.

Next time?

An hour later, the students performed their forms—*Cata* in Japanese, *Hyung* in Korean. The motions were sometimes graceful, sometimes choppy and intense, depending on the student and the form. Master Elliot instructed Ned to show Ben his first form, a series of blocks and strikes in an "I" formation. The motions were confusing, inspiring a kind of dyslexia in Ben, who was certain he could never reproduce them. Ned told him not to worry, he would have plenty of practice. This was a process, he explained, not a race.

Master Elliot then demonstrated self defense against a knife, using Ned as the simulated attacker. He took from a pile of weapons and shields that lay off to one side of the mat a short stick that would act as a knife. In this situation, the instructor explained, the quickest, safest escape—not doing damage to your opponent—is most important.

Ned waved the knife menacingly and Master Elliot dropped back into a fighting stance, both fists up, screaming *"Kiiiaaap!"* Then he stopped to explain that one's willingness to fight in itself may startle the attacker who, like most knife-wielders, is likely a coward at heart.

"He may run away," Master Elliot said. "In that case, you run in the other direction. Another possibility is that the *"Kiap"* will startle him for a moment, and in this moment, you attack. Notice the position of his weapon. Is it truly poised for attack or does it need to be chambered or brought into an attack position? If this last is the case, you can attack, so—"

The instructor somehow slid or hopped several feet forward, blocked the knife out of the way and struck Ned in the face with the heel of his palm.

Ben tried to analyze the motion but it was too quick, the footwork too light, to break down. The master had seemed to appear where he had not previously been.

"Then, when the palm heel forces his middle section forward, you follow with a knee, then an elbow to finish him off." Master Elliot and Ned bowed to one another—apparently the instructor had missed Ned's face, not quite striking him—then the instructor clapped twice, similar to the gunshot claps Ben had observed Ned using at the office, everyone bowed and the class was over.

Afterwards, he and Ned stayed and watched some of the higher belts spar and Ben was startled by the way the students seemed able to absorb the heavy contact so easily, coming back each time for more. He wondered if he would ever be able to do the same.

The following morning, Ben woke up and found that his body, particularly his lower body, was stiff and sore. It was a different soreness than the old pain of his bruised ribs.

Getting into the Cougar was difficult and he thought about complaining to Ned, who was meeting him at the hospital to go over ad proofs and the hospital's budget. He turned to look for cars behind him, felt a hint of the older pain of his bruised ribs and decided that such a decision might be premature.

* * *

The room was green except the table; even the short stubble of carpet was a dirty pea color and the vertical blinds were a darker tint of lime. The light, which was yellow, threw an oz-like glow over the room. Ben glanced at Franklin, who was sitting at one of the three round tables, a heavy glass ashtray in front of him, his black spiral notebook open and his expensive silver pen scribbling energetically.

He thought of saying, "Pay no attention to that man behind the ashtray!" in a deep voice, but thought the better of it. Beside him, Ned was silent, his black leather case across his lap. Presently, Franklin stood up and put out his hand, which each of them shook. Beneath his notebook lay a manila folder which he opened and from which he slid a series of color proofs. He sat back, lit a cigarette and peered through the smoke. "Yes, Ned. I like these. Did I tell you, you folks do nice work? Mm, yes.

The relationship between the facility and its patients—you've really captured that. I like it, I like it."

Ben's chest filled with air and he sat back; his jaw relaxed. Next to him, Ned was not quite so relaxed.

Franklin continued. "And I like the copy. Well written, succinct." He nodded.

Ben wanted to burst into song. His first job a success! And a big one! He remembered being six and going fishing with his dad and catching the lunker of the day—a five and a half pound large mouth bass. Beginner's luck, he was told by his dad's best friend. Too good to be true, was the way he had seen it. He hadn't slept at all that night.

"Yes," Franklin puffed and blew smoke at the proofs, shuffling them like cards. "Mm, quite good. What I'm not so sure of is…the color."

"Color?" Ben blurted out. "But…it's a hospital. It's green, gray." Ned shot him a warning look.

Franklin continued examining the proofs, giving no sign he had heard. "Color is crucial, of course, to any project, no matter what the subject. The hue, the saturation—it's got to be right. No, the more I see it, the more alive and rich I think it has to be. This is not just a hospital—it's *the* hospital. I want that to come across and we have to do it with color."

Bennett wanted to tell the man he was out of his mind. He could feel the tension coming from Ned; his boss had been coiled, as though he might leap from his seat. Now, he relaxed. His motions were deliberate, his voice calm, yet Ben could feel that same intensity that had been present at the *dojang*.

"I see what you mean," Ned nodded. "We show the vibrancy of the healing environment. We make that environment super-real. We…bring up the clarity of the images."

Franklin pointed at Ned. "There you go!" He glanced up at the door. "Ah, Barbara's here." He stood up; Ned and Ben did the same. "You gentlemen know Barbara Kaplan?"

"We've met," said Ned, nodding. "Barbara."

"Pleased to meet you," said Ben.

"Hello," said Barbara. She was an attractive woman, in her mid-forties. Her dark curly hair framed a face that could not accurately be called beautiful, Ben thought, but was stunning nonetheless. No single feature stood out as particularly attractive but when she looked at Ben, there was a power behind her eyes—a force of emotion and intensity that added impact to her appearance.

"I was just telling these fellas," Franklin said, between puffs, *"mwah,* how much we like their ads and what we can do to fine tune."

"They're excellent." Barbara looked at Ned, who smiled.

"Thank you," he said.

"Barbara, of course, is the money person. She represents our financial or fiscal responsibility, and she's brought up an important point. I see on the invoice that you've added twelve hundred for proofs."

Ned nodded.

"That isn't appropriate. We never pay additional for proofs."

Ned opened his leather case and took out several papers. "It's right here on the original estimate."

Franklin did not take the papers from Ned. "Mmm. But we never pay for…Barbara?"

"I believe we have, on occasion, bought proofs, Mr. Franklin."

Franklin sat forward. He stubbed out his cigarette. "Barbara!" He sounded hurt.

Ben wanted to scream, but forced himself to sit quietly; Ned had explained that there might be what he had referred to as a "budget waltz."

"And as long as we're talking about the invoice," Franklin said, "I'm confused. This was supposed to cost seven thousand and now it's up to nine. How did that happen?"

Ned started to speak; Barbara laid her hand over his. It was a subtle, perhaps insignificant gesture, but Ben noticed it. And he saw that Ned did not pull his hand away.

"We did ask the agency to change the focus of the ads," said Barbara, looking at Franklin.

"…After the initial proofs were tentatively approved," Ned explained. "That's really half of a new set of ads—all new photography, different layouts, revised copy…"

"All right, all right." Franklin held up a hand. "If my budget officer says it's right, it's got to be, I guess." He shook his head, an expression on his face as though he had eaten something bitter. "But I fail to see how you can be doing your job, Barbara, if you're in bed with the damn client."

Ben felt a tiny jolt of energy from Ned, whose only visible reaction was a darkening of his gaze. His heavy brow shaded his eyes even more than usual.

"I don't see sides here," Barbara said. "I'm laying out the facts."

"Facts are open to interpretation," said Franklin. "But I don't want to get into a debate. While we're in here picking at this invoice, the public perception of this facility, which is really a wonderful, life-saving facility, is getting worse. I have cops in here all the time…"

Ned interrupted. "All the more reason to finish up and get those ads out. We already missed one newspaper deadline because of one change—"

"That change was necessary!" Franklin sputtered. "If we had gone to press—"

"I'm aware of that." Ned's voice was soothing, contrasting with Franklin's emotion. "As you say, the public's perception isn't getting any better. At some point we have to cut bait."

Franklin turned to Barbara. "What do you think?"

"Mr. Doyle's right. What's the purpose of the campaign in the first place? To put a friendly face on the facility; to minimize or counter the effects of this situation—"

Franklin shook his head. His forehead reflected the yellow light from above the center of the table. "That's exactly why you're the CFO and not the CEO. Stick to your money responsibilities, Ms. Kaplan."

Barbara did not blink. She appeared used to such treatment. Franklin turned to Ned; a subtle red line was creeping up Ned's neck.

"The reason for the campaign is to get the truth out," Franklin explained. "And the truth is this facility gives an unprecedented quantity and quality of care. We love our patients. Talk to some of the AIDS patients. Ask them about me. We're like family."

For the first time, Ben spoke. "That's certainly true, Mr. Franklin. I saw that for myself during the shoot."

Everyone looked at him. Franklin's face tightened around his mouth. "Who is this young man? I've seen him around, but can't place…"

"Bennett James," Ned explained. "He's my art director and he ought to learn not to be such a yes man."

Franklin grinned. "A little brown-nosing never hurt anyone—you might try it, Doyle."

The red creeping up Ned's neck blossomed into full blush. He glanced at Barbara, who was trying to hide a smile.

There was a knock at the door, followed by a cough. George Franklin got up, opened the door and stepped back.

"Sergeant Michaels, come in. How are you? How's Mrs. Michaels feeling?" He did not wait for an answer. "Good. And the little girl? That jaundice clearing up, I hope? Great. Folks, this is Sergeant Danno Michaels. He was brought in by the Board of Health to sort of keep an eye on things. But don't hold it against him. He's a good man. His daughter, Debra, was born here last week."

Sergeant Michaels carried his hat into the room, smiling at Barbara, nodding to Ben and Ned. He was tall, greying and slightly balding, thickening around the waist.

"Congratulations," Ned held out a hand. Ben did the same.

The police officer touched one of the chairs at the table they had been sitting at and, when Franklin said "Please do," he sat down, picking some lint from the cap he held in his hand.

"Gentlemen," he nodded to Barbara, "and lady. I, ah, would venture to say," he rubbed his nose between his thumb and forefinger, "that the ah, press have been largely kept away from our situation—"

"And we appreciate that, Danno," interrupted Franklin, who had sat down next to the police officer.

"Yes, thank you. But that's becoming more and more difficult. The ah, tabloids have been offering money to certain members of the hospital staff, and—"

Franklin sat up straight. "Who? Whoever they offered money to will cease being members of the staff if they so much as breathe a word of—"

"Yes, well, I would say that is all well and good," the officer went on, "however, the point is," he ran his hand back through his thinning hair, "the insurance companies, HMOs, the legal establishment, HIV special interest groups, the Medical authorities are all pressuring us—"

"Come to the point, officer," said Barbara.

Sergeant Michaels turned his gentle blue eyes to the hospital's CFO. "The point, ma'am, is that, we're going to have to work with the Board of Health to quarantine the affected areas of this facility."

For a moment, no one spoke. The only sound was George Franklin's faint wheeze. Then, in a quick motion, he whipped a cigarette pack from his inside jacket pocket, popped one from the pack and took it into the corner of his mouth. He began talking quickly, his tone taking on a military cadence.

"What you're talking about, Sergeant, is a significant portion of the hospital, all of the Med. Surg. floors, in fact."

"I would venture to say that is true."

"Well, I would venture to say that is impossible. We can't operate that way. This is a hospital, not a clinic! The greater good, the majority of patients—"

The officer was unblinking and calm. "When previously uninfected patients become HIV positive as a result of the actions of some member of this hospital, suffice it to say that the greater good, as you call it, sir, is affected."

"You can't prove that anyone in this facility—"

"Now, until we have some idea of who that person is, until an arrest is made, we cannot allow—"

Franklin leaned forward, his elbows on the table, the cigarette quivering in the air. "Who are you to allow anything? You're a police officer. You should be out looking for—"

"When I say we," he looked down into the blue of his hat, "I'm talking about the medical and legal establishments, the insurance companies, the HMOs...the Board of Health."

Franklin glared at him. "What'll we do with these infected patients?"

"They'll have to be transferred."

"Not so easy for some of them. And do you know how long that would take, what kind of operation?"

"Then you'd better get started."

"George," Ned spoke gently. "From a public relations standpoint, if the story might break any day now anyway, we've got to beat it to the public, get our point of view out there first, maybe even spin this as a good thing. We're out in front of it."

Franklin's eyebrows went up as he digested this.

"How can we avoid it getting out?" Barbara added.

Franklin stubbed out his cigarette and slapped the table with both palms. "I don't buy that anyone on my staff is doing this. I don't see where this conclusion's coming from. How can this be called murder? Where's the evidence? How do we know it's not just a series of unfortunate coincidences? Maybe they all had the virus before they..."

"Please, George." Officer Michaels looked down. His voice was quietly compassionate. "The evidence is there. The murder part is still strongly circumstantial, but these are no coincidences. We have the medical records of all the patients. None had the virus before. None were high risk. The virus was acquired here and we're quite sure, off the record at least, that it was given to them intentionally."

Franklin tapped his fingernails on the table. "I've got to talk to our lawyers, Sergeant. I'm willing to bet you can't do this without a court order. And I'll make you get it." He took out another cigarette, lit it and blew a victory breath. "I'll make you get it," he repeated. "Off the record won't cut it here, officer. You say you're thinking of the public? I'm thinking of the public." He pointed a finger at Sergeant Michaels. "The greater good is not the couple of patients who're getting sick, it's the hundreds, the thousands who are getting well! You're neglecting them! In fact, you're abusing them. And now that I think of it, I can't believe that the medical establishment would back this. You've got to be bluffing, officer, and I'm going to call your bluff." He smiled and blew a smoke ring.

Ned and Barbara exchanged glances.

Ben had the feeling he was watching a play where the actors had forgotten their lines and were careening off in a dangerous, unknown direction.

Barbara swallowed. "George, the HMOs are asking a lot of questions. They have their own investigators and it's only a matter of time before they come to their own conclusions and stop payments. A fiduciary crisis is only a matter of time."

"Everything's a matter of time, dammit!" Franklin exploded, waving his arms. "We're all going die, for heaven's sake. A comet will eventually hit the earth, the universe will fly apart. It's all a matter of time. Let them come after us. We have our own legal department. We'll rip them to shreds in court!" He lay his cigarette in one of the corners of the ashtray and pointed his finger. "They've got to document these things. They've got to prove beyond a shadow of a doubt. Dammit, Barbara, this is business!"

Barbara nodded slowly, her eyes glazed.

Sergeant Michaels stood up, picked up his hat and nodded to Ned and Ben. "Pleasure seeing you folks."

As the officer left, Ned spoke quietly. "This is more than business, Mr. Franklin. This is public safety. And stonewalling isn't going to get to the bottom of—"

"Who's stonewalling? I'm not stonewalling. I want to solve this thing. What kind of person do you think I am? And what kind of person are you to—? Look at how you're treating me. If everyone would stop trying to throw the blame of this on me, we'd all be able to move forward. It's you people who want to grind everything to a halt—not me! I want to keep caring for people. I love those patients. I never said anything about stopping any investigation." His hands were shaking as he lit another cigarette, forgetting the still smoking one in the ashtray. He dragged wetly on it, inhaling noisily. "Neddy, I wouldn't expect you to understand. You're really a hybrid artist. But Barbara, you're a business woman. I'm surprised at you."

An hour and a half later, after everyone else had gone home, Ned and Barbara stood next to her gray Chevy Lumina, the key ready in her hand, as it had been for forty five minutes. Not far away, under the street lamp in the corner, lay several dozen beer bottles and a faint red stain.

Ned had been doing most of the listening. Now, he spoke. "I've had some difficult clients in my day—people who imagined whole conversations and then proceeded to tell me what I said and what I promised and what I supposedly agreed to do. I've worked for screamers and desk bangers and I found all you can do is let them scream and bang the desk and then do what you feel is right." He leaned back against the car, his hands flat against the cool metal.

"One difference was, you could leave," said Barbara.

Ned looked at her and saw that her mascara had smeared—was she crying? He reached forward and touched a spot near her eye with the side of a finger. She did not draw back. "Do you think he meant all that?"

She nodded, was about to speak, and waited as a jet passed overhead, its lights blinking against the lightly falling snow; Ned smiled. Barbara did not. "Oh, he's capable of incredible levels of paranoia. One thing he is though, is honest." Her tone dropped to a whisper. "Waking up's just really tough some days, you know? Knowing what might go on during the day. And the next, and the next..."

The snow had begun falling harder—thick, wet flakes that stuck to the roof of her car. Ned traced something in the new snow, then scribbled it away. "You know, you've really helped me cope these last few days."

She laughed. "Is that what you call it?"

He gave her a sudden, serious look. "Yes, it is. Things at home are...difficult. I get these little, I don't know what you'd call them—digs, from my wife. She doesn't just tell me what needs to get done. She plays this word game, and it's not very nice. I'm learning to dread coming home the way you dread going to work."

She rolled the rubber handle of the car key between her forefinger and thumb. "Maybe we should meet somewhere in between."

She had meant it as a joke but his serious expression did not change. "I'd like that. I feel I can really talk to you in a way I can't talk to anyone else. Well, I have this one friend I can talk to, but," he smiled, looking down, "he's not quite as sympathetic as you are."

"Oh, who's that?"

Ned shook his head. "Doesn't matter." He touched the side of her face with his palm. "I'm glad you're here."

7

BEN

Bennett was sitting in a metal chair with an attached wooden desk front in a dark panelled classroom in Stillman House, the Fine Arts facility which was down the hill from his dorm. Through the window he could see the arc of tiny pointed leaves from the Japanese maple that grew on the north side of the building. He had been sick, a lung ailment that made his chest hurt when he breathed. His illness had forced him to miss a month of classes, yet here was Mr. Duke handing out the midterm exams. His breaths grew shorter and shallower. He felt rather than heard a silent moan in his mind. How had this happened? Everyone else was writing. He looked down at the paper on his desk and the questions might as well have been in Chinese. He looked more closely and saw that some of them were indeed written in what appeared to be Chinese.

Mr. Duke, imposing and Zeus-like with wild, blond mane and heavy, entwined beard, was laughing with serious eyes.

Ben blinked awake. Thick flakes of snow were falling outside his window. He sighed, and closed his eyes again, then turned the other way and buried his face in Eleanor's bare back. She breathed deeply and turned from her side onto her back, her red-brown freckles nearly matching the color of the blanket. He rested his chin on her shoulder. This had been the second time in two weeks that he had dreamed about that test.

She had not been next to him when he had fallen asleep. A restless sleeper at best, Eleanor came to bed after he did and even on those nights when they made love, she would get up and watch TV or listen to music in the living room. He ran his hand down her neck and between her breasts. She smiled in her sleep and her lips parted; her eyelids twitched.

Ben's side ached faintly and he rolled over and reached for his black chinos, which lay on the light blue throw rug on the floor next to his bed. He went through the pockets but the pills weren't there, so he got up and went to the bathroom, and inspected his sleepy face in the mirror. He opened the medicine chest, but the pills weren't there either. He tried to remember if he had finished them. Could he have left them in the car?

He stepped unsteadily into the black chinos, thinking he would change into something clean later. He slipped a green polo shirt over his head, and looked for his down vest so he could go out to the car for his pain pills.

But the vest also seemed to have disappeared. He giggled as the silly, still-drunk part of his mind conjured up an image of the escaped pills and vest on the run, handcuffed together. When was the last time he had worn the vest? He had not worn it to the karate—he corrected himself: to *taekwondo* class.

Then he remembered. He had taken it off at Doctor Epstein's office and never put it back on. How could he have done that? It was his favorite vest! That vest had been like a brother to him! He giggled again, trying to think of how he might get the vest back when the doctor was home. Perhaps he ought to make a pitcher of Bloody Marys to help him think. He could hear Ned in his mind telling him he didn't have to do that. *Get the hell out of there!* He chased Ned away but it was too late, the drinks were no longer so attractive.

An idea came to him. The nurses and technicians worked on a rotating schedule. He remembered that heavyset technician with the red glasses—the one who had been so interested in going out for coffee or cake. She had seemed to have been into everyone's business. If anyone could get him Dr. Epstein's home number, she could.

He went into the kitchen and dialed the hospital. After a few minutes of talking to operators and getting through to wrong departments, he heard that familiar nasal whine.

"Bennett? Behhnnett! It's sooo nice to talk to you."

"It's nice to talk to you too, Janice. I was wondering if you might be able to help me."

"I'll try, Bennett. Anything I can dooo." Her voice dropped to a conspiratorial sotto.

"Well, I left a vest of mine in Doctor Epstein's office. I'm sure he's not in today, but I was wondering if you might tell me how to get his phone number so I could get it back. I'd sure appreciate it."

"Oh. Well, we aren't supposed to have access to that kind of personal information."

He paused, waiting for her to follow up. When she didn't, he tried to sound as disappointed as he could. "Mm, never mind. It was a long shot to think you'd be able to help me. But I knew if anyone could, you could. In fact, I was hoping to stop by the diner and I thought we might...well no, never mind."

Janice's tone changed. "You know, come to think of it, I'm friendly with Tony, the maintenance man. And I'll bet I can get him to open the main personnel file cabinet at the nurse's station if I tell him there's a medical emergency. He doesn't know what's in there and the doctors really do have to be on call..."

"Could you really?"

"Call back in fifteen minutes, Benny. And I'll see what I can do."

He hung up. *Benny!* No one but his mother got away with that.

Something brushed against his back; a hand wrapped around his stomach and pulled him down. He jumped and tried to turn, but was off balance and nearly fell.

"Ooh, I'm sorry. I didn't mean to startle you." Eleanor was leaning, sleepy-eyed, on the counter, her reddish brown hair lit orange by the sun that poured through the kitchen window. She had put on one of the four or five of his tee shirts she had adopted as morning wear. Her eyes were bright and she started toward the bedroom, casting a glance at him over her shoulder.

He turned her around and hugged her, running his hands under her shirt, over her smooth back. "Um, I left my vest at the hospital. I'm waiting for a call that'll tell me how to pick it up."

"Mm. Wait a minute." She held up a hand, then sneezed.

"Bless you. I don't know if I should tell you to put something on or not."

She sneezed again, then went into the bedroom and came back with a small box wrapped in black paper. "Here," she said, handing it to him.

"What is it?"

"Open it."

He sat down on one of the four stools at the counter and tore the paper off the box. Inside was a purple velvet jewelry case filled with cotton on which lay a length of gold chain. He lifted the chain out, laying it over his palm and saw the item at its end. "A gold artist's brush."

"Well, you're so creative; I've always admired creative people. I wish I could be one."

"Well, you are in your own way." He paused. "I'm sure you are."

"Don't bother. I'm not. Believe me. My sister is—she writes, you know. Even my mother knits, or she used to. I'm the analytical one in the family. My brother Georgie was the really creative one. He could—"

"I didn't know you had a brother."

She stopped in mid sentence. "Oh. Well, I did. He died a long time ago."

"Oh, I'm sorry."

She looked at the floor. "…not your fault."

He held the chain to his throat. "I love this. Help me put it on."

Once the chain was around his neck, he looked down, examining it, and noticed that she was wearing something similar. "What did you get yourself?"

"It's a painting palette."

"Oh, I like that." He took it in his fingers. "I thought you weren't creative."

"Only by association."

He nodded. "I see the curve in it and the little dabs of paint, and I guess this is a thumb hole."

She laughed, touched his chin with her finger and looked down. "You really have to go?"

"Well, I'm waiting for—" The telephone rang. "That's her, now."

"Her?" Eleanor's features hardened; her hand dropped to her side. She turned away. The phone rang again.

"El! One of the technicians at the hospital was going to try to get me this doctor's number so I can get my vest. She's your sister's friend, Janice." He hoped mentioning Janice would take away any threat.

"Oh, I know Janice." She looked back at him, bit the inside of her cheek and went into the bedroom. "You'd better get the phone," she called over her shoulder as the door closed behind her.

He picked up the receiver and listened, taking a pen from the old red coffee can that held pens, pencils and scissors. He jotted the number on his blue message pad. "Thanks, Janice. I'll meet you afterwards at the diner. Sure. I said I would, didn't I? Soon as I get back." He hung up, looked around self consciously to see where Eleanor had gone, then dialed Dr. Epstein's home number. The doctor picked up on the second ring, explained that he had brought the vest home for safe keeping, and suggested that Ben come right over to pick it up.

"I sure appreciate that, Doctor. Gerald Avenue in Freeport? No, I don't know…oh, Atlantic Avenue. Sure. And from there I—yes. Got it. Thank you, sir. I'll be right over."

Humming, he went into the bedroom to get dressed. Eleanor had put on a pair of jeans and a coat. She barely looked at him.

"Thanks again," he said, grabbing for her hand. "I really like the…"

She pulled away. "I'm going out," she said.

"I'll be at Dr. Epstein's getting my vest. He said to come right over." He slipped on his work boots, which were on the little square of green carpet near the door.

She left the room without answering.

Outside, the snow was well above his shins. Heavy and wet, it was good snowman snow. The three teenage brothers across the street were wearing identical black wool caps and pulling sleds along the side of the street, tossing snowballs with their free hands and shaking loose little avalanches from the trees.

Ben took the shovel from beside the door and started shoveling, trying to use his legs rather than his back. Immediately, the pain in his side increased. The *taekwondo* seemed to have made it worse. He remembered building snowmen with his father when he was five. Halfway through, he cleared his car of ice, started it and went back to shoveling.

Bennett enjoyed the drive to Freeport. He enjoyed driving in snow, and the streets in Oceanside and Baldwin along the way had several inches of fresh snow on top of the early plowing.

People were digging out stuck cars. Tires spun, back ends fish tailed, sending up white showers and sprays. Trees and power lines glistened, and he forgot about the pain and Eleanor's sudden jealousy.

Dr. Epstein's house was a large light brown colonial on the right side of the street several houses in. Ben parked and went up the unshoveled walk. The top layer of snow had melted and refrozen; it crunched with each step. He stomped his boots clean and rang the bell.

Dr. Epstein opened it; he was unshaven and wearing a beige, terrycloth bathrobe and a wide smile. "I hope you don't mind my not inviting you in. My wife's asleep and I'm not quite up myself."

"No problem," said Ben. "I just appreciate you letting me stop by your home like this."

The doctor opened the door and handed Bennett the vest. "Thanks," said Bennett. "Enjoy your weekend."

Doctor Epstein waved. "If you have any other questions at all, feel free to stop by my office. I mean that."

Ben waved and made his way towards the white Cougar. Epstein was one of the few doctors at the Medical Center he liked. No condescending tone of voice, no cold impatience—what a pleasure!

An enormous crow flapped low over his head toward a car in the driveway to his left. Bennett watched it land, started back towards the Cougar, then turned and stared.

The car in the driveway was a blue Mercedes. He stepped towards it, stopped, thinking about the footprints he was making, and decided that if this were not the car he was looking for, an innocent Dr. Esptein would not mind his admiring it.

He went around to its front, brushed the snow from the fender and stood up, his hands on his hips. He took off his glove and held it and the vest in his left hand while scraping at what looked like snow with a fingernail of his right hand.

It was not snow; it was white paint like the Cougar's, and it was streaked throughout a prominent dent.

Putting the glove back on, he jogged to his car, glancing up at the house, and drove away, wondering what to do next.

* * *

Ben pulled into the diner's lot and sat in the car, breathing white puffs into the cold day. Dr. Epstein was, by all appearances, a friendly professional. Nothing threatening about him. Yet his Mercedes was the one that had tried to kill him!

Ben's side ached and he rooted through the vest pockets, but his pills must have fallen out. He wondered if the pharmacist would give him a refill without the original bottle.

Janice had picked a booth near the back of the diner, along the window, facing the railroad tracks. She smiled when he sat down, then looked concerned.

"Everything okay?" she asked.

He didn't answer right away.

A young waitress with short black hair and a Mediterranean complexion placed red laminated menus in front of them and asked if they wanted coffee first.

Bennett nodded.

"Tea, lemon," said Janice.

"I, I just had the strangest experience," Bennett said.

"Relax," Janice said, patting his hand with hers. "Everything's okay."

He allowed the story of the two attacks to spill out, followed by his most recent discovery.

Janice took off her glasses, and bit one end, thinking. "Do you think you should go to the police?"

"I don't know. Probably. But I want time to think. I have a lot of trouble picturing Dr. Epstein chasing me in his car."

"Then it'd be really hard to see him injecting all those people with HIV." Janice shrugged. "But you never know." She put on her glasses. "Benny, I really don't think you should be alone today."

His eyes focused on her and for the first time it occurred to him that confiding in Janice might have been a mistake.

"If you don't want to go to the police right away," she was saying, "you could confront Dr. Epstein, give him a chance to explain. Watch his reaction carefully. I've learned how to do that. You'd be surprised what you can tell about someone by their body language, the subtle movements and expressions, the way they sit, and so on."

Bennett shifted in his seat. Outside, a Long Island Railroad train rumbled slowly past and he watched its dark blue and silver patches through the white lattice of snow covered trees.

The tea and coffee arrived. The waitress waited, pen poised.

"Tuna and lettuce on rye toast," Janice said.

"Blueberry muffin, no butter." Ben looked down at his hands, which were folded in front of him. He grasped the end of a packet of sugar and shook it, then tore it open and poured it into his coffee, added a little milk and took a sip, comforted by the warmth and familiar taste.

"Ben," she touched his hand again. "Just make sure there are people around when you talk to him, okay? I don't want to see anything happen to you. Then, if you want, we can get together again and talk about what his reaction was. We'll go to someplace nicer next time—near my place, in Cedarhurst."

"The nurse who works with you..."

"Marilyn Franklin? She doesn't work with me. She's a Well Baby..."

Ben nodded. "A Well Baby nurse, I know. What's she like? I, I, ah, know her family, and..."

"You know George Franklin?"

"Well, in a professional way, yes, I have to deal with him regarding the ad campaign."

Janice squeezed a slice of lemon over her tea. A piece of seed plopped into the hot liquid and she fished it out with her spoon. "Oh, I'd like to hear about that," she said.

He smiled. "Well, afterwards. I'm curious about Marilyn."

"You think she had something to do with—"

"She just sounds interesting."

"Oh." The enthusiasm went out of her voice. She looked down at the place mat.

"She certainly had the opportunity," Ben added, "and, before this thing happened with Dr. Epstein, I'll tell you, she's one of a few nurses who seemed from a distance anyway to have some kind of ax to grind." He shrugged. "That's all I've really had to go by."

"I wonder if she could be having an affair with Dr. Epstein!" Janice's eyes widened with excitement; she clasped her hands in her lap.

"Well, I don't know. It's possible, I suppose. Tell me about Marilyn."

Janice's eyebrows went up and her mouth tightened. "She used to be my best friend, but she's so moody. It's hard to get close to her." She looked earnestly at Ben. "Sometimes it's hard to be good friends with someone you work with, you understand, Benny."

"I do," he said.

She dabbed at the corner of her mouth with a napkin, then peered at his shirt pocket. "You have a spot." She wet the napkin in one of the untouched glasses of water on the table. "Here, let me—" She started to rub it with the wet napkin but he pulled away.

"No, no thank you. It's okay. Really. I *like* that spot."

"You—?" She shrugged. "Okay." She sipped her tea, folding the tea bag into the napkin. "Anyway, Benny, Marilyn's very bright and you know," she looked up at him over her glasses in a confidential way that made him nervous. "I've never seen anyone work so hard. But you can only get to know her to a point. She's private and there's this, this wall you can't get past. Very frustrating. We had coffee a few times, and Danish. And we talked about art, she likes Impressionist painting, you know. And music. Oh, and writing. She loves writing. Modern—but not too modern—American writers, as well as the classics. Poe's her favorite, I think. She writes a bit herself, you know."

"Really?" Ben sipped his coffee, saw Janice staring at him and finished it in a quick swallow.

"I hope I've been of some help." Her eyes grew wide and girlish.

"You have. Thank you." He reached for his wallet—a signal, he hoped, that he was ready to leave.

"Oh, one other thing," she said. "She has these mood swings."

"What do you mean?"

"Well, she'll be happy and sweet and interested in what you are saying, then she'll just shut off, like a faucet. You can't talk to her or get her to talk to you. She'll get this depression—you can see it on her face. Like a storm coming over her. And if you bother her, this awful temper comes out. She'll bark at you to leave her alone. But she won't be quite so nice about it."

He leaned forward. "Really? And she's always been that way? How long have you known her?"

"Six years." She patted Bennett's hand. "And yes, that's just the way she is. I used to take it personally, but I learned that it has nothing to do with me." She smiled into his eyes. "I'm very sensitive, you know."

* * *

"Come in!"

Ben opened the door, thinking that perhaps confronting Dr. Epstein directly in his own office had been a mistake. Going to the police might have been wiser.

"Well, young man, come in!" The doctor smiled and Ben imagined he saw the detached madness of a serial killer hidden in his face. He stepped into the office.

"I, ah—" Ben looked at the ceiling. How did one begin to accuse the Chairman of Pathology at a major hospital of committing a crime?

"You have your vest, I see. Glad to see it. Have you come up with anything else in your investigation?"

"Well, that's why I'm here. Actually the two things you just said are sort of…connected."

Dr. Epstein tilted his head, and paused. "Your vest? And…?"

"Well, you see, sir. I was attacked—twice, actually. And I think it's because I'm getting close." The room had become quite warm, the air stuffy and difficult to breath. Was this wise? Would the doctor attack him right here in the office? Would he kill him? Did he keep syringes of HIV infected blood around the office? Ben thought back to what he had seen in the *taekwondo* class. Could he hold off this sixty year old man, should a physical confrontation arise. "Most recently it was a gang of kids in the hospital parking lot, but the first time it was a car that tried to run me off the road."

The doctor's high forehead wrinkled into a frown. "Really? I had no idea. Do you know who—"

"And when I went to pick up my vest, sir, I ah, noticed that you have a blue Mercedes."

There was a long silence. Doctor Epstein's eyes narrowed. "And you think that I—young man, do you know what you're implying?" His voice deepened, taking on an air of impersonal authority. "In the first place, have you any idea how many blue Mercedes' there are in the New York metropolitan area? And in the second—"

Ben interrupted. "Very few sir, I would think. At least very few with dents covered with paint that match my car."

The doctor stopped talking. His head remained motionless, his mouth slightly open. Only his eyes moved. They looked from side to side in what Ben thought was an odd way.

What was he going to do? He couldn't kill me right here in the office, could he? Who would do that, during business hours on a busy day?

The Chair of Pathology began to blink. Two, three blinks in quick succession. Then, he stood up suddenly, strode to the door without even a glance at Ben, and shut it, flipping the bolt. He walked back to his desk and sat down, leaning forward on his elbows and folding his hands in front of his mouth. He breathed into his folded hands, as though they were cold and he were trying to warm them.

Ben's stomach churned, trying to send a message to his brain and, failing that, to his legs. The message was "get out. Run!" The rest of his mind was frozen, blanketed with a white coating of adrenaline. Could he jump up, unlock the door and be out of the office before the doctor could reach him? Epstein looked healthy for his age, not particularly overweight, and most important, tall, his legs long.

The doctor slid his chair back and opened his desk drawer and began digging through it. It occurred to Ben that this might be his only chance to get away. He managed to turn his chair slightly toward the door and lean his weight toward its edge. What was the doctor looking for, a syringe? Was he going to stab him with an HIV infected needle? Ben's mind showed him a quick flash movie of a few years of medical treatment, a shortened life of pills and doctors. What would Eleanor say? He would lose yet another true love.

Perhaps the doctor was reaching for a gun. At least it would be over quickly. Ben wondered if the sound of a gunshot would be heard in the hallway. If it were, would it be noticed? Would the doctor be crazy enough to shoot him in the middle of a busy day in a bustling hospital?

Epstein's hand lifted out of the drawer and extended towards Ben.

"Gum?"

"Uh, no thanks."

Epstein took a piece for himself, unwrapped it and popped it into his mouth. "Bennett, of course you're absolutely right. That was, is, my car. I did try to run you off the road." He shook his head, which was shining with sweat. "I'm terribly, terribly sorry. I don't know what I was doing." He looked down at his desk. "Actually, I do. The pressure in this facility is incredible. You have no idea what it's like to work for George Franklin."

Ben realized that he was gripping the metal arms of his chair. His hands were hot and wet, his fingers cramped. "Let me get this straight," he began. "You didn't kill anyone. You only attacked me because the questions I've been asking were bringing pressure down on you?"

The doctor looked as though he might cry. He wiped his forehead with his sleeve, leaving a gray stain on his arm. "The investigation—by the police, by you, by anyone—affects all of us. You have no idea. They've been threatening to shut down the whole facility for years and it may yet happen—and maybe they should." His voice dropped to a whisper and he leaned forward, looking Ben in the eye. "Bennett, I have problems, personal problems. Marital, financial—but they're not your problems. And now I have legal problems." His voice cracked. "The pressure around here, from the investigation, from this whole awful thing, has been unbearable. And Franklin, Franklin's like a buzz saw; he cuts right through you, threatening your livelihood, your family, your future. He says he'll see to it that I'll never work again. He's crazy. I mean it. I think he'll do these things. Please Bennett, don't ruin my life. Don't turn me in. I did a terrible thing. I know that and I'm sorry. Anything I can do. If there are doctor bills, I'll take care of them. Please, allow me to do at least that. And, of course, I'll take care of your car. Hell, I'll buy you a new one. And then if you really feel you have to turn me in, I won't do anything to stop you." His face fell forward and Bennett found himself looking into the shining top of the Chair of Pathology's head.

* * *

The painting was a study in browns and muddy greens. It appeared formless to Ben, until he looked at the title: "Landscape at Nightfall." Then the landscape took on life, as it might have if he had been peering into the dusk. He allowed the voice in the headphones to penetrate his thoughts.

"Van Gogh's letters tell us that he was insecure in the development of his drawing skills, but that he had faith in his art as a process. He believed that he had a strong artistic force within him. He called himself an artist, meaning that he would seek without ever really finding."

Eleanor was across the room, looking at a painting of a wheat field at sunset from a distance of about ten feet. He wondered what she thought of the paintings. The landscapes, particularly, were formed with so much paint, it seemed to Ben that Van Gogh was creating not so much a painting but the landscape itself!

She came over and put her arm through his. He lifted off the headphones.

"I love this," she said, shaking her head slightly. "Whenever I see Van Gogh, I feel as though I'm coming home. Everything is...more real than real. It's like he painted in the fourth dimension."

Faintly, Ben could hear the voice on the headphones telling him how much Van Gogh wished to be able to paint, disease-free.

"Does your family appreciate art the way you do?" Ben asked.

"My God, look at the way the light just shines off the water." Eleanor was shaking her head. "My family? My mother did. She took us to museums when we were little. But my father wanted her home, doing things around the house. He said there wasn't time for that sort of nonsense." She looked at him, her blue eyes questioning, her short hair standing out orange like one of the paintings against the stark white of the gallery walls and ceiling. "It's amazing because my father's the talented one. Why do you ask?"

"Just curious. What about your sister?"

"Marilyn? Not so much. She liked to stay by herself and read fiction. She wrote a lot as well."

They stood before a painting called "Public Garden with Round Clipped Shrub and Weeping Tree." They looked at it together, taking it in. "How he got the feeling of leaves bursting out from the trunk or weeping down like that—it's incredible." Bennett's eyes stayed on the canvas.

"I know. And the light—it's so elusive, yet he found it and reproduced it and it shines off leaves and through them and, yeah." She rocked against him as though blown by a wind.

"Sounds like your father was kind of tough to get along with—for all of you, I mean."

Eleanor nodded, still looking at the painting. "Well, you've met him. He was no easier on his family than he was on anyone else. Quite the contrary."

"What about your sister?"

Eleanor looked at him, brushing a bang from in front of her eyes. "Marilyn?"

"Yeah. How did she get along with him?"

Eleanor's body shifted away from Ben. Her hip thrust out on her other side and her hand curled at the wrist and rested on that hip. She looked at him from the corner of her eye, her head shaking. "Why do you want to know so much about my sister? What's that about?"

His tone became defensive; his voice went up in pitch. "It's not about anything. I said I wanted to learn more about you and your—"

"Yeah, yeah, you said, you said." Her voice flattening into sarcasm. "Don't give me that romantic crap. You can't bullshit me. You're in that hospital all the time, aren't you?" She backed away. "I should have thought of this before."

Ben realized what she was implying. "Oh, my God. Eleanor. I don't even know your sister."

"How well did you know me the first night we slept together?"

Ben looked around; all twenty or so people in the room were looking at them while trying to appear not to. Faces pointed toward paintings, but eyes shifted their way. Innocent, bland faces caught his eye, then whisked away.

"Eleanor," he whispered fiercely. "Your sister and I aren't—we never—let's drop it, fergodsakes!"

They went through the rest of the gallery in silence, looking only at paintings, never at one another.

* * *

The train ride was a silent standoff. She wouldn't look at him, even as they left the train and walked the short blocks west along Park Avenue to his building. The winter air whirled through her hair; a half smile played on her red mouth.

He turned the key and opened the door and she pushed past him, disappearing into the bathroom behind a slammed door. He stood in the open apartment doorway, smelling marinara sauce cooking somewhere nearby and looking at the beige paint on the bathroom door. He slowly withdrew his key, closed the door and took off his coat. He moved the gauge on the thermostat from sixty eight to seventy two, and glanced at the answering machine.

A deep, pulsing rhythm emanated from the bathroom, vibrating through the apartment. Glasses and plates shook in their cabinets; windows rattled. He looked outside. Dull yellow headlights made their way through blue gray dusk, crisscrossing barren sidewalks.

The red light was blinking on the answering machine. He pushed the play back button.

"Benny, I have some interesting information for you. My number's 555-1026. Call me when you have a chance. Oh, this is Janice." The voice giggled.

He hesitated. How much did he really want to solve this case? He was, after all, an art director, not a detective. He pushed the erase button, listened to the whirring that was making Janice's voice disappear, then dialed her number.

She answered on the first ring. "Hi, Benny."

She must have been waiting for him. "Hello, Janice. How are you?"

"I thought you'd be interested in some things I found out. I feel like I'm your partner. Like we're on "NYPD Blue" or something, you know?"

"I don't watch much TV."

"Oh, it's a great show. Maybe we could—"

"So, what did you learn?"

"Well," her voice dropped and he could picture her looking around to see if anyone else was listening. "Well, first of all, Marilyn's been out sick for two days."

"So? People get sick. She's entitled."

"Not Marilyn. She hasn't been sick in all the years we've been working together."

"Well, then, I guess she was due."

"No, there's something strange about it. She has a runny nose all the time, you know? But she doesn't take time off. She's had a lot of physical problems. She's been to see doctors in the hospital about things—don't ask me what things, I don't know. But she's been sick plenty, I know that. And she never misses work. Never. But now she has. I'm telling you there's something weird."

"Is that why you called?"

"Oh, that's just the start of it. You know her sister, right?"

He glanced toward the bathroom door. Abruptly, the music stopped. He blinked. "More or less."

"Well, Eleanor wanted to be a nurse, too. But she never made it. They have a fierce rivalry over just about everything. Work, men—everything. We used to be pals."

"You and…?"

"Eleanor. Very good friends. And you? You know Eleanor well?"

"Well, you could say."

"But did you know she had a brother?"

"Um. I did, yes. George Junior."

"You know about George Junior?" Her voice squeaked with surprise. "Benny, you're some detective. But did you know he was gay and that his father shamed him about it and that eventually he committed suicide?"

Ben paused. "No," he said quietly, looking again at the bathroom door. "I had no idea." He was picturing Franklin, smoking and yelling and taunting the way he had seen him so often in meetings. He pictured a young red headed boy on the receiving end. "That's very interesting, Janice."

"So? What's it worth to ya?"

"Excuse me?"

"Let's get together, Benny, and talk about it. You can come up to my place and we'll piece it out."

"Oh, ah, well, I'm kind of busy."

"Benny," her voice became small, timid. "I can make myself more attractive for you."

There was a silence, then a barely audible sigh. "Marilyn works ridiculous hours, even for a nurse, you know." Her tone was back to normal. "I used to call her 'The Terminator' because she just doesn't quit. She works all the time. I mean, day and night! And it gives her the opportunity to be all over the hospital at all sorts of times. She would certainly have had the opportunity to commit these crimes. And I used to wonder how she could do it, but you know, I think she's on some kind of drugs. Cocaine, maybe. She has a runny nose all the time. Did I mention that? And I know some people shoot it, you know, with needles. At least, that's what I've heard. And if she shoots cocaine, maybe she shoots heroin! Maybe, maybe she has AIDS. She'd certainly be at risk! Imagine that? With all that anger over her baby brother and maybe blaming her father?" She paused. "Wow. Benny, I'm good, aren't I?"

"You're something, Janice."

"Well," her voice became sultry again. "I can *really* be something, if you'll give me a chance."

He nearly dropped the phone; instead he held it to his ear, gingerly, with two fingers. "Janice, you really have done a heck of a job. I've got a situation here, though. Give me time to digest some of this and I'll, I'll get back to you, okay?"

After hanging up, he walked past the bathroom door and looked at it, then touched it with his palm. "Eleanor?" No answer. He wanted to say, "I miss you" but for some reason he couldn't bring himself to say the words.

He sat down on the couch and closed his eyes, thinking about George Franklin. Janice was on the right track, but maybe she missed something. Marilyn Franklin may indeed have committed the murders. She may be a crazed drug addict, but there was another Franklin who had the opportunity, who was in the hospital night and day, and whose presence anywhere on the premises would never, ever be questioned. And Bennett was beginning to wonder about that Franklin's sanity.

8

SYMPTOMS

The cold—in every sense of the word—had come. A runny nose and vaguely sore throat and an exhaustion that ran through the legs, from the bones outward into the muscles, as though you had exercised too much and had been lightly bruised all over at the same time. A bursting pressure was building behind the spot where the eyes met—some kind of killer sinus headache.

And at the same time it was winter everywhere. Though the heat was on full blast, you couldn't stop shivering; your skin was all goosebumps, your toes ice.

But the Man with the Hat knew the perfect short term treatment. And for a long term treatment, what better place than a hospital? What lovely therapy they offered, and everyone helped. Old people, young people, men, women, children. Such a giving, sacrificing environment.

You could give as well as receive.

But first you stop, and write down what you're feeling, which helps. Not enough, but like a cold pill: it's a temporary, small solution. It feels like someone's there, even if it's just yourself. You're talking and someone's listening. You turn up the radio and write and feel better, your toes warmer now, under the green wool blanket. Then it's time to go and you turn off the radio and the voices that say nothing come back. The old voices, led by the loud One. The personal One.

You take a few of the pink tissues from the box on the nighttable and stuff them in your pants pocket. Then you check your pouch for works, blood vials, gloves, put on your hospital clothes and go.

* * *

BEN

George S. Franklin's office was a cut, sanded, polished forest. The walls were covered with a dark wood paneling while the furniture—the CEO's desk and a round table nearby as well as the chairs at that table—were a shining, reddish cherry. Matching prism-like glass ashtrays were on both the desk and the table. The room was dimly lit and smelled of cigarette smoke.

Ben and George Franklin sat next to one another at the table. Color proofs were spread out before them. Ben was trying to think of a polite way of suggesting that they move to a room where there was more light.

"This is not the headline I want here," Franklin was saying. "It's too obvious, too overstated. It's as though we're telling people outright to have more faith in the Center rather than showing them situations where that'll come about naturally."

A battle was raging in Bennett's mind. He wanted to blurt out that this headline, as well as the other two Franklin had already rejected, had been Franklin's own idea. Personally, he had never liked any of them in the first place. In fact, the very point Franklin was making was exactly what Bennett had told him weeks earlier. He wished he had a tape recording of that conversation. "Excuse me, sir. May I make a quick call?"

Franklin indicated that he could.

Ben dialed the office. "Annie? This is Ben, get me Ned. He's—okay, give me that number. Sure, I'm fine, just—five five five, six two oh three? Thanks." He dialed again. "Maureen? Bennett James. Oh, pretty good. You know how it is. Yes, you heard right. Her name's Eleanor. Um, well, actually I'm not sure what she does. Something to do with art. Thanks, I would. Yes, I'll wait." He glanced at Franklin, who was looking through the proofs. Hurry Ned, before he finds something else he hates.

"Ned? Hi. I'm here with Mr. Franklin." He cupped the phone. "Ned says hello."

Franklin nodded, his eyes half closed.

"And he feels the headline is too overstated, too obvious." He listened carefully. Ned's instructions were explained slowly and clearly but their effect on Ben was immediate, like a high voltage charge: listen and learn from the client. Internalize what he wants. Sublimate your ego until you're sure of the right road—then go for the jugular.

Ben took a deep breath. "Thanks, sorry to bother you at home." He hung up.

George Franklin lit a cigarette. "Man keeps you on a short leash if you have to call every time we disagree."

"Oh, I didn't have to—"

"Never mind. Now you say these will go on the posters as well?"

Bennett nodded and brushed back a hair that had fallen over his eyes. Lately his hair was making him crazy. Still annoyed with him, Eleanor had stopped applying her pomade, and no matter how much cream he combed into it, one rebellious strand insisted on falling over his eyes. He was seriously thinking of shaving his head.

"That's right. Once we agree on all the details, we make the big prints, for posters, bus shelters, and so on." He ventured a smile. "They'll look terrific, Mr. Franklin."

Franklin was about to answer and, perhaps, clue Ben in on how he really felt about the direction the campaign was going, when there was a loud rapping on the door.

"It's open," said Franklin, smoke whistling from his mouth.

Sergeant Danno Michaels and Doctor Adrian Lord came in, trailing a third person, a fiftyish man with dyed brown hair and sharp eyes. When Franklin saw him, the blood drained from his face, and his expression, which had been mildly welcoming and expectant, disappeared and was replaced by a wary mask.

"Mr. Franklin, this is Richard Elkins, Mr. Archer's superior at the Board of Health."

"We've met."

Mr. Elkins gave a thin smile, then looked at Ben. "Would you mind excusing us, sir?"

George Franklin put up a hand. "No, that's all right. This gentleman is with me."

Ben was startled when George Franklin grasped his wrist, as though for support.

"Well, then," said Mr. Elkins, "I'll get right to the point. Until now, the elusive nature of the HIV virus and the difficulty of tracking its source in so complicated an environment as this, combined with your lack of cooperation, have kept this facility open. The incubation period of the virus, which as you know can be six months or longer, was another factor making it difficult for us to pinpoint the source of infection. There are those at the Board, in the legal community and even in the state legislature, who haven't agreed with our procedure. They think we should have just declared a public health crisis and shut you down. But we know each other well, Mr. Franklin. You'd have gone out and gotten an injunction and the next time around our job would have been that much harder. So we waited until we could make some kind of connection—until we could demonstrate that patients absolutely were coming in contact with HIV here in the facility."

"And you think you've done that?" Franklin asked.

"Oh, yes. And I'm here today to shut you down."

"Really?" Franklin's hand still gripped Bennett's wrist. Now it squeezed and let go. "Show me your proof. What documentation do you have?"

Detective Michaels and Dr. Lord looked at one another, and then each looked pointedly at the stained oak paneling on either side of the room.

Mr. Elkins appeared to be enjoying himself, as though this were the third act in a long play, as though he had been waiting for the day when he would have the upper hand. "The only papers I need to show you are the ones ordering you to inform physicians affiliated with this Center to transfer their patients to other facilities and ordering you to shut your doors by next Friday."

Franklin's tone became condescending. "No one is contracting any disease, much less HIV, in this facility. Show me your documentation and my lawyers will show you why it's faulty. We're not moving anyone or closing anything, Mr. Elkins, so get the damn smile off your face and—"

Mr. Elkins nodded to Detective Michaels and Dr. Lord. "Let's go," he said softly. "Good day, Mr. Franklin." He nodded to Ben and the three left the room, with Sergeant Michaels closing the door behind them.

"Maybe I'd better go." Bennett began stacking proofs so that they would fit into his black vinyl case. He felt as though he were at the base of a volcano that was about to erupt.

George Franklin was looking at a knot in the oak paneling behind Ben. His nose had begun to run and he lay his cigarette in the ashtray and reached into his suit pocket for a handkerchief. After blowing his nose several times and rubbing his temples with the thumb and forefinger of his left hand, he resumed smoking.

"Yes, maybe you'd better," he said.

* * *

The sun was in Ben's eyes. He blinked and rolled over, the blankets warm around him. Eleanor's freckled back was to him, her red hair light and delicate on her shoulders, her spine bumpy and vulnerable. He snuggled close to her, spooning his naked body around hers. She sighed and reached back; her warm hand lay on his thigh.

After a few minutes, she turned over, stretching and grinning. "Mmm, that was fun, wasn't it? You sure know how to show a lady a good time."

He turned around, looking behind him. "Me? Were you talking to me?"

She pressed herself close against him. "This is my favorite sport."

"And you, you conduct yourself like a pro."

Eleanor held him at arm's length, slapping him on the shoulder. "A pro? A pro!"

"No, no, I didn't mean that kind of pro. I mean, like in sports, pro—as in you're good at this. Here, let me show you." He held her by the small of her back, pulling her close, kissing her neck.

She laughed and kicked the covers away. "Let me get a beer first. You want one?" She walked, naked, toward the kitchen.

He looked at the clock, squinting through the sun, which filled the room with glowing stripes of dust as it shone through the blinds. "At ten o'clock in the morning? All right."

They made love and drank beer for several hours and Ben knew that he ought to be at work but something kept him from going—something more than the fun he was having with Eleanor. And it was more than the fact that Eleanor seemed to have forgotten her jealousy towards her sister and her annoyance towards Ben. Whatever it was, that same thing was encouraging him to drink more and earlier than he normally would have.

He was avoiding something.

Eleanor was laughing, her head on his stomach, her hair tickling him. "Did I ever tell you you're a funny guy?"

He hugged her to him. "Did I ever tell you I love you?"

She stopped moving, stopped breathing. The moment froze, and she looked up at him. Instantly he knew he shouldn't have said it. Without a word, she got up and went into the bathroom.

A swelling feeling started somewhere between Ben's throat and his stomach. He was suddenly dizzy and nauseous. He held onto the side of the bed, feeling as though he were really somewhere else, watching himself slowly get sick. He was in two places at once, and ill in both.

And then he was in the kitchen, watching the toaster. He was still naked. The little television on the countertop was turned on. The trumpeting theme of the morning news was playing. He looked at his watch. Eleven AM. He had somehow lost an hour. He glanced into the hallway; the bathroom door was closed, so Eleanor was still in there. What the hell was going on?

And then he saw something that made him forget the time he'd lost, forget his declaration of love and how it had offended Eleanor. The front of the Medical

Center was on the news. The newscaster was standing next to George Franklin, who looked concerned. Ben turned up the sound.

"An arrest was made this morning in one of the most horrific crime sprees in recent memory, a crime spree that is only now coming to light as something other than a series of bizarre coincidences. Dr. Jonathan Sticker was arrested at his Great Neck home, and charged with three counts of homicide. The Chairman of the Hematology Department at the New York Metropolitan Medical Center, Dr. Sticker was said to be using heroin and injecting patients with the HIV virus. With me now is George Franklin, the hospital's CEO. Mr. Franklin, what do you have to say about this shocking arrest?"

"It's a terrible thing," George Franklin said, "a tragedy for everyone involved. Apparently, Dr. Sticker is a sick man. Thank God he's been caught and will get the treatment he needs. As for the victims, everyone's a victim. The patients he's murdered, and those who are sick, their families, the staff, the public, even the media, which has been forced to paint an inaccurate picture of this facility."

"Tell me, Mr. Franklin, might there be as yet undiscovered cases of patients who've been given the HIV virus by Dr. Sticker? Might patients continue to get sick, given the long incubation—"

"That's all for now." George Franklin pushed the microphone away.

Bennett's legs went weak. He grabbed the counter for support. This was, of course, terrific news. Why then, didn't he feel so terrific?

* * *

NED DOYLE

"And they lived happily ever after." Ned closed the book. Frankie, who along with his brother, was lying across his father's lap, sat up, took the book from Ned and turned it around to the front.

"Moh," he said, his dark eyes happy.

"More? But I've read it four times."

"Moh."

Little Ned jumped up. "How about..." he pushed his father backwards and jumped on his chest, "if we beat you up instead."

"Oh, no!" Ned cried out, arms flailing.

"Oh, no!" imitated Frankie and followed his brother's example, until the three Doyle men became a tangle of arms, legs and hair, coming to rest with Ned on his hands and knees and the boys riding on his back, slapping his thighs and Little Ned crying, "Giddyup, Daddy!"

"Giya, da!" copied Frankie, gamely holding on as he teetered in every direction.

Maureen watched from the doorway, arms folded. Ned looked up.

"I guess you're not such a bad dad, after all," she said, chuckling.

Ned didn't answer. He looked at her for a moment, then lay down, sliding his sons around to his belly and bouncing them up and down. He stopped after a few bounces. "I love you guys," he said. "And you, too," he called towards the doorway.

"Keep bouncing, Daddy," yelled Little Ned.

* * *

That night, Ned rolled over and reached for his wife's shoulder. He tried to turn her toward him. She didn't move. He tried again. This time she turned but the look on her face made him pull back.

"Do you know where Little Ned was today?"

"I, ah, a birthday party, right?"

"That's right, and do you know what kind of entertainment they had there?"

"Is this some kind of quiz? Do I have to answer in the form of a question?"

"I'll tell you, a clown."

"Great, what's the point?"

"Did you tell someone over the phone to 'go for the jugular' or use an expression like that?"

Ned shook his head. "I fail to see—"

"That's just it. You fail to see. You just go full steam ahead—with whatever." Her nose was twitching, the way it did when she was really furious. "Well, when you told whoever it was to go for the jugular, Neddy must've overheard you, because today, they had this clown at the party, and as soon as he started juggling, your son attacked him, ripping his wig off and pulling his nose and disrupting the whole party. They called me and made me come get him and what does he tell me on the ride home? Daddy told him to go for the juggler!"

Ned's shoulders shook.

"Don't you dare think this is funny, Ned Doyle! You may not know it but you are hanging by a thread! You are out of control. You don't have control over what you say, you don't have control over what you do!" Her eyes accused him. "You've gotten dangerous, to your children, to me, to yourself." The threat in her voice frightened him, but not as much as the suspicion that she could read his guilt.

* * *

Mr. Stein would be there at any moment, so he'd have to talk fast. Ned dialed Sam's number. He was almost never there, so he'd have to—

"Sam, I can't believe you're in."

"You must've needed to talk to me."

"Sam, I've done something—I'm out of control. I met this woman, the Medical Center's CFO, and—" He explained in one breathless paragraph about Barbara, then waited for Sam's reaction.

"When we alcoholics get going, we don't screw around." Sam chuckled. "I'm sorry. Bad choice of words. Listen, I can only tell you how insane I get. Remember when I won that trip to Hawaii with the travel association last year? Fantastic, wasn't it? Well, I almost didn't go. I got so depressed the week before. In my mind the whole trip became more trouble than it was worth. And it was all because I knew I'd have to leave Hawaii and come back home. I didn't want to go because I was depressed about having to come home! I projected on the negative and got out of control. Isn't that crazy?"

Ned smiled to himself. "That's exactly the phrase Maureen used. Out of control."

"Listen, Neddy. I wish I had some magic words for you, but I don't. First off, whatever happens, whether you stay married or not, you'll be okay. Try to do the right thing. Ask for help. Know what I mean?"

"Yeah. Thanks, Sam." He hung up, took a deep breath and glanced gratefully up at the ceiling. "I could use some help," he whispered.

* * *

BEN

Mattis's tiny eyes grew large. He slapped Bennett on the back. "Benito! Finito! All right!" He pointed to the loveseat. "Sit down, we'll celebrate. You want a beer or a beer?"

"A beer'll be fine."

"All outta those. Here, have a beer." He handed Ben a bottle and aligned the top of his with the edge of the table. A quick, hammer-like punch with the side of his fist and its cap popped off. "So you can finally move ahead with your first account, get some recognition, and...get your second account."

Ben nodded.

"Hey, calm down, Ben-kenobi. Your enthusiasm will rip the house apart."

Ben shrugged and opened his beer. "I don't know. This guy got arrested awfully fast and—"

"Come on!" Mattis sat down behind his computer and absently flicked it on. "You just thought someone else was responsible for the murders and now that you were wrong you want to force it to be that person. Your ego can't take it."

"Look who's talking about ego."

"I know it. That's why my entire salary—my entire reported salary, that is—goes to therapy."

"You know what? You're right." Ben stood up. "Let's go out and celebrate. I'm buying."

Mattis gulped. "Sounds good." His face began to turned red.

"We can go to the Club and afterwards, I know of this..." He peered at his friend. "What's the matter?"

Mattis's eyes had begun to bulge and his forehead was covered with sweat. "It's okay!" Mattis screamed. He took a gasping breath and looked wildly toward the window. "Gotta throw up!"

Ben rushed to the window and opened it. "No! There's schoolkids down there! The bus just let out. The bathroom. Go to the bathroom. Where's the garbage can?"

"I just…use the floor. Ptah, hah, hah." He gasped and gripped the edge of the table. "Woh, everything's spinning. I, I think, I think I'm okay. Whew, that was a bad one."

"A bad what? A heart attack, what?"

Mattis swallowed, calm now. "No, panic attack. My therapist explained that I'm agoraphobic. I don't like going out because I'm avoiding certain places, certain kinds of situations. Big, open places. Parks. They scare the hell out of me and I guess when you talked about going out, that triggered it. I just have to remember…that I'll be okay." He rubbed the side of his face and looked at the beer in his hand as though he were seeing it for the first time. He drank it in a series of loud gulps, then went to the fridge for another.

"I'm making progress in therapy. The middle school is the center of this whole thing for me, somehow. I've been avoiding that one place, and that spread and became a general fear of going to places like it and eventually it became a fear of going out at all. I have to get a particular head going, which reminds me." He opened the desk drawer and took out a clear plastic envelope from which he removed two large round white tablets, three brown and clear capsules and an oblong green pill. "These usually put me exactly where I need to be."

"Really?" Ben said. He had begun to quietly question his own drinking and felt a little guilty now when he drank, especially during the business day, and especially when he ran into Ned.

Mattis ate one of the fat round pills and one of the capsules and shoved the rest in his pants pocket. "I'll be ready to go out in about fifteen minutes."

"Yup," said Ben.

"What, you got the hiccups?"

"Nope." Ben gave a little nod toward his friend. "Aren't you afraid your brain'll explode taking all that?"

"Are you kidding, this stuff is what's keeping my brain *from* exploding."

"A weird thing happened to me recently. I lost an hour. I was hanging out with Eleanor, goofing around in bed, having a few, and somehow I lost an hour."

"You were probably asleep."

"Uh uh. I was just there and then it was suddenly an hour later. I know it when I fall asleep."

"Ahh. Time travel."

"I don't think so. I think—blackout."

"So? I do it all the time. Don't think another thing of it. It's a modern way of moving through the time-space continuum. Come on," he flipped on the computer. "Let's go to a Cyberbar."

"I'd rather go to a real bar."

"Too dangerous. Need protection. Wait 'till the drugs kick in." The computer screen glowed blue as Mattis's modem dialed into its connection. "This cafe is totally plug-n-play. You go and you're there. Whew! Whaddya say, Ben-nington? I bookmarked this place just for you. Lot-sa Cyberbabes."

"But you don't know what they look like."

"That's not a bug, it's a feature, Ben-Franklin. Come on. Talk to her, Ben-ito Mussolini! Talk, do your thing! It's not cheating. Step up to the Cyberbar, give her a little of that old Ben-evolent magic." He cocked his head, as if listening. "Up, up. I'm starting to feel better. Yes, I think the boys're kicking in."

Fifteen minutes later they were in the White Cougar on the Loop Parkway, hurtling towards the Meadowbrook.

"Mattis, close your window. It's twenty degrees out!"

"Chill, Benbo."

"Yeah, chill's right. Shut the goddam window!"

"Wheewww!" Mattis leaned out, the wind blowing his wild hair back. He lobbed his beer bottle like a hand grenade into the air, and watched it splatter between cars twenty yards behind them.

Ben looked at his friend. "Are you out of your mind? You could've killed someone!"

"Oh, lighten up, Ben-Dover. No one got hurt. Besides, if they did—you've got a connection at the hospital!" He rolled up his window and fumbled for a tape, but had trouble coordinating his fingers properly. The tape banged against the dashboard, never quite making it into the slot. Mattis giggled, then gave up. "So, what's the deal with this doctor who shoots up?"

Ben shrugged. "He's the Chairman of Hematology, so I guess he's in a position to control what goes on with the blood supply. They caught him shooting dope, started questioning him, and got him to confess this whole thing. At least that's how it sounded on the news. I haven't heard anything else. He had financial problems, psychological problems, you know the deal."

Mattis frowned at Ben. "Was that a shot? You taking a shot at me?"

Ben shook his head. "No shot. I'm just saying..."

"Because that's not cool, taking a shot at a sick person who's trying to get better."

Ben thought of asking whether Mattis's therapist had prescribed the pills he was taking, but he kept the thought to himself.

"You'd think they'd have figured out that all the people getting AIDS were this guy's patients," Mattis said.

"They aren't. The whole thing doesn't make sense," Ben said, as he looked in his rear view mirror and signaled to get off the highway. "The cop and doctor who ran the investigation are smarter than that. I'm sure they checked into who the attending physician was in each case. There's no way the same doctor could've been assigned to each one. And that would mean that Sticker would've had to have gone around giving each of these patients the virus on his own. Patients he wasn't assigned to. Someone, a head nurse, an intern, someone would've noticed. A patient, even."

"Well, the patients sure wouldn't have if they weren't conscious. You'd be surprised how much you miss when you're out cold. Woh, look at that babe!" He looked into a car that passed them as they veered onto the exit ramp. He banged on the window. "Hey, Sweetie! Ben-evolent. Get back on the highway."

"Come on, if you were face to face with that girl, you'd be too scared to speak."

Mattis didn't answer. He looked over at his friend. "Nice guy," he said, quietly.

Ben laughed. "Besides, did you see the guy with her? Steroid-chin."

Mattis grinned. "You can have him."

Neither of them spoke for a moment as Bennett navigated the back streets north of Hempstead Turnpike towards The Club. "I don't know. I don't know if I buy this guy's confession, though I met him and he is a wacko. It's just that it would've been hard for him to commit all those murders and much easier for an intern or a nurse."

"Well, you wouldn't have thought he could be a heroin addict."

"No, that's true. I don't know. From everything I've seen at the Center, the nurses, particularly, are on top of things."

"Ooh, I'll bet."

"Shut up, you moron."

"I love when you talk to me like that. Oh, shit." He gasped for air, closing his eyes. "One, relax. Two, relax. Three..."

"Come on, you're okay."

"We're getting near a park, a schoolyard or something, aren't we?"

"Well, yeah, there's a park over that way..."

"Then go the *other* way! Hoo, hah." Mattis leaned back, then leaned far forward, his head between his knees.

"Okay, okay, we'll turn here."

"I think I shouldn't have taken the speed," Mattis said, his voice weak. "It makes me hyperventilate. You've got to get just the right mix of pills to avoid the attacks. I did it the first time."

"It's never like the first time..."

"You laugh, but you're right." Mattis looked around, more relaxed now. "You know, I should've stayed in college, finished my psych major. They taught us about all sorts of wild medications and I'd know how to deal with this better if I'd—"

"So, why didn't you finish college?"

"Psych had too many early morning classes. It was a big pain in the ass."

9

DRIVEN

Late winter brought an expectancy of spring. Nature's colors were heavy, thick on the sky's canvas. A few birds seemed to have returned, scouts perhaps, for the flocks to come. Warmer days were augured, spring inevitable.

The banquet stretched in every direction and to every sense. Symphonies of sound and color, delicacies without end waiting to fill up the palette, belly and mind. Soft, subtle textures, feathers and down, caressed the skin, beckoning one's hair to stand up—mesmerizing. And the tastes were rich, creamy, bitter and sweet. Spring was buds and flowers, grasses, newborn babes. All on their way.

But underneath and behind it all was a vague beat, a permanent insistent throb that would not be defeated. A backbone, a thumping bassline that might bounce beneath the surface, only to reappear closer and grinning. An irresistible notion, like the voices of Sirens to Ulysses, and this voice said, "have your fun, enjoy the coming spring, for I will be here, too. Watch the leaves and animals, breathe the perfumes, feel the textures. I will be waiting."

Like an insistent song that played in the back of one's mind, the thought, the feeling, the notion was there, and would not leave. It harped and reminded and cajoled. And it grew.

Soon you saw that it was not a tune, not a temporary thought that would be flushed out by larger thoughts. It was a virus, or worse, it was the whole and you were part of *it*.

It was the nightmare itself, the irresistible urge for revenge drumming through your mind, its clouds rolling over the senses like a thunderstorm, a tornado over the new spring season. It filled your mind's eye until you could not turn away, until there was no room for thought or consideration, no appreciation of art or music.

You must, you will go out and kill. Like sex or hunger or the need for air: you will do what you must. There is no thought of revenge. There is only this single sense, this overwhelming need that cannot be denied.

And you rush to the hospital, and you kill, carefully. And the thing is satisfied. It creeps away, yawning.

Until tomorrow.

* * *

CHARLIE SPOON

"Daddy and Rob-Rob sitting in a tree. K-I-S-S-I-N-G. First comes love, then comes marriage, then comes..."

Robin hesitated, then pointed at herself.

"...Robin in the baby carriage. Hooo!" She hooted with laughter and bounced harder on her father's knee. Charlie smiled and sang the song again, and when

Robin pointed to him, he sang "Daddy in the baby carriage," and she laughed again, harder.

A woman seated across from them was wearing a translucent emerald scarf. Robin had been peering at it and now she hopped off her Daddy's knee and went over to the woman and took an edge of the scarf between her fingers. The woman had been looking off into the distance and she started, her body shaking for a moment as she stared at the girl, then at Charlie.

"Robin don't mean no harm. She just wanted to get a closer look, seein' as how it's so pretty."

The woman looked at Robin, whose curly hair and fair complexion were so much like her father's, and noticed the wide set eyes and slack features.

"Of course," she said, and Robin continued to handle the scarf, curling it around her own head and grinning back at her father.

"Very nice, honey, now let's leave the lady alone."

Robin ran back to her father, bent low to the ground and began walking her fingers upward. She sang at the top of her voice. "The itsy bitsy spider, went up the water spout!"

A wrinkled woman with gray hair and birds-egg blue eyeglasses came to the entrance of the waiting room. "Hello Robin!" she said, smiling also to Charlie.

"Jane, Jane, friend of mane!" Robin cried, running to the woman and nearly crushing her in a hug. Charlie followed his daughter to her therapist and waited.

"I will see Robin today, Mr. Spoontag, but you know the situation. It's not a question of what I want to do." The woman looked regretful.

Charlie scratched his head and shifted his weight. Inside his heavy work boots he could feel the sweat pouring off his feet. "Dr. Maynard, I know this isn't your fault. And I'm not here to make my problems yours, but to tell you the truth, Robin's condition is this hospital's fault to begin with. Now I'm not here to get into that, but if you're not going to be here for her anymore, then please look her in the eye," he pointed to Robin's face, which was focused up at her daddy's, "and tell her you won't be seeing her after today. Go on."

Dr. Maynard sighed. This was the flip side of her job. She loved working with challenged children. They were so happy, so unaffected by the complexities of modern life. Sometimes she wondered if these children were more advanced than the rest of us, discarding worry and resentment in favor of beauty and love. "Mr. Spoontag, I will see Robin today. But that's all I'll say. How's that?"

Charlie nodded. "It's not good enough but, okay…for now."

Robin's hands were high over her head, her fingers extended and shaking in all directions and she lowered her hands slowly. "…down came the rain and washed the spider out!"

Charlie could feel his throat closing. Damn! Every time he had to do this, as good a thing as it was, he got all choked up. He took his little girl's hand and extended it towards Dr. Maynard, who looked Robin in the eye, smiling warmly. "Robin, I missed you so much. It's sooo good to see you."

Robin shook her hand away and raised both arms over her head. "Out came the sun and dried up all the rain—hey! Jane, rain, Jane, rain. Rain! Jane! Friend of mane!"

"You stay today for class, we'll have fun, okay?" She looked at Charlie and mouthed the words, "only today."

Charlie wiped his eyes with the sleeve of his coat. "No, we'll be here every week."

Dr. Maynard sighed and led Robin into the ward. Charlie went back to the waiting room, sat down and picked up a magazine.

* * *

MARILYN FRANKLIN

Marilyn leaned close to the bathroom mirror and looked for strands of gray in her short red hair; she found only a few. Satisfied, she patted the sides in place and went back to the lab's closet and began piling diapers onto the gurney.

She felt flushed and wondered if she had a fever or if the lab was hot. She looked over at Janice to see if she showed any signs of distress, but Janice was wearing a sweater, and appeared comfortable as she sorted through the test tubes and vials on the counter. She wanted to tell her that she ought to have the first tray of vials sorted and stored away before she even touched the second, but she bit her tongue. Janice was already annoyed with her, at least it seemed that way. More than a few of the nurses had been looking suspiciously at her. Before Dr. Sticker's arrest that sort of suspicion was common and understandable throughout the hospital. Everyone suspected everyone else, and, as usual, the worst opinions were reserved for the nursing staff, the least appreciated and most overworked population at any hospital, at least in her opinion.

Nothing surprised her anymore. She had, over the years, grown a thick enough skin to tolerate whatever anyone said or thought of her.

They had been friends, she and Janice. Since Eleanor had been seeing her new boyfriend Janice had kept away from her sister, and had gravitated more towards her. But these last few weeks, she had been cool, distant. She was a strange, suspicious woman. Perhaps it was just as well, Marilyn thought, refocusing on the closet and the items she needed for her ward. Ointment, bottles, nipples, more diapers, blankets…

She had thought about saying something to Janice. She drew a breath. What could she possibly ask her? She knew enough about herself to know that anything she said would likely come out as anger. The only thing she could think of was asking how she was getting along with Eleanor's boyfriend. As sensitive, even paranoid as Janice was, she would certainly take that as a dig…and she would be right.

The room tipped and spun, and Marilyn grabbed onto the gurney's metal rail to keep from toppling over. When the feeling passed, she turned her attention back to the closet.

The last time she had tried to talk with her, Janice had cut her off, claiming that she had asked her to come out to lunch several times and that it was she, Marilyn, who had refused. Marilyn stopped what she was doing and looked over at Janice. She didn't remember ever talking to her about going out together. She just assumed their friendship had soured like so many others. Well, she was here to work. This was business.

The room was getting hotter. An itching had started on the outside of one of her legs, as though something were crawling on her skin; the feeling was familiar; she ignored it. Her body knew this routine and it would continue no matter what her mental state. She was proud of that ability. No thinking, just working. Autopilot was necessary for one to get through the work day in a hospital that was so poorly run.

When care for the patient became secondary to budgetary considerations: which units were full, which made the most money, which were favored by the insurance companies and HMOs—a nurse's job became exponentially more difficult. Only a crisis would direct more money into the hospital towards those who were really sick. Emergencies tended to put the system on hold. The uninsured were suddenly paid for—if only on a temporary basis, and the fallout would wait. Care might, just might, be administered if a real crisis were apparent. That was the only way the system responded. Indeed, since the AIDS crisis had stopped being swept under the rug and had become the focus of semi-public investigations, the general quality of care had risen…a little.

The gurney was prepared and she was ready. She glanced at Janice, who didn't even look up, and she imagined in an instant what it would be like to leave work and go out to the diner for a cup of tea, and chat about her life, her loneliness, her wanting to fall in love some day. What would it be like to be a little less alone her head?

She shook the daydream away; the vulnerability was too much to imagine. Exposing herself like that would be unwise. Better to go home, shower and dress in her night clothes. Then, after writing for a half hour in her journal, go out to the bar to be alone in a sea of faces.

* * *

BEN

"Come on in. Hey Ben! Got the final proofs ready?"

Ben nodded and sat down in one of the chairs in front of Ned's desk. "Yeah, they look good. That photographer, Charlie, did a nice job."

Ned was smiling down at his desk. His eyes came up to meet Ben's, and they sparkled with half concealed amusement. "The responsibility for the job rests with the art director. And that means he has to be big enough to take the credit when the job goes well." He waggled a finger and nodded as though this were a sad fact.

Ben looked down into his own lap, noticing a faint outline of a coffee drip on the right thigh of his gray pants. He wondered if he were to marry Eleanor whether she would know how to get stains like this one out—whether she would wash his clothes at all.

"That's why I'm here, Ned. I'm wondering about this guy they arrested, Dr. Sticker. My friend and I were out the other night and we were discussing it and, well, if you'll forgive me, it just doesn't add up."

Twin vertical creases appeared in Ned's forehead. "What are you talking about?"

"I'm saying that it doesn't make sense that a doctor, a department chair, who would be noticed in units that are not under his jurisdiction, would have committed these murders. I'm saying that..."

Ned's eyes receded into bony caverns and widened, staring. "You don't think this doctor, this heroin addict, committed the murders?"

"That doctor isn't the only heroin addict in the world. Ned, it just makes a lot more sense that a nurse or a technician would be able to—"

"You're an art director, Bennett, and a good one, although you're hanging by a goddamn thread right now." Ned spoke slowly, succinctly. Ben sensed a dangerous tension building in his boss. "You have a way of sabotaging your own success, Mr. James, did you know that? Are you sure you want to succeed? Let's leave the police work to the police, okay? We have this special deal with them. We do that, they leave the artwork to us."

"All I'm saying is..."

"I don't care what you're saying!" Ned thundered, eyes bulging. His voice suddenly dropped again, becoming placid, controlled. "I apologize, Bennett." He waved an open hand. "I have things on my mind. Things at home have been—difficult the last few weeks." He shook his head. "Listen, why don't you get back to work? Like I said, you did a heck of a job on these ads. Franklin was very happy with them. Did I tell you that?"

"No. Was he? Really?" Bennett was pleased, momentarily forgetting his reservations.

"Umhmm. As was the CFO of the hospital."

"Oh, that woman..."

"Right. And don't worry so much about the police and that end of it. They know what they're doing. Sometimes you've got to trust the process." He chuckled, as though at a private joke.

* * *

"Just put the tape in, and forward it to the beginning of the movie," Mattis called. "I'll be right out!"

Ben sighed and walked over the dirty yellow carpet to the television, glancing at the window. The sky had darkened and filled with low, gray clouds. A heavy spring snow was forecast. He looked at the spine of the tape. "Space Creatures—Back for More" was 96 minutes long.

Two quick screams came from the bathroom.

Bennett jumped up and bolted into the hallway towards the bathroom, crashing into Mattis who was running in the opposite direction.

"Oaff of mff wff!" He shoved Ben out of the way and flung open a closet door and ripped a towel from a shelf, gagging and burying his face in it. After a moment, he lifted his head; his face was flushed, there was a white foam around his mouth. "Oh, my God. Oh, my God," he gasped.

"What? What happened?" Ben asked.

"C'mere." He walked to the bathroom, and pointed to a wicker basket that sat on the back of the toilet. "See that? I keep all my stuff in there, including toothpaste and acne cream. I, I, I got the two mixed up." He shook his head. "Acne cream tastes like damn poison."

Ben nodded. "But look on the bright side, I'll bet you never get another zit on your tongue."

"Zit on my tongue?" Mattis looked at Ben. Slowly it dawned on him that his friend was not serious. "You son of a bitch…"

"Come on, let's watch the movie. I gotta tell you, you did make me forget about what's going on at the hospital, if only for a few minutes."

Mattis took a sixpack of 16 oz. beers from the cardboard case in the refrigerator, and they sat down on the couch. Mattis pushed a button on the remote control and the movie began with an orchestral flourish that represented a space flight.

"The Galactic Council had spoken!" said the narrator, whose voice was so deep that the television's speakers vibrated.

Mattis looked over at Ben. "You know, I have this idea for learning more about whether these murders are still going on and who's committing them." He paused and when Bennett did not answer, he continued. "I get myself into the hospital as a patient, and—"

"Not as a doctor?" Ben asked.

"Well, that would be a thought. Hey! I'm serious. I can keep an eye on the nurses, find out their routines, what they do on their rounds. I can talk to your girlfriend's sister, maybe. Feel her out."

"Oh, you'll feel. I'm sure you'll feel."

Mattis looked disgusted. "I'm talking about doing a little police work on our own. If the cops have the wrong guy, then maybe we can help find the right one."

Bennett looked at Mattis, raising an eyebrow but deciding to say nothing.

"Okay, genius," Mattis said. "If my idea's so dumb, what's yours?"

"I'd go to Epstein and get names of victims. And I'd interview them and find out who treated them, what doctors they saw, what nurses came to see them, technicians, and so on. I'd try to find something in common."

Mattis nodded. "That sounds like a pretty good idea. What are they feeding you over at the agency? Brain food?"

"At least I don't brush my teeth with acne cream!"

On the television screen, the space hero was patting his tritanium-alloy friend on one of his telescopic arms. "The universe is lucky to have us around to protect it, eh, Hackroid?"

A long whistle and four beeps was the answer.

"What do you mean, without us, there'd be nothing to be afraid of?" The space hero stopped walking and gave the robot a push. "Why I ought to rip out your translipo-tase control!"

Mattis gestured towards the screen. "What he said."

* * *

MAKING ROUNDS

As soon as the drugs hit, you were here, in Med. Surg. 3, acting out revenge although you long since stopped feeling the joy of it. You had no choice. As soon as you got off, once you could walk or came out of a nod, you had to get to the hospital. No one questioned you. The duty nurses stopped to chat, the doctors smiled. The goddamn patients told you their problems, and all the while you wished you could stop it. Get out. Break the chain. It was enough. But that voice was soft, no match for the airplane roar demanding revenge.

You check the CPT Codes and the ICD-9 classifications for ideal candidates. They had to be expected to live six months, preferably a lot longer. What would be the point of killing them slowly if they were already dying quickly?

You suppress a laugh.

A young man named Adam is smiling while he's sleeping. His dark hair and long lashes remind you of someone. His chest rises quietly and lowers with each breath and his eyes move behind their lids.

But you have no choice, no control. This is a closed system. So you administer the needle to the port in the IV and make sure he will die.

A white-skinned seven-year-old named Eric with an endotracheal tube connected to a respirator has a nighttable littered with colorful books about Winnie the Pooh. Someone must have been reading to him before he fell asleep. You have a memory of wanting to be Christopher Robin so you could be so popular with so many friendly, clever little animals, but then it is gone and you are powerless over what you must do. You explain that you have to give him some medicine and it's not going to hurt a bit. He cheerfully agrees, explaining that he's very brave and his daddy is very proud of him. The needle goes into the port in the boy's IV line.

A Japanese girl in her early teens who has had a lung transplant has long, fine hair and you admire it for a long moment before doing what you have to do. Afterwards, you watch her sleep and you're startled when she opens her eyes and looks you in the face. You pat her on the head and whisper "it's okay," and she smiles and drifts back to sleep.

* * *

BEN

The door to the Freeport home opened and the tall, bald man smiled briefly, then recognized Bennett and stopped smiling.

"Yes?"

"Hello, Dr. Epstein. We need to see you."

"Yeah," said Mattis, and Bennett turned slowly to look at him.

"I don't think you do. This business is over with."

"No sir," Bennett said. "Look, we just want to talk to you for a minute."

"Who's he?"

"He's my friend, Ricky Hatters. He's helping me sort this out."

Dr. Epstein stood his ground. Gone was his friendly bedside manner. "The police have already sorted it out. Dr. Sticker's in custody. You've had my apology. What more could you possibly want with me?"

"We have reason to believe that Sticker didn't do it."

"Oh you do? And your years of police training make you quite certain?"

"Tell me, doctor. A prominent physician like Dr. Sticker would have been pretty noticeable going around administering needles to patients who were not necessarily his, don't you think?"

Dr. Epstein paused. "Well, that's probably true."

"So we want to interview some of the patients—the, ah, victims."

"Impossible. Confidentiality prohibits—"

Bennett cut him off. "Prohibits finding the real killer? Prohibits an appropriate, politics-free investigation? Sticker's an addict, Dr. Epstein. That much is true. And they're trying to hang the murders on him, isn't that possible? They're trying to free the hospital from the burden of having bad judgment, of having hired a doctor with a problem." He snorted a laugh. "Pretty convenient having a criminal on staff right now, isn't it?"

Dr. Epstein glanced up and down the street. "Come in."

They stepped into the carpeted living room and Bennett sat in a leather armchair. Mattis squatted on a matching ottoman. Dr. Epstein stood, arms folded. "You want to interview patients who've been infected?"

"That's right. We want to find out who'd been in to see them, who their doctors were, the nurses and so on."

Mattis nodded. "We think a nurse would have had a whole lot more opportunity to do this without being noticed."

Epstein nodded. "Agreed. But giving you the names of patients would be most inappropriate."

Ben nodded slowly. "You know what's inappropriate, doc? Assaulting someone with a car."

Mattis whistled softly. "Ooh, yeah. Very inappropriate."

"That's also blackmail, guys."

"Hey, we're just trying to find the truth." Bennett stood up and took a step towards Dr. Epstein. "We're not screwing around here. Who knows who could be acquiring the virus while we're having this discussion?"

Epstein hesitated. “All right. Give me a day. Stop back here tomorrow evening and I’ll have some names for you. Then you’re on your own and you’ve got to promise to leave me the hell out of this from now on.” He rubbed his forehead, which was red and glistening with perspiration.

“One other thing,” Bennett said. “I’m still not quite clear on how it was determined that this was a person committing murders and not a fault of the blood system. I know the computers are fool proof but that’s really circumstantial, isn’t it? How can anyone be so sure these are murders?”

“I’m glad you asked that. It’s simple really. One of the victims had been given autologous transfusions.”

“What’re those?” Mattis asked.

“An autologous transfusion is when a patient stores away his or her own blood prior to surgery. His blood didn’t come from the bank. And he’s HIV positive, now. That’s how the blood system was ruled out.”

* * *

What little hair Kenneth Sullivan had left was gray and clumped with sweat and was entirely on the right side of his head. The left side was shaved and covered with gauze and a bandage. A drainage tube was attached to the center of the bandage. Another tube was attached to his throat and a third, thinner tube to his wrist. Next to him, in an upholstered chair sat a tired looking woman and next to her sat a similar-looking woman, equally tired but younger. As Ben pushed the curtain aside, he turned to Mattis and held a finger to his lips. “Mrs. Sullivan?”

The woman looked up. “Yes?”

“My name is Bennett James and this is Richard Hatters. We were wondering if we might ask your husband a few questions.”

A worried look crossed Mrs. Sullivan’s face. Her daughter explained, “He can’t talk, you know.”

“Well, we can keep these to yes or no questions and he can answer by nodding or shaking his head or tapping the nightstand if he prefers. He can even squeeze your hand. It’s about…how he got sick; it’s for the investigation.”

Mrs. Sullivan looked them up and down. “Are you…police officers?”

“No, our connection is with the hospital. These would be questions about who might have been in to see him when he was here originally.”

Mrs. Sullivan raised an eyebrow. “That was nearly ten years ago, Mr. James. You don’t expect a man, a very ill man, to remember…?”

Mr. Sullivan’s hand rose slowly, shaking. A finger pointed at Bennett, then bent, beckoning him over and motioning him to sit down on his side of the bed.

Mrs. Sullivan’s lips pressed together. “Well, I guess it’ll be okay. But since you’re with the hospital, you must know, my husband’s been positive for nine years and has been full blown for a year and a half. His T-cells are nonexistent and he has five different opportunistic conditions, counting the brain tumor.”

The daughter tapped Bennett’s arm. “What she means is, don’t get him excited.”

Mrs. Sullivan nodded. “That’s my daughter Megan. She looks out for her daddy, along with her three sisters.”

“Of course,” Ben nodded. He felt as if he were dealing with a particularly delicate customer. “I have a duty roster, Mr. Sullivan. It’s ten years old and was given to me by one of the Department Chairs who was here at the time. It includes physical descriptions of each doctor and nurse, even technicians. I’m going to read from it and I want you to close your eyes, sir, and remember. Now this might take a little while. I want you to take your time. Remember, okay? Think of who was in to see you, who took or gave blood, who administered your IV. Now some of this was done while you were sleeping, so there will naturally be people you cannot recall. Just do the best you can. I’ll start slowly.” He turned to the two women. “If either of you thinks Mr. Sullivan is getting tired, please let me know and I’ll come back another time.”

The hand waved, signaling that this would not be necessary, then pointed to Ben to begin.

* * *

MARILYN FRANKLIN

Marilyn sat in front of the fish tank watching the goldfish and guppies frantically try to get away. She wiped her nose with a tissue. She had put them in only moments ago and the Dempsey had not even shown itself, but the smaller fish seemed to know enough to be afraid.

She knew how they felt. In a half an hour she’d have to go back to work. Another long, long shift and then back home to write in her journal, get high, then go out to the bar to get higher. Then she’d let the night and whatever help came her way take her where they might, maybe get a few hours of sleep before going back to work.

He was in there somewhere, like the Dempsey. At work she sometimes had to fight the impulse to run. Writing helped. There was no one to talk to except her journal. Janice had been available for a time, but she had changed. Perhaps he had somehow gotten to her, converted her somehow to his side. She could picture him calling Janice into his smoky office and offering her a raise if she froze his daughter out.

She threw the tissue away and watched the goldfish and the guppies dart in and out of the leaves and coral, their efforts becoming frantic when they encountered glass and were forced to swim in smaller and smaller circles. Marilyn smiled to herself. That’s an important difference between us, she thought. I can adapt to my circle. I can work with what I’ve got.

* * *

BEN

An hour later, they moved to the next patient. Maria Toval was sixteen and had contracted the HIV virus at the age of eight, apparently while in the hospital for a tonsillectomy. Ben asked the questions; Mattis stayed silent, whispering a suggestion or observation now and then into Bennett's ear.

Since she had been so young, Maria was not able to remember many details and without finishing, they moved on to Larry Steinberg, who had been in the hospital for gallstones and who was reasonably healthy and living at home.

"As I understand it, many of the patients either haven't gone full blown yet or are healthy enough to be going about their lives," Bennett explained, as they drove to Mr. Steinberg's home, which was in the poor part of town not far from the tattoo parlor.

They walked up the cracked pavement and knocked on the door of the bungalow. It opened immediately.

"I've been expecting you." Larry Steinberg was tall and thin and his face came to a point at his nose, from beneath which sprouted a heavy brown moustache. He wore a knit green shirt and blue slacks. Aside from a reddened face and chrome cane, there was little outward sign of illness.

"Come on in." He led Ben and Mattis into a small room with peeling beige paint revealing irregular patches of white. Splotches of color dotted the dark wood floor.

"Coffee? It's made."

"Sure," said Ben.

"Got any beer?" Mattis asked. Ben slapped him.

"Sorry. Can't have any alcohol," Larry said. "Want a coke?"

"Fine," said Mattis.

Ben and Mattis helped with the drinks, and Mattis and Steinberg sat down on the floral print couch in the living room. Ben sat on a folding wood chair. Mr. Steinberg stood up suddenly. "Oh, let me put on some music."

"You don't have to do that," Ben said.

"I certainly do." Melodies, harmonies and textures of an orchestra filled the room. "Mozart changes everything," he said, smiling. "You know, when you told me what you were doing with the investigation, I vowed to give you all the help I can."

"Thank you," said Mattis.

Ben shook his head and sipped his coffee. "Mm, this is good. I can't understand why no one's done this before."

"Maybe you don't visit people who like coffee." Mattis sounded offended.

"No, I mean investigate who was in to see the victims," Ben glanced at Steinberg. "I mean the patients."

"That's okay. I'm a victim, all right. A crime was committed and I'm a victim of it. You can bet on that. And I know why no one's carried on an investigation. Money. Politics. What do you think?"

"Tell me about yourself, Mr. Steinberg," said Bennett.

"Well, I had been a realtor, the most successful one in town. But after 7 years of illness my insurance ran out and I began paying for my care with my savings until I was forced to sell my home and rent this shack. Ironic," he chuckled and cleared his throat for some seconds. "I used to sell the nicest homes in town, and look at this," he shook his head, smiling. "Life is funny sometimes, don't you think?"

Ben and Mattis looked at one another. Bennett opened his log book. "I have this list of doctors, nurses, technicians and we're going to go through it slowly. Take your time, close your eyes, think, remember…"

Mr. Steinberg sipped his coffee and sat back on the couch. "Let's get to it."

10

BEN

Ben and Mattis stood at the intersection of the two corridors and peered around the white walls, down the shiny tiled floor toward the conference room just as its door opened and doctors, nurses and administrators poured out. Marilyn was one of the first out, her father, one of the last. Ben looked at Mattis.

"Want to follow her?" Mattis asked.

"I don't know; I think we should do what we came to do. Let's just see this last patient and go back to analyze the data."

Mattis nodded. "Fine. Let's go."

Ben didn't move.

"Well? I'm agreeing with you. Don't look so stunned."

"No, it's not that. One of the doctors. I think I recognized him. Dumpy guy with sort of orange hair and big eyes." Ben looked at the ceiling. "Where've I seen him before?"

"Sounds a little like that tattoo—"

"Yes!" Ben shouted. "The tattoo guy. One of the doctors who just came out of that meeting was the guy at the tattoo place. Charlie!"

Mattis looked at Ben out of the sides of his eyes. "If that's true, then he'd be the most upwardly mobile person on the east coast."

"No, Eleanor said something about him. He's got a daughter, and something happened to her here. I know it's him." Ben started in the direction he'd seen the man go.

"Wait a minute, boy wonder." Mattis grabbed his sleeve. "If that guy is the tattoo artist and if he is a murderer, let's try not to antagonize him. Why don't we just include his description in our interviews with these folks? Put him out there a little more prominently."

Ben let out a breath. "Good idea."

* * *

Genevieve Shull was in her mid sixties; her face was thin, sunken, but her skin was soft and luminescent. Her almond shaped eyes looked up when Ben knocked on the wall just inside the door of her room and her full lips pressed together and moved before answering as though they had to prepare before presenting themselves.

Her head was swathed in a turban of bandages and she slowly explained that the maze of wires and tubes connected to the machines at her bedside would set off alarms if particular readings were exceeded at any time.

"But I'm not worried." She batted her eyes at Ben. "Why should I when I have two marvelous men like you to protect me? So? Where should we start? I had a wonderful business and I loved it."

"What kind of..." Ben started to ask.

"I'm going to tell you, sweetheart, if you'd only let me." She touched his wrist. "I'm teasing you, dear. I'm an unmitigated flirt and you certainly are a cutie." Her eyes focused on Ben's face for an instant, then blurred into the past. "You do have a girlfriend, don't you? I'll bet she knows how to keep you happy." She giggled. "In my day, I was quite a catch, you know?" She sighed. "But it isn't my day anymore, I suppose. Anyway, I had a clip-on concern."

"What're clip-ons?" Mattis asked.

"You attach them to your glasses to keep out the sun. We did very well with them. We're still doing well, if Esther and Cassandra aren't running the business into the ground. They're my sisters. When I started getting sick, which was about a year ago, we had a new ad budget and we were going places. First, I went mental. I was never so scared. I'd only read about this illness in the papers and even then, only skimmed. Back then, if it wasn't the financial pages, I didn't read it. But then I accepted it. It's stages, you know? Anger, denial, acceptance. I don't remember them now. My memory's been a problem. Having a head full of cancer isn't particularly great for your memory, you know? But, you know what else?"

"What?" Ben asked.

"I believe in God. I do. More than ever. I love God and God loves me and we're going to get together for coffee and donuts real soon...Now, let's get to that list of people you wanted me to look at."

* * *

Mattis was looking out the window on the passenger side of the White Cougar, and when Ben asked him what he thought of Genevieve, he turned and Ben saw the tears in his eyes.

"I've never seen anyone so brave in my life," Mattis said. "God, I wish I could be like her. And no, I don't mean in the 'head full of cancer' sense." His face froze and his eyes opened wide. "No! Turn here! Turn, I said! We're near the park! Turn the goddamn car!"

Ben turned the wheel and they drove back the way they came.

"Take the goddamn highway, ferchrissakes," Mattis implored.

"Jeez, what's that about?" Ben asked. "Have you gotten to the details of this park thing in your therapy?"

"Well yeah, but no, not really." Mattis sounded depressed. "We're working on it. It's so old, real old. And at this point it applies to any park. I get near a park and I get panic attacks. The origin is hard to remember. My mind's protecting me, not letting me remember. I don't want to talk about it. But, of course I do want to talk about it. God, sometimes I have no idea what I want."

"So we're going to have to spend at least a day going over these interviews and collating and cross referencing..."

Mattis brightened. "You know, I have a computer program that'll do that for us. Of course, we can just feed the information in, tag common items and...but we'd need it typed onto a disc and that's going to take a while."

"Yeah, right." Ben was silent. "You know, I think I know someone who might type it for us."

* * *

As Ben walked into the office, Lydia began whistling the theme song from a popular television detective program.

"Bennett," Art held up a mug of coffee in greeting, "the final proofs on the hospital ads are in. They're on Neddie's desk. He's out with some clients. Why don't you have a look?"

"I'll get to it. There's something I have to do first." He walked to the back of the room. "Annabel?"

Slowly, the mop of red hair rose from behind the computer screen. The freckled face beneath it flushed. "Hi, Bennett. Sure, I'll do it."

"I ah, wonder if you could do me a favor. What?"

Her hands were folded on the desk in front of her. She looked down at them. "The typing? No problem."

Aware of a creeping sensation on the back of his neck, Ben turned quickly and saw that the rest of the office had gathered a safe distance away and was watching them.

Annie saw them too, and stood up. "Are we in a zoo?" she said, in the most authoritative voice Ben had ever heard from her. "Don't you all have something to do? Lydia, there are two lines ringing. Why don't you answer them? Art, one of those calls is for you!"

Lydia and Art looked at one another.

"Who does she think...?" Lydia started to say, as the phone rang. Just as she picked it up, a second line rang.

"Hold on," Lydia said, into the receiver, with a frown and a squint towards Annie. She looked at Art, her eyebrows raised. Art picked up his phone.

"I, ah, have some information I need typed and put on a disk..." Ben began.

"I know," Annie said, holding out her hand and smiling eagerly. "I'll have it by three."

"I appreciate it." They looked at one another for a moment.

"You go, girl!" Lydia called from the other side of the room.

"I've been trying to get her to type for me for months," Art said.

"Well," Lydia answered. "You don't swing that way."

Art shrugged. "I might consider that stuff if it'll get my typing done."

Ben looked back at Annie. "Have you seen Lou?"

Annie nodded and Ben was aware that she was doing something more than looking at him. Her eyes had attached themselves somehow to his heart. They looked inside him, holding not just his image but his being.

"Annie, don't look at me like that."

She blushed. "Like what?"

"Like...where did you say Lou was? Stop it!"

"Coming back from the diner with his coffee...now. Stop what?"

He was saved from answering by Lou, who did indeed walk through the door at that moment.

"Thanks, Annie." Ben smiled, shrugged and waved to Lou, pointing to the artist's desk. Lou held up the bag he was carrying.

"Got two. Knew you were coming."

Ben took one of the folding chairs from the side of the room and sat down at the edge of Lou's desk. "I know you're busy. I'll just take a minute."

"Take all the time you want. I'm dreading starting this layout anyway. What's up? This woman giving you the—"

"It's the hospital, the campaign, the whole thing." Ben swallowed. "It's, it's..."

"Getting a little stressed out?"

Ben nodded. "More than a little. And burned out. I'd probably be burned out by the campaign alone, but Mattis and I've been interviewing patients at the hospital, to see if they remember anything from—"

"Why are you doing that? Why not just let the police handle—?"

"Because my conscience won't let me do my job under these circumstances."

Lou hesitated. "Maybe this isn't the right account for you. I know you don't want to hear that, but—"

"Maybe it isn't, but I'm not giving it up." Ben grinned. "If I do, Ned may not give me another chance until, God knows when."

Lou nodded. "Art and I've been keeping an eye on you. We're proud of you. The way you've handled the account, the decisions you've made, the way you've handled Mr. Franklin. Even the inquiries. Whatever we might feel about that, we're proud of the way you've taken the bull by the horns. And the campaign's going beautifully, from a strictly advertising standpoint. Public relations-wise, you couldn't have known about this arrest, so I hope you're not looking at that as something—"

"No, I'm not. It's out of my control." Ben shook his head.

"That's the boy," Lou slapped his shoulder. "Listen, why don't you come out to Tara next weekend? Art's done with his manuscript, and—" He saw the surprise on Ben's face. "Didn't you know? He sent it in last week, via some connected people we know. In fact, you'd be doing me a favor if you'd visit again. Maybe let him take you clothes shopping or go to the Art Center with him. Since he's finished that script, he doesn't know what to do with himself." He gave Ben a merry look. "You writers..."

"I'll think about it," said Ben. "I'm pretty swamped actually."

"Let me know. Like I said, you're a big boy. Art and I are there for you. I mean it."

Ben nodded. "Thanks." He again experienced the feeling of belonging that he'd first had at the lake behind Art and Lou's country house. The experience was so moving and emotional that he had to grab the edge of Lou's desk.

"You okay?"

Ben nodded.

"So? Tell me about the young lady."

* * *

That evening, Ben struggled to keep the white Cougar below the speed limit as he brought the disk to Mattis's house in Valley Stream. He took the steps two at a time and found Mattis relaxing at an Internet Cafe. "Just hearing some Cybertunes and a Cyberverse reading by a well known Cyberpoet."

"You sure he's a real person?" Ben asked.

Mattis sipped his beer and answered him seriously. "I suppose it doesn't matter."

"Let me ask you this. You have relationships, even sex on the Internet, right?"

"Sure, Cybersex is the best. The only virus to be had is of the computer variety."

"But what if that girl you've been screwing around with is really a guy, putting you on?"

Mattis looked dubious. "I'd know."

"Really? I don't think so. How? What if the guy were sincere?"

Mattis shivered. "Just give me the damn disk and stop trying to ruin my fun."

Ben handed over the disk and Mattis popped it into the computer. His fingers began moving rapidly over the keys. Five minutes later, he called out, "We have a lucky winner!"

"Who is it?" Ben asked. He had been watching an old western on TV from the couch and having a beer.

"Only one entry is a match on all the patients."

* * *

MARILYN FRANKLIN

The sides of her head at and just above the temples ached pleasantly. A familiar bitterness worked its way up the back of her throat, causing her to swallow. Pink splotches danced before her eyes, growing brighter when she blinked. She'd been on duty for thirteen hours and the last bit of methamphetamine was wearing off. Somewhere in the cavernous yellow room a swarm of bees seemed to be buzzing, drawing nearer and then edging away, growing angry, then calm.

Marilyn bit her lip and blinked. Doctors and nurses, from the highest department heads through residents and interns, registered nurses and LPNs were crowded into the room. Everyone was talking at once. She saw Janice across the table, against the far wall, standing next to Davenport, a tall, thin intern who hoped to become a cardiologist. She caught Janice's eye, but Janice looked in the other direction and then up at Davenport, saying something to him that caused him to smile and shake his head, no.

"Excuse me, coming through. Yes, hi. Fine, thank you. Achem!" George Franklin edged quickly through the crowd, nodding and acknowledging the greetings that came his way. "Oh, she's fine thank you. I'll tell her you asked."

Marilyn watched her father in the clinical way she used to enjoy watching her sister's ant farm. His greetings and salutations were phony. He couldn't have cared if the room and everyone in it blew up, as long as he wasn't in it and hospital profits didn't suffer. The meeting would have to be short, she decided, since even he wouldn't dare to smoke in a room so crowded with health professionals.

He cleared his throat, and the rumbling of phlegm went on for some seconds. "Folks! Folks! I've asked you here this morning to, first of all, make it official. The sick, twisted individual who has spent the last decade committing the most heinous crimes here at this institution is finally behind bars and will soon be brought to justice."

Applause started in the front of the room and quickly spread to the back. George Franklin beamed and nodded and held up his hands for quiet.

"So the threat to the public's health and welfare is over, as is the threat to the dignity and viability of this institution. In this light we are instituting a vigorous ad campaign to restore the public's faith in our ability to provide not only adequate, but superior care and in a friendly, and in fact," he paused and his voice softened, "truly old fashioned way."

Marilyn wondered if he had worked on that touch with a voice coach. She smiled to herself, and leaned back, her palms against the wall behind her. She looked up at the little holes on the ceiling and wondered what her father was really here to say. He never, ever made his presence felt merely to deliver good news.

"Now there are still new HIV cases," he said, shifting his glasses lower on his nose and raising an eyebrow. "Because of the virus's incubation period, these would have been introduced before Dr. Sticker's arrest. So while the public threat's been eliminated, the perception of it may not be. I urge you all to keep this situation in mind and understand that prudence and tact are of the utmost importance." His voice softened again, and Marilyn shook her head and laughed to herself. A kinder, gentler daddy was so uncharacteristic!

"This is a time for us to move forward. Let's do it together, tactfully. Let's deliver the care we're here to deliver, but let's understand that this is not a time for alarms. We know who was responsible for these atrocities. He's in custody. We have closure." He smiled. "That's it, people. Let's get back to work."

Marilyn closed her eyes against the surreal scene. His smile brought a terrifying vision. When she was little, she had seen him smile only when some new and terrible pronouncement was going to come down, some verbal whipping that would be delivered with a frozen appearance of benevolence so that he could claim that the perception of malice was all in her head—or Eleanor's or Georgie's.

She hadn't thought of Georgie in a long time. As it always did, the thought of her baby brother brought up a volcanic rage, and she turned and pushed blindly through the crowd and out of the room, holding her breath, before it got the better of her.

* * *

BEN

Nothing was what it appeared to be, but there was an answer—that was the TV show's message. Ben's head was in Eleanor's lap. A bag of potato chips, a box of tissues and two beers lay on the floor next to the couch.

"See, you can't tell them from humans at all," Ben was saying. "The only way to tell is when one of them gets cut. As soon as it's exposed to air, the blood turns to metal. It's all in the blood."

Eleanor blew her nose. "No way."

Ben nodded, then sneezed and ground his head purposely into her lap until she giggled.

"Way!" he countered.

"I think we're supposed to identify with them," she said. Her hand cupped the side of his face.

"Ooh, your hands are cold! Yeah, I agree with that, but only to a point. Sometimes the enemy is among us. That's really the point of the show. We never know quite who is who, and even when we do, there's something we identify with about the killer and there are usually things we don't like about the heroes."

"And heroine."

"Hmm?"

"Heroine."

"Oh."

"Ben, can I ask you something?"

"Nah. You can only tell me things. It's Saturday. No interrogatives allowed. Only declarative sentences on Saturday."

"What?"

"I'm kidding, silly. Ask away."

She slapped the side of his head. "You know, you're very weird."

He looked up at her. "Yeah, well at least I'm from earth! You're the one who identifies with the martians!"

She lifted her hand to a point over his face, pointed two fingers downward as though she were going to poke him in the eyes. "You have seen nothing and will remember nothing!"

"So?"

"Well, about this hospital thing. You really think my sister committed those murders?"

He sat up next to her, took a sip of beer. "I didn't say that."

She got up and walked across the room, turning to face him at the doorway. "Well, I'm telling you she didn't do it. Marilyn's a sweet girl. She's a loner, she has a bad temper, she's angry at my father because of what happened to Georgie, but that doesn't make her a killer. Does it?" She glared at him.

"No."

She turned off the television, and was momentarily silhouetted by its fading glow. "And they do have a suspect in custody, don't they? Don't they?"

"Calm down, El. I'm just trying to get to the bottom of..."

"I don't know what you're trying to do, Bennett. That's the problem. I mean, what is this about? Your first big account?" She waved her arms and walked toward him. "You need to be sure your account will be successful, right? So you've got to solve a goddamn crime, right?" She kicked her beer over for emphasis, and watched the foam dissolve into the rug. "I mean, Bennett, please. Can't you leave her alone?"

"El!"

But she stormed into the bedroom, her red hair whirling.

Bennett sat in silence for a moment, then turned the TV back on.

The special agent was looking up at the sky, and then down again at his partner. "They're not from here. I can tell. They're from…out there."

When he had walked in, he had left his notebooks and papers on the bookcase near the door and he went and got them and sat back down on the couch, thumbing through his notes. Once he found what he was looking for, he reached over to the end table for the phone and began to dial.

"Hello? This is Ben James. Hi. It's nice to talk to you, too. Well, sure. I'm fine. No, it hasn't gotten to me yet, but I'm keeping warm and—oh, I drink orange juice in the morning and—vitamin C? Not specifically but, okay, I'll keep that in mind, Janice. Thank you. You did? Well how did you know I'd call?" He glanced at the bedroom door. Loud rock 'n roll shook the walls behind it.

"What's that? Well, I'm flattered. I think you're very nice, but I have a…in fact she's right—" The music had stopped. He lowered his voice. "Well, I just wanted to ask you a few more questions. Oh, that's okay, we can do it right here over the phone." He could hear Mattis's voice in his head shouting 'no, no, go out with her! A good detective sacrifices his personal life for the good of the case!' He ordered Mattis out of his head.

"Well, maybe we can meet, but Janice, please don't have any illusions…no, I'm not fighting it. I'm—okay, okay, five o'clock tomorrow. Yes, I know where it is. Me, too. See you then."

As he hung up, the bedroom door opened and Eleanor came out. She was wearing a red terrycloth robe that came down only to the top of her thighs.

"Aren't you cold?" Bennett asked.

She sat down on the couch, lifting the notebook out of his lap and tossing it aside. Papers slid from between its pages and spilled onto the floor.

"El, I need that stuff." He leaned over to collect them but Eleanor pushed him back.

"Who was on the phone?"

"Mattis. I'm meeting him for dinner tomorrow."

She looked surprised. "I thought he was agoraphobic and didn't like to go out."

"If he has a few drinks first, he can usually tolerate going out."

"I know what he means." She spun so her legs were over his lap; her arms went round his neck. She kissed him and slid down to the carpet. "Come on down here," she murmured, as the red robe slid from her shoulders.

* * *

As Ben walked into the Hewlett restaurant, a tall, slightly stooped man in his fifties in black slacks and a white short sleeved shirt that was open at the collar nodded and beckoned him in. "One?"

"Well, I'm meeting someone…Ah, I see her." Janice had stood up next to one of the red cushioned booths in the non-smoking section.

"Enjoy," said the man.

Ben approached the table with his hand out. "Nice to see you again. How are you?"

Janice used his hand as a handle to pull him toward her. Before he could pull away, he was locked in a tight embrace. Something thick and wet sloshed against his face.

"Benny! I'm so glad to see you again!"

The move was so deftly executed that he thought to ask if she had martial arts training.

A waitress appeared with two brown leatherette menus. "Would you like something to drink?" she asked as she slid the menus in front of them.

"Diet Coke," Ben said.

"Tea, lemon," said Janice. She paused, fingering her spoon until the waitress left. "You know they're saying diet drinks can give you headaches." Her eyes narrowed. "There's a lot they don't know about artificial sweeteners. You might want to stay away from them."

"Thanks, I'll keep that in mind. I, ah, wanted to ask you about Marilyn. Um. I know you've worked closely with her in the lab and around the hospital. I know she was your friend…" Janice was looking into his eyes, her expression, eager, rapturous—frightening.

Bennett willed himself to concentrate. "I was wondering if there was anything about her behavior that sticks out in your mind as odd or incongruous."

"Well," Janice lay one hand on top of the other in front of her and looked out the window at the traffic on Broadway. "She keeps to herself. She's very efficient, a good nurse. Works hard. I'd say she's angry."

"Why would you say that?"

"Well, she's quick to think you're criticizing her."

"Are you saying she's paranoid or angry?"

"Well, both, now that I think of it. She's paranoid. Off in her own world, I'd say. And she acts as though everything I say irritates her. She's quick to get annoyed. Quick to be wounded. Like she's a martyr, you know?" Janice looked at him, eyebrows raised, a hopeful smile on her lips. "She hates the way the hospital's run. I know she thinks it's not efficient. It doesn't do the best it can for patients. She feels the nurses are overworked, the bureaucracy's too unmanageable. She thinks the patients don't get the care they deserve. She gets really angry about that, and she feels her father has a lot to do with it."

"You've heard her say that?"

The waitress arrived with the drinks and waited. Janice ordered a tuna salad platter, Ben a cheeseburger and fries. "I know it's not good for me, but I like it," he said, seeing her take a deep breath.

"There's something I don't understand," Janice said, as she dipped the tea bag repeatedly into the steaming water. "They have Dr. Sticker in custody. He's a heroin addict, not that that makes him guilty of anything, but apparently he confessed. So why are you, an art director, looking for another suspect?" She lay her hand on top of his, and parted her lips in a toothy smile. "If you don't mind my asking."

"I don't mind...your asking." He pulled his hand away, took a sip from his drink. "I don't want to get too into that now, but there are aspects of the case against the doctor that just don't add up. A nurse would have more and better opportunity to commit the crimes without being noticed. And, you know what? My reasons don't make sense, even to me. I guess I feel some responsibility, because my job involves painting the hospital in a positive light."

"Ooh, you're so...moral. That's so—upstanding."

"And I just don't think Dr. Sticker did it. I'm not sure Marilyn did it, either. These are monstrous crimes and we have to check out all the possibilities." He paused. "I, ah, also am in a position, as art director for the hospital's ad campaign, to see that there's a certain amount of political pressure to pin this on someone. Of course they'd like to get the right person, and of course, everyone would agree that it would be a horrible mistake to accuse and convict the wrong man or woman, but this is a business, a for-profit institution. Nothing is worse, for everyone involved than not having anyone in custody."

Janice nodded slowly, a faint smile on her lips. "But what if the murders go on even after Sticker's convicted—if he's convicted?"

"Good question. Maybe they cover them up. These're patients getting a virus, after all, not gunshot or stabbing victims. It would be easy for hospital personnel to keep *themselves* in denial about it." He took a deep breath and leaned back. "That being said, I'd like to think that isn't what would happen. I'd like to think they'd re-open the investigation. Maybe they'd figure Sticker had an accomplice or they were copycat murders. It still wouldn't be pretty for Sticker, even if he is innocent. I'd just like to see that they get the right person, for the right reasons. And that all of this stops."

"Wow," Janice shook her head. She cleaned her glasses with a handkerchief she took from her purse. When she put them on, she seemed more focused, more serious. "Well, I don't really know if Marilyn does drugs, but she certainly has been moody lately."

"Keep in mind that these killings have been going on for years."

"Hmm. I can't honestly comment. She's always worked long hours, but so does every nurse. She has a lot of energy."

"Well, heroin would tend to have the opposite effect. She might fall asleep suddenly. Or seem tired, lethargic."

"She isn't lethargic, really." Janice shrugged. "Just moody. Sudden bursts of temper. Then, very nice."

Ben nodded. "Well, that might be valuable. Does she get sick often?"

"We've been through that. Yes, recently, it does seem that she's been sick more often. Of course, she might not have full blown AIDS yet. Oh, I just remembered something. She's in therapy."

"Lots of people are..."

"I remember that her therapist commented that she has a lot of repressed anger. Now for a therapist to say that, wouldn't you have to have more than—?"

He nodded slowly. "Maybe so. Thanks, Janice. Good job."

She smiled and looked down at her hand, which had moved to only an inch or so from his. "I'd like to ask you something. I, um, hope you don't mind my asking. It really isn't any of my business, but, ah, how's Eleanor?"

"Eleanor? She's—"

Janice interrupted, speaking very quickly. "I was just wondering because, you know, I like Eleanor a lot, and she doesn't seem as angry as her sister. But you know, I worry about you and your spending so much time with this woman who might be related to a very sick individual and, well, I've been concerned. She and I were close for a while, you know." Janice was looking him in the eye. "I'm concerned about you, Benny."

"Thank you."

The waitress arrived with the food and they began eating in silence.

"What're you looking at? Do I have some tuna on the side of my mouth?" Janice dabbed at the corners of her lips with a napkin.

"No, no. I was just thinking. You know, I saw a doctor in a short, white coat with longish blond hair and very wide eyes who looked exactly like—this is going to sound weird—but he looked just like a tattoo artist I met once." He shrugged and tried to look embarrassed at his overactive imagination. "I was just wondering—indulge me here—could someone pose as a doctor? Is that too far fetched?"

Janice laughed. "Around here, Mickey Mouse could probably perform heart surgery. Actually it would be pretty hard. Where'd you see him?"

"Coming out of a staff meeting."

"Now that'd be an especially hard place to pull it off. Around patients who don't know or are sedated, it'd be easy, but around other staff..." She shook her head. "By the way, if he was wearing a short coat, he was probably an intern. The longer the coat, the lower the rank. If he were impersonating a doctor, that'd be the way to go."

Ben nodded.

"It's hot in here," Janice said, unbuttoning the top button of her blouse and looking up at the aluminum air ducts that wound around the edges of the ceiling. Each time she reached for her tea, she leaned forward, and Ben was sure she was doing so for his benefit.

He hurried through the food, in part to get away from Janice, but also because he had decided on a course of action and had to get back to the hospital. Time was running out.

* * *

Bennett followed the dull blue light up the old wooden staircase. The only sound was the creaking of his own footsteps. He paused at the top of the stairs, listening for computer keys or music, but there was only silence and a distant fire siren. He stepped into the dimly lit room and flipped on the switch.

"Turn it off!"

The sudden screeching command startled him and his heart gave a violent lurch, but he turned the light off, and for a moment saw only fading purple and yellow flashes.

"What's the matter? Why're you sitting in the dark?"

Across the room, a mass on the floor stirred. "What's it to you?"

"Mattis, are you okay?"

"Ben-nefit, oh, man. I didn't know who it was. No, I'm losing it. I can barely go out anymore."

"What do you mean? We've got to get to the mall. Come on, Mattis. It's a mile from here! Marilyn's there. I followed her from the hospital. I figured you'd help me check out what she's doing. Who's better at stealth operations than you, man? Come on. Have a beer or whatever you need to go out, and let's go."

"I know about the park, now. The middle school. My therapist and me, we figured it out."

"So we won't go to the park, or the middle school. Listen, can't we talk about this later? We're going to the mall."

"The mall, the park, it's pretty much the same. We'd have to go past Mill Pond, right? It's a park, that's all that matters. I can't go. You don't have any idea how these attacks feel. They're a nightmare. They shouldn't be allowed. I'm not going anywhere."

Ben's eyes were becoming accustomed to the darkness. He could see Mattis, his stringy hair around his shoulders, obscuring his face as he sat on the floor on the other side of the room, covered up to his neck by a blanket.

"Something's out there. And whether it's tangible or not doesn't matter. I can't go out. My legs won't do it. Talk to them, if you want." He was biting his nails, chewing the ends of his fingers, his teeth clicking as he cut through each nail, his head turning as he tore it away.

"Listen to me, Mattis. You know nothing terrible's out there. You've been out there and you've been fine. You're okay, Mattis."

"No." He shook his head. "I'm not okay." His voice rose to a scream. "I'm LOSING MY GODDAMN MIND!"

Bennett took a deep breath. "Did it ever occur to you…that you do an awful lot of drugs and drinking?"

"Yeah, that's what keeps the little bit of my mind that's left in a comfort zone. It keeps what's out there—" he nodded towards the little window over his computer, "from getting in here." He tapped the side of his head and began biting his nails again. "And what're you, my father?" He pointed all of a sudden to the door. "Get out of here. Get out of my apartment."

Bennett sat down on the couch.

"What am I speaking, French? Get out!"

"Look, I know I do a lot of that, too. Maybe I'm a hypocrite, but I'm just wondering if you ever thought about cutting down a bit. I know someone who's been through something like that. In fact, he's been trying to get me to cut down a bit. Says I can talk to him about it, and...I don't know. It's...a thought."

"That's the first intelligent thing you've said. You don't know. That's right, you don't, so if you don't know, maybe you ought to shut up, don't you think? I'm telling you, I can't go out. You're going to have to check out your leads yourself. The problem is, people're looking in the windows. I can't stay in here either."

"No one's looking in any windows; we're on the top floor. What're they in, helicopters?"

"I'm not kidding..."

"Did you see them?"

"No, but I feel them. I know they're there. And they have cameras. It might be the FBI..." He uttered a little cry, "I'm bleeding!" He looked down at his fingernail and pressed it into the blanket.

Bennett sat back on the couch, his hands folded behind his head, his feet on the ottoman.

"Don't put your feet up there, you'll get that thing dirty. What, do you live in a barn?"

Ben shook his head. "Listen to you! You're trapped in here, all paranoid, and you're worried about me putting my feet up? Isn't that a little odd?"

For the first time, Mattis's tone calmed to a conversational level. "Not at all. If I'm going to have to spend all my time in a room, I want it to be the way I want it. It takes a certain amount of self esteem to feel that way."

"I'm sure it does. So if you can't go out and you can't stay here, what're you going to do?"

Mattis's voice shook. "I don't know. I'll, I'll have to, to stand in doorways or live in some kind of iron lung or be on permanent medication. I thought about killing myself but, talk about claustrophobic—can you imagine being trapped in a coffin for eternity? And I hate the smell of wood or cloth or whatever. I'd go nuts."

"Listen to you! You'd be dead!"

"I'd be staring into the same piece of wood, inches from my face. I've given this a lot of thought, Ben-Kenobi. Maybe being burned would be better! But what would they do with my ashes? I'd be in a jar! A tiny jar. Oh, I'm so claustrophobic! See, the options get worse—smaller and smaller containers! What am I going to do?"

Ben got up, glanced out the window.

"What, what do you see? What's out there?"

"Nothing. I'm watching a cop who's writing tickets to see if he's writing me one. I'm going to the mall to check out what Marilyn's doing. I can't pass this up, but I'll be back and we'll work this out together, okay?"

Mattis didn't answer.

* * *

INSPIRATION

They said the Man with the Hat was dead. Had a batch of the worst—or best—dope anyone had heard of in a long time and couldn't resist the temptation to find out if what he'd been hearing was the truth. The pull of dope like that was like the pull of sex, but better. You didn't need anyone else.

Your nose has been running for two weeks and the back of your throat is in constant contact with the front and your toes are numb from standing out in the cold looking for someone to cop from. It's so easy to find dope in the city; the Island's a different story. It's here but you've got to look. Hookers usually know.

"Hey sweetheart. Come here. Shh. You know where I can get?"

"For who? You? I don't think so." She looks you up and down. "I know you wearing a badge under there."

You laugh and tell her you'll pay double and she agrees if you pay half first, and stupidly you agree, knowing there's a seventy five percent chance she won't come back. And if she doesn't, you know you'll do the exact same thing again.

God damn the Man with the Hat! How can you make him pay? You walk around the block three times and the third time a police car slows and the driver watches you so you turn up the next corner and go into the all night diner, buy a pack of cigarettes, praying that the hooker doesn't come back right away.

You get back to the corner, your mind compressed into a tiny pressure cooker from the cravings, your stomach hurting and legs starting to ache. The police are gone and the hooker's back and she says "Okay, I only did this because you're not one of them, you know?"

And you're thankful and trying like hell not to look too eager. She gives you the bundle and you stuff it into your pocket, half hoping it's the same batch that killed the Man with the Hat.

And you have an idea. A new, inspired thought. A location, actually. Location, location, location. And this one will work wonders of revenge. You know where you can go after you get off, if not this time, then the next. A place that will provide a fresh new level of satisfaction. A new way to shock him, scare him, turn him inside out. All summed up in one word.

Babies.

11

BEN

Two men, one in a faded green ski parka, the other in a leather jacket covering a hooded sweatshirt, were forcing a hanger into the space above a car window. They glanced at Bennett as he passed them in the mall's parking lot. Bennett looked away.

He mentioned what he had seen to the blue uniformed security guard he saw inside the double glass doors at the nearest entrance. The officer, who appeared to be in his mid-fifties, shrugged. "What do you want me to do?" he asked. When Bennett continued to look at him he said, "Was it your car?" Bennett walked away.

The large drug store was part of a national chain. He watched Marilyn go in, looked in the window, then went inside. She had been wearing a kerchief. Her red hair peeked out in the front. Large dark sunglasses covered her eyes. He checked each aisle, looking at candy, inexpensive children's toys, magazines, beauty aids, stockings, contraceptives and soaps. Marilyn was gone.

He left the drug store and wandered out into the mall, wishing Mattis were with him. Mattis could think like a drug addict, could put himself in her place. There had been a time when Ben wondered about his friend's possible connection to the murders. Who, after all, would commit crimes like these? If the police and doctors were right about it being an addict, it would have to be one with a grudge against the hospital, and he'd heard Mattis rant about just about everyone and everything, the hospital included. He certainly had a paranoid streak; and he did ingest drugs regularly, though as far as Ben knew, heroin was not among them.

He passed a telephone island inhabited entirely by cigarette-smoking teenage girls. They alternated on the telephones and Ben had a sudden memory of talking to unknown women on "party lines," perhaps ten years earlier. It had seemed exciting then.

He saw a flash of auburn and sunglasses. She was on the phone, on the other side of the island. He circled around. Two of the teenage girls looked him up and down and snapped their gum at him. Marilyn was nodding and saying something. She coughed several times into her fist, then hung up and felt around in the coin return. Looking around, she hurried into a department store. Ben followed and watched her take a pair of pants from a rack without looking at the tags and go into a dressing room.

Five minutes later she came out without the pants but with a new, self assured walk, head up, shoulders back. As she left the store and reentered the mall, she took a tissue from her pants pocket and blew her nose twice. Ben followed her up and down the mall; she seemed to be window shopping, pausing now and then to look more carefully at this item or that, then moving on.

She approached the telephone island from which she had made her call and walked more slowly, looking around. A middle aged man, nondescript except for his black cap, was standing against a wall, smoking a cigarette. She approached him and shook his hand. As he had learned from Mattis, Ben watched the handshake closely and thought he detected a flash of white pass between their hands. They continued to talk; Marilyn sneezed several times, wiped her nose with a tissue and looked in his direction, her eyes sweeping the crowd and stopping at Ben.

She straightened her sunglasses, whispered something to the man in the cap and began walking rapidly away and to Ben's left. The cap man walked directly to the left, but neither away nor toward Ben. As Ben followed her, he tried to pass the man, who blocked him. Ben tried to move to one side, excusing himself when the man seemed to inadvertently move that way. He tried to go around the man's other side. The man moved the other way and laughed.

"Quieres bailar?" the man said.

"Sorry," Ben said again, finally moving around him, but when he looked, Marilyn was gone. He looked behind him but the man had vanished.

* * *

NED DOYLE

Ned was relieved to see that the restaurant was nearly empty. Coming to Benito's early, before six, ensured that there would be free tables and a suitable atmosphere for two young energetic boys. Maureen wore her black turtleneck and leather skirt, despite the cold. She looked sleek and sultry—ten years younger—when she dressed up. She wore the diamond pendent he had given her for their tenth wedding anniversary.

"It's so nice to see you again, Mr. Doyle," said the maitre d', a wan, elderly man wearing a thick toupee. "Hello, Mrs. Doyle. You look lovely! And the boys!" He stepped back, palms on both sides of his face. "I wouldn't have recognized such big boys!" Little Ned smiled his "good boy" smile. Frankie tugged at the cuff of Ned's pants.

"Cake!" he cried, pointing to a Viennese cart. "Daa! Caaakkke!"

"After supper," said Maureen. "First supper, then cake."

"Nooo! Cake!" Frankie insisted.

"We have a nice table near the window." The maitre d' gathered two menus and led them to the back corner of the room.

"Thank you, Micelli." Ned patted him on the shoulder. "It's nice to see you again."

As soon as they sat down, a busboy brought a basket of bread and breadsticks, which the two boys devoured, leaving piles of crumbs on the white linen.

"I wonder how Benito's been doing?" Maureen said.

"I hear they're okay. They get a good lunch crowd from the businesses over on Newbridge Road and the office buildings on Merrick Road."

She nodded and he noticed how pretty she was in her makeup, which made him realize how pretty she was without it.

"Well, it's a nice quiet place. Good for talking business. They don't rush you."

"No," Ned laughed. "That's one thing they don't do."

"Remember last year, on your birthday? We were here hours before they brought your veal!" Maureen giggled.

"I know, and you were on your dessert. We had to eat in shifts."

"Ahem. Drinks?" A young latino waiter, wearing a long sleeved white shirt and shiny black vest, was waiting, hands behind his back.

"Well, it wasn't the waiter's fault," Maureen said, smiling. The waiter nodded and smiled back as though he understood completely, then looked questioningly at Ned.

"Club soda," said Ned.

"Nothing for me," said Maureen.

"I'll have a scotch!" announced Little Ned.

"Scaa!" echoed Frankie, and he hurled half of a roll at his brother. It landed in a glass of water on the next table.

Maureen covered her mouth. "Oh, I'm so sorry!"

"Neddie!" Ned looked hard at his older son. His voice dropped to a threatening level. "And Frankie. No throwing!"

"It's all right," said the waiter. "No problem." He whisked the glass away. The couple at the next table pretended not to notice.

"Boys. Behave."

A man and woman had come in and were seated two tables away. A jolt went through Ned's body just below the skin; the woman was Barbara. He looked at Maureen but she was wiping bread crumbs from the front of Frankie's shirt. Little Ned was looking at him.

"What's wrong, Daddy? Mommy, Daddy's making a face like he just ate some pickles."

"Nothing's wrong, Neddie. Where's my soda?" He looked around for the waiter and managed a glance at the woman. It was not Barbara after all, but a woman who looked vaguely like her. Same dark, wild hair but the eyes were different. These were vacant, whereas Barbara's were alive and saw somehow into your heart. Ned exhaled and his body relaxed.

"So has the hospital account gotten back to normal?" Maureen asked. Frankie picked up a fork and jabbed it into one of his eyebrows.

"No!" Ned cried and grabbed the fork, slamming it down. "Jeez, Mo, can't you watch him?"

Maureen's eyes widened. "I am watching him." She took the silverware from Frankie's place and moved it to the center of the table.

"Mine! Mine!" Frankie said, and he began to cry.

"Frankie, it's okay—" Ned tried to keep the anger out of his voice, but it was a losing battle as Frankie's voice rose and became more piercing.

"Frankie Doyle, I'll take you out to the car!"

Frankie nodded. "Car! Go car."

Maureen closed her eyes, then opened them and looked at Ned. "Great. Now we'll have to eat at Benito's drive in."

"No, we'll eat here." Ned spoke slowly, controlling the simmering feeling high in his chest. His head had begun to ache, a pressure far in the back, where his neck met the back of his skull. “Actually, the account is doing well. We’ve shown the second set of proofs to Franklin and he likes them. You know, you’ve got to decode the way he talks. He’ll never tell you he likes something, but you can figure it out by the way he says he doesn’t like it. If his comments are about minor details, then you know he likes the general layout, the picture, and so on, as well as the service we’re providing. So I think we’re on the right track.”

The waiter arrived with the two sodas and took their order.

“And how’s Ben doing?” Maureen asked. “Is he more confident with his first big account than he was at the beginning? I remember he was terrified.”

Ned laughed. “He’s better, yeah. He’s doing a good job but I don’t think he’s comfortable with the way the police seem to have solved the murders, and of course, I think he might have a bit of a drinking problem.”

“And you’re trying to cure it?”

Ned looked annoyed. He mimicked her. “No, I’m not trying to cure it…”

Maureen sipped her soda and patted Frankie’s head. Little Ned was bouncing up and down in his seat. “I want spaghetti. I want spaghetti!” Frankie grinned and started to bounce in sync.

“Boys!” Ned pointed and glared at each of them. He clapped his hands sharply the way he did in the *dojang*. Everyone in the restaurant turned to stare.

“Ned,” Maureen whispered fiercely. “When you do that it sounds like a firecracker. It’s worse than anything the boys do.”

“Don’t tell me it’s worse.” He was suddenly simmering again. “This is a controlled situation, whereas the boys get out of control and can disrupt other peoples’ meals. That’s not appropriate and we have to do something about it.”

Maureen looked down into her lap for a moment. “So Ben doesn’t think that doctor’s responsible for the murders?”

Ned shook his head.

“So, who did it then?”

“I don’t know. You’d have to ask him.”

She paused. “Honey, what’s wrong?”

Ned didn’t answer. He looked in the direction of the woman who looked like Barbara. Maureen touched his chin and tried to turn his head toward her, but he resisted.

“Sweetie, what? Tell me…”

“Ooh,” said Little Ned. “Daddy’s mad at Mommy!”

“Yaah!” Frankie cried, throwing a napkin into thc air.

“Hey!” Ned’s voice whipcracked. “Boys! I said quiet!” Adrenaline course through him, exactly as if he were about to break a stack of cement blocks.

“Ned Doyle! Whatever’s bothering you, stop taking it out on your sons!”

* * *

He slipped between the cold sheets, pulling the blankets to his neck. Maureen was facing the other way; he couldn’t see if she was sleeping. The guilty ache in his chest had grown as the evening went on, undiminished by ice cream or time.

He kissed the back of her warm neck, and she turned, smiling, to him, and pulled him to her. He was surprised to find her naked, her skin hot, hands welcoming on his back. He rolled onto her and ran his hands down her sides, kissing her throat, and she returned his kisses and began to move against his legs in that circular Maureen way and soon they were in the natural flow that had become theirs over ten years of marriage and she was making those tiny Maureen sounds he loved so much.

Suddenly, they stopped. No one moved. A distant airplane approached, its landing gear descending, and roared off toward Kennedy Airport.

"I'm sorry," Ned whispered. He had barely been able to get the words out. They were the first words he had spoken since the restaurant.

"It happens," Maureen whispered.

"Not to me."

"It did once."

"Shut up."

"It's okay, honey." She touched his shoulder. "What's been the matter all night?" She tried to turn him to her but he pulled away.

He pressed his lips together. How could he answer her? "Nothing," he said and closed his eyes and rolled onto his side, facing away from her, the covers wrapped protectively around him.

After several minutes he heard her sigh, sniffle and reach for a tissue. Then the covers rustled and he peeked her way and saw she was facing the far wall.

The motor in his belly chugged and burped and he tossed and turned and finally, after an hour and a half, he went into the den and turned on the television. This combination of guilt, anger and self pity was how he had felt back when he was drinking. He knew he ought to talk to Sam, but on the other hand he really didn't want to. And he knew that it was exactly that stubbornness that was the biggest reason he ought to call. He had been through enough feelings like these to know the symptoms.

He picked up the phone and dialed Sam's number. The machine came on and he looked at the phone, knowing he ought to leave a message, let Sam know he was hurting. Screw it, he thought, hanging up. He stared at the phone in its cradle, fighting with himself, knowing what was right yet feeling old, powerful impulses. Finally, he went to the dining room table, got his work notebook and sat back down next to the phone. He opened the notebook, found the page he was looking for, and dialed Barbara's number.

* * *

MARILYN FRANKLIN

"Well, Mrs. Ellison, how are we today?"

Mrs. Ellison's eyes were half closed. "As well as you'd expect from someone who's lower half has been through World War Three, dear."

Marilyn smiled and held her hand. "You're doing just fine, dear."

"And how are *you* doing? Oh, you have a cold, Marilyn."

Marilyn nodded. "One of those winter things that grabs on and won't let go. Don't worry, I don't think it's contagious."

"Why don't you have a husband?" she glanced at Marilyn's finger. "Well, a boyfriend, then, to take care of you?"

The emotion disappeared from Marilyn's face. Mrs. Ellison saw the change and blinked, startled.

"I don't need a boyfriend to take care of me. I don't need anyone to take care of me. I do just fine."

"Well, I'm sure you do, honey. But a little love and affection never..." But Marilyn was already drawing the curtain around the bed. "Hmf. You just can't talk to some people," Mrs. Ellison said to herself, as she drifted off to sleep.

* * *

Sheryl was the new Well Baby LPN. She had started yesterday and while she had a basic understanding of proper medical procedure, Marilyn quickly saw that she had no knowledge of protocol or personnel or of the layout of the Medical Center. She would need an experienced nurse to show her the ropes, and Marilyn was elected.

She chose to ignore the fact that Sheryl was young and rather attractive in a blonde, mousy sort of way. Not everyone was capable of such professional detachment, Marilyn thought, noting that she frequently disliked patients as well. Some were racists, misogynists and worse. But hell, if she could work for her father, she could forgive anything!

"We'll be going over procedure for basic well baby care. It's not difficult, but we have a system."

"Don't I also have to know about other units? What about the ICUs and Maternity?" Sheryl asked.

"Those are specializations," Marilyn explained. "The nurses in those areas stay in those areas."

They walked quickly out of the elevator and down the long corridor. "You'll be answering to Dr. Beck and to me. Beck's the one with the gray beard."

Sheryl struggled to keep up; every third step she broke into a run. "What's Dr. Beck like?"

Marilyn shrugged. "He's by the book. If you keep everything sparkling and in order, you'll be fine. And treat the mothers right. Half of them don't know what they're doing. They're scared and think they don't know the right way to be a mother."

They rounded the corner and dodged a woman in a wheelchair being pushed by an orderly.

"So what do we do besides tend the babies?"

Marilyn stopped so short that Sheryl had to hold up a hand to keep from slamming into her. "Weren't you listening just now? We tend to the mothers almost as much as to the babies. We also help the physicians. We're an emotional as well as medical support staff."

Sheryl shook her head. "Sounds like we ought to get two paychecks for the two ends of the job, you know?"

Marilyn looked at her. "No, I don't know." She mimicked the girl's tone. "*Sounds like*...we're doing what we've been trained to do, *you know?*"

Sheryl looked as if she'd been slapped. "Yes, ma'am."

Sheryl watched while Marilyn quieted and turned the babies and supported the mothers. After a while, they switched roles, with Marilyn watching, arms folded over her chest. Now and then she offered commentary, terse and to the point.

"I hope you don't mind my asking," Sheryl looked at Marilyn, who had picked up a baby who had been crying so hard he had begun to choke, "but is George Franklin your father?"

Marilyn rubbed the baby's back, her hand making soft circles. Her eyes crawled up Sheryl's legs and body to her face. No other part of Marilyn moved. "Someone tell you that?"

"Yeah. At lunch. A technician in the blood lab."

"Heavy woman, red glasses?"

Sheryl considered for a moment. "I believe it was."

Marilyn's tone did not change. "Who my father is, is none of your business. If I wanted to be associated with that man, I'd wear a sign." Her eyes started to close, she raised a hand and Sheryl flinched, thinking she might hit her, but instead, Marilyn's hand went to her nose and her head jerked forward in a silent sneeze.

Sheryl's eyes widened. "O-kay...bless you."

Marilyn stepped toward her. "No, not okay. Not at all! You don't ask your superiors about their personal lives. You think that's appropriate? What, because I'm a woman you can do that with me? Would you ask Doctor Beck about his childhood? Would you ask Doctor Lapuda about his sex life?"

"Can I hold him?" Sheryl asked.

"I don't think so. Look, your hands are shaking."

* * *

JANICE

Janice was eating lunch in the lab. She wasn't supposed to, nor was she supposed to have the radio she had begun bringing with her. But she was lonely. Marilyn would never have tolerated these minor breaches of protocol. On the other hand, she thought, as she squeezed open the pop-top of her diet soda, glancing around nervously at the "pfft!," the fact that Marilyn spent so much time with her in the lab was itself a minor breach of protocol. Marilyn often bent rules—minor ones, yes, but rules nonetheless—so that she might write her report in the lab. Now that they seemed no longer to be friends, Janice thought it only fair to continue to bend rules to fill the void created by Marilyn's absence.

The packets that had come in from the blood bank were to be arranged by type before being stored, so Janice began what for many might have been tedious work. She sang softly to herself. It was amazing the way a little music could make a job more fun. Which Disney character had said that? An elf? A cricket?

The music stopped and Janice turned. She screamed.

Marilyn was standing next to the radio, arms folded, eyes fixed on Janice.

"How dare you," she said quietly. A hoarseness crept into her voice and she cleared her throat.

"H-hi, Mar. Long time…"

"Don't give me that. You know you're not supposed to have a radio in here." She reached up and yanked the cord from the wall socket, pulling the radio from its shelf above the counter. It crashed to the floor, its back panel flew off and batteries scattered on the shiny tiles.

"S-so? I'll bring it home."

"That's right." Marilyn took a step toward her; she cleared her throat again and coughed several times. "You know, you've got a big mouth." She pointed a finger and Janice stared at the tip of the finger as though it were a weapon, her eyes showing white around the pupils.

Janice tried to laugh. "Yeah-ah, I've been told."

"You told the new girl who my father is, didn't you?"

"No." Janice's voice quivered. "No!"

"I cannot tolerate lying!" Marilyn's face began to turn a deep red; the muscles in her forearms tensed. Blood drained from her face. Her eyes scoured the countertop.

Janice began talking very quickly. "If I did, I'm sorry. I didn't know what I was saying. You know how I like to gossip. If I did, that's all it was. Talk, harmless talk. I might have been trying to impress her with who I know. I'm like that. It's a lack of self esteem. An old issue, and I'm dealing with it. And you're, you know, one of the most experienced nurses, daughter of the CEO of the hospital. I know it's selfish to say I know you but, but that's all it was. It was about me, Mar, I swear." Her eyes welled and remained on Marilyn's hands.

Marilyn stopped moving toward her and for an instant all motion in the room stopped. A battery that had been rolling across the floor came to rest underneath the refrigerator. Marilyn relaxed, though she continued to look at Janice. In nearly ninety seconds, she had not blinked.

Now, the muscles in her face suddenly relaxed. Marilyn smiled. "How are you getting on with my sister's boyfriend?"

* * *

CHARLIE SPOON

Robin had hummed the same tune over and over again on the drive to the hospital and she was still humming as they walked across the parking lot. She stopped every few seconds to examine her footprints in the snow.

"See, daddy? I'm over there now!" She pointed to a footprint.

Charlie shook his head. "No, darling. That's just a footprint. It's not part of you. Just what your shoe does to the snow."

"I like snow! Snow likes me!" She resumed humming and Charlie took his daughter's hand and they began walking again. He had calmed enough to devise a plan. He would tell Dr. Maynard that he was changing insurance companies and that the next carrier would cover her program until Robin was eighteen. The paperwork was filled out and in the works. It just hadn't come back yet. That would buy him time to figure out something else. What that would be, he didn't know yet, but he'd think of something. He had to. Robin had to be in this program. As soon as she'd started with Dr. Maynard, she'd started speaking better, understanding better, and best of all, she'd been happier. Fewer tantrums, more singing, more loving and kisses for her daddy. He'd go to hell and back, just as he had before, to keep her with Dr. Maynard.

He held the door for Robin and together they entered the hospital, walking right past the security attendant at the front desk, and into an open elevator.

"Going up?" Robin said, smiling and pushing the two button and then, after a pause, the three, four and five buttons. "Elevator go for a ride," she said, giggling. Charlie smiled and shook his head.

A bucket and mop stood on the shining floor outside the elevator on the second floor; a rope and a paper sign stretched across the hall. "Wet Floor" read the sign, and Charlie led Robin around it and toward Dr. Maynard's office. They paused outside the door; Charlie strained to hear the class, but there was no sound. Was the therapist reading to the class, showing them a movie? He edged the door open. The room was dark.

* * *

BEN

Bennett took a can of tuna fish from the cabinet over the refrigerator, went to the sink and fished around in the soapy water until his fingers found the can opener. Dressed in tight jeans, a leather vest and a t-shirt, Eleanor watched him from the couch.

"Want half?" he asked. She shook her head, still watching him. "When's the last time you ate?" She shrugged. "When's the last time you spoke?" She smiled, her eyes never looking at him, but at a space on the wall where light played from the stained-glass chandelier hanging over the kitchen table.

"You pissed at me?" Bennett asked, reaching into the sink and opening the drain. He waited while the water and soap ran out, then drained the can of tuna and brought a bowl and fork to the counter.

Eleanor didn't answer.

"How're we going to get anywhere if you don't tell me what's on your mind?"

"Just because Marilyn was one of many nurses to care for the people you talked to doesn't mean she killed anyone."

He opened the refrigerator and took out the mayonnaise and a plastic bag containing a washed head of lettuce. "No, I suppose it doesn't."

"That's what they call circumstantial evidence."

He turned to face her. "I'm glad we're talking about this, because there's other circumstantial evidence. Did you know your sister's a drug addict?"

Eleanor gave a quick breath out through her nose; Bennett wasn't sure if it was out of surprise or amusement. She looked into her lap. "A drug addict? Marilyn? I don't think so."

"Well, I think so. You deny she's involved with drugs?"

"Who isn't involved in drugs, Ben? I know you've done cocaine with your computer-head pal, or at least been present."

"Scuse me. Been present? Yes. Done it? No." He sang the last two words. "Thank you."

"Well, aren't you putting a little guilt on *me* by association? My sister works hard. She has one of the hardest jobs and she gets very little credit for it. Do you have any idea how hard an RN works? The hours? The stress?"

Ben looked up. "And working for your father, it's got to be that much harder."

Eleanor stared at him. "What do you mean?"

"I mean, from what you've told me, working for your dad isn't easy, that's all. I've met the man. I've done business with him, and I'll bet growing up in that house wasn't easy."

For an instant, tears came into Eleanor's eyes. "No, it wasn't." She swallowed and her voice grew strong again. "But Marilyn's a strong lady. She can cope just fine."

"By getting high?"

"If she does, it's recreational. I'm willing to bet."

"I'm not so sure I am. Not with hundreds of lives."

"You mean because she's a nurse? Stop being melodramatic."

Ben tore a paper towel from the dispenser over the sink, laid it on the counter and placed two pieces of rye bread on top of it. "Did you ever want to be a nurse?"

Eleanor looked surprised. "Why would you ask me that?"

"Just a feeling I get from the way you talk about your sister. Like you admire her—what she does, yet you know how hard it is."

"Actually, I worked at the hospital years ago."

"What happened?"

"It...didn't work out."

He wanted to ask more, but the look on her face told him not to, not now. He finished making his sandwich. "Sure you don't want half?" She shook her head. "I can cut it. I'll cut it diagonally. Remember sandwiches cut diagonally? My mom used to do that. Did your—"

"I don't want to talk about my mom."

He blinked. "Okay. All right. We don't have to talk about anything you don't want to talk about."

Eleanor took a deep breath. Her eyes came into focus and looked at Ben. "I was a pre-med student a few years ago, believe it or not, and I worked at the hospital, first as a candy striper, then as a sort of LPN."

"But you didn't have the training to do a lot of things an LPN would do..."

"So I didn't do those things, but I helped out as much as I could. I stayed around Marilyn a lot."

Ben carried the paper towel with the sandwich over to the couch and sat down next to Eleanor. "What happened?"

She shrugged. "Some problems I had got in the way."

"Like what?"

"What difference does it make? It's too late to do anything about it now."

"It might be nice to talk about it."

"It is." She touched his leg. "It's good to have someone to talk to, but that only goes so far."

"What about Marilyn?"

"It was hard for her at first, working for my father. He's a bastard. Not a feeling bone in his body. But she's the toughest of us and if any of the three of us could cope, she could."

"The three of you?"

"You don't know about Georgie?"

"I think you told me about him once..."

"He was the kindest person I've ever met in my life. My father—my father didn't approve of his lifestyle. And so...he killed him." She looked into her lap, then into Ben's eyes.

He stopped eating and held up a hand. "You're saying your father killed your brother?"

"He might as well have. Technically, it was a suicide, but my father drove him to it with his intolerance and the way he tore Georgie apart. He did that with all of us. Just ripped into us with words. How do you think that made us feel? I mean we were kids."

Bennett put the half eaten sandwich on the end table. He leaned toward Eleanor and massaged her thigh. "It must have been awful."

She slapped his hand away. "I don't need sympathy. I learned how to cope with all this years ago. Ever hear the saying 'What doesn't kill you makes you stronger'? Well, Marilyn and I are plenty strong. And whatever you might think, you'll never get me to believe that Marilyn killed anyone."

"Okay." He leaned back on the couch. "But you have to admit it all makes sense. Especially with your father running that hospital. It's a helluva way of getting back at him." They sat in silence. Outside, garbage cans rattled as they were moved and covered. "So, how did you guys learn to cope?"

Eleanor lay back against him; he could no longer see her face. "We found things to occupy our attention. My sister got into writing. She kept a journal; she wrote stories."

"And you?"

"I've always liked science. Even though she's the nurse, I always liked chemistry, nature."

Ben didn't answer.

"I know you think my sister's involved in these murders, Bennett, and you're welcome to your opinion. But wouldn't those patients—"

"Victims..."

"Wouldn't the patients you talked to have been medicated? Wouldn't some of them have had a tough time being sure of who they saw and what was going on, particularly since they acquired this virus years ago? I mean eight years, ten years after all!"

"I guess that's true."

"And even if Marilyn did tend to them, what does that mean? Does it mean she purposely infected them with HIV?" She sat up, spun around, grabbed him by the shoulders. "I don't think it means a damn thing. I think you're just coming after my sister because it fits your little theory. They have someone in custody, you know."

"I know. Look, El. I think it's admirable that you defend your sister. And I feel for all you've been through—"

"You don't feel anything." She pushed him away, got up and went into the bathroom, slamming the door behind her. A moment later, loud music crashed and boomed from behind the door.

Later that night, she climbed into bed and to Ben's surprise, she pulled him close and they made love, and she had never been so tender. Afterwards, she clung to him, her face wet against his chest, and he felt the feathery flutter of her eyelashes.

* * *

Ben climbed the creaking wood stairs the following day. His legs ached. He no longer cared about the Medical Center account. When he was excited about work, it crept into his thoughts when he was doing other things. Creative ideas came to him while he was shopping or driving or even as he was falling asleep. But the murders and who might have committed them had occupied so much of his energy that the fun, creative part of his mind had been forced to work on that single, tantalizing problem to the exclusion of all else. He had become obsessed.

He paused at the top of the stairs, listening for keystrokes. He wanted to be polite, to let his best friend know he was coming.

"Mattis?"

He remembered that Eleanor had once suggested that Charlie, the tattoo artist, had committed the crimes because he had some sort of personal grudge against the hospital. He remembered the intern who had looked so much like him. Last night, she had mentioned the tattoo artist again. Ben remembered the man as angry, a drinker. The man took his problems to a bar stool. Was that the appropriate thing to do, as someone had said? Who had that been?

"Mattis, you there?"

He walked toward the room, which was lit only indirectly by the single yellow bulb in the bathroom off the other end of the bedroom. That was odd, Ben thought. Normally, the computer would be on, its glow visible from the hallway. Perhaps Mattis, with his therapist's help, had learned to let go of his computer and live on his own in the light of day.

Ben stepped into the room. No one was there. That was even more odd. Mattis never went anywhere alone, and the only person he trusted enough to allow into the house, the only person he would leave with...was his best friend.

So where was he?

Ben looked around. The apartment looked as it always did. A mess. Beer cans strewn around the floor along with t-shirts and socks. Ben moved closer to the computer on the desk and saw that it was on, but its screen was black. On the keyboard was a slip of paper on which one word was written.

"Bennett."

He picked up the paper and turned it over. On the back were written two sentences:

"Press any key and when the screen comes on type in my password. Once you've logged onto the Internet, type in the following URL address: www.mattis.net."

Having been with Mattis hundreds, perhaps thousands of times while he was either conducting business, trying to meet "cyberdates" or surfing, Ben knew his password. After pressing the spacebar and seeing the "connect to internet - enter password" screen come up, he typed "help," followed by "enter." He sat down and entered the URL Mattis had given him and, after a moment, a dark green screen came up with what he thought was Mattis's photograph. Only when it blinked did Ben realize that what he was looking at was not a photograph, it was Mattis himself.

12

BEN

"Ben-ificient! I knew you'd come. I've never been so glad to see anyone."

He looked terrible. Dark circles rimmed his eyes, his hair was more disheveled than usual and lines of fear crept out and downward from the corners of his mouth. He glanced continually to either side.

"Where are you?" Ben stammered. "Let me know and I'll come get you. What the hell's going on?"

"I've given up my RL for a URL, an internet address."

Ben searched his memory. "I know what a URL is, but what's an RL?"

"Real Life. I can't live like other people anymore—out in the open." He shivered. "I, just can't. So I'm going to exist through the Internet. You can talk to me at this address. Even take me with you, if you can get a hold of a laptop. It's the only way I'm willing to experience the outside world."

"Where are you? What are you talking about? What the hell happened?" Ben grasped the sides of the desk, bracing himself and taking deep breaths.

Mattis looked down and seemed to be trying to make a decision. "I had a breakthrough with my therapist. I've found out what's been scaring me about parks, why I've been so terrified of them, why I can never go out unless I'm half in the tank…I remembered being buried alive, when I was—I dunno, six or seven. Not just that it happened, but the details of it!" His voice went up into a squeak and Ben thought he might cry. Mattis took a deep breath, swallowed, and looked at his friend. "Anyway, I don't feel safe anymore. Anywhere. I can't go out or see anyone. The world's just too much for me. It's won. So, I'm going to stay in cyberspace from now on, where it's safe."

Ben wanted to blurt out how ridiculous that was, but knew his friend too well. He generally thought that about two thirds of what Mattis had to say was ridiculous and not particularly connected to reality, but telling him that would only drive him away permanently. Mattis had never been willing to trust people, and the reason he trusted Ben was that Ben took him seriously. So Ben listened.

"But that's not why I wanted you to contact me. I want to continue to help you solve the murders. Together, we can do it. Your nurse friend. I remember her, I think, from the time we went to that lab and met her and that technician with the red glasses. Since then, I'm pretty sure I've seen her at the club, and I'm almost positive that she puts enough chemicals into her body to…well, to make me back off."

"You?" Ben made a gesture of surprise and accidentally touched the keyboard and the screen went blank.

"Hey! Who turned out the lights!" Mattis yelled. "Quick! Hit Control Enter Shift 'Y.' Ah, ooh, that's better. Yeah. Jeez, don't do that again."

"Do what? I have no idea what I touched."

"Then don't touch anything. You might erase me, or corrupt my disc or…it's too horrible to think about. Anyway, that nurse is at the club all the time. So I can't see that she should be in charge of taking care of people, at the very least. That doesn't make sense. It's got to have something to do with that father of hers. What do you have on motive? What'd her sister tell you?"

Ben nodded. "Some interesting facts. Did I ever mention that they had a brother, Georgie, and it seems that their father was somehow responsible, at least by neglect or verbal abuse, for this kid killing himself years ago? Eleanor really loved her brother. I've never seen her so shaken up as when she told me about it. I can only assume that Marilyn loved him, too. It sounds as if he was the opposite of his father. Sensitive, compassionate."

Mattis raised an eyebrow and brought his face close to the screen. "And you wonder why I'm in here? World's a delightful place, isn't it, Ben-there-done-that?"

"Anyway," Ben continued. "Eleanor blames her father and if Marilyn's warped by chemicals and anger and whatever genetic material makes this whole family so wacky…"

"You know, I've learned a thing or two in therapy. If this father's as tough a son of a bitch as everyone says…"

"Believe me, he's my client, so I know. He's a tough bastard. Not a nice man…nobody likes this guy except the patients at the hospital. Them he treats like gold."

"So? What does that mean. No one likes me, but that doesn't mean I'm not a nice guy."

Ben frowned into the screen. "If you don't stop feeling sorry for yourself I'm going to shut the screen off, now." He reached for the "escape" key.

"No, no! Don't do it! Okay. I'm sorry. I was feeling sorry for myself. Listen, what I was going to say was maybe Marilyn feels impotent towards her father. There's no way to get at him, so she gets at the hospital, ruins its reputation and his along with it. To her, the hospital *is* him. And she works there, so she has the means. So now we have a motive, a means, and circumstantial evidence in that victims seem to remember her."

Ben nodded, raised both eyebrows. "Seem to, seem to. Either way, now's the tough part: convincing the cops and the hospital staff that the CEO's daughter committed the crimes because the CEO was responsible for the death of his own son. Not much tougher orders than that, especially when the cops think they have their man."

Mattis sighed. "No? Ever tried to satisfy a real appetite with a cyber-burrito?"

* * *

DR. MAYNARD

Dr. Jane Maynard opened the door, but tried to close it again when she saw Charlie. "I'm sorry, Mr. Spoontag, there's nothing I can do for you. You'll have to settle this with the administrative office. I'm sorry but it's a reality of business."

"Where's the class?" Charlie asked, his fingers barely touching the smooth painted surface of the door.

"It's in another part of the hospital, but I cannot—"

"She needs to be in the class, dammit. You know that!"

"I'd like to see Robin back in her class too, Mr. Spoontag. The disruption in her routine is not good for her. But it's up to you to handle the insurance end."

He pushed the door open. Dr. Maynard looked startled and backed away, her hand pressed to her chest.

"We'll take care of the insurance. But in the mean time, isn't there something you can do for her?"

"Jane, Jane, friend of mane!" Robin cried, when she saw Dr. Maynard. She ran forward but Charlie caught her by the shoulder and pulled her back. Immediately, she began to wail.

The doctor looked pained. She knelt down. "Robin, I'm sorry, honey. I can't see you today. Your daddy and I are talking about how we can get together soon. Another day."

Robin's wail turned to a shrill scream.

"See how you're hurting her?" Charlie said. The scream was a serrated blade, sawing into his chest.

"Mr. Spoontag, I cannot be responsible for every individual's insurance." Dr. Maynard stood up, shaking her head and taking off her blue rimmed glasses. "It's a shame. Robin's been making significant progress."

"But can't you do something, even temporarily?" Charlie dropped his voice to a whisper. "Look the other way? You're in a position…"

"I'm sorry," Dr. Maynard said, "but there's nothing I can do. Really." She closed the door.

Charlie and Robin, who was sniffling now, stood outside the door.

"Reeeaallllyy?" Charlie drawled, to the door. He dragged Robin outside. He had to get outside, quickly. It was coming, he thought, and he couldn't stop it. They burst through the exit, just as the screaming roar erupted from his chest.

"Lllliiiiiaaaarrrrr!"

He would get a babysitter for tonight, then he would come back to the hospital. It would be just like the old days. At least he'd feel a little better doing things his own way. In fact, he felt better already. He glanced at his daughter.

Robin's eyes were wide with fear. She began to cry. "Where's Jane Jane Friend of Mane?"

"The Doctor's sick," he said.

"Nooo!!" Robin cried. She turned to her father and began beating his stomach with her fists.

* * *

BEN

"No, Mr. Franklin. I'm positive." Dr. Epstein waved Bennett to a seat in his office and switched the phone to his other ear. "It was, oh, about seven thirty last night, definitely dark out. I was working late, and I came out and there it was." He smiled vaguely at Bennett, and held up an index finger. "Well, what anyone would have done. I called Sergeant Michaels to report it."

Ben took the gold and black ball point pen from his top pocket and the pad from his rear pants pocket and wrote down "Sergeant Michaels." That would be his second errand.

"Yes, I did. Yes, I will. Three o'clock? I'll be there." He put the receiver down in its cradle, picked up a pencil and sat down behind his desk, holding the pencil horizontally between two fingers. "Well, Mr. James. I thought we'd finished our business."

"I'm not here to give you a hard time, Dr. Epstein. I'm asking a favor. I need a picture of a nurse."

Dr. Epstein gave a short nasal laugh. "I would have thought a young, athletic boy like you ought to be able to get the real thing."

"She's a suspect in the case. I need to show it to someone."

"Really?" The balding doctor adjusted his glasses and leaned back in his brown leather chair. "I was under the impression that Doctor Sticker was in custody, and he's far from being a nurse. Are you sure that's what you want the picture for?"

Bennett took a deep breath and shifted his weight in the hard wood chair. "My associate and I believe that the police are holding an innocent man—a heroin addict, yes, but not a murderer."

"Your associate?" Dr. Epstein tapped the point of the pencil in Bennett's direction. "And who would that be? Joe Mannix? Ironside? Sherlock Holmes?"

"No, a very intelligent young man who's...an expert in certain kinds of paranoid behavior."

"Really. And where is this..."

"He's, he's doing field research at the moment."

"I see." Dr. Epstein sat up straight and placed the pencil on the desk. "Well, I'm afraid that our personnel files are confidential, and even if I wanted to..."

"You know, Doctor, whatever the penalties for assault and battery are, they are probably not as nasty as George Franklin would be if he heard about it. We meet on a regular basis, you know, to discuss the ad campaign I'm art directing for him." Ben tapped his chin as if remembering. "He was so shaken to see that I had been attacked. And he was so sympathetic. We've developed an excellent rapport, really. I'm sure he would be thrilled to have some idea of who was responsible." He shook his head sadly. "Though finding out it was one of his own doctors, and another Chair at that, would undermine his confidence, not only in you, but in the whole personnel procedure..."

* * *

As he drove toward the precinct, Bennett glanced over at the passenger's seat to make sure that the picture would stay in its envelope, which he had closed but not sealed. Epstein had given him a note to take to the Director of Human Resources, a procedure Ben was happy with, since he had feared that even had he agreed to provide the photo, Epstein might have balked when he saw who the subject was.

Sergeant Danno Michaels sat in a windowless office behind a desk that was as plain as Epstein's was ornate. The wood it was made of was so old it was gray, and the legs had squared bottoms as though they were not lathed, but sawed off. The paint on the walls, once white was now gray, cracked and peeling. A picture of the President was hung behind and above the Sergeant, the President's neatly clipped hair and smiling face contrasting with the Sergeant's mussed, rumpled appearance and dour expression. His tired eyes lay in a bed of wrinkles, giving his face a dark, sad expression. He did not look up when Ben knocked.

He knocked again.

"Umhmm."

"Excuse me, sir. May I see you for a moment?"

A hand pointed to a backless bench opposite the desk and went back to writing.

"I'm here about the murder cases?"

The Sergeant looked up, stopped writing. "Which cases?"

"The HIV cases at the Medical Center."

"What about them?"

"I have some information I think might lead to an arrest."

Sergeant Michael's eyes circled the area around Ben's head, as though a fly were buzzing around him, then landed on Ben's face. "There's already been an arrest."

"Yes, sir. But I believe that person to be innocent—or at least innocent of murder."

"Oh? And why's that? Aren't you the ad guy from Three S Advertising over on—" He snapped his fingers twice, trying to remember the name of the street.

"Yes, sir. And as the art director of the Medical Center account I've had the opportunity to have contact with a great many hospital personnel, including the CEO, quite a few doctors—including your suspect—nurses, technicians, and many patients, including some of the victims. I, ah, was wondering, sir. Have the victims, people who've come to be HIV positive during their stay with the hospital, have they been questioned as to what they remember about their stay?"

The officer didn't move. "We don't comment on ongoing investigations. Why do you ask?"

"Well, sir. I've had the opportunity to meet quite a few of these patients and one thing they all have in common is a memory of one particular nurse." He took the photo from the white envelope and handed it to the gray haired police officer. "Marilyn Franklin, sir. She was recognized by a majority of the surviving victims."

"Isn't she the daughter of—?"

"George Franklin. The hospital's CEO."

Michaels ran his fingers back through his hair. "Jesus Christ," he said.

"My associate confirms that this nurse has a drug problem—"

"Your associate?"

"Well, yes. He's really a friend. Richard Hatters."

"Is he an investigator…or another artist?"

"Neither, sir, although his powers of deduction are remarkable. He sells computer programs on the internet."

"Ah, well then, he's certainly qualified to investigate..."

"But he has had some involvement with the, ah, element of people she's associated with and he confirms that Ms. Franklin has an involvement with drugs." The effort to talk the way he imagined a police officer would was becoming exhausting. Phrases like "involvement with" and "method of" spun in and out of his consciousness.

"She also has an ax to grind, sir."

"Really, against who?"

"Whom, sir."

"What?"

"Against whom. Never mind. Her younger brother, Georgie, committed suicide years ago, and she blames her father. So she could be committing the murders to get at the hospital and thereby get back at her father."

Sergeant Michaels nodded slowly, his eyes never leaving Ben's. "You've been a very busy fellow. You must be one crack ad man to have this kind of free time."

Ben shrugged. "It really has kind of fit with my current assignment sir."

"I'd venture to say that what you've told me, young fella, troubles me deeply."

Ben let his shoulders relax. "I'm glad to hear that, sir. Shall I leave the picture—?"

The sergeant's eyes hardened. "It troubles me that someone in no way connected with the force would be out there, a loose cannon, taking police matters into his own hands." The officer pointed at Ben. "It also concerns me that citizens—ill citizens, possibly dying citizens—have had what little time is theirs disturbed by someone in no way connected with the case, in such a way that their cooperation with the police might be compromised."

"Sir, I—"

The officer's eyebrows lowered, and both heavy palms came down hard on the desk. "Now you listen. You've tampered in a police matter. I could have you arrested right now. I ought to have your boss's ass in a sling for letting you run loose like this. So, if you've been counting, that's two things you ought to lose: your job and your freedom. I want you to be very, very grateful when I let you walk out of here with both those things still in your possession."

"But, sir. The circumstantial evidence is—"

"Do you have a hearing problem? I don't want to know your opinion of the evidence. Just say 'Thank you Sergeant Michaels' and then get the hell out of here!"

Ben pressed his lips together, looked down into his lap. "Thank you, sir." He put Marilyn Franklin's photo back in the envelope, stood up and walked toward the open door.

Sergeant Michaels called after him. "And don't take any sudden vacations!"

* * *

MAKING ROUNDS

"How are you feeling Mrs. Hoffman?"

The woman looked up from her bed. "Oh, I'm okay, thanks. My baby's not eating much, I'm afraid. I bring him up to my breast but he doesn't seem to want to eat."

What to say, what to say. Try to remember. Smile, smile, smile. "It happens, dear. And you'd be surprised how often. There's nothing to worry about. Nature will handle it. When he's ready to eat, he'll eat. He's just not used to using his mouth. He'll have to learn. Just keep bringing his mouth up close and know that it may take a while. He'll get the idea."

"I'm glad to hear you say that. I was beginning to think there was something wrong with me." She clutched the blue hospital gown close around her. "It's chilly in here. These don't do much for keeping you warm, do they?"

"I'll order you a blanket, Mrs. Hoffman. And don't worry, there's nothing wrong with you."

Not yet, anyway. This wasn't going to be easy. Not a lot of IVs around. There had to be a way. Injecting the virus was a possibility, but the patient would probably wake up. Unless…

"You've changed something, haven't you?" Mrs. Hoffman said. "Your hair, or you lost weight. You look different somehow."

But no one was there to answer.

* * *

ANNIE FLOWERS

Annabel Flowers sat bolt upright in bed, the green and blue tartan blanket up around her neck. She looked quickly at the window. A tree branch swayed in the wind; a plane blinked as it flew west, towards Kennedy Airport.

He was coming.

She felt that Kenneth-fear that cut her lung capacity in half and drew the blood toward the center of her body, away from her suddenly cold skin. Her home was no protection against him. This had been his home until she had thrown him out; he had supervised its building; he knew every inch of it, including the alarm combination.

Sweat broke out on the back of her neck and ran down her back, sticking to the thin white cotton of her pajamas. She sat utterly still, listening. Perhaps she had been wrong. She had known her sensory ability to be wrong once or twice, though usually about insignificant matters that were more questions of interpretation: she had sensed that she would win a small lottery payoff and had instead benefitted from a surprisingly generous tax return. And at the diner last year she had warned Ned Doyle about undercooked eggs when in fact a man at the next table had been served contaminated fish.

Then she heard it.

A series of intermittent beeps. The sound of the house alarm being tripped. Someone was in the house.

She waited a few seconds: either the alarm would go off or, if not, it would have been disabled. She wished it would sound, waking up the neighborhood, but it didn't.

Kenneth had entered the combination.

She stared at the phone on the windowsill on the other side of the room, and rushed suddenly for it, picking up the receiver and dialing 911.

"Please state the nature of the emergency."

"My husband's broken into my house and he's about to—"

"What is the address, ma'am?"

"Six eighteen—"

The door flew open and he was on her, ripping the phone from her hand, hanging it up and hurling her to the bed. "Honey, honey. Who are you talking to in the middle of the night?" His long brown hair hung over his eyes, which were wide with adrenaline and beer. Bits of saliva clung to his moustache.

"Nno, one. Lydia, from the office."

"You don't have to call the police. I'm not going to hurt you. I love you. You're my wife and I'm here to work it out."

"Kenneth, we've been through that already. We're getting divorced. After what happened—"

He leaned over her, pinning her down. "I told you I was sorry about that. How long are you going to punish me for one mistake?"

"It's not one mistake, Kenneth. This isn't about that one time. It's about your getting help and..."

"Help for what?" He bent close and she smelled alcohol and sweat. How long had he been wearing those clothes? She tried shifting her weight but couldn't move.

"Where're you going?" he wanted to know. "It's okay. You don't have to be afraid of me."

She looked hard into his eyes. "Then why don't you let me up?"

"I will. If you promise not to go running out of here or do anything stupid."

"I promise." She tried to imagine she were somewhere else. With Bennett. *Bennett, oh, where are you? What are you doing right now?*

Kenneth stood up but was tensed, waiting for her to run, so she lay there, looking at him but thinking of Bennett. *Bennett, do you still love your girlfriend? You never talk about her. You have no picture of her on your desk, so it can't be serious, can it? Is she just a rebound from Beth?*

"There, that's better. Not so bad, is it, Ann? See? I'm not going to hurt you." He grinned, uneven teeth showing below his moustache.

He was going to rape her; the sense said so.

"Kenneth, if you want to work this out, you'll have to leave and talk to me about it over the phone until I'm ready to see you."

He lit a cigarette and took a deep inhale, looking around for somewhere to throw the match. He lay it on her dresser. Their dresser. "So, if I go, you'll call me Monday and we can talk and then I can come back?"

"We'll talk about it and see." Her legs were shaking.

He sat down next to her on the bed, his hand on her back, the other hand still holding the cigarette. "Wish I could believe you, Ann. But I don't. I don't think you'll let me back in if I leave. Don't think you'll ever make love to me again, without…a little help."

As he spoke, her eyes focused on an object on the other side of the room. It was an object she had forgotten about and now she could not believe she had forgotten about it. It was a Panic Button—part of the house alarm. Pushing it alerted the Central Station who would then send the police, without any confirming phone call.

She forced her body to relax, even to curl around his a tiny bit. "All right. Maybe you can stay a little while. We did have some nice times. But you've got to be gentle and you've got to put out the cigarette. There's a cup on the dresser with a little water in it. Why don't you put it in there?"

He smiled down at her. "That's my Annie. I knew you'd come to your senses." He got up and walked over to the cup. "You won't regret—"

She flung the blankets back and was out of the bed in one motion. With a leap she was across the room, her finger on the button. She pushed it.

Recognition was slow to dawn on Kenneth's face, but when it did, the rage boiled over instantly.

"You liiiiieed!" he screamed, grabbing her by the shoulders and hurling her back against the wall. The air was slammed out of her and she was temporarily unable to breathe, her chest heaving in little convulsions as it tried to get back its ability to take in air. She swallowed, her throat making a clicking sound.

"The police are on their way," she managed to croak.

"So? This is a domestic dispute. They hate getting involved with families."

"This is an attempted *rape!"* She hurled the word at him. "This is assault and battery! This is it, Kenneth! It's over! Get out! *Get out!"* Her voice was a hoarse scream and she grabbed for anything she could find—European painted-glass figurines she had collected for years, many of which Kenneth had bought for her for birthdays, anniversaries and Christmases. One hit him in the arm; another shattered against the door.

"Hey! Those're expensive!" The absurdity of his words made her laugh through her rage.

"The police'll be here any second, Kenneth. Wanna wait around?" She suddenly felt safe again. Her sense said the police were on their way and the danger was over. For now.

"I'm never going to leave you alone, Ann. We're meant for each other." He pointed a finger at her, gave her a hard look and then he was gone. She heard the back door close downstairs.

She took a deep breath. Tears were running down her cheeks and she was trembling. She had never felt so alone. The boys at the office, Art and Lou, were her only confidants but they were so different, like sweet old aunties who doted on her and covered their mouths in shock whenever she shared a personal revelation.

She got up, put on her slippers and shuffled across the room, carefully avoiding the broken glass. She looked at herself in the mirror that hung on the back of her door. She looked like a clown: all orange hair and lips.

A noise downstairs made her shake, the air rushing out of her. She realized it was the police.

* * *

BEN

The computer dialed the seven digit number, then beeped and wheezed like an old Ford as its modem connected to the host computer.

Establishing connection...successful...

Mattis's face appeared on the screen, yawning. "Hey."

"Hey," said Ben. "Howya feeling?"

"Cool."

"Cool. Ah, can you work in there?"

"Work? Sure." Mattis grinned. "I have the perfect job for this. In fact, it's like I'm living at my job. Think of it. I sell computer equipment on the internet and now my only connection with the outside world *is* the internet. It's like I've moved into my job. I can bank from in here, even order food."

"Yeah, and I know about the sex."

"Nowhere better." He laughed. "Though it's a little third person. So, inspector, how goes the investigation?"

"That Sergeant Michaels isn't too thrilled with me. Says I'm messing with police business."

Mattis grinned. "They hate it when you do that. Guess it's our ballgame, then. How you holding up? Learn anything new from your girlfriend?"

Ben shook his head. "Not since she told me about Georgie. I think that brought us closer together. She trusts me and, and something about that changed everything. It's like we crossed over and now she's really my girlfriend. Like she was hard to get to know, hard to trust. She didn't really let me in. But now she has and, it's like everything's changed, for both of us." Bennett looked up, suddenly blinking back tears, at the ceiling. "I think Beth's finally out of my head."

"Cool." Mattis nodded. "But don't let it get in the way of this investigation. We may have to turn in your girlfriend's sister. Think you're up to that, Ben-Gurion? If she suddenly trusted you when you accepted the news of her brother, how's she going to react when she finds out you turned in her sister?"

"Yeah, I've thought of that." Ben swallowed and looked hard at the screen. "It pisses her off that I think Marilyn's involved. They don't seem close at all, yet she's protective as hell. But look, girlfriend or not, if Marilyn's killing people in that hospital, and we're the only ones who know the truth...what are we going to do? Keep it a secret? If she holds that against me, then maybe this wasn't going to work out from the beginning. Besides, I'd hope she'd see the reality of the situation—how this might relate to what happened years ago."

Mattis's hand reached out toward the screen and his image bounced for a moment. "Attaboy, Ben-kenobi."

"Besides," Ben went on. "She has problems. She's been hurt. I can help her."

"Ooh, be careful about that. Don't play nurse."

"All right, all right. Let's focus on the subject at hand. How're we going to catch Marilyn in the act? That seems to be the only way we're going to convince the cops that this Dr. Sticker isn't the killer."

"Not easy." Mattis bit his lip. "Follow her around? Interview patients?"

Ben shook his head. "Maybe we can hire some kids to get involved. Like candy stripers or some sort of interns. That's how Epstein came after me…"

Mattis's expression didn't change. "So let's stoop to the level of the criminals here. Good idea but, ah, I don't think so."

Ben glanced at his watch.

"Oh, am I boring you?"

"What? No."

"Maybe you have to be somewhere else? Go! Go on." Mattis waved him away.

"Don't pout, man, it doesn't become you. Can I check the time please, without you taking it personally?"

But Mattis continued to sound put off. "No, no, never mind. It isn't important. Go on. I'll be fine. Don't worry."

"I guess I could try talking to her. Maybe I can trick her into confessing."

"This isn't television, Ben-Cartwright. And you aren't a lawyer, or even an actor playing one. People don't just blurt out their involvement in years of murders in answer to a trick question. Why don't you go see her friend, the technician again? She might have some more information. And she seemed very willing to cooperate."

Ben stared into the screen. "I thought you'd be happy for me. That I've found the right woman, gotten over Beth. That I'm in love. But you aren't, are you? You're jealous and you're trying to sabotage the whole thing by feeding me to the lions."

Mattis tried to hide his smile. "No! I'm not. The technician's the closest person to the suspect, and certainly the most cooperative."

"Oh, she's cooperative, all right. You know, this detective business can be more dangerous than I thought."

Mattis winked. "Just make sure you dress like a detective. Wear a raincoat."

Before Ben could answer, the screen went gray and a message came up: *'Signed Off.'*

* * *

MATERNITY ROUNDS

The nursery had been experiencing overcrowding for years and debate had raged on the pros and cons of expansion of space and staff. Which units brought in the most money had been a debate at staff meetings for decades.

Bassinets were crowded together. The placards sporting magic marker names were adorned with blue bunnies and pink flowers. A few babies cried, their tiny chests heaving and shaking, their arms waving while their mouths, which filled half their red wrinkled faces, opened wide and did what they did best.

The red-headed nurse stood outside the glass. Most of the babies were wrapped in blankets; many, particularly those whose heads had been squeezed to a point during birth, wore cotton caps. A few still showed forceps bruises on their cheeks and other purple or red signs of the ordeal of coming into the world. Bright lights shone over three particularly jaundiced babies.

The pain of who you were or where you came from could not exist if you were exactly the same as everyone else. No one could hurt you by singling you out as different if you were part of a larger whole. Like an ant, for instance.

A baby's cry broke the illusion and the nursery became a room full of differences.

Here was a population that would not mention an extra injection or two.

* * *

BEN

The elevator had a stale smell that was somehow homey and when it stopped on the third floor, it gave a little jolt before it came to rest and the heavy door slid open. As he stepped into the dimly lit mirrored hall, Bennett heard Barbra Streisand's voice soar up and over the traffic noises outside on Central Avenue, the Cedarhurst strip. Intuitively, he knew the music came from 3H.

Janice's apartment was red, matching her glasses. But she wasn't wearing her glasses when she answered the door. Her face was different without the red frames: the curves of her cheekbones were accentuated and her eyes seemed more open, lids fluttering. She wore eyeliner and heavy, orange mascara.

"Ben!" she laughed. "Come in."

Streisand sang about "Superman" and love and Bennett had to resist an impulse to fling himself into the hallway in a backwards somersault. He reminded himself that lives were at stake as she closed the door behind him.

Everything about the apartment was soft and most of it was red. Janice sat down on the L-shaped scarlet vinyl couch and patted the spot next to her. Without removing his jacket, he sank slowly into the pillowy material.

"It's so nice to see you outside that horrible hospital." Preceded by a wave of heavy perfume, she leaned close to him and began unzipping his jacket. "It's so warm in here; you'll be much more comfortable without this."

Ben coughed.

"Oh, where are my manners? What can I get you to drink?"

He thought of answering her first question with a veiled reference to her dress, which consisted of semi-sheer layers draped strategically around her shoulders and chest. Anything might be hidden in so much material.

"Water's fine," he said.

"Oh, don't be silly," she fluttered her hands like some massive bird. "At least let me get you a beer."

Grateful she had moved away, he nodded.

"What you do must be so interesting," she purred, as she rummaged through a refrigerator on the other side of the red panelled wet bar that divided the living room from the kitchen. "Creating the atmosphere for each product must be such a challenge." She closed the refrigerator. "I know the feeling; I love to decorate." She handed him a tall, vase-like glass. "Allow me." She popped the flip-top and leaned toward him as she poured.

"We'll talk in a moment," Janice said as she walked delicately, on tiny bare feet with scarlet painted nails, into the kitchen and set the empty can on the counter. "But first things first."

Next to the refrigerator was a closed door. She opened it, looked at Ben and said, "Enjoy your beer. I'll be just a sec," and closed it behind her.

Bennett tried to relax and think of a way to ask about Marilyn. The apartment, which had the appearance of what he imagined a New Orleans bordello might look like, had a disconcerting effect on him. His concentration was thrown off. Perhaps it was the perfume, which was powerful, like a toxin in the air. He wondered if he were allergic to it. And Janice was like a different person; her transformation was frightening.

"Beennnnett?"

The door creaked open a crack.

"Beeeennnnnnett?"

He cleared his throat. "Ah, yes?"

"You can come on innnn, dear."

"Come in? In there?"

"Of course. Come! Bennett?"

He got up and went to the door and gave it a little push with the fingertips of his left hand. At first he didn't see her. The room was darker than the living room, still red, but lit by dimmed tracks of light along two sides, so that much of the room was in shadow. A white wicker table and two chairs sat next to a window and two dressers. A closet behind them was open, revealing outfit after red outfit. The closet floor was covered with spiked pumps that were various shades of red.

But dominating the room, stretching from its center to within three feet of the doorway and each of the pink walls, was a high, round bed, over and around which hung a canopy and veils of the same sheer material as the sarong Janice had been wearing.

A motion from the bed and, oddly, from above it made him realize two things. First, that above the canopy the entire ceiling was mirrored; and second, that Janice was indeed no longer wearing the sheer sarong. Bennett's eyes were accustomed enough to the dark to make out her white skin rippling over the edge of the covers as she held them close to her chest.

"Don't be shy, Bennett. Put your beer down on the table and…come closer. I won't bite," she giggled. "Unless you want me to."

She leaned toward him, the satin falling away from her body. Her eyes were bright.

Mattis had once explained to him what a panic attack felt like: the sudden message every cell in his body sent to his brain, telling it to get away…now. He couldn't wait to tell Mattis that he finally understood.

"Janice, I'm, I'm, I'm flattered." He stuttered, his mouth dry. He tried to swallow and coughed instead. "And you're, you're—I don't know what to say." He gulped the rest of his beer. "I, ah, can we discuss—?"

"Oh, we'll get to that. I have plenty to tell you," she patted the bed. "After you give me what I want." She leaned back, smiling serenely.

Ben's forehead was suddenly burning and a dizziness overcame him. He reached out to catch himself but there was nothing to grab onto.

The next thing he knew, she was bending over him, her dress and glasses back where they belonged.

"I'm so sorry! I didn't mean to—I have that effect on men sometimes."

He sat up. "Just give me a little room. I'll be fine. It's warm in here. There, that's better. Why don't we go back inside and discuss what I came here to discuss."

"Of course." She cupped his cheek with her palm. "I'm so sorry. We'll take it slow. You're such a delicate man. I had no idea!"

Once they were on the couch, she turned off the stereo and brought Ben a glass of water while he took out a pen and paper.

"Well, I have reason to believe," Janice began, "that Marilyn's taking drugs. She has violent mood swings and goes to the bathroom every half hour. Each time she comes out, her mood's different."

"Different?"

"Usually, she's irritable going in, and calm, almost relieved coming out."

Ben nodded, writing. "Good. That's very good."

"Another thing is that she withdraws her pension money regularly."

Ben looked at her, not understanding.

"We have a matching funds plan at the hospital. A SEP. As long as we keep the money in, the Center matches it and it grows. It's a pretty good thing as long as you don't withdraw the money. And you know, it goes into stocks or funds or whatever you want, really. CDs, whatever. But if you take it out, there are big penalties. Well, she takes it out, regularly. Like she had some regular need for money above and beyond her salary. More water?" She got up and went to the kitchen.

Ben nodded. "Sure. How, if you don't mind my asking, do you know all this?"

"I checked into it. I know everyone at that hospital and all of us, at least all the normal people, cooperate. And this whole HIV situation—it's our jobs and it's a lot of other people's lives—we want to see it resolved. You know?"

"I know. Thanks. Oh, that's okay, I'll pour it myself."

She sat back and crossed her legs, arranging her dress to show as much thigh as possible, which was, Ben noticed, quite a lot.

"Another thought about her taking her retirement money out: she must not think she'll live very long, if she doesn't want it for retirement. Which brings me to the last point. We're having physicals this week and next. Everyone has to get one. Everyone. No exceptions—in part because of this situation. I'm the technician handling that blood, so I can get my hands on a sample of hers. We can check it really easily for drugs, for HIV. We can even test her blood type."

Ben leaned forward. "Why would we do that?"

"Well, if she's going around giving people the AIDS virus via her own blood, she'd probably be a universal donor. That way, she can give without the recipient getting sick from her blood mixing with theirs."

"Well, what does she care if they get sick? She's killing them, after all, in the long run. She wants them to get sick."

"Slowly. And she doesn't want to clue anyone in by causing a reaction that's traceable."

"A reaction to the wrong blood type is traceable?"

"Well, I'm not sure. Anyway, it's more information that might be available. So, what do you say?"

He nodded. "I think it's all valuable. And hey, if it helps catch her in the act or provide the police with anything they don't already have—we have a duty to do it."

"Exactly how I feel." She put her beer down and edged closer to him. "Now, are you feeling fully recovered yet?"

* * *

After giving the most plausible excuses he could think of—several of them—he was back in the white Cougar, thankful that nothing red was anywhere in his line of sight. He closed his eyes, and allowed the thought of the sweet smell of soapy perspiration on Eleanor's delicate shoulder to wash away the events of recent hours.

He listened to the car's rough idle, then stepped on the gas and pulled out of the parking lot onto Central Avenue and from there onto Route 878 heading towards the Atlantic Beach Bridge and home. The sun had just gone down, but he felt he could see for miles in the blue dusk. He felt the weight of losing Beth finally lifting and he drove a little faster, looking forward to getting home to Eleanor.

13

BEN

As the car bumped around the final bend and the familiar blue tarp came into view, Ben wondered why he was surprised. The construction on Art and Lou's home did not appear any different from the last time he had seen it.

"Thanks for inviting me, guys. I could use a break."

"Oh, we're not just doing this for you," Art said. "We all need a break. You get into this long stretch of cold weather without holidays and it gets brutal."

"I'll bet the place is freezing."

"Don't worry," Lou said. "We've figured out a few ways of coping."

When they brought their bags inside, Ben saw what Lou had meant. Each room had at least one often two electric space heaters. And since the area around the chimney had been finished and no tarps were anywhere near it, Lou deemed the fireplace ready to use.

"The workers wouldn't be happy about my using this, but they're lucky they're getting checks at this point," Lou explained, as he piled on wood.

"I can't wait to just relax, put my feet up…" Ben plopped onto the couch and put his feet up on one of the pillows.

"Relax?" Art said. "Well, maybe you'll relax, but you won't be lying around."

Lou chuckled. "Our tour guide has planned an itinerary."

Arthur counted off on his fingers. "Tonight, we barbecue…"

"But it's thirty degrees!" Ben protested.

"Invigorating! And tomorrow, we get you dressed. Maybe a corduroy blazer…"

"Corduroy!"

"Or tweed. And Oxford shirts, monogrammed ties. You'll have Ned's job in no time."

"But I don't want…"

Art waved two fingers. "You say you don't, but when the time comes, you won't turn it down. Fate, you'll call it. Anyway, tomorrow night, some music befitting your new wardrobe. The symphony? String quartets? Bridgehampton is known for—"

"I'm kind of a rock 'n roll man, myself."

Lou waggled a finger at Art. "And he isn't Liza Doolittle."

Art folded his arms, and tapped his foot.

Lou smiled. "I love it when he pouts. Brings out that puckish charm."

Art shrugged. "I know when I'm not wanted." He stormed from the room.

"He'll be back in a minute or two," Lou explained. "He's probably hungrier than we are. Easiest guy in the world to wait out."

"I heard that!" Art's voice called from the next room.

Ben laughed, and as soon as he did, he realized he hadn't laughed in weeks.

Lou was watching him. "It's wearing on you, isn't it?"

Ben didn't answer.

"The whole damn situation is depressing. And it's getting worse. That's why we wanted to get away. I'm so sorry this had to happen on your first account."

Ben nodded.

"There'll be others."

"You think?"

"I think. You're handling this well, and everyone involved knows it. It'd be hard on anyone."

"Thanks, Louis. It's just...seeing people die. And on top of that, knowing it's somehow tied up with my account. I almost want to quit."

Lou closed his eyes. "Tell me about it."

"And I'm also scared, you know?"

"Of what?"

"I don't know, exactly. It's like camping out in the woods and you know stuff's out there, but you don't know exactly what or when or if it'll get you, but you know it might."

"The world's scary, Ben, but it's also beautiful and fun, and there's a lot of love and caring in it. Arthur and I want to make sure you know that we're here for you, anytime. Anytime you need anything, from advice to money to a place to get away, whatever. You come to us."

Ben nodded, unable to answer.

Singing loudly, Art came back into the room. "Suppertime! I think it's...suppertime!"

Ben saw him exchange a glance with Lou and noticed the little nod Lou gave him, and that tiny gesture along with Lou's kind words were the keys to an emotional floodgate somewhere inside him. Out flowed a torrent of pent up fear, insecurity, loneliness and into its place rushed the warm water of safety, security and love.

He rushed to the bathroom and let the tears overflow, a part of him amused at the fleeting feeling of shame that appeared, then vanished from his consciousness.

At dinner, Art tried to put him at ease. "I won't even get into an airplane, you know. It just isn't natural, all that heavy metal flitting about the sky. Now fear *is* natural. God's way of saving us from the saber-toothed tiger."

"And the North American right wing homophobe," Lou added.

"Same thing."

"No," Lou disagreed. "The saber tooth just did what it was genetically engineered to do. It had no choice. And it, by the way, is extinct."

"Ah," said Art, nodding to Ben. "A science lesson."

Ben smiled.

* * *

The following morning, as he and Art headed for several clothing stores, the winter air filled Ben's chest with a pine freshness that opened his mind. As Ben picked out pants, shirts and ties, Art told stories of his own early days in advertising. Stories that were harrowing both from the viewpoint of a young art director coping with difficult clients and bosses, and from that of a young, gay man unsure of how to present himself to a not-yet-accepting industry.

And what Ben learned was, whatever the circumstance, try to keep a sense of humor. He shook his head at Art's ability to laugh at himself and at his troubles, and he resolved to develop that ability himself.

"Be patient," said Art. "It'll happen," he grinned, "but things have to get awful first."

* * *

That evening they went to the Art Center to hear a string quartet. Ben knew nothing about classical music, and wasn't sure he even liked what he was hearing, but there was a quality about it, not necessarily the music itself, that he did like. He spent much of the hour and a half trying to pinpoint what that quality was, and it was only when they were walking down the red carpeted steps to the exit that he knew.

The music was civilized.

* * *

Afterwards, he, Art and Louis shared a fruit salad and late night latte.

"And how is your lady friend?" Art asked.

Ben shrugged. "It's a bit weird. She's inconsistent, sometimes really loving and caring, taking care of me when I'm sick. Other times, she just...disappears." He took a deep breath. "I think she's afraid her family's involved in the murders. She gets so angry when I ask about her sister." He looked into his coffee for a long moment, then up at Art with a forced smile. "The sex is great, though."

"Sex isn't everything," Lou commented dryly.

Art looked hurt. "Really? We'll have to talk."

"Love can be strange," Lou mused, his spoon clinking as he slowly stirred his coffee. "It can show up, disappear, seem inconsistent. You can find it in odd places."

"Where've I heard that?" Ben said, scratching his chin. "I know—" He reached for his wallet. Had he kept that fortune?

"Do you want a little more?" Art asked.

Ben picked up his coffee cup and held it out for Arthur to fill.

"Ben," Lou said, "there's something you ought to know."

"I don't like the sound of that," Ben said, with a tremor in his voice.

"Arthur and I are giving notice next week."

Art grinned. "They're buying my treatment!" He shook his head at the ceiling with open joy.

"Arthur, that's fantastic! Why didn't you tell me before?"

Lou shrugged. "Because we're leaving the company and you aren't; we wanted the weekend to be about our being there for you."

Art nodded and became serious. "That's what's important now."

Ben waved them away. “No, no. Tell me about it. You’re going to Hollywood?”

Art nodded. “We’re going to watch production of the pilot. I’ll be a script consultant and possibly a writer. There’s a whole union issue about getting credit. Anyway, *The Addition* will be on cable, so it’ll be no holds barred.”

“Outstanding.” Ben shook his head with a half smile. “Congratulations!” He got up and hugged Arthur. “I know how long you’ve wanted this.” He stepped back, biting his lip. “I’m going to miss you guys.”

Art waved him away. “Don’t be silly. We’ll be out every couple of months. And you can visit us, maybe do a guest shot. You’ll be the ah, let me see, the hunky plumber who installs the jacuzzi and while teaching the daughter, Kimberly, how to turn it on, ends up in it with her!”

Ben laughed. “Just point me to the set, but I don’t do nudity.”

“We’ll get you a body double.”

“And if Brad Pitt’s busy?”

“Listen,” Lou pointed a finger at Ben. “You keep an eye on Annabel. She has a tough situation with her ex. Promise me, you’ll keep an eye on on her?”

Ben nodded. “I will. I promise.” He sat back and sipped his coffee, which was exactly the way he liked it.

* * *

READY

Well Baby was one of the hospital’s more active units at night due to the feeding needs of the babies. This presented a problem. Surreptitiously injecting babies would be difficult if nurses were wheeling them in and out of their mothers’ rooms.

“Hello, Marilyn.” A nurse she did not recognize was waving from the nurses’ station. She waved back, then turned again to the nursery, gazing at the babies through the glass. The glass prevented the sound of the babies crying from reaching the nurses and made seeing the babies that much more important. The babies were turned toward the glass at viewing time, but at other times were visible from the sides and front.

That was the answer! Only one wall of the nursery was glass, so positioning herself between the baby and the glass—having her back to the window—would hide her actions from the nurses’ station. And no one, no one, was quicker with a needle and more expert at finding veins than she was.

Everything was in place. The logistics were worked out. The Man with the Hat would meet her tomorrow night with double the usual order: four bundles. And she was set in her own mind. That had been the tough part. Could she truly separate herself enough to do this? It was what she was best at, what she’d been doing for so many years. For this ultimate challenge she would have to truly become…an ant.

As she watched the little red and brown bodies squirm and cry, she remembered Georgie's infectious laugh and the patience in his voice as he helped her with her science homework. She knew she could do it.

* * *

BEN

The main room at 3S was decorated with the first series of Medical Center ads. Magazine tear sheets, high resolution proofs, massive poster prints were tacked to the walls and ceiling at various angles. The same huddled group of AIDS patients stared toward the center of the room from everywhere—hundreds of surreal, sad eyes.

Annie Flowers was standing near the far window in her black cocktail dress, holding a drink and talking quietly with Art and Lou. She glanced towards the door with orphan eyes and her face took on a Christmas expectancy.

"Ben!" She ran towards him, threw her arms around his neck. Her pillow chest pushed against him. "Congratulations!"

Faces turned and a cheer went up.

"Great job! Congratulations! Good work! Super campaign! Don't the ads look great?"

An informal receiving line formed in front of him, waiting for Annie to let him go. She held him at arm's length.

"Ben, I'm so proud of you."

He thought of saying, "Your hair smells terrific," but instead said, "Thanks."

Her smile faded; she looked around uncertainly and stepped aside. Ned stepped forward and squeezed Ben's hand. Ben winced from the force and size of the handshake. For such a small man, Ned had huge, powerful hands, his knuckles misshapen from breaking boards and cinder blocks.

"Hell of an account to have for a first one." He was shaking his head, the twinkle in his eye switched on high. "Goddamn public relations nightmare. But you've gotten through this, and now you'll get through anything. The ads are beautiful. Franklin says so himself."

"Don't hog the line!" Art called, holding up a plastic cup and jiggling it until the ice rattled. He handed Lou his drink, then hugged Ben to his turquoise Hawaiian print party shirt and Lou, in his brown jeans and red flannel shirt, patted Ben's shoulder.

"Ben, Ben, Ben." Art looked him up and down. "It's like, it's like your Bar Mitzvah! Look at him, Louis, all grown up!"

"Don't get choked up now," Louis said. "You're liable to set off your stomach ulcer."

Art turned to him. "Stomach ulcer! Of course, I'll set off my stomach ulcer. It's a measure of how important Ben's success is to me! And anyway, the only thing that will quiet that little monster is food and who can eat with all this excitement?"

Lydia was next on line. She gave Ben a quick peck on the cheek. "You did real good, Benny." She looked at Arthur. "Thank God someone around here's been working."

"Don't go *there*, girl!" came Art's warning. "You're playing with fire."

"Don't threaten me," Lydia shot back. "I'm twice the man you are."

"Strap-ons," Art whispered to Lou.

"A compliment from Lydia." Ben folded his arms. "Now I know I'm dreaming."

"Yeah," a smile fought for control of Lydia's mouth. "Well just don't tell anyone. I don't want to ruin my reputation." She leaned close to his ear. "Besides, I'll deny it."

Ned dragged a chair to the center of the room and clapped his huge palms together. "People! Hello! We have a congratulatory occasion." He cleared his throat. "Lydia, get me a ginger ale, would you?"

Lydia frowned. "What am I, your wife?"

Ned closed his eyes for a moment. When he opened them, Annie was holding a cup up to him. "I need to talk to you later," he said, as he bent over for the cup.

"Sure, whenever you say." Annie moved away.

"Ahem. I'd like to say congratulations first to Arthur, for being discovered by Hollywood. We all knew it'd happen some day." He held up his glass. "Arthur, I knew we wouldn't be lucky enough to keep you to ourselves. Now the world will get a little taste of what we've seen all along. And Louis. We'll miss you, too."

Louis looked at the ground, hands on hips. "An afterthought. Always, I'm an afterthought."

Everyone applauded. Ned continued. "I'd also like to congratulate Bennett on a job well done on his first independent assignment. He had a difficult set of circumstances and some interesting personalities to work with and he came through like a champ." He clapped his heavy palms together, and the applause swelled. "Annie, would you open the door to the outer hall, please? Oh, you already…I should have known. Thanks."

He hopped down and went through the doorway and came back wheeling a chair draped in clear plastic. "In honor of your success, we are presenting you with an executive office chair, complete with—drumroll please—lower lumbar support!" He ripped the plastic from the gray woven chair and again the cheers began, coupled with "ooohs" and comments like "now you've really made it."

"That ought to straighten you out," called Lydia.

"Well, sit in it already!" Art said.

Ben sat in the chair and Art gave it a push, sending him spinning across the floor. The staff took turns taking rides until Lydia ran over Art's foot and Ned suggested putting the chair away.

Against the glass walls at the far end of the room, three round white plastic tables had been set up with matching chairs. After moving along the food and drink lines everyone found seats, except Art, who went into his office and brought out a boom-box radio. He fiddled with the tuner and settled on a 50s rock 'n roll station, then began dancing around Louis, hands clapping over his head. Louis sang along with the bass line in a deep, surprisingly clear voice that was not at all like his speaking voice. Everyone else ate and watched. Annie Flowers tapped the table with her fork.

Two songs later, Art, his face red and sweating, sat down with Lou at the center table.

Ben gave himself a mental slap on the wrist for not bringing Eleanor, who seemed to be from a different world than that of his job. But she did love to dance.

"Disgusting," Lydia was saying to Art, "the way you transform at parties. Jimmy Stewart, ad man becomes Norma Desmond, surreal diva."

Art was gulping beer. "Hear that, Louis? Lydia thinks I'm a diva! Thank you, dah-ling."

"I said sur-real. And that beer will go right to your head if you swill it like that after such a workout."

"You can dispense with the 'sirs'," said Lou. "We try to stay informal around here."

"The beer will go to my head?" Art echoed. "You say that like it's a bad thing."

Lou went to the mens' room and Art knelt next to Annie.

"How's it going, Annabel?" She looked up, shrugged. "About the same. He's not allowed within 50 feet of me, but he swore he'd get to me." She pressed her lips together and made a helpless gesture.

"Blue moooon…" the radio crooned.

"He's a resourceful guy, you know?" Annie dabbed at her mouth with the napkin, then stood up. "You?"

"You know my Louis. We're comfortable. Maybe you ought to get a can of pepper spray and one of those loud sirens and stalk *him*. Turn those tables."

"He'd take it as a challenge."

"Or as a come on."

She laughed.

"What about Ben?" he asked gently.

Her eyes filled with tears. "What's there to say about that? He has a girlfriend."

"She isn't here, is she?"

"No, but—"

"And you are. You know what they say about a bird in the hand…"

She pouted. "I know it can get your hand awfully dirty."

Art squeezed her shoulder. "Why don't you just try talking to him?"

Her voice broke. "I can't. I just can't. I could never get a guy like him."

He looked her in the eye. "That's what I thought about Louis. So successful, out of reach. That's what I thought about my script as well. But, you certainly can't succeed 'til you try." He bent over and kissed her lightly on the cheek and she hugged him.

Lou returned from the mens' room. "Trying to steal my man?" he asked.

"If anyone could, she could," Art said, holding onto her and rolling his eyes. "Once you go red you stay in bed!" He stood upright, suddenly. "Look."

Annie turned. Ben was beckoning to her. Her lips parted and she looked first at Art, then at Lou. "This is a setup, right?"

"Nope," Art said.

Annie took a step toward Ben, who was smiling and saying something to Lydia. Art and Lou sat down. Annie started toward Bennett, but stopped. Lydia had diverted his attention.

Annie felt as though she were standing in a vacuum. The air around her had evaporated; there was no sound. The chairs, tables, food, people—even the brown and beige shapes on the wall—began to swirl and meld. Her head swam and she felt the fluttering of her own eyelids.

"You okay?" a deep voice asked.

She strained to focus and clear her head. Falsetto voices swam in harmony somewhere above her. Ned was holding her elbow.

"Yeah, I think I'll be okay. I ate some of that Chinese fish. I think I might be allergic to it."

"Come on." He walked her through the glass entrance and into the office. "The cool air in here will help." He sat her down at his desk and got her a glass of water from the cooler in the hall. "Is there anything I can do?"

"No. The water helped."

"I mean about Kenneth."

She shook her head. "That's all over. If he comes after me, it becomes a police matter. If not, great. I'll have nothing to do with him."

He nodded. "Ann. That's what I want to talk to you about. Kenneth's a sick man. His stalking you, the way he's mistreated you. Obviously that's wrong, and ought to be dealt with by the authorities. Of course. But he's sick. You've got to understand that and forgive him."

If he had slapped her, she couldn't have been more startled. She took another sip of water, her eyes wide. "Excuse me?"

Ned swallowed. "You've got to forgive him. He's a sick man, Annie. A sick man. He's not in control of his actions. You think he wants to hurt the woman he loves most in the world? He doesn't." He sat down on the edge of his desk next to her. Reflexively, she pushed her chair back with her feet. That he was so emotional over her situation struck her as odd. Was he drunk?

"I want you to listen to me, Ann. Your husband loves you. I'm not asking you to let him back into your life. I am asking you to understand that he's sick. He can't control his behavior." A gilded frame standing on his desk held four photographs of him with his wife and two sons at various ages. He glanced at it.

"He knows what he's done is wrong, and whatever he has to pay for it, he has to pay. I'm only asking you to understand that he's weak, in his way…on some level."

He stood up and looked at her for a moment, his face serious, lips tight. She did not say anything, but looked back at him. "Are you okay to go back, now?"

She nodded, then stood up and walked past him. Ned picked up the gilded frame and looked at the pictures in it as Annie left the room. He did not hear the words she muttered under her breath.

"Fat chance."

"I was just going to tell you," he whispered after she was gone. "I wanted someone to know," he held the picture up in front of his face, "that I cheated on my wife."

* * *

BEN

Mattis's face flickered and broke up. When it returned, the motion was uneven—he would move for a moment, then freeze, then move again, as though the connection were bad.

"The office party was great." Ben patted his stomach. "Lots of rich food, though."

The static made his words intermittent. "They…you…award?"

Ben nodded, wrinkling his nose. Mattis's room smelled of old socks. "For my first big account, yeah. It was…nice."

"What…should give…a percentage of…"

"Mattis, you're on a bad line or something. Is your modem okay, or do you think it's the weather? It's raining pretty hard, you know. Um, listen. I just wanted you to know, I'm going over to the hospital to interview Marilyn. Maybe I can get her to say something contradictory or incriminating. I promise I'll be back by eight tonight to let you know what happened."

Mattis's face reddened. The scarecrow head leaned close, springy hair bouncing, tiny eyes skeptical.

"Well, you…careful. Let me know…my phone service here is all screwed up and some little company is sending the school bills...can't say anything because…not supposed to be…is that screwed up or what?"

Not sure he understood, Ben took the safest course of action and nodded in agreement.

"…was a deal between the school and the...company, letting me stay…unlimited...Now those bastards…" Mattis's small eyes sank into their sockets, his long face sagged, jaw dropping and jutting with righteous fury; his snake-hair quivered as if ready to strike on its owner's behalf. "They just sneak in, basically lie and suddenly, I don't...phone access…like someone cutting off the water in your…" His voice was rising. "Do you know how important…I'm in a jail here!"

"Well, it is sort of a self imposed jail."

Mattis stared. A distorted hand reached forward and the image bounced. "What's the matter with you? You think I like being…? You think I wouldn't rather be able to go where I…? You think I ASKED those guys to bury me in that park and basically *ruin my life?* Are you crazy?"

"No."

"And I am? That's what you're saying, old pal. Isn't it? *Isn't it?*"

Ben closed his eyes for a moment and shook his head.

"No, I'm not saying that. But I do think you can learn to cope with—"

"Cope? You think I'm not coping, you pretentious, unfeeling piece of—hey," his tone changed, instantly calm and conversational, "did you say you're interviewing Marilyn today?"

Accustomed to such gear shifts, Ben was unfazed. "Straight from here."

"But you promise to get back online by eight tonight, right? No freaking me out by being late, okay? She's a goddamn serial killer. Let's not screw around...old Mattis's feelings, okay? I'm close enough," the rage came back into his voice and he was suddenly screaming, "I'm close enough to, to...*goddamn edge* without you talking to murderers and then standing me up, okay? *Okay?"*

Ben nodded. "Okay. I just have to stop in on El at seven thirty, then I'll call."

"Because I wouldn't want to see anything happen...you. You know? Be careful. Maybe it isn't such a...idea. You don't want to go around antagonizing murderers, or is it murderesses?"

"I've got to go, man." Ben leaned forward to click 'Sign off.'

"Oh just turn me off. That's how it is, right? Just—"

The screen went dark.

* * *

Though it was only six o'clock, heavy gray storm clouds sapped the daylight from the south shore sky; white lights around the fringes of the Medical Center's parking lot illuminated arcs of rain, which slammed the asphalt and raised a fine, ankle high spray. Red lights whirled, spinning off the sides of the building and cars, and as he pulled the white Cougar between the painted yellow parking lines, Ben wondered if Marilyn had been caught. Two police cars formed a "V" and a bevy of blue uniforms surrounded an individual in the corral formed by the cars. Ben could not see the person through the sea of blue and steel. He flipped on his interior lights, patted his hair in place, rubbing the pomade between his fingers. He donned the Yankee cap that lay on the passenger seat, then got out and walked towards the building, craning his neck to try to make out what was going on. Nearby, a half dozen parked cars sagged to one side, their tires slashed.

The handcuffed figure was not Marilyn Franklin. It was a burly, bushy-haired man, his eyes unnaturally wide. Bennett looked closer and recognized him. Charlie Spoon, the tattoo artist. He made a mental note to tell Eleanor.

The hospital's waiting room smelled like floor cleaner and coffee. He explained to the woman at the information desk that he was "family" and that he was looking for an RN named Marilyn Franklin. The woman made a short phone call, then told him that Marilyn worked in the Well Baby unit. He took the elevator to the second floor but the nurse at the station there would not let him pass because he was not an expectant father and visiting hours were not for two hours. After standing at the desk for a few minutes, he spotted Marilyn coming out of one of the private rooms. He hoped she had not spotted him watching her at the mall.

"Nurse Franklin?"

She peered at him, approaching cautiously. "Yes? Do I know you? Are you one of the fathers?"

"Well, no. My name is James, Bennett James. I'm with the ad agency that—"

"You're my sister's boyfriend. I remember." She nodded, looking, he imagined, a bit less happy to see him.

"Well, that's right. Do you mind if I talk to you for a few minutes?"

"I'm sort of busy—"

"I can cover for you," said the nurse at the desk. "Cary is here. She can watch the babies. Cary?"

A wrinkled woman wearing silver wire-framed glasses, a hairnet, and very red lipstick popped her head out of one of the rooms. "Yes, Doris?"

"Would you mind watching the babies for a few minutes while I cover for Marilyn?"

"Oh, sure. Just give me a second."

Marilyn looked warily at Ben. "Okay, then. We can go to the coffee shop and you can buy me a decaf. But just for a minute."

"Thanks. I appreciate it. And I won't keep you long." As they rode the elevator Ben thought how ironic it was that a heroin addict would drink decaf.

He examined her out of the corner of his eye. Marilyn's eyes were more serious than Eleanor's, more lined, her nose perhaps a little longer and not quite as straight. Eleanor had a thinner, younger-looking face, though their red hair and basic features were similar.

The coffee shop was dark and nearly empty. A tired waitress poured coffee beans into a grinder. Through the swinging doors behind the counter, Ben could hear mens' voices blending with the clatter of pots and pans.

They sat down at the table. Ben smiled; Marilyn did not smile back. The waitress appeared, pad ready.

"Coffee," said Ben.

The waitress nodded and looked at Marilyn. "I know, decaf."

"Thank you, Paula."

Marilyn had not taken her eyes from him. Expressionless, unblinking, her green eyes held his. Was she curious, angry, eager to cooperate? He had no idea. The hairs on the sides of his legs rose, tingling, as though a light breeze were blowing, only there was no breeze and he was wearing coarse jeans.

He felt present yet not present, his sense of reality slipping away. He might be having coffee with a serial killer. How could this have happened? His muscles, particularly in his legs and stomach, were sending his brain an urgent message. *Run!* For the second time, he thought of Mattis's panic attacks.

"Excuse me," he said, getting up. "I'll be right back." He forced a smile as he stumbled towards the mens' room. He really had to go.

When he returned, the coffee and decaf had arrived and Marilyn was stirring hers and tapping the spoon on the side of the off-white mug.

"So," he announced, clearing his throat as he sat down. "What's your take on what's going on—the murders, I mean?"

"Why are you asking me?" She looked at him, still emotionless. "You'd better ask the police. They have the murderer. You know about Dr. Sticker, don't you?"

"*Alleged* murderer."

"Oh," she said. A light dawned in her eyes. "So that's what this is about. You think the killer's still...you think, you think," she pushed herself back from the table, her jaw dropping, eyes wide. "You think I know something...?"

Ben felt a series of tiny jolts, like electric shocks, on the back of his neck. Adrenaline coursed through him and he had to breathe deeply to restore calm to his body. "Actually, I was wondering if you think perhaps a nurse might be more anonymous, more free to get around the hospital—have the run of the place, do what he or she wanted, have access to medications as well as patients..." His voice trailed off. "I mean, let's put aside, even hypothetically for the moment, that the police may have the murderer."

Marilyn's eyes narrowed; sarcasm edged her voice. "Nurses are the only people around here who have a clue. Nurses are the glue that hold this place together. That's what you should put in your ads, you know. Yeah, sure, we have the wherewithal." She sat up straighter, palms flat on the table. "But you know what, we're also the real caregivers. We're the ones who give a damn and work double and triple shifts. And as usual, in your campaign just as in general around here, we get none of the credit." She stared at him. "And that makes me sick. It's disgusting." Her knuckles were white where she gripped the table.

"Are all personnel routinely tested for drugs?"

Her tongue clicked the roof of her mouth and she looked at the ceiling. "You know what? I'm not answering any more questions. Hypothetical or not. The police do have the murderer, alleged or not. So why you're running around, questioning people on your own is beyond me. It's irresponsible. Do the police know you're doing this?" She had taken the spoon in her fist and was gripping it like a knife, shaking it in his direction at the end of each syllable.

"If you'd stop to think about what's really the responsible thing to do here, you'd see that your ad campaign is what's insane. Why mislead the public? That is what you're doing, you know. It's what your whole industry's about. So if you're going to question anyone's integrity, why not look in the goddamn mirror?" The spoon carved the air between them.

Ben's mind had begun to side with his legs. He looked at the clock behind the counter. Six thirty. He had to meet Eleanor in an hour. And Mattis at eight. He kept his voice calm, professional. "Well, I do thank you for taking the time to speak with me, Marilyn. I really chose you more because you're a friend of the family than for any other reason. Anyway, I have an appointment in a half an hour, so I've got to go." He reached for his wallet and tossed two dollars on the table.

"With my sister?" Marilyn sat back, the spoon lowered.

"Well, yes, as a matter of fact."

"Say hello."

He couldn't get out of the hospital fast enough and once in the car, he locked the doors and drove as quickly as he could without attracting police attention. The interview had unnerved him and told little that was new. What had he been thinking to meet with her? Had she said anything worthwhile? Had anything in her demeanor been telling? He'd have to report back to Mattis to get a more objective point of view.

He rushed into his apartment. The phone was ringing.

* * *

SET

The Well Baby unit was so full there was barely room to walk. Mrs. Lutz had given birth to triplets that morning and every bassinet had to be rearranged. Nothing was where it had been the previous evening. Musical beds, came the crazy thought. Just looking at the sea of pink and blue cotton made your skin itch, as if it wasn't itchy enough already. The belt holding the syringes and vials of virus blood was too tight. A quick look around. No doctors, only the one LPN whose job it was to take blood pressure and temperature. There would be no ports in IV lines here, and since the patients cried so much anyway, a squall from a needle wouldn't be noticed. It would be the final nail in the coffin. The end of that ridiculous ad campaign. The hospital's and His ultimate failure. The administration would have to fall and He would finally be humiliated, forced to see His own inadequacy. And everyone else would see it, too. The final victory.

Where to start. Maybe the triplets. Walking over to the single bassinet they shared you become suddenly aware of how much your legs hurt and you have to stop. You're going to vomit right onto their blanket. Clamp down on that! Only one way to stop that, but it's got to wait. The Man with the Hat will save you. Knowing he was there, that he was the real One, brought a measure of calm.

The LPN was still on the other side of the glass, not looking but not leaving either. Did she know? Was she waiting for you to make a move? Did she recognize you?

Swollen fingers slip a ready syringe from the leather pouch. Both hands ache now as much as both legs. It's been so long, your insides feel like dead trees in winter—no flowers or colors. Everything brown and dead and hurting.

Keep the syringe low, at your side until the nurse leaves and it can be up and into one, even two of the triplet's legs and down again before anyone sees. And at this point, if someone sees, who cares? You'll be off and down the street with the Man with the Hat.

You glance up at the nurse. She's gone. It's time. You glance at the clock.

Oh my God!

It's seven o'clock. Everything, the clock itself, stops. There wasn't time! You'd miss the Man with the Hat and you'd miss the appointment too!

The needle breaks as you force it back into the holster and you rush past the nurse who calls "Hi, Marilyn," after you. No time to answer. Got to find the Man with the Hat and get home—all in half an hour.

* * *

BEN

Bennett's hips had begun to vibrate and for a moment he wondered if Eleanor's couch had a hidden massage control she had never told him about. Then he reached down, unclipped his pager and squinted at the numbers, trying to remember whose they were. Then he picked up the phone.

"Ben?"

"Annie?"

"Ben, do you have a minute? I'm sorry to bother you. You're at your girlfriend's, right?"

"Annie, it's okay." He exhaled, his shoulders relaxing, the chill leaving his legs. "Are you okay? You sound—"

"It's my husband, Ben. He's, he's been threatening me. He won't leave me alone. He's been violent, and—"

"Are you home? Is he there now?"

"No, I mean yes. I'm home, but no, he isn't here. At least not yet. He says he'll never let me alone and I believe him, Ben. I talked to Ned but he was no help. He wanted me to try and understand, but Kenneth's crazy, Ben. He's psychotic. He'll kill me!"

The door opened and Eleanor came in, carrying a bag. She waved and went into the bathroom and Ben waited for the radio to come on.

"Annie, Annie, calm down. Nothing like that's going to happen. I want you to listen to me."

"But Ben, you don't understand, the police won't intervene in a domestic dispute until after the crime's been committed. Nobody cares about—"

"Annie, listen to me. I care."

* * *

ELEANOR FRANKLIN

Eleanor pressed against the bathroom door, panting. Sweat poured down the insides of her thighs. Her stomach had become a tiny, compressed heavy thing and it was trying to hurl itself out of her. She ripped the blue uniform out of the bag and stuffed it into the laundry duffel that hung from the metal hook on the back of the door. Her hand reached for the radio knob, but she heard a phrase that stopped her. It was Ben's voice, and it sounded comforting.

"Annie," he was saying. "Listen to me. I care."

And the pain gave way to rage.

14

1984-1985

SHIRLEY FRANKLIN

Nestled in a cozy residential neighborhood between Sunrise Highway and Rockaway Avenue in Valley Stream, the house was coated with red shingles that were faded to orange on the south side. It was an oddly shaped house; rooms cropped out where past owners had found the need to add them, and the oddness was more pronounced inside, where those additions had become dark hiding places, secret clubhouses to generations of children.

"Okay, mom, I'm done." Eleanor snapped the book shut, stood up and looked at her mother, who glanced at her other red-headed daughter, the older one, who was sitting in the yellow flowered arm chair, chewing on the blue cap of her pen.

Marilyn waved their mother away. "I've got a few more pages to read. You and El start the decorations without me."

Shirley had been watching the girls do their homework—Marilyn for nursing school and Eleanor for her Catholic day school. She had been daydreaming about better days. She remembered the way, even at 8 or 9, Marilyn loved to write about whatever she saw or thought or felt. Eleanor had her old ant farm then and they used to joke about how she was becoming an ant, so engrossed was she in their little comings and goings. And Georgie, little bright eyed Georgie, of course, would turn his natural talents towards whatever pleased him. Indoors, he sang in his strong choir boy's voice and played that old piano that used to stand amidst the leafy ficus plants in the corner of the living room. Out in the street and in the schoolyard he ran and jumped higher than any boy any of them had ever seen. He gloried in what his gifted body could do and pushed himself happily every chance he could to do more. Shirley worried that he might hurt himself, but he never seemed to. His wonderful body never failed him.

And the questions those children used to ask!

"Mommy, where does music come from?"

"Mommy, why did God make Marilyn and Elly look like each other and I look different?"

"Mommy, what do they stand on when they build the floor?"

She laughed to herself, and allowed her mind to continue remembering. George would generally call in at some point from his study: "Make yourself useful, Shirley, and type this letter for me!" And on her way to do so she would hear: "Mommy, I want to play the animal game!"

"Shirley, I told you last week to rewrite these notes so I can read them."

"But George, you wrote them."

"What? What did you say to me? You watch your tone of voice, Miss."

"I'll be right there, George."

"Mommy, I said it's black and white and lives in the forest and its behind smells really bad what is it?"

"Girls will you please stop yelling."

"Mommy, it's a skunk, mommy. Now it's Elly's turn."

"I said stop yelling!"

"George, will you stop yelling?"

"What did you say? What did you say!"

"Girls, please wait until I get back inside and we'll play some more."

"Georgie will you stop playing that damn piano!"

"Mommy, I want Daddy to play the animal game."

"Marilyn, I have to work now. Please be quiet."

* * *

Remembering the tears in Marilyn's eyes and the pout on Elly's lips, Shirley lit a cigarette and brought herself back to the present, staring at the faded spot on the pine floor where the piano had been. The ficus was long gone.

"Don't be silly, Marilyn. Eleanor, you go back to studying until your sister is ready to help. Marilyn…"

Eleanor interrupted. "But I said I was finished. What am I supposed to study?" She rubbed her palm on the rough black denim covering her thigh.

Shirley ignored her. "Marilyn, when you're finished, I'll unroll the crepe paper and you and El can hang the streamers and the banner. By the time that's done, the cake ought to be ready." She looked like a middle aged version of her daughters, her once too-red hair had grayed and now required help to achieve its more subdued and appropriate brown hue, and her smooth complexion was lined from the stress of raising three children and living with an ambitious, inattentive husband. Yet Shirley Franklin's sweet disposition was still apparent in her eyes. The natural kindness and tenderness that radiated from the features of all three Franklin women was their singular common characteristic unaltered by time.

"I'll check on the cake," Shirley said, and went through the white swinging door to the kitchen.

"Do you think Daddy will be home before Georgie?" Eleanor asked, settling back into the deep pillows of the red and brown plaid sofa, her school book in her lap.

Marilyn looked up from her text; she was halfway through nursing school and felt she had given up every second of her free time for the pursuit. She also felt the effort was more than worth it. Altruism and philanthropy were more than Franklin traits—they were part of a heritage. "I think so. He knows we're setting up and, you know, everything's got to be right for Georgie." She smiled at the image of her father insisting on this.

Eleanor shut her book again. "I hope you're right. Daddy's so good at those little crepe flowers. Remember how he used to make them for our birthdays and mom used to tape them to our presents?"

"Mmm." Marilyn looked past her sister, lost for a moment in that day dream. "Just let me finish this chapter. I'll be with you in a minute."

The front door creaked and slammed and George Sr. rushed through the room. "Hi, everyone," he said, breathing hard. The white wood door to the living room swung shut and the study door beyond could be heard closing, followed by the metallic snap of its lock.

The girls looked at one another. Their mother appeared at the kitchen's entrance. "Did I hear your father come in?"

"He went into the study," said Eleanor, with finality.

"Ohh," said Shirley, and she leaned back against the door frame. "Well, I guess he has important work then." She forced a smile. "Well, we can finish the decorations just fine ourselves. Why don't you ladies put your books away and we'll get started."

Marilyn closed her text and went to the dining room table, which was covered with colored papers, streamers, scissors, glue and tape. She sat down and began cutting and bunching small circles of magenta crepe paper. Her mother stood on a chair and began taping a long "Happy Birthday" banner across the ceiling.

As she worked, Marilyn's eyes filled with tears. As they began to overflow, she stopped what she was doing, got up and went through the dinette and knocked on her father's study door.

Her voice drifted back to the living room, the words unintelligible, her tone increasingly shrill, followed by George Sr.'s sharp, booming answer. The study door slammed again, its lock snapped shut and Eleanor, unable to bear seeing her sister's face, did not wait for her to reappear. She ran out of the house, looking only once at her mother as she ran.

Marilyn went straight to her room, turned on her record player and lost herself in the colors and textures of violins and woodwinds. Once settled there, she began to write.

Up on her dining room chair, Shirley was taping the edge of Georgie's seventeenth birthday banner to the spot where the wall and ceiling met, careful to snap off the correct length of tape and to smooth each edge evenly.

* * *

ELEANOR FRANKLIN

As she traveled east on Sunrise Highway toward Stompers, where she and her girlfriends danced on Friday evenings, Eleanor passed Belle's Ice Cream Stand, its parking lot jammed with high schoolers, fresh from after school clubs and sports. Crowds of students stood around cars and the bright orange garbage cans that were part of Belle's motif. In wintertime, Belle's sold pizza and soup and sometimes someone dropped a match in one of the cans and teens gathered close around the fire and smoked cigarettes, drank fruit flavored brandy and warmed themselves in the orange glow.

At the far end of the lot, well past the other cars, Eleanor noticed her mother's Ford with Georgie in the front seat next to another boy she did not recognize. The image did not particularly strike her except that she noticed her brother and felt sorry that his birthday party would lack any evidence of their father's attention. She also hoped that the other boy was at least eighteen and had a permanent driver's license, so Georgie would be driving legally. The thought that Georgie did not appear to be wearing his baseball uniform entered and then vanished from her mind. Georgie frequently changed back into his school clothes if the field had been wet or muddy. But as her car was passing the field and her brother and his friend were disappearing from her field of vision, she saw something that startled her and she nearly turned the car around to get a better look.

Her brother's arm was around the other boy's shoulder.

* * *

GEORGE JR.

Georgie was throwing a baseball into a white net backstop and hurling himself to either side to catch it as the ball snapped back at him.

"Mom, let's come back outside after supper." Marilyn looked up from the textbook she'd been highlighting.

Next to her, Eleanor agreed. "It's such a nice day."

"And then we can go in and watch Geraldine Ferraro debate George Bush on TV."

Shirley went on raking leaves, not looking up. "After supper, dear. But please stay out of your father's way. The way Willis has been running that hospital board has him on edge and there's no telling what state of mind he'll be in at any given moment—and I can't say's I blame him." She stopped raking and looked over at the other side of the lawn at George Jr.

"Georgie, why don't you give Barb Robinson a call and ask her to the dance they're having over at the Y tonight."

On the brick stoop, Eleanor, who was reading a magazine, closed her eyes and took a deep breath. Marilyn continued to read, her yellow highlighter squeaking.

George Jr. continued to throw the baseball, harder now, against the white netting. He leaped high, his gloved hand stretched over his head to catch the ball, which smacked with an echo into the pocket.

Shirley Franklin's voice went up a half octave. "Georgie Junior, are you ignoring me again?"

George stopped what he was doing, put his hands on his hips and turned around, smiling. "No, ma. I'm not ignoring you."

Unable to meet his eyes, Shirley looked down at the leaves, and moved them around a little with the rake. "Well?"

"Ma, I'm just not interested, okay?"

She began to rake again, talking to the leaves. "Well, I just don't see how you're ever going to meet a nice young lady…"

"Yeah, I know, and have the wife, the kids and the nice picket fence, and so on and so forth." He dropped the ball on the ground at his feet, put the glove under his arm and began walking toward his mother. "Well, maybe that's not what I'm after. Maybe that's not the lifestyle for me. I love you a whole lot, Ma, but I suggest you stop getting involved or you might bite off more than you can chew." He was standing in front of her, looking hard into his mother's eyes.

Shirley continued to look at the ground, slowly shaking her head. "I'm only trying to help…" She began to blink.

He swung his head up, looking at the sky. "Oh, jeez, don't start crying. Whatever the subject is, it changes to the fact that you're crying, that I'm hurting you. That's why nothing ever changes around here. We don't deal with anything." He pointed his finger at her. "Why don't we stick to the subject, Ma? You want to know why I don't go the dance with Barbara? Is that what you want to know?"

A dark green late model Pontiac pulled up in front of the house. On the stoop, Marilyn went on reading; Eleanor closed her magazine and whispered, "Georgie."

The Pontiac's driver's side door opened and George Sr. got out, pulling a brown leather briefcase after him.

"Well, I'll tell you why," George Jr. said as Marilyn looked up from her book. Her mouth began to form the word "no" but Georgie went on. "It's because I don't like Barbara. In fact, I'm not interested in women at all."

Still blinking and talking to the leaves, Shirley gave a little shrug. "I can appreciate that you put so much into your work and into your baseball, but if you found a little time for a girlfriend—I only want you to be happy, Georgie—" Her face contorted and she began to cry.

"That's not it, Ma," George Jr. said. "I'll tell you what it is. I'm not interested in women because I'm interested in men. What do you think of that? I have a boyfriend, ma. We're very happy, thank you, so I don't need any advice in that department. Okay?"

George Sr. had put down his briefcase and was walking quickly to his son, his chin in the air, eyes wide and unblinking. "You talk to your mother like that? You make your mother cry?" He grabbed his son by the lapels, hands tight and twisting until George Jr.'s shirt bunched up like a straightjacket. "What's the matter with you? Who do you think you are?"

But George Jr. was not cowed. An energy had come into him, a proud, defiant momentum he had never known. "Don't change the subject, dad. We were talking about your son, the homosexual. That okay with you? Did you want to discuss that or did you have some work to do in your study?" He tried to nod toward the briefcase. "Got some papers in there that are more important than your son, dad?"

"I'll not have you talking to your mother that way," George Sr. said through clenched teeth. "You may not be abusive to your parents!"

"No, that's not the subject, dad. Get on track, dad. The subject was…your dear little boy's a fag!" He shouted the last word, and Shirley moaned softly and leaned her forehead against the top of the rake handle.

"Too much for you liberal, generous folks to deal with, isn't it? It's one thing in the voting booth or the newspaper. Ohh, those terrible repressive politicians, but when it's your own son, you—"

George Sr. slapped his son across the mouth, instantly drawing blood. Everything stopped—but only for a moment. Marilyn jumped up, leaving her book on the stoop and ran to her father and her brother, grabbing her father's wrist with both of her hands. The yellow highlighter rolled down the walk into the gutter. Eleanor closed her eyes tight and with the crack of her father's heavy palm against her brother's mouth, slowed rose and walked into the house. Shirley hugged the rake handle to her chest.

"I will not have you using that sort of language in my house!"

"We're not in the house," George Jr. shouted. "And you know damn well it's the language you'd use in your head, anyway. So why not use it in the open?"

George Sr. hit his son with his open palm, making a loud "craack." He hit him again with the backswing. "I will not be called a bigot!" George Sr. bellowed, pushing Georgie away with both hands. Georgie fell to the ground and lay there, panting and wiping his mouth with the back of his wrist, squinting at his own blood. "You don't hear me, do you?" He smiled. "Well, I'll make you hear me."

He stood up, gathered his mitt and the baseball, got into his car and drove away. Marilyn had put her arms around her mother, who was crying quietly. George Sr. shook his head, muttered to himself and lit a cigarette before going into the house, his briefcase under his arm.

* * *

"Pass the rice, please," George Sr. reached across the table and took the blue and yellow serving bowl from his wife. She looked at the bowl as he spooned liberal portions of rice onto his plate. "I think it would be good for the country to have a woman in the White House." He set the bowl down. No one answered.

"Marilyn, what do you think?"

His elder daughter raised an eyebrow. "Sure, I guess. The more important question dad, is what do you think of her policies, would she be the right person for the job, what do you think of Mondale—not what her sex is."

Having received the answer he was looking for, George Sr. grinned and winked. "That's my girl—cutting right to the heart of the matter. And I didn't mean that as a nursing pun, you know." He laughed and looked around. When he saw that no one else was laughing, he grunted and went back to chewing noisily, his mouth half open.

Eleanor, who had been looking down at her plate, dropped her fork and sighed, looking off toward the stairway that rose from the hall beyond the kitchen to the bedrooms upstairs.

"See, I don't think so," George Sr. said, chewing and pointing his fork at Marilyn. "Having a female vice president would affect every—well maybe not every, but a majority of women in the country. They'd feel they're more a part of the process and the process itself would benefit."

"Do you think I ought to go out for potato chips before the debate?" Shirley asked, looking at George. He shook his head without taking his eyes off Marilyn. "And even more—"

"How can you people sit here and not talk about him?" Eleanor's face was shaking; her eyes were tearful slits. "How come no one's out looking for Georgie?" Eleanor said. "How can you…just eat?"

For a moment George Sr. looked at his younger daughter out of the corner of his eye. All motion at the table stopped. No one spoke. No one chewed.

And then everything resumed.

"You see, Marilyn," he continued. "Even more important than the day-to-day details of how the government's run, the policies, the decisions, what bills are signed, etc., is the satisfaction—"

Eleanor slammed her fork down and ran from the room.

"—of the people with the system. This is a symbolic—Shirl, would you pick the fork up, please—this is a symbolic thing, I admit." He swallowed the mouthful he had been chewing and took a sip of water. "Now, once you have half the population more satisfied, you can get more accomplished."

The telephone began to ring. Marilyn started to get up but George put up his hand. "Not during dinner, dear."

The telephone stopped ringing and there was a pause and then a long, high pitched scream. Eleanor came running down the stairs. "Georgie's tried to kill himself. He's at the Ice Cream Stand and he's bleeding to death!"

The EMS workers were there when the Franklins arrived.

"I'm a nurse. How can I help?" Marilyn said.

"You can hold this bandage over the wound on his right wrist," an Emergency Services person called from inside the van, "while I hold the one on his left."

"He's lost an awful lot of blood," said a second technician.

"You can take blood from me. I'm a universal donor," Eleanor said. The technician nodded and led her into the van where her brother was strapped to a stretcher.

George Sr. herded his wife off to one side; she cried quietly into a handkerchief, occasionally blowing her nose. "They're doing everything they can," he said.

"Why would he do this?" Shirley said.

"I don't know," said George Sr., hugging her. "We gave him everything he could ever want. Sometimes it's just not enough. I don't know."

* * *

THE SOLUTION

The tag on the door in the CCU read "Beverly Edelberg." Her Chief Complaint had been tachycardia and she had received a CABG—Coronary Artery Bypass Grafting—taking veins from her legs to replace the blocked sections in her heart. The betablocker Propranolol was being administered intravenously.

She was sleeping on her side, covers pulled up to her neck and her arm thrust out towards the IV. Her face was lined with friendly wrinkles and the Man with the Hat had worked such a wonderful magic tonight that there was plenty of time to stop and look at her face and imagine she was Grandma. She had that look, as though she was used to giving Christmas presents. Her rouged cheeks and upturned lips were festive reminders of merry-go-round Saturdays in the park with paper bags of sandwiches and penny candies.

From the other side of the curtain that ran down the center of the room a man coughed and cleared his throat and Grandma was again just an old woman. *Thank you.* The filled syringe jammed into the IV's port, the plunger pushed and the solution emptied into her.

That ancient, lonely ache had traveled from its old place in the pit of the stomach to the fingertips, which had grown thick and red. The magic was gone. The show over. Time for business. Holding the syringe and handling the tiny needles was hard, yet it had to be done. This was all one necessary process now. One big continuing payback that no one else could administer. The pain in the fingers had to be ignored or at least endured as had so many other pains.

This was business.

* * *

The second door tag read "Albert Maguire." He was young, barely forty. His dirty-blonde hair was thick and curly and edged down over his freckled Irish face. His shoulders were heavy and his nightstand was covered with football magazines. He had a bone infection: Osteomyelitis, requiring long term intravenous antibiotic therapy via an arterial line. Beyond the normal cautions for phlebitis or sclerosis, his prognosis had been good. Until now.

Looking at him for more than a moment was distracting. Memories and old thoughts appeared—of black and white games on small screens during grilled cheese Sundays. No time to waste on sentimental bullshit. The needle went in and it was on to the next room, at the other end of the hall.

* * *

"Joshua Abraham" lay in the second room on the right. He had received a Craniotomy to relieve hydrocephalus, water pressure around the brain, resulting from a fall. He was nearly bald and perhaps in his sixties. A creeping red stain showed from behind the gauze that stretched over much of his high forehead. Intravenous antibiotics—Vancomycin—had been prescribed. House staff was to be alerted to the possibility of septic shock, or infection.

Mr. Abraham's brown hand clutched a small, silver locket containing a photograph of a younger version of himself in a suit next to a smiling bride.

It proved he'd had his good times, his love, his days in the sun. It was only fair to share the wealth and give someone else a chance, and that meant that they had to see the other side. Mr. Abraham had to fulfill his larger purpose.

The needle found its mark.

* * *

BEVERLY EDELBERG

"Well look who you've brought me!" Mrs. Edelberg laughed and sat up on the bed. She automatically reached across her chest for her pocketbook, which was on the nighttable, but the IV pulled her up short. She smiled and waved it away. "Oh, you don't need to see lipstick on old Bubbie, do you?"

Howie, who was six, shook his head and climbed up on the side of the bed and lay his head on his grandmother's leg, rubbing his nose in her gown. "If you couldn't come to my party, mommy said we could bring the party here!"

Howie's mother, Mrs. Edelberg's daughter, nodded. "But it was Howie's idea. Howie's a thoughtful boy."

His grandmother agreed. "I know he is." She kissed the top of his head. "And a delicious boy."

Howie looked up. "You can come to my party next year, Bubbie. And the year after that and the year after that and the year after that."

"Of course," said Mrs. Edelberg. "And the year after that." She looked reassuringly at her daughter. "The doctor's say I'm fine, my heart is strong. If I eat a little better and walk in the afternoons—" she shrugged. "I'll be just fine, sweetheart."

"And the year after that and the year after that," Howie said, counting on his fingers.

* * *

ALBERT

Albert Maguire sniffled. "Ah, what do you know about covering a receiver." He looked disgusted and started to turn off the television, but instead he put down the control and sat back, his attention caught up once again in the game. "Hut, hup—oh, nice deflection. No! Ref! How could you say it was interference!" He started to throw a punch at the television, but the IV line flapped against his arm and he decided against it.

Pretty soon he'd be healthy again and back to his Saturday League—drinking beers and covering the best receivers out there, though not necessarily in that order. Albert smiled to himself, thinking of his fiance, Vivian, who came to the games and cheered for him at the top of her lungs. By this time next season, they'd be engaged, and by the season after that, they'd have their own little linebacker on the way, God willing. Their five year plan would be under way as soon as he got out of this gown, and got back in the game!

"Ah, come on, Ref! I hope ya drop dead!"

* * *

JOSH

He had been dreaming about Jesse and a long ago Memorial Day Parade. He'd been seeing the sunlight glinting off the trumpet's bell and how handsome and grown up Jesse looked in his dark blue, V-neck sweater and pressed navy pants. That boy looked smart, even if the school's choice of material for such a hot holiday wasn't so smart. But no matter. Jacqueline would squeeze his hand and he would bite his lip to keep the tears from coming into his eyes when the parade went by and little Jesse, a bit small for his age, stood tall and looked straight ahead, knowing his mom and dad were watching.

What a wonderful moment, Josh Abraham thought, grateful that the procedure was done with and he could get this nightmare behind him. He hoped that his body's ability to heal would be as stubborn as this hydro-whatever it was. As Jacqueline said, if anyone could do it, he could. And Dr. Farrell assured him he would be just fine as long as he kept his family close and believed in himself. He felt so good each time that doctor came by. He wiped a tear from his eyes, brushing the IV line out of the way. And the best of it was, this would be the first of so many parades.

* * *

1995

BEVERLY EDELBERG

"I'm going to stay home with you, okay Bubbie?"

Mrs. Edelberg smiled and stroked Howie's hair. "Nonsense. You're sixteen years old. You should be out dancing with some young lady."

Howie laughed. "Tonight you can be my young lady, Bubbie." He took her thin fingers in his hand, stood and pulled gently. "Come on, Bubbie. Dance with me."

His grandma smiled, her lips pressed together. "I don't think I'll be doing much dancing anymore."

Her daughter watched from the doorway. "Maybe I'll stay up with Howie. Maybe you ought to go to bed, ma."

Mrs. Edelberg shook her head. "Fran, stop worrying what I should be doing. I've been taking care of myself since before you were born…"

"But you haven't had this virus since before I was born."

"AIDS shmaids. I'm lucky to have lived this long."

"Okay, ma." Fran shrugged and walked out of the room, her bare feet padding through the thick green carpet. On her way out, she glanced at the portrait of her father that hung next to the doorway; it had been painted soon after he returned from Midway. In one sense, she was glad he had passed away.

Thank God he didn't have to go through this. Dad was terrific in a crisis. He knew what to do, where the emergency exit was, the right number to call, how to cover a fire with a blanket. But drudging through each day, watching Mama wither away, her eyes alive but the rest of her shriveling, shrinking, giving up to first this and then that AIDS-related syndrome. This was a different kind of enemy.

She opened the newspaper and looked without seeing at an ad for spring fashions. Howie was living for his grandma. She wished he wouldn't and she knew mama wished he wouldn't—at least that was what his grandmother told him. He could be out practicing basketball. But his Bubbie had AIDS and he said he had to be with her.

Fran closed the newspaper and looked up at the brown plastic clock on the shelf above the sink. 11:30. She could hear Howie reading aloud to her. Sholem Alechem.

* * *

One afternoon several months later, Howie walked past the front desk toward the elevators.

"Young man? Excuse me, young man? Visiting hours don't begin for another fifteen minutes!" The blue haired receptionist with the gray framed glasses pointed a bony finger toward the rows of chairs lining the wall of the waiting room. "I'll let you know when you can go in."

Howie lay the flowers over the schoolbooks on his knee. He had gone directly from his last class to the flower store, skipping out on Steven, who had invited him to come over and shoot some hoops in the driveway. Bubbie said his visits meant everything to her and that meant everything to Howie. No one loved him more than Bubbie did. If she felt better when he was here, then he'd be here every day.

"Visiting family?" asked a tall, heavyset man sitting opposite Howie. The man wore gold wireframed glasses, what appeared to be an expensive suit, and a fancy, gold watch.

"My grandmother."

"Was she in an accident?"

"No," Howie said. "She's just sick."

"Ah," said the man, and he turned his attention to a dark haired woman in a purple dress sitting off to one side. "Visiting family?"

The woman nodded.

Howie wished they would let him in. Bubbie had been getting worse over the last few months—some kind of rare pneumonia that seemed to have shrunk her to half her normal size. Her skin had gone gray and her breathing become so difficult that her laugh, which had once filled a room and infected anyone in it, dissolved into choking coughs when it made an appearance at all.

Howie picked up a magazine and thumbed through it, not seeing the basketball players, though basketball was his favorite sport. After a few minutes, the blue haired receptionist said, "You folks can go in, now."

As Howie got up, he saw the heavyset man take something from inside his jacket pocket and hand it to the dark haired woman in the purple dress.

"Sounds like you may have a case for litigation. Why don't you give me a call first thing Monday morning and I'll look into it for you?"

Howie found the room with Bubbie's name on the card on the outer wall. Two doctors in long, white coats were standing outside the door, talking and comparing notes. He could not hear what they were saying but he heard the words "hyperalimentation" and "undernourished," followed by something about a "catheter." He knew what undernourished meant and knew it applied to Bubbie. He pulled aside the curtain around her bed and, once inside, pulled it closed behind him. He knew she was sick and frail and no longer his jolly, laughing and loving Bubbie, but nothing prepared him for the shock of those frightened eyes peering out from the shrunken balding skeleton of a person.

"Hi, Bubbie!" Howie managed to croak, in what he hoped was a cheerful voice.

A sigh whistled from what had been Bubbie.

"Mom'll be a little late. She had to pick up some things, but she promised she'd meet me here within a half hour. These're for you!" He held up the flowers, then put them in the vase on the nightstand, replacing the flowers he had brought three days before. He was grateful for the diversion. If he were turned away, Bubbie might not notice he was crying.

* * *

ALBERT

"It's funny," Albert McGuire said. "I never gave a damn about anything but football. I took you for granted."

Vivian put her hand over his, ignoring the noises in the hall—sometimes this floor got so loud; there was always some equipment clattering by. "You never took me for granted." She was trying to forget what the doctor had told her that afternoon. Albert's T-cell count was down to single digits. And he was so weak, they didn't expect him to live more than a week or two.

Albert tried to laugh, but could only cough. "Oh, yes I did. I could've cared less whether I lived or died. I thought life wasn't worth a damn. And now look at me! Is this justice or what? Ha!"

Vivian wanted to yell at him, to slap this self-pity right out of him. She knew her Albert was a generous, loving man, no matter what his physical condition, and she would be here for him. Just as she knew that if she were the sick one, he would be there for her. She didn't see the purple splotches of Kaposi's Sarcoma that covered his face or the lesions on his legs and back. She barely noticed the weight loss and labored breathing. And what did she care if he had lost forty six pounds or whatever it was? He had complained about his weight since she met him!

"I know what we should do this weekend!"

He looked at her, the old humor on his face. "Go camping?"

"Get married."

He didn't say anything for a moment.

"Don't say it," Vivian said, holding up a hand. "I don't want to hear that morbid shit today."

"I was just going to say," Albert said, taking her wrist, "that I know the real reason you're marrying me."

"Really? What's that?"

"For my money!" He shrieked a laugh, and his eyes half closed from the effort.

She wiped his shining forehead with a tissue she took from the box on the nightstand, and patted his arm just above the spot where the IV went into the back of his hand. "I mean it, Al. We planned to get married. We've never let anything else stop us. Why should your being a little under the weather cramp our style?"

His eyes clouded. "This is some weather I'm a little under. I'll tell you what. I'll marry you if you sign a prenup."

Vivian nodded. "You got a deal."

A nurse poked her head into the room. "Time for your medicine, Mr. Maguire. Visiting hours are just about over."

* * *

BEN

Bennett stood quietly on the perimeter of the formally dressed crowd; the quiet tones of the funeral service lost in the wind and the rumble of trucks from the highway which bordered the cemetery. When the service was over and the plain brown casket had been brought in from the silver hearse and lowered into the ground, Bennett waited for the family and friends to pay their respects to Jesse and his widowed mother, Jacqueline. Finally, he approached them.

"I'm so sorry, ma'am. Jesse." He hugged Mrs. Abraham, whose mouth tightened into a dogged smile.

"It's over, anyway. We can go on."

Jesse was looking at Ben, trying to place him. Then recognition dawned in his eyes. "The bar, right? With Ricky."

Ben put out a hand. "Bennett James."

"Where's Ricky?"

"Well, Mattis has been—sick." Ben looked around at the neat lawns and plentiful trees which looked so much like a park. "He couldn't make it."

Jesse nodded. "Tell him I hope he's feeling better soon."

"He said to send his sympathies. He speaks very well of you and of...your father."

Jesse didn't answer. "Mama, why don't you stay with Aunt Elizabeth for a few minutes. I'll be right over."

He guided Ben down a rock path between plots. Ben glanced at the smooth headstones and stone benches and felt the blanket of quiet that lay over the cemetery.

"Thank God this is finally over." Jesse shook his head. "It's been hell, especially because they don't know how it happened."

Ben nodded sympathetically.

"Oh, they have some official explanation, but it's so empty. It's insulting, really. My father was a proud man with hopes and dreams, particularly for me. And he didn't just want them to come true; he wanted to see them happen."

Bennett didn't know what to say. "I'm sorry," he offered.

"Mmhmm. He wasn't very reasonable. We used to fight over how much he expected of me, and from everyone really." He stopped walking and looked at Bennett. "This suspect I understand they have. They'll be able to get a conviction?"

Ben hesitated. "I don't know. I'm not really that close to the case."

Jesse nodded. "Well, if you should learn anything…my mother's ready to move on. She's already forgiven the man. But I'm not ready for that. I want to see him punished. I want to see it myself, the way my father didn't get to see me do all the things he wanted me to do."

"If I learn anything, I'll let you know."

Jesse put his hand on Ben's shoulder. "Send Ricky my best."

"I'll do that."

* * *

GO

Eleanor came out of the bathroom wearing faded cutoff jeans and a tight t-shirt advertising a Jewish deli in thick black letters; she stood for a moment in the hallway, watching him. Pressing the receiver to his ear with his shoulder, Bennett waved and winked. Her expression, which was no expression, did not change.

"I just want you to know you'll be okay. You can call me anytime," he said into the phone. "And I want you to do it—don't just know I'm here. Call. And be careful, okay? Now, get some sleep." He cradled the phone to his shoulder and squinted at Eleanor. "What happened to your face, your neck? You have scratches all over you! Wait, wait a second." He spoke into the receiver again. "Like you said, leave the TV on if it helps, but get some rest." He paused. "Oh, don't be silly. Well, you're welcome, okay?" He hung up the phone. "What happened? Are you okay?" He started to get up. Her arms, neck and face were covered with red welts and deep scratches. Had she run into her sister?

"Don't get up," she said, her voice calm. "I'm okay. Don't worry. How 'bout I make us a nice, cold drink?" Eleanor smiled suddenly, fingering the gold palette pendant at her throat. "Would you like that? One of my lemonvodka-ades?" She went into the kitchen and opened the freezer; there was the cracking sound of ice breaking free from an ice tray and crashing to the bottom of two glasses.

She came back, handed him a glass, put hers on the table, and sat down on the sofa, her legs crossed. She watched him, her shoulders hunched up around the sides of her face in what struck him as an odd way. What could have caused such deep, red scratches? It was as though an animal had attacked her upper body. She wrapped her arms around herself, watching him.

The drink had an odd taste. Different...and before he could finish his thought, he threw up, violently, his body retching and twisting inside. And two strange ideas struck him. Eleanor had not moved to help; she remained seated comfortably on the couch, watching his sickness the way one might watch a particularly interesting movie. The other thought was that he did not mind being sick at all. Throwing up was part of a larger feeling, part of a song of which his body was the chorus.

These would be the last coherent thoughts he would have for a long time.

Within minutes he was reveling in his sickness. A wonderful sensation had taken over the center of his being. A rainbow grew inside him; he was warm all over. Snot seemed to be pouring from his nose, but he couldn't be sure. *He had become a faucet!* And anyway, that was unimportant. The murders, too, had faded to background. What mattered was this new feeling, these flowers and rainbows and melodies inside him—or was he inside them?

Her arms were around him and there did not seem to be anything strange about that. It did not occur to him that he had lost again at love, or that this person kissing him had violated and assaulted him. Bennett did not seem to be thinking or feeling in his usual way. He had lived such a linear existence; he had been an artist, but now he was art.

Something slammed into his chin. It was his chest. *Had he fallen asleep?*

Eleanor was gone.

He tried to think, to remember, but then his chin was bouncing again; *who had given him this rubber chin?* And then, there she was, back again. And she was clawing at her own shoulders, arms and neck, squirming and crying.

"Get them off!" she screeched. "The ants! They're all over me! Bugs, ahh! Ben, get them off!"

She was wearing a leather belt with a pocket in its front and she managed to slip her hand into it and come out with a syringe. She inserted the needle into a spot behind her knee, then collapsed on her back, groaning. A few moments later, she rose up, fresh welts on her neck and shoulders. And she was yelling, bellowing, as she bent over him, her canyon mouth about to swallow him, her hoarse voice braying. Something about hypocrites and healing.

"...and Georgie, Georgie, Georgie! How can you help anyone, the poor or the sick, before you help your own family? That's the real disease, the real low T-cell count. Nobody loved Georgie like I did! And nobody!...Fucking!...*Listened!*"

She was standing over him, her fist waving. "Well now they're paying attention, aren't they? Oh, I've got their attention, haven't I? Well, it's all for Georgie! Now He has to see what He's done. His little sonny boy, his precious little baseball player wasn't really so fucking precious! Was he?"

She leaned close to him, her hand at his throat, and lay the gold artist's brush charm that hung around his neck across her palm. "Where'd you get this? From that technician? From my sister? From your friend on the phone?" She yanked it, tearing the chain and throwing it across the room. He could not force his mouth to remind her that she had given him the gold brush as a gift and that it matched the palette around her own neck.

"I'm not selfish. You see that, don't you, Ben? I'm not doing it for me! It was all for Georgie. He's dead and I'm dying and Marilyn's alive but she hasn't felt anything in twenty years, so she might as well be dead." She sat down on the couch. "And you know what, Ben? It's all goddam business. All business, like He says. That's what it is."

And the song continued; follow the bouncing chin.

* * *

JANICE

Janice sat back on the couch, one finger tapping her lips; her foot bounced to the funky jazz. She was watching the evening news with the sound off and had just seen Dr. Sticker being led from the county courthouse, a free man. She rushed to turn up the sound. Lack of evidence, the announcer said. She turned the sound down again.

She had done some checking after her last meeting with Benny, and what she had learned disturbed her.

She picked up the phone, which was as red as the couch it sat next to, and dialed Ben's number, taking off her glasses and biting an end of the temple while waiting and listening. After five rings she heard his voice. "Ben, listen to me. I looked into the medical…" His voice continued; it was a machine. She left a message warning him to stay away from Eleanor at all costs, then she hung up, dialed Eleanor's number, changed her mind and dialed the police.

"Sergeant Michaels, please. That's quite all right. I'll hold." She waited, still chewing on the eyeglass frame, until the Sergeant's voice came on the line.

"Danno Michaels."

"Yes, hello. I'm a lab technician at the hospital, the Medical Center, and I have some information that may be of interest to you, particularly in light of Dr. Sticker's release."

"Just a moment. Your name?"

"I, I'd rather not give that right now."

"Well, what's the information?"

"Well, sir. All employees have to take physicals and I was going through some records and one of the nurses here, a known drug user, actually, she has a B positive blood type—"

"And this would interest me because…?"

"Well, it wouldn't really, but her sister—it's an interesting thing, Sergeant. Both sisters, particularly when taken together, are fascinating people. Angry young ladies, if you'll forgive me for saying so. And they live such a wild lifestyle, a lot of partying, clubs, drugs, that sort of thing, but the sister who I'm embarrassed to say used to be a good friend of mine, once worked at the hospital, and her blood type is O negative."

"I see. And the significance of this is…?"

Janice sighed. *Didn't the police know anything?* "Well, sir, she's a universal donor. She can give blood to anyone without causing a reaction. Don't you find that interesting?"

"I see." The sergeant sounded tired. "So, that and the fact that she lives a wild lifestyle and maybe she's a little angry—this information is supposed to lead to an arrest?"

"Well, I wouldn't be so presumptuous as to say that, sir." She put her glasses back on. "Oh, and one other thing. These women are the hospital CEO's daughters." Without waiting for a response, she hung up the phone, put on her glasses and turned back to the news, where it was time for the only important segment as far as she was concerned: the weather.

* * *

MATTIS

Mattis paced the floor of the gray computer room at Morrisville College in Rockville Centre, glancing at the dial of his tiny black plastic watch. The blank faces of two dozen computers screamed at him. *Bennett was never late.* He ought to go to Ben's apartment to make sure he was okay; he ought to stop by the Medical Center to see if he had ever arrived for his interview with that nurse. He ought to check the parking lot for his car, and every road between the Center and Ben's or his girlfriend's apartment.

But he would do none of those things. He couldn't bring himself to leave the building. He paced in front of the blackboard, which still held bits of partially erased C+ code. He clenched his hands at his sides, and tightened his forearms to ropes. He let out a frustrated, strangled cry.

He had been six years old and playing on the piles of excavated sand and mud behind the middle school, finding stuck-together bits of dirt—dirt bombs, he and his friend called them—and throwing them at his friend, Harry. They would hit a leg or chest and explode with a satisfying thud, sending brown showers in every direction, like bombs in the movies.

They had heard a child crying. And when the two friends climbed over the piles of dirt and rounded a yellow bulldozer, they had found a half dozen teenage boys standing over a 9-year-old girl, her dress up around her neck, her panties down. The boys were taking turns doing things to her with dirty wooden sticks, and little Harry and Mattis—he had been Ricky then—watched for a few minutes, trying to understand what they were seeing. When one of the boys poked the girl particularly hard, Harry let out a gasp and the boys turned and one of them yelled "Let's get 'em! Joey, you stay here, make sure she doesn't get away."

Harry, the fastest boy in the first grade, got away, but Ricky was caught from behind and dragged to the ground, his arms pinned and his chest sat on, until it hurt to breathe. After a short, heated discussion that Ricky couldn't quite hear, the boys threw him to the bottom of a newly excavated hole. He landed on his shoulder, which flashed white pain and he lay there for a few moments, panting, glad to be away from the boys.

A moment later the dirt began raining down on him. At first it was a cool shower, welcome in that it further distanced him from his tormentors; but then it began to get in his eyes and mouth and soon he was covered with a layer of gritty filth. He cried out: "Hey, c'mon! Stop it! Stop!" but the threats that rained down along with the dirt were so horrible and the image of the girl being poked with that long stick so fresh in his mind that the dirt became preferable and he kept silent.

Instinctively, he curled into a ball, chin to his chest, maintaining a pocket of air. He could no longer think; there was only dirt and darkness and animal fear. No thought, no future. Only faint thuds somewhere above him. Soon, they too stopped.

He waited and breathed in shallow puffs. Dirt crunched between his teeth and scratched his eyelids, but he did not move. The dirt was better than the boys, so he stayed still for what seemed like hours and when he finally did move it was only a wrist. The wet dirt pressed down on him and it was minutes of sweaty struggling before he could free even one of his arms and turn his body so that he could use his more powerful leg muscles. Every part of his body ached and cramped and fought his decision to move. His muscles wanted to lie still in the cool dirt, but he managed to free himself and crawl up, like some larvae, out of the excavated hole, brown and dripping muddy tears.

His father and the police sergeant spent an hour and a half getting the truth out of him and once the little girl was found and their stories corroborated, the boys were caught and punished.

Ricky's therapist later explained that his mind had since protected him by purging the incident from his memory, leaving him only with a fear of open spaces, particularly parks, schoolyards and construction sites. The murders he and his friend were now investigating threatened him, triggered the old terror, and worsened his agoraphobia until he could not go out at all.

He stared into the green computer screen, and his own frightened face stared back. He wished it would all go away.

* * *

GEORGE FRANKLIN

It was cool outside, even for March, and the windows were open. The room had a summer-like heat—a wet, tense humidity born of fear and sweat more than temperature. George S. Franklin paced the front of the room, head shining behind the veil of smoke, eyes leering at doctors, nurses, administrators and at the three people in the room not connected directly with the hospital. The breeze blowing in cooled the sweat on his forehead and he stopped for a moment to enjoy the feeling.

They sat next to one another, against the back wall. Sergeant Danno Michaels leaned his metal folding chair backwards on two legs, his head bobbing; he appeared close to falling asleep. Mr. Stephen Archer folded forward, his chin lolling near his chest, his once white shirt sweat-stained and wrinkled. Ned Doyle sat upright, his deepset, iron eyes took in the whole room at once. He was combat-ready for anything.

"Mr. Elkins sent his underling, this Archer again. The Board of Health again wants to shut us down." The end of Franklin's cigarette glowed. "What's the matter, Archer, your boss playing golf?" Little clouds of smoke snorted from each nostril. "The State, County, everyone's after us. And it's all because the police couldn't make the charges stick." He shook his head contemptuously at Sergeant Michaels, who, he was satisfied to see, was now wide awake.

"I would venture to say, Mister Franklin, that if a suspect cannot be linked to a crime or incident, that person ceases to be a suspect. We had to let the man go, whatever your public relations needs may be."

Archer was waving a hand, as though he were a student in school. "And that's the only reason I'm back, Mr. Franklin. I'm sorry, but the public's interests are not being served by your institution's inability to protect its patients."

Franklin stopped pacing, picked his burning cigarette up from the ashtray on the table, and took a long drag. It glowed and shrank as he rolled it between his fingers, popping another from the pack in his shirt pocket and lighting it without bothering to put the first one out. "*Wheeww.* Exactly, Sergeant." He ignored Archer entirely. "And your failure to link him to that crime is not even going to be discussed at this meeting. We," he accented the word, "intend to move forward. Don't we, Ned?"

"I sure hope so."

"Now the public agencies have said all along that they can't shut us down without proof that these patients were contracting HIV here. They don't have that."

"Oh, but Mr. Franklin," Archer whined nasally, "while we have no smoking gun, we have tremendous circumstantial—"

Dr. Jennaro, a youngish intern with curly dark hair and thick eyebrows, put up a hand. "Didn't they say that if a certain amount of cases pointed our way, they'd have to shut us down as a precautionary—"

"Circumstantial evidence!" Franklin roared, a finger in the air. He began pacing again, puffing furiously. "We must consider the rest of our patients, not to mention our good standing with the public, with patrons at our fundraisers..."

Sergeant Michaels was shaking his head. "This is not a court of law, sir. Health precautions protecting the public do not carry the same requirements as the burden of proof in a criminal trial."

Heads nodded around the room, but Franklin was not listening.

"Do you have any idea what our CFO's report for the first quarter is going to—?"

"Mister Franklin!" Ned's voice whipped so forcefully to the front of the room that it bounced back, creating a faint echo.

Franklin blinked. "Yes Ned?"

"My business also stands to lose quite a bit of money since we're the ones buying space in health journals up and down the east coast, and—"

"Exactly!" Franklin pointed with the cigarette, then poked it through the smoke ring it had made.

"And I have no choice but to put that aside. Of course I had hoped that the killer had been caught. I'm disappointed that he hasn't been, but this Dr. Sticker is apparently a sick fellow, not a murderer. We cannot allow another single individual to become ill in this facility." The diminutive ad man looked around the room. "Many of you have sworn oaths not to be a party to that." He looked at Franklin. "I hate to lose an account—a fabulous account—but I cannot in good conscience continue this ad campaign."

Franklin's eyes rolled imperceptibly upward, as though he were dizzy, and he sucked on the cigarette for support, grunting with the effort. To Ned, he looked as though he were melting, wicked witch-like, into himself. He would have to have Ben...Ned slapped the table with his palm and everyone in the room turned around. He had left Ben a memo asking that he be at this meeting. And Ben never missed a meeting without calling or paging him!

He checked his beeper to make sure that it was on, and saw that he had no new messages. *How could Ben have forgotten this meeting?*

* * *

BEN

A tiny beige beetle with black markings on its wings crawled up and down strands of carpet, inches from Ben's left eye. A faint noise above him made him attempt to push himself up from the floor, but his neck seemed to be on a spring, his head heavy, and while his shoulders rose up a few inches, his face stayed down, cheeks pressing the floor, neck bent like a jack-in-the-box's.

The noise above him continued and he wondered if he were near an airport and perhaps planes might be landing nearby.

"Oh, there's not a thing you can do about it, can you? *Can you?*" Eleanor was standing over him, waving a set of keys, his keys. She was wearing a nurse's uniform. "You know, I cared about you. I let you in." She touched her chest. "And I don't let anyone in!" She lowered her voice. "My mistake...I'll be at the Well Baby unit," she smiled, "working."

The door slammed shut.

He had to get to the phone. He crawled, following the beetle.

How did they make this sort of carpet, anyway? Did they weave separate fabrics together, or—?

His eyes weighed more than his whole head.

Who was he supposed to call, again? Was there some water he might have, even a half glass?

He fell asleep trying to figure out a way to lift his head high enough to look for water. A few moments later, the phone began to ring.

* * *

MATTIS

Mattis put the receiver back in its cradle, stared at it for exactly two seconds and picked it up again. He hit the "redial" button and waited, four rings, five rings—then hung up, walked to the door of the computer room, which led to the school's parking lot, stepped through and felt as though he might faint or throw up.

Dizzy. His heart tried to jackhammer through his sweat drenched t-shirt, but he took another step towards the college's front gate. Every cell in his body screamed at him to *get back in that room*. The parking lot, the sun, the fact that Bennett was missing, all became secondary to this physical terror to which his body was hostage.

Unable to bring himself to leave, Mattis stepped back into the computer room, staggered to the soda machine and knelt before it. He reached forward and up, snaking a wiry arm into its opening and upward, into its metal guts. He drew out a cola and went back to his seat in front of one of the multimedia stations. He popped the soda's top and slurped cold fizz.

He examined his feelings, attempting to sort his own demons from the reality of circumstance. He found two distinct sources of dread. His panic attacks were an old enemy grown powerful. They had never cowed him like this, rendering him unable to leave a room. He guessed he'd been moving in this direction for a long time; he could hear his therapist in his head, telling him that allowing himself to feel his fear was growth.

Easy for her to say. For all the money she made, she ought to be the one feeling this.

His anxiety towards parks and schoolyards had grown, he knew, to nearly complete agoraphobia. Was it because of these murders? Did they threaten him personally? Or was his own therapy taking him to this place naturally?

His second fear was for Bennett. His best friend was ridiculously punctual, disgustingly prompt. Every hair pasted in place, his car practically *licked* clean, his clothes *spotless*, never wrinkled.

That anal retentive, obsessive-compulsive...so why wasn't he on time now?

Because something had happened.

Because this Marilyn had done something to keep him from calling at 7:30.

So, which fear was stronger?

* * *

ELEANOR FRANKLIN

She had finally become an ant. A worker. No emotion, no regret. Only purpose. Her fingers hurt. Years of heroin use had caused them to swell. She was calm now, high, and would be for some time. Plenty of time to get to the Well Baby unit and put the finishing touches on her masterpiece. When babies started testing HIV positive, they would have to close the Medical Center. Shit would hit fans; politicians would wake up.

You can ignore drug addicts, but you can't ignore babies. Future voters.

And the doctors, nurses, and especially the administrators—even the CEO—would be disgraced. Publicly humiliated.

She got out of Bennett's car and hurried into the building, checking the leather belt rigged with syringes beneath her loose white blouse.

"Hi, Marilyn," waved the receptionist. "What happened to your…?"

Eleanor waved as she went by, pulling her collar up to cover as much of her face as possible, careful not to look directly into the woman's eyes.

* * *

MATTIS

Mattis staggered from the phone to the doorway to wait for the cab. A small plane buzzed overhead.

Was there really a plane or was the noise in his mind?

He'd done it; there was no turning back. If he puked or fainted in the back seat, so be it. He'd explain the situation to the driver on the way, so someone would know and might be able to carry on if he couldn't continue.

His head was swimming, his arms cold, his thoughts and emotions swallowed up by this creeping, glacial fear.

The cab arrived and beeped its horn. Mattis closed his eyes, took a deep breath and stepped out of the building, his eyes to the front. Breathe, walk, breathe, walk, open the door, get in, sit down, tell him Ben's address…

He moaned as they drove past a park.

"Hey, are you okay?" the driver asked. "What're you doing? What's that? Can't you talk? Ha! That's funny! Say, you're playing charades aren't you? I love that game! Let's see, I've seen a face like that somewhere…I know, the movie *Alien.* No? Is it an older movie? *The Wolfman? Frankenstein?* Hey, why are you opening the window? Whoa, be careful leaning out like that! Oh, I'll bet it's an old war movie! Something with planes!"

Mattis kept his face out in the cool March air. Keeping his eyes shut made him dizzy, but the passing trees and grasses kicked up his anxiety, so he tried looking at the white lines on the road as they blinked past, mesmerizing him. A bit of his sock was stuck to his toenail and he stamped his foot, trying to shake it loose. He was ready to explode. Where were his cigarettes?

15

MATTIS

Once in the hallway outside of Ben's apartment, Mattis felt a little better. While it was closed in, there was no hint of dirt or any of the outdoor scenery that frightened him, so he knocked on the door, knowing from his earlier calls that there would be no answer.

He looked around, holding his breath, but saw no one and heard nothing other than static bursts from the radio in the cab he'd instructed to wait outside. So he slipped his wallet from his back pocket, took out his plastic telephone calling card and slid the card into the slit between the door and its jam. When it encountered resistance at the level of the knob he pulled back and then shoved quickly forward and to the left.

The latch clicked and the door opened.

On the dining room table lay Ben's notebooks and work related papers, and Mattis scanned these for any clue as to what might have happened to his friend.

A red light was blinking from the table in the living room, and Mattis sat down on the couch and pushed the button on the telephone answering machine.

"Benny, listen to me. This is Janice. I hope you're okay. God, I hope you're okay. I'm calling about Eleanor. Stay away from her, whatever you do! Trust me, Ben. I know what you must think of me but I don't mean this for any selfish reason. Eleanor's a universal donor. I did some checking into the records that were taken when she worked at the hospital. She's O negative. That would account for why there haven't been any reactions on the part of victims for receiving incompatible blood. It makes sense, Ben. And she looks enough like Marilyn to pose as her if she moves quickly and doesn't talk to anyone. Oh, Benny, I hope you're okay..."

Choking back nausea, Mattis found Ben's tan personal phone book next to the telephone.

Thank God Ben's so compulsively neat and organized, Mattis thought, remembering that his own personal phone numbers were scrawled on scraps of paper in his wallet, his pockets, on countertops, in crayon on his refrigerator door. But Ben-ito the Neato, God bless him, kept them right in this little book, right next to the phone. *How pre-goddamn-dictible!*

Mattis opened the book to the Fs, found Eleanor's address and was out the door and shouting at the cab driver within seconds.

On the way to Eleanor's apartment, he tried to put himself in her place. He understood rage, even dysfunctional rage. Wouldn't he want to kill the boys who buried him? Sure! But given the opportunity, would he actually do it?

Probably not. He'd be afraid to.

But what if he had a sister, the baby sister he'd always wanted but never had. And what if he loved her with that fiercely protective big brother love. And what if she had been driven by someone to kill herself...?

They pulled up in front of Eleanor's building and as he jumped out of the cab, Mattis realized that his fear was gone. Don't dwell on it, he told himself. Find Ben.

He banged on the apartment door. No answer, so he took out his phone card again. The commercials were right. Once you start using it, you'll use it all the time!

The door was bolted with a second lock that his card wouldn't open, so he backed up to the other end of the hall, ran as fast as he could at the door and slammed into it with his shoulder. The lock gave way and he fell into the room.

Wow, pretty cool, he thought, wondering if he might join a winter league football team. His mind examined that possibility as he picked himself up off the floor. Did those leagues have cheerleaders? Would he have to play second string until he got to know the coach? They were probably corrupt! The city council's kids probably got to start. To hell with that!

The room was hot and smelled of vomit. Breathing through his mouth, Mattis looked around. He heard a vague hissing and after listening to the regular hiss and pause, hiss and pause, he attributed it to the old building's heat.

A glass on the table next to the phone was half full and Mattis went over and dipped a finger in and licked it.

"Eehh." He shook his head violently and made a bitter face. Sour lemonade with a familiar aftertaste.

Heroin.

Something moved on the floor. A beetle. It crawled up the side of Ben's face.

"Yahh!" He jumped a foot in the air and his heart jumped even higher.

The hissing he heard had been Ben's snoring.

"Benson-hurts!" He dialed 911, then began slapping Ben's face.

"Benno! Ben-tana! Ben Hogan! Where is she? Did she go to the hospital? I called an ambulance, pal. You're going to be okay." A thought hit him so hard he had to sit down and force himself to breathe.

Ben's been sleeping with her. She's got the virus...

"Ben!" He shook his friend's shoulder. "Ben, just tell me one thing..."

The one eye facing Mattis opened a tiny bit, showing only white. Ben's mouth moved. "Moshti baba. Danf, danf." The eye closed and he was snoring again.

* * *

ELEANOR FRANKLIN

The nursery smelled of ointments, antiseptic and another, earthier smell. It took a moment to realize that it was the babies themselves. A thirtyish Well Baby LPN was bending over one of them, describing something to a slightly younger intern.

Eleanor adjusted the light to shine directly on a jaundiced little girl.

She allowed herself a glance out of the corner of her eye, but the doctors were still there.

She began straightening bassinets. One of the babies, Sherry Collier, her tag read, began to cry, turning red in the face and shaking with the effort of each out-breath. Eleanor patted her softly on the back and said, "It's okay, Sherry. Your mommy's just down the hall. She's going to feed you again later, okay?" But Sherry was already asleep.

The doctors were still talking.

She considered slipping a needle into a tiny leg, but did not entertain the thought long or seriously. The leather belt sagged to one side and bit into her waist, but she did not want to straighten it within view of the two doctors, so she left the nursery and went into one of the private rooms.

Once again she had become an ant—working, busy, not thinking or feeling but waiting to do her job. The knowledge that what she had done to Ben would probably get her caught had been relegated to a holding cell in the back of her brain—the same cell that held the knowledge that the virus would eventually kill her if the state didn't do the job first.

Unimportant facts, stored by a worker for use when relevant to the greater good.

She found a gurney and began collecting unused food trays from the womens' rooms. As soon as those doctors moved, she would begin.

* * *

MATTIS

The Emergency Services workers lowered Ben onto a stretcher.

"Where're you taking him?" Mattis asked.

"Closest hospital is NYMMC."

"No! You can't take him there! She's there and if you take him, she'll—"

"Excuse me, can I do my job, please?"

"Listen, you guys should know that Ben might be HIV positive."

The larger of the two workers, a dark, burly man with five o'clock shadow that ran from the middle of his face to his shirt collar, eyed Mattis. "You his partner or something?"

"His...no! But I know. Just...just take my word for it." He quickly explained what had happened to Ben.

"Jesus," said the second worker, an equally burly woman with close cropped hair. They lifted the stretcher and started out the door. "That...would be a police matter."

"Nes-wee. Bees!"

"Wait! He said something." Mattis grabbed the side of the stretcher, nearly tipping it over, and bent over his friend, but Ben was snoring again.

"Careful!" said the woman.

Mattis looked at her. "What do you think he said?"

"Messy trees!" she said, without hesitation.

"Nasal breathes," said the man.

"I don't know," Mattis shook his head. "I think it might have been Nursery—babies. Oh, my—!" He closed his eyes. "All right, you go ahead, I'm calling the cops."

He went back to the phone and began to dial. Sweat dripped from his hair and ran into his ears. "Sergeant Danno Michaels, please. I'm calling with regard to the hospital AIDS cases. That's right, NYMMC. Well, I'll hold but it's really—shit." He held the receiver away from his face, gave it a dirty look, then hung up and redialed.

"Uh, yeah, this is Detective Watts from over at the," he covered his mouth with his free hand and made a garbled sound. "I need Sergeant Michaels, stat." He realized that "stat" was a medical rather than police term and was about to correct himself when the police operator came back on the line.

"What do you mean 'in reference to what'? It's a four sixty two dash five odd six...What do you mean, 'what's that'? It's free dinners donated by two of the restaurants in your precinct especially for him and Congressman You-Know-Who, that's what it. Oh, you'll put me through now?" Mattis rolled his eyes. "Well, aren't you lovely." He cleared his throat. "Yes, Sergeant Michaels. This is Ricky Hatters. I'm a friend of Bennett James'...of the ad agency, yes. The murderer, or should I say murderess got a hold of Ben and dosed him with heroin. No, orally. No, I don't think it had anything to do with her blood, but he managed to say she was on her way to the Medical Center, to the Nursery. Yes! Right now! Yeah, I'll meet you there!" He looked at the receiver, then shouted into it. "No! If you show up with half a dozen uniforms, she's liable to panic and go wild with a needle in that nursery. I know where she's coming from. I live that lifestyle. Well, I'd, I'd rather not get into that now, just meet me there, okay?" Without waiting for an answer, he slammed down the receiver and rushed out of the apartment and into the waiting cab. "Medical Center," he said, handing the driver a twenty.

The driver, a pale blonde young man in his twenties gave him a sleepy stare.

Mattis flipped his hand backwards three times at the wrist. "Let's go! Up through Oceanside, left over the tracks, then right on Ocean Avenue, to Sunrise."

The switch in his brain had flipped on; the fear was back. *Wasn't there someone to help? To tell him it was okay? To notice? Even the killer got noticed. The whole city was trying to understand* her.

And all at once he saw the lure of murder and suicide. People noticed. There was a kind of glory in tragedy that was absent from this silent terror.

Killing himself would make people *care*—maybe not in a personal way, but they had to pay emotional attention and wasn't that a kind of caring?

He knew he didn't have the guts to kill himself. He wished for an instant that he were HIV positive so that people might sympathize, then had the ultimate horrible thought: maybe no one would.

He lit a cigarette.

"Can't smoke in here!" came the laconic voice from the front seat.

Mattis threw the cigarette out the window. *When was it going to end?*

* * *

ELEANOR FRANKLIN

Eleanor glanced through the nursery glass, but the doctors were talking calmly, so she went back to piling food trays on the gurney and fluffing mothers' pillows. A woman who had delivered twins that morning needed a cushion to sit on and someone to talk to, so Eleanor brought the cushion and, in a soft voice, reassured her that she would heal soon and that, once healed, she would be better able to care for her newborns. The voice and response had been automatic. It was part of the worker ant's job, a vestige perhaps of her relationship with Georgie, but now just her job, just as killing as many babies as she could as soon as those doctors moved was also her job.

Another woman, Mrs. Faber, had her baby with her because the baby had refused to eat during the previously scheduled feeding. The baby was still not taking to her breast and Mrs. Faber was desperate, so Eleanor soothed her, stroking her hair and the side of the baby's face while sitting on the edge of the bed. When the baby got hungry enough, she explained, she would eat.

She took the baby, whose name was Jasmine, from Mrs. Faber and laid her in the warm bassinet. The baby's face kept switching in and out of reality and Eleanor stood there for a moment, looking at it. It was a doll; it was a baby; it was a doll again...She had an impulse to distract the mother by suggesting she go to the bathroom to wash her tear-streaked face. She could jab the baby with the syringe while she was gone.

But an ant, a good ant, stuck to the plan. And she was a good ant. She knew enough not to trust her impulse. Stay with the greater good. This was business, and she had a business plan.

She looked up at the clock over the doorway. Nearly feeding time. A surge of energy welled up inside her. The babies would be wheeled into their mothers' rooms in ten minutes. Her window of opportunity was closing. She looked out into the nursery but the doctors were still talking.

She pressed her lips together and strode into the nursery.

"Excuse me, doctors. One of you has a phone call at the nurse's station..."

"Who's it for?"

"I'm afraid they didn't say—"

"Then how do you know it's for one of us?" The doctor sounded annoyed and Eleanor mentally talked her hand out of whipping a syringe into his thigh.

"The RN just said there's an important call and to grab the doctor in the nursery." She kept her facial muscles slack, expressionless.

The doctors looked at one another with raised eyebrows, then headed out of the nursery in the direction of the nurse's station.

She closed the door behind them, unbuttoned a single button and reached for the pouch.

* * *

MATTIS

"Sergeant, over here!" Mattis jumped out of the cab, waving his arms over his head when he saw the police officer. He pointed to the emergency entrance. "We're looking for a red headed nurse in the Nursery."

The sergeant nodded and they hurried inside.

"Excuse me, gentlemen," said the blue haired lady at the front desk. "Visiting hours don't begin for an hour and a half. You'll need a pass to—"

"Police business," said Sergeant Michaels, flashing a badge, "where's the Nursery?"

"That would be the Well Baby unit. Second floor—take that elevator over there—then make a left when you—hey, I wasn't finished!"

* * *

ELEANOR FRANKLIN

Eleanor felt around the pouch, found the first of the four syringes, and slipped it out, cupping it expertly while looking around out of the corners of her eyes. Her swollen fingers ached a little, but she could feel enough to do what she needed to do.

"Okay, kids, who's first?" She looked around. "Today, we're having a lesson in the American system of justice. The lesson is, it doesn't work, and you've got to take matters into your own hands." A blue elephant on a card taped to the side of one of the bassinets caught her eye. The baby squirmed inside yellow pajamas. The blue cap covering his slightly pointed head was pulled down a little too far, so that it covered the spot where an eyebrow might eventually grow in.

She stepped to the bassinet.

* * *

MATTIS

Mattis and Sergeant Michaels burst from the elevator, ran to the left, slowing at the nurses' station.

"Police! Where's the Well Baby unit?" The sergeant yelled.

The nurse was explaining to two doctors that neither of them had a phone call, no matter who told them what. She paused, her face blank. The doctors looked at one another, shocked understanding dawning on both their faces at once.

"My God!" said one.

"Behind the glass, end of the hall!" said the other, and he started running in that direction, his long coat flying behind him.

Sergeant Michaels pushed past him. "There she is." He drew his gun, and hesitated outside the huge window.

Eleanor was bending over one of the babies, her hand shielded from view by her body.

"Shoot her!" Mattis cried.

"I can't!" Michaels' eyes darted around. "A ricochet might hit a baby."

Eleanor turned, saw them and ran to the nursery door, kicked it shut, then rushed back to the baby. The needle caught the light as she bent over the flailing little body.

Mattis froze. They would never get to her in time. She was going to kill that baby and there was nothing he or Michaels could do to stop her.

* * *

ELEANOR FRANKLIN

Eleanor brought the syringe up to the pudgy arm. Something on the card next to the baby's head caught her attention. It was the letter "G" drawn in blue magic marker, and she angled her head to see the rest of the name.

Georgie.

Not him. She moved to the next bassinet.

* * *

MATTIS

And in that instant, Mattis jumped.

His stomach had been filled with frustration, loneliness and paranoia, all balled up, unable to go anywhere but to his brain, where they re-formed as fear. But in that one instant, they found an alternative.

He crouched and sprang, one magnificent leap. Up, up over the railing and through the plate glass, which rained shards and splinters in every direction.

He landed on a table, knocking lotions and baby wipes in every direction. He forced away a fantasy about the Olympic high hurdles and allowed his momentum to carry him to the floor. He leaped again, between bassinets, tackling Eleanor at the knees. He concentrated equally on two things: bringing her down, and keeping track of the syringe.

She had jumped back, but he caught her with his hands instead of the intended shoulder, and she fell forward, onto his back. He felt a sharp pain.

The needle's in me. I'm going to die.

He reminded himself that he had wanted to be HIV positive only a moment ago. Now he would get the attention, the sympathy, the notoriety he craved.

No, please God! I was wrong. I want to live. Please! Allow me this one mistake. Let me be there for Ben if he has the virus, let me be okay. I want to live!

And as he heard the footsteps and the handcuffs snap around Eleanor's wrist, he opened his eyes and saw the syringe on the other side of the room and knew that he had heard it land before feeling the pain in his back.

One of the doctors helped him up. Sergeant Michaels lifted Eleanor off the ground and turned her towards the wall, her hands cuffed behind her.

"You really didn't have to jump like that," the sergeant said. "She never locked the door."

He turned to Eleanor and took her by the arm, turning her towards him. "You have the right to remain silent..."

16

BEN

He dreamed of lime and olive greens dotting rolling hills, sprinkled with yellow and white buds and flowers. Annuals and perennials: impatiens, geraniums and daffodils accenting lawns in the east end foreshadowed lusher greens and cottony dandelions, all warmed by the salt water breeze of the coming summer in Long Beach.

Ben awoke with fresh air cooling the back of his throat, and blinked at the harsh lights as the hospital room came slowly into focus. An IV line ran into the back of his wrist and as bits of the last few days seeped into his consciousness, he confused his own experiences with memories and thoughts and his eyes went wide with horror as they took in the tube taped to the back of his hand.

"It's okay. It's only Ringer's Lactate to replace bodily fluid. You were dehydrated."

Ben blinked and turned his head to the right and there were Mattis, Ned Doyle and Sergeant Michaels. It was Ned who had spoken. Behind them stood two doctors, one he did not recognize; the other was Doctor Epstein.

"It's good to see you awake," said Dr. Epstein. "This is Doctor Lardner. He'll be taking care of you."

"I feel like Dorothy at the end of the Wizard of Oz," Ben said. "You're out of the computer," he said to Mattis, who smiled and shrugged.

"How else was I going to save your life?"

"I'd venture to say that this young high jumper risked his life to put that young woman behind bars." Sergeant Michaels nodded toward Mattis.

Ben's eyes filled. "It was Eleanor, wasn't it? Oh, God." The tears spilled over and down the sides of his face. "M-maybe you guys ought to…go"

The doctors looked at one another and nodded to the others. Ben gripped Mattis's forearm. "You can stay."

Ned slapped Ben's shoulder. "Hurry up and come back to work. Your campaign is being seen all over town, in the papers, on bus stops—everywhere. And we've got more for you to do. A nice new account."

"Nothing medical, I hope."

"Snack food," Ned laughed and winked.

"You just rest, son." Sergeant Michaels waved and he and Ned left.

"There's something we need to know," said Dr. Lardner. "It's about your relationship with the young lady and it's of a delicate nature, so if your friend will give us a moment—"

"No, it's okay. I think I know what you're getting at. We always, always used protection, every time. I even stopped everything just to—"

"We get the idea," said Dr. Epstein.

Mattis jumped three feet in the air. "Yes!" He looked embarrassed. "Sorry." He sat back down, then thrust his head close to Ben's. "Benito-the-Neato, you compulsive, retentive…"

Dr. Epstein scratched his forehead. "We thought you'd like to know that she once worked at the hospital, about ten years ago. Her father managed to keep it completely off the record. She used her resemblance to her sister as a cover, of course."

Ben felt emotion overwhelming him again. "She never really trusted me, did she? I loved her. At least, I think I—" His voice broke.

"She got Beth out of your system," Mattis said quietly.

Ben laughed though his tears. "She did that! Mattis, you have a way of saying the right thing, you know? I, I guess when she was a little girl she did trust someone. Her brother, Georgie. And when her father took him away and it got swept under the rug…"

Dr. Esptein nodded. "She was going to ruin her father's life for that—and a whole lot of others."

"She already has ruined quite a lot of lives," said Dr. Lardner. "Remember that."

Ben nodded. "What's Franklin's reaction to all this?"

"Not much, on the outside, anyway," said Dr. Epstein. "Business as usual. Put the criminal behind bars. That sort of thing. No outward evidence other than the family name that they're even related."

Ben could only shake his head. "I really think…I need to be alone."

"We've got all the medical information we need for now," said Dr. Lardner. "Sounds like your HIV test has a good chance of coming back negative, depending on what sort of condoms you used, especially since that heroin she gave you was dissolved in a drink and you never shared a needle."

"No, we never did that."

"You'll need to be tested periodically for a while, of course," said Dr. Epstein. "Dr. Lardner and I will be back later, on regular rounds." The two doctors left.

"So, what about you?" Ben asked, and Mattis tilted his head.

"What?"

"Now that you've gone out in public, will you be able to get a regular job, date real women…?"

Mattis looked at the edge of the blanket, never raising his eyes toward Ben's. "I don't know. If this were a movie or a book I suppose I'd be ripe for a romance, a real job—maybe even as a counselor here in the hospital. But," he shook his head, "I don't think it really works that way. I've been doing things my own way for a long time and I don't expect that one different day's going to change everything. Besides, I extended myself because your life was at stake." He smiled. "And who *said* I want to live like everyone else?"

Ben laughed.

"Bennnny!"

Ben's eyes followed the sound, then went wide with fear. There she was, filling the doorway. A scarlet dress draped over shoulders and hips.

"Well, hello!" said Ben. "Y-you didn't have to come." He tilted his head towards Mattis. "Don't leave!" he whispered, clearing his throat. "Mattis, you remember Janice? She works here at the hospital. She was very helpful..."

"Of course, I do." He put out his hand, which Janice allowed to take her own by the fingertips. "It was your call to Ben's machine that alerted me he was in trouble. Ben you owe this woman your life." He kissed the tips of her fingers. "Thank you...for him."

She smiled sweetly, then turned her attention towards Ben; her lips parted in a personal smile. "He's right, isn't he? You *do* owe me your life. And...I'm here to collect." She stepped into the room. "Don't be afraid, Benny."

"I've got some work to take care of," said Mattis, giggling.

"Don't you leave!" Ben reached for the edge of his friend's shirt, but Mattis was too fast.

"See ya," he said, and slipped out the door, giggling.

"Benny, I'm so glad you're okay. I knew that Eleanor wasn't for you." Janice sat down on the edge of the bed.

Ben groaned, his hand rubbing the side of his head.

Her hand covered his. "Where does it hurt, Benny?"

* * *

The next morning Ben dialed the number Sergeant Michaels had left for him.

"Sergeant, I do have a favor to ask. I'd like to see her, talk to her. Is that something that can be arranged?" He paused. "I loved her. Whatever she did—I understand she's sick, but I would have married her. I can't just leave it cut off like this. I, I want to...say goodbye." He swallowed, listening. "Well, I understand that and I appreciate your concern, but whether you think so or not, I know I meant, mean a lot to her. Yeah, I know she has a weird way of...well, see what you can do. It'd mean a whole lot to...thanks."

* * *

MATTIS

Mattis heard the truck and was looking out the window before the horn sounded. Downstairs, the 14-year-old he had hired was nearly done cutting the lawn. He'd have to venture downstairs to pay him.

When he got to the door the man in the brown uniform was about to knock. Mattis signed for the package, left it inside the door, and paid the boy, who had finished mowing. He looked at the freshly cut grass and the old oak that spread outwards from the center of the lawn and he felt a chilly twinge, a remnant of old fear. How would he feel when he stepped outside?

He brought the package into the kitchen, tore it open and removed its contents, running wires to their appropriate connections, inserting batteries, performing installations until, an hour later, he was ready.

He stood at the inside of his front door, new laptop computer in hand, and ran his other hand back through his coarse hair. He took a deep breath and stepped out into the warm air.

His first thought was that it was too hot, but he forced himself to continue walking until he was beside the old oak, where he sat down, allowing the numbing fear to come and was surprised when it was only a mild, physical sensation and he was able to feel it, yet continue. An extended phone wire trailed behind him. He smelled the mowed grass and tried not to see the piles of dirt that had been washed down the hill by the weekend's rains.

He sat down, opened the computer and turned it on. "Oh well, it's a start," he said to himself, as he logged into a chatroom and looked at a list of names.

"Hi, Debbie…" he typed.

* * *

BEN

Eleanor was being held in a special section of the jail. Ben had to empty his pockets in a sterile outer lobby, leaving his keys, wallet and change as well as his belt and tie in a locker. He gave his driver's license to the guard at the desk. Then he and Sergeant Michaels walked through a huge visiting area where a series of tables snaked around in a u-shape. Inmates were allowed to sit on one side of the tables, families and friends who came to visit sat on the other side.

Ben's head was a highway of thoughts and feelings. *How could she have lived with such secrets for ten years? Didn't she feel any guilt? And how did she interact with her father? What could life have been like when they were kids? Had she really loved him, or had that been an act?*

"I've arranged for you to see her in a room usually reserved for inmate-lawyer conferences. She's on a variety of mood drugs," said the sergeant, as they arrived at the room and he unlocked the door. Ben didn't answer.

She was sitting in a wooden chair, one hand cuffed to an armrest, the chair itself cuffed to a desk. Otherwise, the room was empty. She looked past him.

"I'm sorry," she said.

"Are you?"

She nodded and seemed to see him for the first time. "For what happened to you. Not for anything else." She wore an orange prison uniform. Her hair had been cut short and she had lost weight.

"How could you have—?"

"Don't even start. You don't know—"

"I guess I don't."

"If you're going to go *there*, you might as well leave. You didn't grow up in my house, you didn't know my brother, you—"

"Okay." He stood up.

"Wait." A familiar look came over her face. A vulnerable look that was privately his. "I'm glad you came. I want you to know, whatever they do to me, at least I'll know I found love. I do love you, Bennett. I always will."

"Oh, God."

She looked at him for a long time. "You don't love *me* anymore?"

He didn't answer.

"I'm sorry," she said again. "The doctors tell me I'm…damaged." She laughed. "Like a package or something."

"It looks like I'm probably not HIV positive."

She leaned forward, a pained expression on her face. "I didn't mean for you to—" She shook her head. "I'm sorry. I know it doesn't mean much, but I'm glad you don't have the virus."

"They're going to keep testing me anyway for a while."

"I know."

"Goodbye, Eleanor."

"Ben…? I wanted to—"

Without waiting to hear what she had to say, Ben walked to the door, which Sergeant Michaels opened from the outside.

* * *

A hole had formed in his chest. And the hole affected the nature of matter around it. Weight, for instance, seemed greater in the vicinity of that part of his chest. Ben could feel the pull, sucking what was left of his emotions towards the hole. He'd read something like that about the black holes in space. That was the way he pictured this hole.

He had begun drinking again. Alone.

Despite everything Mattis had been through, Ben was surprised to find that his friend was less interested in drinking than he had been before.

After work, Ben would come home, crack open a beer and read the junk mail. Then he'd have another beer and read a few pages of *Newsday.* Then he'd start on the scotch. He had once liked vodka, but that last "vodka-ade" Eleanor had given him had taken away his taste for it, so now he drank scotch.

He ate TV dinners. The only other item in the freezer was ice. Besides beer, the fridge contained a little milk, for his instant coffee in the morning. Now and then he ordered a sandwich or a muffin with the rest of the staff at work, but he had lost much of his appetite and ten pounds along with it.

* * *

An hour into the second morning back at work, Ned buzzed him.

"Would you come in here a moment, Bennett?"

Bennett did as he was asked.

"Sit down." Ned indicated one of the chairs opposite his desk. As he sat down, Ben's eye was caught by the gold karate trophy on the shelf behind Ned.

"When'd you win that?" Ben asked.

"Two weeks ago. My instructor was asking when you were coming back." Ned smiled.

Ben shrugged and dropped his eyes.

After a pause, Ned took a manila folder from the stand on his desk and handed Ben a sheet of stationery. "Read this."

Ben scanned the page. "It's from the Medical Center. From George Franklin." He smiled at his boss. "Or, from his desk, anyway." He began reading to himself. "He's commending us—"

"No, he's commending you."

"—for my work and thanking me for helping solve the case…despite his personal sorrow."

Ben looked up. "You don't want to hear what I have to say about him. You think he had someone write this?"

"I don't know. And that last part—I know what you must think of him…Who knows what happened ten or twenty years ago? Who knows what goes on in families?"

"I have a pretty good idea."

"My point is to congratulate you on a job well done and to show that I'm not the only one who recognizes it. Even…someone you might not think capable of recognizing good work did in this case." He looked Ben in the eye. "Your work is that good." He put out his hand. "Congratulations, you're now our Senior Art Director."

Ben took his boss's hand. "We never had one of those, did we?"

Ned shook his head. "I made the title up. There isn't any junior art director. In fact, you're the only art director, but you do deserve it. The hospital's already gotten positive calls. Who knows, you may win us another 'Addie.' Remind me later, I have tear sheets for you. Oh, I also have," he cleared his throat, "two new accounts for you. In fact," he peered through the glass wall of his office, toward Ben's desk. "I think I see Annie carrying the folders in there now."

"Thanks." Ben turned to go.

"And listen—"

Ben stopped but didn't turn around.

"You can choose the way you want to live."

Ben gave the tiniest of nods, showing he'd heard, then walked out into the creative room.

* * *

He missed Art and Lou terribly, and found himself wishing he could let them know how he felt, how much losing Eleanor hurt, how frightened he was about his medical situation, how lonely he had become. He wished he could go shopping with Art, and pictured him, hands on hips, appraising Ben outside some fitting room, like some hybrid mother-fashion designer. And he wished he could go fishing with Lou, on a quiet Montauk afternoon in sight of their perpetual construction, the only sound being the birds and crickets. He missed the couple's gentle jokes, their casual but insistent praise.

"Hey, Bennett," Lydia called, "I mean, boss. How's it feel to be one of the rich and famous?"

Ben looked in her direction, but she was turned towards her computer screen and he could see only the computer's light reflected in her eyes.

"What're you talking about?" he asked.

"Have you read today's paper?" Lydia picked a *Newsday* up from the corner of her desk and opened it to a page near the front.

The phone rang. "Art," Ben said, wishing his name were Art so he could carry on the traditional pun. "Hold on." He pushed the hold button. "Lyd. There's another one of those humans on the phone. Try to transform yourself into one so you can communicate with it."

Ben went back to the newspaper and immediately saw his own face staring back at him. The picture was his employment record photo, taken around Christmas time just over a year earlier, when he'd first come to 3S. The headline read: "Boyfriend of Accused Ran Hospital Ad Campaign."

He handed Lydia the paper just as she hung up. "I thought I'd managed to stay one step ahead of the reporters. You know they're camped outside my apartment every night. I spent the last three nights at Mattis's."

"Oh, come on," she said. "You love the publicity. You're a hero. Act like one. Go on out, help an old lady across the street. Go ahead, I'll cover for you. I'll even find you an old lady."

"Ooh," said Ben, laughing, "a little jealousy! Sounds like someone's not getting enough attention."

"Attend this," Lydia said. "And quit moping. You can become a police consultant in your spare time. Or a talking head on CNN. Oh, they'd love you, especially if you're a little unlucky in love." She turned from her screen to leer in his direction.

"Heel, Lydia," Annie's voice called from the back of the room.

"Oh," Lydia turned around in her chair. "So you want to get involved?"

"No, that's okay." Ben smiled at them both.

"Sure, poor baby, you go ahead and feel sorry for yourself in the wake of all this success."

Bennett went into his office. Annie came in and began laying out papers on his desk.

She touched his arm and smiled grimly. "I wanted to leave you alone yesterday. Congrats. Good job."

"Thanks, Annabel. These're..."

"Your new accounts. InvestSend is direct mail. All the information is in the folder. Contacts, job description, copy, layout, appointments. Best Health Foods is an ad campaign for a healthy snack food, but first you've got to design the packaging. We've already signed the contract. We figured you'd need a couple of weeks to come up with a couple of concepts and mockups. Oh, can I ask a favor?"

"Sure."

"I need a ride to Motor Vehicles, to register the used car I bought now that Kenneth's driven off in the old one."

"Sure. Eleven o'clock okay? I'm interviewing replacements for Art and Lou before and after…"

"Fine."

* * *

After an hour and a half of making calls and working on design concepts, Ben went into the creative room to tell Annie he was ready to go and found she already had her pocketbook over her shoulder.

When he held the door for her on the way out, she smiled, as though surprised, and he marveled at how she was able to predict the future but could not fathom simple acts of kindness.

When he held the door to the Motor Vehicle Bureau she smiled again, more nervously and looked around the huge, bustling room, squinting at the long lines.

"Wouldn't you know if he were here?" Ben asked.

"Kenneth? Well, no. He blocks me or something. Shows up unexpectedly all the time."

"Don't worry, Ann. Nothing's going to happen to you."

"You don't know Kenneth."

They stood quietly on line, and Ben realized he was comfortable. He did not feel pressure to fill the silence with idle talk.

Once her registration was finished they got back into the white Cougar. As they pulled out of the lot and began driving up Route 878 towards Peninsula Boulevard, she reached over and pressed a palm against his stomach. "Slow down," she ordered. He saw no stop sign but slowed.

In front of them, a tractor trailer hurtled through the intersection. He had slowed just enough.

He swallowed and looked at Annie.

"You want some coffee?" she asked. "There's a new little restaurant in Rockville Centre that makes a great cherry pie."

"How'd you know I like cherry pie?"

She opened her pocketbook and rummaged around in it. "You don't mind buying, do you? I seemed to have misplaced my money."

"I don't mind."

She was right about the pie. And the coffee was good, too.

She talked a little about Kenneth, and Bennett said he understood; neither of them had been particularly lucky in love.

"That's a funny expression," she said.

"It's all luck."

She looked around. "He could be anywhere, anytime. And he's apt to do just about anything."

Ben sipped his coffee. "Mmm. You know, a few months back, Ned took me to his karate—excuse me, *taekwondo*—class. It was kind of interesting but I was, I don't know, a little bored maybe, or intimidated. It might be more fun if there were…two of us, going together…"

She looked at him, surprised, then broke into a smile. "Me? You want to go…with me?"

He returned her smile. "It might be fun, and you might learn something useful."

Her eyes wandered in little jumps around his face. "I don't know." She glanced towards the door. Her body tensed. A short man with long brown hair and bulging eyes had come in. Ben turned to look. She relaxed.

Ben remembered how horrible he felt in that moment when he understood Mattis's fear. "Let's do it, Ann. I've been looking for an excuse—"

"Okay," she said, before he could finish.

The check came and Ben reached into his back pocket for his wallet, opened it and pulled out a wad of bills. A strip of paper fluttered to the floor. He picked it up. It was from a fortune cookie; he vaguely remembered it.

It read: "You will find love in an unlikely place."

Ben smiled, carefully smoothed the fortune with his finger, and slipped it into the front pocket of his wallet.

About the Author

David E. Feldman lives in Long Beach, New York, with his wife, Ellen, and two sons. Previously, he published *Born of War: Based on a True Story of American-Chinese Friendship*. Mr. Feldman is currently working on a second Long Island Mystery: *The Universe Principle.*

Printed in the United States
4373